A DEAL SEALED WITH A KISS

"What if I said I didn't want money for saving your brother's neck," Drake asked, watching her closely. "What if I said I wanted something else?"

"What else is there?" Hope countered mockingly.

A crooked smile played over his lips as his eyes resumed their bold exploration of her body. "Take a guess."

The insinuation was clear enough and she could feel the hint of a blush kissing her cheek. Her skin felt as though his fingers were trailing hotly over her flesh instead of just his gaze. That the feeling *should* have bothered her, and *didn't*, was more than a little unnerving.

"Money is the only thing being offered here, gunslinger," she said hoarsely. The next thing she knew, she was in his arms. She had no opportunity to turn away as his lips claimed hers. Like the man, the kiss was hard and probing, demanding and insistent. He pulled her closer than she had any right to be, but she was beyond trying to stop him . . .

WATCH FOR THESE ZEBRA REGENCIES

California Caress

Rebecca Sinclair

Kensington Publishing Corp.
99 Third Avenue
New York, NY 10022

ZEBRA BOOKS
KENSINGTON PUBLISHING CORP.

ZEBRA BOOKS

are published by

Kensington Publishing Corp.
850 Third Avenue
New York, NY 10022

First printing: September, 1989

Printed in the United States of America

10 9 8 7 6 5 4 3 2

— This book is dedicated to —

Kathy Horton, always more than a friend . . .
for "above and beyond."

Joyce Flaherty, who gave me wings . . .
and to Carin Cohen, who gave me the chance to fly.

And, of course, to Steve . . .
a man who is more special than he knows.

This one's for you.

Chapter One

Thirsty Gulch, California, 1851.

"And this time *keep* out!"

The gritty voice and loud squeak of hinges startled Hope Bennett from her anxious pacing. Quietly, she stole to the end of the narrow alley. Peeking around the corner, she was just in time to see the body of a man thrown head first into the dirt.

The swinging doors banged shut as the drunk slurred a curse and staggered to his feet. Brushing the dirt from stained, threadbare trousers, he lurched forward, wobbling down the street with a lopsided gait. By mere inches, he missed falling into one of the holes an overly eager prospector had dug in the center of the street.

Hope checked the man's build against the sketchy description firmly embedded in her memory, then immediately dismissed him to resume her pacing. Her booted feet crunched over the gravel as she stalked to the end of the alley, sandwiched between The Brass Button Tavern and the general store. At the back of the alley, she turned to retrace her path. Barely two steps had been taken when she felt the weight of a hand settle on her shoulder. Another wrapped itself around her mouth as she opened it to scream.

Air whooshed from her lungs as she was brought up hard

against a firm male chest. Without a second thought Hope closed her teeth on the fleshy palm. The taste of dirt and leather was strong on her tongue as a grunt of pain whistled in her ear. It was a small victory she took no time to savor as she raised her foot and slammed the sharp edge of her heel into her attacker's shin.

Hope staggered at the suddenness of her release, but recovered fast. In one lithe motion, she regained her balance and slipped her hand inside the pocket of her dress, her trembling fingers searching for the ivory-handled revolver. The loose folds of her cloak billowed around her ankles as she withdrew the weapon and whirled on her attacker. Her thumb twitched over the cold metal hammer and she squinted into the shadows, receiving her first good look at her assailant.

"Luke!" she gasped, her voice a confused mixture of fear, anger, and relief. She lowered the gun to her side, glowering at the pouting countenance of her brother. He was eyeing her cautiously as he sucked the blood from his palm. "What the hell do you think you're doing?" she demanded, her husky voice thick with a southern drawl that refused to fade. "You near scared me half to death."

The full lower lip trembled as he turned his attention to rubbing his aching shin. His forehead was baby-smooth, his dark brows raised high with surprise. Like a young boy, no hint of menace marred his sulking expression. Of course, there wouldn't be. While his body dwelled well into the realm of maturity, Luke's mind was no more advanced than that of a child of eight. "I wanted to surprise you," he said finally; his lower lip still thrust in a pout. Though his voice was deep and masculine, his tone was sweetly innocent.

"Well, you succeeded." Slowly, she raised the gun, the Colt dangling from her index finger for Luke to see. His brown eyes widened in fright, as though Hope had just waved one of the water snakes he feared so much under his nose. "You succeeded just fine. Don't you see what almost happened?"

8

Her cheeks reddened with anger at the thought. "You snuck up behind me and I didn't even know it was you. How was I supposed to know you weren't a murderer, a robber, or—" she gulped, thrusting back the thought, "or worse?" Her jaw hardened at her brother's look of confusion. "Don't you see? I could have hurt you, Luke. I could have shot you dead."

Luke frowned, his wounded gaze wavering between the gun and his sister. "You would a killed me dead?" he asked, his eyes shimmering with the threat of tears. "Why, Hope? I thought you loved me. You said you loved me."

Inside the saloon, a piano began pounding out a pitifully off-key version of "Hometown Girls." The squeaky notes grated on Hope's already frazzled nerves as she glowered at her brother.

"I do love you, you big lug." Her brother's look of wounded indignation quickly melted into one of delight. The sight frustrated Hope. Luke's boyish mind refused to let him grasp the magnitude of the trick he had just played. Somehow, she had to make him understand. Tucking a stray wisp of chestnut hair beneath the hood of her cloak, she hardened her features and slipped the gun back in her pocket. "Lucas William Bennett, you're my brother and I love you dearly," she continued, her voice harsh and scolding as she watched his grin broaden, "but you can't go around sneaking up on people like that. It just isn't right. Now I want you to promise me you won't ever do anything like that again. Luke?" She sighed impatiently, crossing her arms over her chest and tapping her toe. *"Luuuuke!"*

"All right." The pout was back, but the familiar shimmer of mischief had returned to his eyes. His big feet shuffled in the dirt as he clasped his hands behind his back. "I promise," he agreed with grudging obedience.

"Good," she said, ignoring the hint of a grin that still tugged at her brother's lips. "Now, tell me what you found out. Is he in the saloon or not?"

Luke nodded eagerly, the shaggy ends of his hair brushing

9

the collar of his chambray shirt. The dark strands, lighter than his sister's, glistened in the pale glow of moonlight. "Yup. He's in there all right. But I don't think you wanna find him."

"And why not?" she snapped, still vexed. "That *is* what I came here for, isn't it?" At her brother's wounded look, Hope softened the tone of her voice. "I'm sorry, Luke, I didn't mean to yell. Just tell me, did you see him? Is he playing cards? What table is he at?" Slowly, her gaze narrowed on her brother. "Lucas William, is that whiskey I'm smelling on your breath? And cheap perfume clinging to your shirt? *Luuuke?*"

Luke scratched the top of his head as he contemplated his sister. "I'm not telling," he replied peevishly, drawing circles in the dirt with the toe of his boot. "You already yelled at me once for funnin', and I don't wanna get yelled at again."

"I did not yell!" she yelled. Her mouth snapped shut as she struggled to get a firmer grip on her emotions. When she spoke again, her voice was laced with only the barest trace of annoyance. "I didn't yell," she repeated calmly, "I scolded. There's a difference." Luke opened his mouth to inquire just what that difference was, but Hope rushed on before he could sidetrack her again. "Just tell me what you found out. And be quick about it, we don't have all night."

"I already told you."

"You told me he's in there," she corrected, pointing a finger at his massive chest. "You didn't tell me where."

"Geez, Hope, I don't know where."

Hope nibbled her lower lip as the music inside stumbled, stalled, then started the song anew. She asked with sorely strained patience, "Did you *see* him, Luke? Where was he sitting?"

Luke scowled. "He wasn't sitting nowhere. I just heard some fellas talking about a gunman named Frazier. They said he rented a room yesterday."

"Did they say which room? What number?"

"No."

She wasn't surprised. For Luke to have gotten Drake Frazier's room number would be better luck than she had a right to hope for.

"All right," she sighed, turning on her heel and resuming the pacing that her brother's sudden appearance had interrupted. "At least we know where he is. That's a start. Tell me," she said over her shoulder as she neared the front of the alley, "these men didn't say whether or not Frazier was in his room now, did they?"

"No," he replied, following close on his sister's heels. "But I saw a whole bunch of guys that fit his description."

She spared her brother a reprimanding glare. Luke bowed his head, chastised into silence. He wasn't supposed to go into the saloon at all. That wasn't part of the plan and he knew it. Still, the fact that he had, and had found out in which of the stone-fronted buildings this Frazier character was staying in, *had* helped their cause. She could hardly yell at him for it.

Stopping at the front of the alley, she peeked around the corner. The boardwalk was empty. Horrible music, coupled with the mumble of male voices, drifted out of the saloon's swinging double doors. An occasional giggle, distinctly feminine, floated through the cool night air. It was the only evidence that the saloon's occupants were not all male.

"The description Pa and Old Joe gave us wasn't very good," she said suddenly, speaking more to herself than to Luke. Tall, darkish hair, brawny build, with a gun always strapped to his thigh. That was all she had to go on, and it told her next to nothing. A description so sketchy could easily fit more than half of the money-hungry prospectors who continued to pour into Thirsty Gulch in droves.

She fixed her brother with a scowl. "How do they know what he looks like, anyway? Didn't the guy just get into town yesterday?"

"Old Joe said he met him once," he shrugged, digging his

hands in the pocket of his baggy trousers. "I think he said in San Francisco, back when they called it Yerba Buena."

Hope groaned and stalked back down the alley. "Good God, Luke, that was almost three years ago. What if he doesn't hire himself out anymore?"

Luke followed his sister, kicking a rock with the side of his foot. "Old Joe says guys like that never change — they just die."

"Well this one didn't."

"I don't want you to go in there, Hope," Luke said suddenly. Reaching out a restraining hand, he wrapped his thick fingers around his sister's arm as she tried to move past him. He wrinkled his nose as though he'd just smelled a skunk. "There's bad men in there. Bad men. Drinking, playing cards, swearing up a storm. It ain't no place for my sister to be." Hope opened her mouth to argue, but Luke plunged on. "Let me go in and talk to this Frazier guy. You stay out here where it's safe."

Hope's gaze scanned the alley, and it was all she could do not to laugh out loud. "Here? Luke, it isn't any safer out here than it is in there, believe me. Besides, Pa sent me to talk to Frazier for a reason." She hesitated, meeting her brother's confused gaze. How could she explain the situation in terms Luke could understand? Bluntly, she decided. Eloquent, flowery speech had no place with Luke Bennett. "I was chosen because I'm a woman, Luke," she said finally, her tone very calm and matter-of-fact. "And since I happen to be one of the few decent ones around here, Pa and Old Joe figured Mr. Frazier would be more likely to listen to a woman than to you. Do you understand that?"

"Being a girl don't make no difference," he argued glumly. "All you gotta do is tell me what they told you to say. I may not be as smart as you, but I got a good memory. I can remember what to say, and I can say it just as good as you can."

"I know you could." A soft smile tugged at her lips as she

reached up and caressed her brother's stubbly cheek. "But I promised Pa I'd talk to him, and a Bennett never goes back on his word. Now, let go of my arm so I can go inside and get this business over with."

Luke hesitated. "I don't know," he sighed, shaking his head.

"Luke, I'll be fine," she assured him as she pulled from his slackened grasp.

"But what about the bad men, Hope? What if they hurt you?"

"I can take care of myself." She parted the cloak and patted the side pocket of her dress, reminding her brother of the gun that was concealed there. There was no need to tell Luke about the knife she had tucked in the other pocket — just in case a backup option was needed. "No one's going to hurt me."

The conviction shimmering in his sister's eyes and mirrored in her voice made Luke nod. "You'll be careful in there?" he asked, as she stood on tiptoe and planted a kiss on his cheek. Hope was the only girl Luke knew who was tall enough to do that.

"I'll be careful," she promised. Sending him a brief, encouraging smile, she edged back down the alley. Stopping midway, she turned back to her brother, her features stern. "You'll wait out here for me, won't you, Luke? I don't want you wandering off again. So help me, if I come back and find you're off carousing, I swear I'll—"

"Take me over your knee," he finished the familiar threat as his lips curled into an impish grin. "Yeah, I know."

Hope shot him a look that told him he was incorrigible, then slipped stealthily down the rest of the alley and around the corner.

Luke watched her go with an uncomfortable feeling pulling at his gut. He didn't like this at all. Hope had a way of getting herself into trouble. She needn't court more by walking into a saloon full of drunk men and whores at this hour of the night. But there was nothing he could do. Hope trusted him to stay put, and here is where he'd stay. She hadn't forbidden him from worrying himself sick, however, and until she got back that was exactly what he intended to do.

Hope slinked past the front of the saloon and molded her back against the wall near the swinging doors. Entering a saloon at this hour of the night went against every grain of upbringing she held dear. But there was no help for it. She had to find Drake Frazier. Luke's life depended on it.

Wiping her sweat-dampened palms down the front of her cloak, she pushed herself away from the wall and made ready to enter the saloon — only to have the door swing open and almost smack her in the face.

Gasping, she melted back against the stone as a gaunt, drunken miner staggered onto the boardwalk. The doors squeaked loudly behind him, then banged shut. She held her breath. The man hesitated, struggling to maintain his balance while she steeled herself for a confrontation, glad that her brother was still within calling distance. To her surprise, none came. Instead, the man raised his nose to the cool night air, then smiled as though he'd just caught whiff of the most delightful aroma he'd ever smelled. The contented smile stayed plastered on his face long after he'd staggered into the street, headed toward the crude little shanties on the outskirts of town.

She let out a pent-up sigh, then wondered what on earth she was feeling so relieved about. She'd missed being seen by one drunk miner. *One!* There was still a whole saloonful of them yet to be faced. Relief was the *last* thing she should be feeling right now.

Squaring her shoulders, she took a deep, steadying breath, smoothed down the cloak covering her rose-colored skirt, then pushed open one of the double doors. The hinges announced her entrance as she stepped into the saloon.

Smoke was everywhere. The curling gray vapor filled the

14

room, hanging in the air like a thick fog, only fog didn't smell this bad, nor did it burn one's eyes. Tables were scattered over the floor in no semblance of order. An oak bar stretched from the far wall clear across to the other. In front of it were a variety of stools on which only a few of the many patrons sat. None of the stools matched, and to Hope it looked as if they'd all been salvaged from the trash heap. As for the other customers, they didn't seem to care too much what they sat on. So long as they had a bottle in front of them and a glass, dirty or not, to drink from, they were a happy lot. A deck of cards wasn't mandatory, but it sure was appreciated.

It took her a few seconds of squinting through the haze of pipe and cigar smoke before she could make out the vague lines of the piano in the corner to her left — and it was then she realized the paunchy man who sat in front of the instrument had stopped playing. It was a blessing in disguise, for as she watched, mouth upon bearded mouth snapped shut until it seemed like the attention of every man in the room rested on her. The attention she received from the "ladies" was not nearly as appreciative.

Only the sound of her heart drumming loudly in her ears saved Hope from hearing the whispers of speculation her presence stirred. For the first time in her life, she felt like hanging her head in defeat, and slinking out the door she'd just entered. But Bennett blood ran too thick in her veins to allow such a cowardly retreat. Drake Frazier was here, and it was her job to find him. With her chin tilted at a proud angle, she returned the curious stares and stepped into the saloon as though she belonged there. The sound of the doors swinging shut behind her was loud in the ensuing silence.

A hushed voice to her right made Hope glance down at a nearby table. There, two men well into their cups tipped their hats back, leaned their heads together, and whispered furiously. A bargain was quickly struck. Chuckling obscenely, the men reached into their grubby pockets, and

15

each produced a chunk of gold, almost equal in proportion. The nuggets were placed side by side on the table before the two men shifted their attention back to Hope.

"Well, sweetie?" the toothless one said when he noticed her staring at him and his companion. "You gonna make me rich or you gonna make me happy?" Taking his hat off, he rested it over his heart and sent her a lecherously forlorn look. "Either way, I'll surely die a happy man."

A round of laughter exploded at the off-color remark, but Hope refused to dignify the slimy toad with a response. Instead, she turned her attention to the rest of the room, her gaze searching for any man who would fit Drake Frazier's description. There were a few, but the smoke was so thick and the men so many that she was quickly losing hope of ever finding the gunslinger without some measure of help.

"Don't think she likes ya too well, Hank," the other one said to his toothless companion. The hat he plucked off his head revealed a bald, leathery scalp that glowed dull in the lamplight. "Maybe she cottons more to a man with some meat on his bones." The slurred voice rose with a confidence born from the bottom of a bottle of whiskey. "Hey there, little filly, if Hank here don't suit ya, why not give me a try? Old Mel here really knows how to please a gal." His busy brows rose in lewd suggestion. "Ya won't be disappointed—and that's a promise." Leaning back in his chair, the man hooked his thumbs in his belt loops as his vulgar gaze ran up and down Hope's body.

A hush fell over the room as she slowly turned to the man in question. She fixed her gaze on the one named Mel, and there was no stopping the shimmer of distaste in her large brown eyes as her gaze traveled over the pudgy man.

The toothless one shifted restlessly in his chair as she took a step toward the table. He sent his friend a nervous glance, not at all liking the angry color on the young woman's face. It was a belated thought, but he wondered if any relatives of hers were here to witness his friend's crude remark. If there was a father or brother around, they were keeping their peace. That settled the small man's nerves — a little.

She stopped as soon as her thigh was an inch away from the table side. She was careful not to let the folds of her cloak brush against it, so greasy did the wooden surface appear. Her gaze hardened as it shifted from one man to the other, then down to the two gold nuggets on the table. They hadn't been to the stamp mill yet, she noted, but even a rank amateur could see that both were of fine quality, with hardly a trace of quartz running through the shimmering surfaces.

"A bet?" she drawled, eyeing the gold. The silence that enveloped her was so acute that even those on the far side of the room could hear the softly spoken words. She batted a thick fringe of ebony lashes and regarded the pair with mock innocence. "Over little ol' me? Why, gentlemen, Ah surely am flattered."

The small man ran the tip of his tongue over the disgusting pucker of his lips and nodded. His gaze ran greedily over the curvaceous body, only hinted at by the loose cloak. The eyes were beady and filled with a perversely nervous sort of hunger. It was plain to see he didn't much care what lay beneath the coarse wool. The fact that she was a bona fide, honest-to-God woman was good enough for him. And if she was ugly or disfigured beneath those billowing folds? Well, he could always close his eyes and pretend, now couldn't he?

"Care to settle it, honey?" the bald man asked, his voice a cold, hard challenge. Unlike his friend, he was not as easily intimidated, nor was he as drunk.

"Why, Ah'd be truly honored," she replied, her voice a soft, sweet, deadly purr as she purposely thickened her accent. "Why don't y'all tell me what yer little bet here's all about, first."

The one named Mel grinned. "Why, honey, it's so simple even you can understand it." Hope's lips thinned to an angry white line at the insult, but the man was too busy preening to notice. "Whoever gets lucky 'nough to bed you first gets the gold—if'n he remembers to take it."

"Well now, isn't that just tha sweetest thing?" she asked, her voice dripping with sarcasm. Finely arched brows rose high on her forehead as she resisted the urge to slap his ugly face. But there were better ways to deal with his sort. Lightning quick, she reached out and scooped up the two nuggets. After testing their weight in her palm, she slipped the gold into her pocket, much to the shock of the two men. "Looks to me like you've both lost, *gentlemen*." Batting her lashes again for good measure, she sent them her most charming smile. "Mind you, Ah use the word lightly."

Flabbergasted into silence, the two men watched her pick up one of the glasses of whiskey a buxom barmaid was about to set on their table. She held the glass up to the light, noting its dull, spotted rim. It looked partly clean, she decided, which would probably be the cleanest she was going to get in a place like this. As she tipped the glass to her lips, the hood of her cloak fell to her shoulders, freeing a waterfall of chestnut curls that swayed to below the gentle taper of her waist. She downed the contents in one fiery gulp, gasping as the stuff burned a path down her throat.

Feeling suddenly warm, she wondered whey she'd even bothered with the cloak. Had she really thought the shadowy hood would conceal her identity? How foolish of her. She stood eye to eye with most of the men in Thirsty Gulch, and even a head taller than a few. Certainly, if her height didn't give her away, her soft, husky voice would. Ah well, there was precious little to be done about it now, and she was quickly finding that she really didn't care if the patrons of The Brass Button Tavern knew who she was.

Drinking the whiskey had been a pretty good idea, she decided as she felt her nervousness fading, replaced by a calm numbness that felt almost natural. Liking the feel, if not the taste of the liquor itself, she set the first glass in front of a stunned Mel, and plucked up the second. This drink slid down nice and easy, hardly burning her throat at all as the liquor gathered in a warm pool in her stomach.

She slammed the empty glass on the table with a little more force than was necessary, as her fingers fumbled in her pocket. A silver coin was procured and duly tossed on the surprised barmaid's tray.

"Next round's on me, fellas," she announced, her voice louder and huskier than normal. "Hope y'all enjoy it."

With that, she spun on her heel to face the rest of the tavern. Squinting, she continued her examination of the amused, ragged faces, ignoring the guffaws of laughter that erupted around her. Pursing her lips, she noted that only a few of the men fit the description of the one she was looking for, and gut instinct told her that not a one of them was Drake Frazier.

Scowling in frustration, Hope headed for the bar. Few of the patrons had taken seats there, and she carefully placed herself far away from the ones who had. She settled on the only stool that looked seatworthy. The wooden seat was hard on the posterior and offered no back on which to recline. Still, she perched on its edge in the most graceful way a woman could possibly sit on a barstool. She kept her back to the portly barkeep who was eyeing her intently as he swabbed down the counter with a dirty scrap of rag.

Except for the ribald jokes tossed at the fellows whose gold now lined her pocket, the majority of attention was still focused on Hope. Good, she thought. It would make her chore that much easier.

With slow deliberation, she pulled the two gold nuggets from her pocket. The smile that played on her full, sensuous lips was enough to jolt more than one poor soul into sudden sobriety.

"Ah'm lookin' for a man by the name a Drake Frazier," she said, pausing long enough for her gaze to scan the crowd, and her honey-sweet words to sink into the men's alcohol-dulled senses. "Ah don't suppose any a you kind gentlemen

19

can help me?"

"Depends on what you want 'im for, sweet thing," a voice called out from the back. Hope focused her eyes on a tall, lanky fellow who could not possibly be the man she was looking for.

"That, sir, is mah business," she replied with a coy little smile.

A soft murmur spread through the crowd as she gave them a chance to weigh her words. All the while her fingers played with the two pieces of gold, careful to hold them conspicuously, so all the patrons had an ample view. One at a time, she dropped the nuggets into her lap, then picked them up again, rubbing them together before repeating the process. When no one burst forth with the information she sought, the crowd instead drifting back into conversation, she held one of the nuggets up to the lamplight. Her expression was a mask of feigned ignorance as she pretended to examine its quality. She wasn't surprised to find the room had fallen silent once again.

"What'd you say the guy's name was?" another voice asked.

She glanced at the speaker, a young boy with a crop of sandy brown hair, and smiled. "Frazier," she repeated. "Drake Frazier. Have you seen him?"

The boy shrugged, eyeing the gold that was nestled snugly in her lap. Or was it the lap he was eyeing, she wondered? "I might've." He scratched a smooth, round chin that had yet to sprout its first whisker. "The name sounds a mite familiar, but I can't rightly say where I heard it b'fore."

"Hmmm," she sighed thoughtfully, shifting her gaze from the boy to the men behind him. Absently, she noticed that the table where the first two men had sat—the ones who'd grudgingly parted with their gold—was now occupied by three new faces. There wasn't a sight of the two idiots to be had in the smoke-filled saloon.

"Pity," she said with a wistful smile. "And here Ah was,

thinkin' Ah might part with one a these perty little things if'n it'd lead me to mah Drake."

Again she held one of the nuggets up to the light. This time, she knew with a certainty that she had captured the attention of every eye in the place, and that all were examining the chunk of gold right along with her.

Lowering the nugget back to her lap, she puckered her lips and asked the room in general, "Ah don't suppose any of you know what these are worth?"

The sheer gullibility of the question went undisputed, and not only because she was a woman. It was common knowledge the woman's family had been in Thirsty Gulch little better than a week, and settled down in the Simpsons' old cabin for even less. How could any of these prospectors guess the vast number of camps the Bennetts had traveled through before settling down in this one? For all they knew, Hope Bennett was a simpering female straight off a boat from San Francisco. Besides, only a few women knew much about staking claims, working a cradle, or assessing a nugget's value. By most of these miners' standards, she was ripe pickin's.

She watched as one of the men disengaged himself from the crowd and stepped up to the bar. He was of medium height and build, with jet black hair that was painstakingly swept back from his face. His beady eyes shimmered with greed as they flickered between Hope and the gold in her palm.

She had a feeling she had just found the man who would lead her to Drake Frazier.

"Why don't you let me take a look at those, sweet thing?" he asked, extending a hand that was too soft and smooth ever to have seen the long end of a shovel. "I make my living doing this."

"You mean yer a bona fide assayer?" she gasped, with false delight. She turned the full effect of her velvet brown gaze on him in what she prayed resembled admiration. She didn't trust this man for a minute. He had the look and smell of a weasel of the worst sort. Still, she was careful to keep her suspicion from showing, in either her eyes or her expression, as she placed the piece of gold in his hand. "Well, sir?" she asked with forced eagerness, as he held it up to the light. "Is this mah lucky day? Did Ah strike it rich?"

The man sent her an annoyed glance as he turned the nugget this way and that, rubbing his fingers over the coarse surface, even going so far as to take a sniff of it. One of the most difficult things Hope had ever done in her life was to hide her amusement at *that* maneuver. *Sniffing gold!* she thought. Her father and Old Joe would certainly get a week's worth of chuckles when she told them about it later.

Sending a quick glance over the rest of the room, she was glad to see that most of the men had gone back to their business of drinking, gambling, and raising holy hell. She watched as a giggling, brassy redhead was pulled into a drunken miner's lap. Even the piano player had struck up another chord. Relieved, she turned her gaze back to her companion.

Shaking his head, the man sent her a helpless look as he handed her back the gold. "Sorry, ma'am, but they ain't worth much."

"No?" she sighed, her features melting into sadness as she let her shoulders slump forward. Keeping up her thickened, down-home accent was not as difficult as she would have thought. "No, huh?" she pouted, slapping a palm on her lap. "Dern it all! And here Ah thought fer sure this was gonna be mah lucky day." Another sigh, this one heavy and dejected. "Oh well, Drake'n Ah weren't nevah meant to be t'gether, nohow. Paw told me so, but Ah didn't b'lieve him." She smiled sweetly at the weasel, adding a touch of sadness to her forlorn gaze. "Guess Ah should a listened, huh?"

Taking the gold, she slipped it back in her pocket and began to slide off the barstool. As she suspected, the weasel had no intentions of letting her go so easily.

"Now, hold your horses there, sweet thing," the man said smoothly as he put a restraining hand on her arm. "I didn't say the gold was *totally* worthless."

"Gold?" she squealed, clapping her hands in delight. "You mean this is real gold? Why, who would a thought? And you say it *is* worth somethin'?" Hope turned trusting eyes on him, and at the same time tried to control the impulse to spit in his stinking, conniving little face. The place where his hand touched her arm felt as though a thousand slimy things were crawling over it. She repressed a shudder, knowing she was too close to her main objective to pull away now.

"Like I said, not much," he shrugged. "Maybe fifty dollars between the two of them, but that'd be stretching it."

Fifty dollars, my ass! It's more like three hundred and fifty, if it's worth a cent. And he knows it, too, the bastard.

Wisely, she kept the opinion to herself as she forced her expression into the pantomime of a shocked-into-speechlessness female. Her hand fluttered to her throat as she feigned excitement. *"Fifty dollars!"* she exclaimed. "Why, that's more'n Ah was hopin' for. Tell me sir, if'n you'd be so kind, where 'bouts can a little ol' gal like mahself go to turn these perty little things in?"

The man smiled the weasely smile of a person about to make himself a handsome profit for a minimal amount of work. "Please," he said, cutting her a mock bow, "let me do the honor for you."

"You? Oh no, Ah couldn't pos'bly ask a—ahem—gentleman like yerself to do that. You've done so much already, Mr.—er?"

"Tubbs," he readily supplied with what a completely desperate woman might consider a winning smile. "Tyrone Tubbs, at your service."

"Mr. Tubbs," she said, returning his smile. *A disgusting little name for a disgusting little man.* "Ah thank you so much fer yer help, and Ah really would appreciate you turnin' these little things in fer me. You know, savin' me all that fuss and all,

23

but—" she bit her lower lip as she forced a troubled frown to her brow, "well, this is all the money Ah have in the world. Ah gave my last coin to those nice gentlemen for a sip of their whiskey. And Ah did so hope these two pieces of—what'd you say they were again? Never mind, it don't matter none. Whatever they are, Ah was hopin' they'd help lead me to my b'loved Drake." She gave another sigh, and thought that if she kept sighing with such regularity she would certainly faint from hyperventilation.

Tyrone Tubbs licked his lips and scowled as if searching his memory. "Frazier. Is that what you said his name was?"

"Why, yes," she exclaimed. This time the breathless excitement in her voice was not forced. Nor was the sudden racing of her heart. "Do you know him? Ah heard a rumor he was headin' for these parts, but who knows how long ago that was."

"Quite recently," Tubbs said, eyeing the pocket containing the gold. "In fact, he arrived yesterday. As coincidence would have it, your beloved is in one of the upstairs rooms as we speak."

"Here? Now?" Hope's mouth went dry and she suddenly wished for another taste of that whiskey. It might be a poor substitute for courage, but she'd take it. Suddenly the prospect of coming face to face with the well-reputed gunman was enough to make her slightly numbed senses whirl. The wild trepidation struck her off guard. Although it lasted only a few brief seconds, the effect was severely unnerving.

"Is something wrong?" the man asked when he saw her face drain of color, then flood a becoming shade of pink.

"Wrong?" she echoed stupidly, then caught herself in check. "Why, no. 'Course not. Ah just didn't expect to be so lucky. You say mah Drake is here? Now?"

"That's a fact. I saw him go up those stairs myself." His frown deepened as he held up two fingers in the barkeep's direction. "Are you sure you're all right? You look a little pale."

"It's just excitement, Mr. Tubbs," she explained hastily, slipping her hand inside her pocket. The gold was still there, the nuggets warm from resting against her hip. Tubbs waited expectantly for Hope to hand over the gold, but, to his surprise, she made no attempt to do so.

Two glasses of whiskey were set on the bar, the surface of which was crusted with God only knew what. She didn't give the man a chance to express indignation at what he was quickly beginning to suspect had been a fruitless venture. She'd wasted enough time on the ninny as it was, and there was still plenty more to be done before she could call it a night. "Please, sir," she rushed on. "You must let me repay you fer all yer help." She fixed him with a wide-eyed, innocent stare. "Now I know a fine gentleman such as yerself wouldn't dream a takin' payment from a poor gal like mahself, so Ah want you to let me know if there's ever *anything* Ah can do to help you." She took a sip of the whiskey and asked, "What room did you say he was in?"

He hadn't, they both knew it. Still, Tubbs was hardly in a position to back down now, especially with so many witnesses. He eyed the burly barkeep, who had finished swabbing down the bar and was now leaning only a few feet away. The look on the barkeep's face told Tubbs he'd heard every word that had passed between the woman and himself, and that *she* was the one who had the big man's sympathy.

Swallowing hard, Tubbs turned his attention back to the woman. "Up the stairs, second door on your right." He sent her an evil sneer, the facade of helpfulness peeling away like the outer layer of an onion. "Better knock first, though. He may be — er — busy."

Hope nodded, then belted the rest of the whiskey down in one long gulp. She exhaled hard as the molten fire seared her throat.

"Thank you, Mr. Tubbs," she said, her thickened accent stripped to the bones now. "You can't begin to imagine how much help you've been."

Tubbs didn't acknowledge her words, having already turned his attention to the card game at a nearby table. Pulling up a seat, he threw a few coins onto the center of the table and motioned for the dealer to count him in.

A smile played on her lips, and as she turned back to the bar, she found it was returned by the enormous barkeep.

"Want another?" he asked, throwing a grimy towel over his shoulder and nodding to her empty glass. When she hesitated, he grinned and let his gaze slip to Tubbs. "Don't worry, I'll put it on his bill."

Hope smiled. "Thanks, but I think this should be sufficient." She reached over and plucked up the glass of whiskey Tubbs had forgotten. The barkeep chuckled as he turned to a reed-thin barmaid who was setting a tray of empty glasses on the bar.

Looking at the glass, she contemplated the amber-colored liquid. Her head was beginning to feel light, but not unpleasantly so. Her speech had yet to slur and her vision was intact. If anything, the liquor had bolstered her courage for the encounter that was yet to come. So what would one more drink hurt? It might make facing Drake Frazier that much easier. Or it might get her drunk. It was a chance Hope decided she was willing to take. With a vision of a hardened, arrogant gunslinger floating in her mind, she downed the whiskey. No fire cut down her throat this time. If anything, the drink tasted pretty damn good. If she wasn't careful, she would acquire a taste for the fiery brew.

Sighing, she set the glass down on the bar, then slipped off the uncomfortable stool. The barkeep grinned in her direction as she wobbled past him, and Hope thought she might have sent him a conspiratorial wink, but she wasn't sure.

Why did I have that last glass of whiskey? she thought as she concentrated on placing one foot after the next on the narrow steps. Her knees felt like unthickened strawberry jam, and, at the rate the alcohol was seeping into her system, she would be lucky if she made it to the landing at the top of the stairs without tumbling back into the saloon.

Somehow she made it, though she thought the feat was accomplished more by luck than coordination. Now, if she could only remember what room the little weasel had told her Drake Frazier was in. Was it the second door on the right or the first on the left?

An intoxicated giggle escaped her lips before she could clamp a hand over her mouth to stifle it. She'd just try every damn door until she found the one that housed the man she was looking for. Should be easy enough, she thought as she staggered for the door straight ahead.

"Don't knock first," he had said. Hadn't he? She couldn't remember. Shrugging, she grabbed the handle and turned. The door wouldn't budge.

Not that one, she decided as she moved on to the next. Ah, now that handle turned quite easily. Too easily, if the unclothed occupants of the room had anything to say about it.

"Sorry, honey, you're too late," a brassy, feminine voice cackled as Hope quickly closed the door. The girl wasn't telling her anything she didn't already know. At the first sight of the man's blond hair she had already guessed it to be the wrong room.

She staggered to the one across the hall, realizing as she went that she hadn't tried the one nearest the stairs. That one would be next, she decided as she grabbed the door knob. Which doorknob? At the moment she was seeing three of them spinning before her eyes. Her hand lurched for the middle one, though her mind hadn't given it permission to do so. Miraculously, it turned.

The door swung open into a vacant room illuminated in the soft orange glow of lamplight. This was the room, wasn't it? Oh God, she should never have drunk that last glass of whiskey! Now she was seeing two beds in the center of the room instead of just one. And her stomach was—sick! She was going to be sick!

Without thinking, she raced to the closed door to her left. Flinging it wide, she collided into what felt like a brick wall; a very fuzzy, very warm, very muscular brick wall.

Hope staggered backwards, and by the time two large hands had wrapped around her upper arms to steady her, she had passed out cold.

Chapter Two

The last time Hope remembered feeling this awful was on the ship that carried them around the Horn, bound for that cursed place called California. Her stomach had heaved for nearly the entire voyage, and by the time they'd finally reached port, she was ten pounds lighter.

But this was worse. While the soft thing beneath her now wasn't rocking, it might as well have been. Even with her eyes closed, she felt the world spinning in slow, agonizing circles. Perhaps if she had something to focus on, she thought. Maybe that would help stop the dreaded rotation of the dark world she was desperately trying to lose herself in.

Slowly, bit by painful bit, Hope opened her eyes. The light, a pale orange glow reeking of kerosene, pierced her eyes, and she felt as though a dagger had been thrust clear through to the back of her skull. Stubbornly, she refused to give in to the pain. As she opened her eyes a little more, the fuzzy blur of a wood planked ceiling came into view.

Ah, much better. With her gaze focused on the cracks between the planks, and the tiny nail heads that held them together, her world blessedly stopped spinning. This did nothing to relieve the throbbing in her temples, however.

Deciding her mind needed something else to think of, she let her gaze drift over to the hastily constructed end table by the side of the bed. It was a crude little thing, she thought, confident that Luke could have produced a better piece of furniture than the carpenter who had built that atrocity. The wooden wardrobe was even less elaborate, as was the squat, rectangular table resting against the wall near the foot of the bed. The porcelain washbasin and pitcher atop the rickety table looked like they had seen better days. And as for the chair the man was sitting in, well, that was—

Man?!

Hope's eyes widened in surprise, then squinted as she tried to focus on the boots so casually crossed atop the chipped oak bed rail. They were black, those boots, with low heels worn down where the sole first touched ground. The leather was cracked, molded to curve over the large feet within. Where the surface had once been shiny, it was now dulled with a fine coat of dirt. Her gaze rose to where the top of the boots disappeared beneath the hem of blue denim trousers. The sinewy legs encased in that rough material had muscular calves and thighs that extended for what seemed to be miles before tapering off into lean hips, a taut stomach, and a broad, virile, completely naked chest; a chest that brought a vague sense of familiarity to the outskirts of her memory. There was a V-shaped pelt of soft golden curls there, disappearing just as the broad, muscular shoulders came into view. The tendons beneath the sun-kissed flesh were well defined. It didn't take much exertion on Hope's part to imagine how the muscular biceps would ripple with even the slightest movement.

The nausea that had been forming in her stomach was suddenly forgotten. Boldly, her gaze rose. She wasn't at all surprised to see the thick cord of neck that smoothed itself up into a hard, square jaw. There was just the slightest indentation in the chin resting below sensuous lips. Even the light, bristly coat of stubble shadowing the jaw and lower part of his face could not conceal the high, rugged cheek-bones or the enticing hollows beneath. His hair was sun-bleached blonde and shaggy, accentuating the hard mold of

30

his cheeks as it swept away from the high, broad brow. The color reminded her of endless fields of wheat, rich and ready to harvest as it basked under a midday sun.

Then there were his eyes. Narrow beneath the bushy, golden brows, they were the same shade as the tumultuous seas that had carried her to this godforsaken land. A deep, almost translucent shade of green shot with shimmering silver flecks, the eyes had a penetrating quality about them that both shocked and mesmerized her.

"Should I ask how much you've had to drink?" His voice was a deep, husky whisper that tingled its way down her spine. A smile curled his lips, a gesture not mirrored in the piercing gaze.

Hope scowled, then immediately regretted the impulse. The result was a feeling akin to a renegade herd of cattle stampeding through her head.

"Drink?" she asked, her voice a hoarse, dry whisper. *Whiskey,* she remembered with a groan, *I drank some whiskey.* It took a few more seconds for the memory of what had transpired in the bar to come flooding back — as well as her mission for going there in the first place. "Two glasses of whiskey," she answered finally, squinting at the man as she sent him a weak smile. "Maybe more. I don't remember exactly."

Oh God, I'm in the wrong room. It was the first real thought to pierce the haze of alcohol fogging her mind. She winced as the pain of the realization shot through her already throbbing temples. And what would happen if Luke decided to disobey her instructions and come looking for her? The last thing she needed was for her brother to find her lying in a stranger's bed, with the stranger in question half-naked to boot!

The stranger nodded, his cold smile turning into one of pure deviltry. "Good, we're making progress. Not only have you rejoined the world of the living, but you've also proven you do indeed have a voice. All this in the matter of a few short seconds. Now," his voice grew hard and the smile disappeared as though it had never been, "why don't we move on to what brought you barging into my room in the middle of the night, drunker than a river rat, and who the hell sent you here?" His gaze narrowed. "Keep in mind, I'll settle for nothing less than the truth."

"No one sent me," she replied indignantly, hoisting herself up by way of her elbows as she slid her legs over the side of the bed. The world around her swam with the suddenness of the motion, and her stomach rolled. Gripping the edge of the bed, she waited for the nausea to subside before attempting to stand. Her knees were still weak, but at least they held her weight, albeit with a slight sway. "I—I was looking for someone. Apparently, I picked the wrong room." She cleared her throat, mentally willing the slur from her voice. "It was an honest mistake."

"*If* it was a mistake."

The voice, filled with mistrust, made her slowly turn back toward him. A scowl etched her brow as she peered into the penetrating depths of his eyes. "Of course it was a mistake," she scoffed, slowly plucking up her cloak from where it had been carefully folded at the foot of the bed. "Why wouldn't it be?" Flinging the cloth around her shoulders, she tied a poorly shaped knot beneath her chin.

"I was hoping you'd tell me." The smile was back, but there was nothing at all endearing about it as the man reached behind him and extracted from his belt loop the glistening curved blade of her bowie knife. Hope's eyes widened, her hand awkwardly groping at the pocket of her skirt. She sighed in relief when she felt the small but solid form of her Colt tucked beside the two nuggets of gold. Her relief, she was quick to find, was painfully short-lived.

"Don't bother," he informed her coldly, his eyes glistening with an emotion she didn't dare contemplate. "It's as good as worthless without these."

One by one he tossed the metal bullets atop the bedspread, and she watched in despair as they bounced on the pale ivory surface. Though the effects of the alcohol were beginning to wear off, the sluggishness wasn't entirely gone. Her coordination was slow, her reflexes off, and her head was throbbing fiercely. There was no possible way to get to the bullets before he did, even though an equal amount of distance separated them from the bed.

Hope swallowed hard as her gaze wavered between the bullets and the man she was quickly beginning to dislike. "Is there a point to all of this?" she asked tightly.

"Um-hmmm," he nodded, lazily regarding her through heavy lids. "The point being, you are not going to leave this room until you tell me why you came here."

"I've already told you," she repeated, keeping her voice stern but soft in respect to her aching head. "I made a mistake. People *do* make mistakes, you know. Unfortunately, mine had to be in entering your room." She hesitated, willing calm into the rising panic that laced her words. "Now, why don't you give me back my knife and my bullets so I can leave and find the room I'm supposed to be in."

"Sorry." If it wouldn't have hurt so much, she would have screamed when the man merely shook his head and clucked his tongue. "It was a nice try, that story about stumbling into the wrong room. Very original. But I'm not stupid enough to buy it."

"You're not—"

To hell with the knife and the bullets, she decided abruptly. The rat could keep them for all she cared.

Taking a deep breath, she spun on her heel and bolted for the door. Since the man seemed so intent on keeping her here, she was more than a little surprised that he didn't rush from the chair to stop her. When the doorknob refused to turn under her sweat-coated palm, she realized why.

"Damn it!" she yelled, ignoring the searing pain throbbing in her temples. Pulling back her foot, she hurled her toe into the solid piece of wood. The pain that exploded in her foot

33

was small in comparison to the anger that rushed through her blood. Shifting her weight onto the foot she hadn't been foolish enough to injure, Hope lifted her fists and began pummeling the door. "Help!" she screamed as loud as her headache would allow. "Someone help! Let me out!"

The staccato click of boot heels echoed in the hallway, and her spirits soared. Thank God, help was on the way!

"I'm in here," she called, her heart hammering quick with the relief that warmed her blood. "Quick, please, he's trying to rape me!"

The footsteps approached the door and hesitated. She increased her frantic pounding. Through the crack beneath the door she heard a thick, slurred chuckle, then the footsteps moved on. Shocked into sudden silence, she took a step back and regarded the closed door with all the warmth she would show a rattlesnake. And speaking of rattlesnakes, there was a certain arrogant reptile laughing quite humorously behind her back.

She turned, silencing the deep, pleasantly husky chuckle with an icy glare. "You rat," she hissed, her lips thinning into a hard white line. "You knew he wouldn't stop, didn't you?" She paused, taking a deep gulp of air. "Of course you knew. That's why you didn't stop me from making a total idiot out of myself, isn't it? Because you knew he wouldn't care enough about what was happening in here to even think about offering help."

"Don't be a fool," he scolded, his tone patronizingly dry. "Of course I knew he wouldn't stop. Yelling and screaming goes on around here night and day. Nobody thinks a thing of it. Where are you going?" To his surprise the woman gathered the cloak tightly around her and marched with rigid determination toward the single window behind his chair.

"As far away from you as I can get," she informed him briskly as she gave a push to the smeared bottom pane of glass. Her heart skipped a beat as the wooden frame stuck, then slid high. Unfortunately, it slipped down just as easily, but that minor hindrance could be worked around. She was feeling braver, more confident with the cool night air wafting around her, clearing her senses. Her headache receded to a dull throb.

"We're on the second story," he informed her, his tone dry and unemotional. From the sound of his voice, he hadn't bothered to get up; a fact that hardly surprised her. "It's quite a fall."

"Not if I land on that drunk," she said as she peeked out the window and saw the sprawled form of a man lying face first in the dirt. She wasn't sure, but she would have sworn it was the same one who had almost smacked her in the face with the swinging bar door.

By the time Hope felt the viselike grip wrap around her upper arm, she had already managed to swing both legs out the window and was perched on the sill. She used one hand to prop up the frame above her head while the other steadied her precarious balance. The rose-colored skirt was hoisted well above her knees, exposing more than a proper amount of creamy calves and delicately turned ankles. The folds of her cloak, still inside the room, floated down the wall and draped over the crudely planked floor.

"You're not going anywhere, young lady," the man growled as a hand wrapped around her other arm. It was all she could do to keep the window from falling on her legs as she was forcefully dragged back inside.

As her back came up hard against his chest, she suddenly prayed Luke would disobey her as he always did and come looking for her, fast. The sight of her gigantic brother would certainly knock that overly inflated ego down a peg or two, something this man sorely needed.

"Let go of me this instant, you idiot," she demanded, trying to twist away from his grasp. She might as well have been heaving herself against a brick wall for all the good it did her.

In a repeat performance of what she had done to Luke, Hope pulled back her foot and kicked for all she was worth. Apparently she was worth more than she thought, especially if the man's grunt of pain was anything to judge by.

"Stop it," he ordered as the heel of her boot collided with his shin yet again.

"Not until you let me go," she snapped, slamming her heel down on his toe. Unfortunately, his boots made sure the blow did little damage. She resorted to kicking again.

This time the man waited until her foot was drawn back and ready to strike, then unexpectedly let her go. Hope, unprepared for the sudden release, tumbled backwards, her bottom meeting the hardwood floor in a bone-jarring collision. The force of her momentum thrust her backward, her legs pinned by the twisting skirt and cloak. It was sheer luck that she was able to reach out in time to stop her head from hitting the floor.

So much for fighting fair! she thought as she staggered to her feet and faced her opponent. Expecting a man the size of the rest of the prospectors of Thirsty Gulch, it was not a pleasant surprise to see that this one towered over her by almost a full head. Her courage floundered.

"Are you done?" he asked bitterly. Like a dancer, he balanced his weight on one foot while the other rubbed against his sore shin. He wasn't taking the chance of bending to inspect the damage, she noted, and surmised the reason as rightful mistrust of what she might do next.

"Are you going to let me out of here?" she countered with an indignant toss of her head. A mistake, that, as her pounding temples were quick to inform her.

The gesture made the chestnut curls ripple over her shoulders, swaying freely at the small taper of her waist. In the scuffle, her cloak had parted, the front pleats working their way to the back so the coarse wool now flowed freely over her shoulders. The parting served only to draw attention to the low-scooped neckline of her dress.

36

Noticing where the man's attention lay, she quickly flipped the cloak into place, nestling into its folds as though she hadn't so much as a stitch on beneath. Indeed, from the way those sea-green eyes had ravished her exposed flesh, she might as well not have. There were rumors of the way some men could look at a woman as though undressing her with their eyes, but never had she experienced the sensation—until now.

Planting balled fists on her hips, she valiantly gathered what was left of her courage and proudly returned his glare, measure for angry measure. "I demand you let me out of here."

One golden brow arched, and she would have sworn she saw a fleeting trace of amusement. "You demand? *You* demand?" The chuckle that filled the room was brief and filled with sarcasm. "You are hardly in a position to *demand* anything, sunshine. And I'm not your jailer. If you want to leave, leave." The tanned brow was much too innocently smooth for Hope's liking as he cut a mock bow and swept the interior of the room with a large palm. A crooked smile twisted his lips. "If you can."

Instantly, she turned back to the window, but the voice behind her stopped her cold before the pane was halfway up.

"But not that way."

She dropped the heavy casing as though it had just burst into flames. The thing crashed down onto the sill, the echo of splintering wood loud against backdrop of piano music drifting up from downstairs.

Hope whirled on him. Not since her mother died could she remember being so angry. Her hands clenched and unclenched at her sides, itching to reach out and slap his arrogant face, and at the same time not daring to do so.

Taking a deep breath, she took hold of her emotions and forced her expression into simpering sweetness. "Whah, mistah, Ah don't know why yer so suspicious of a little ol' gal like me." The man turned slowly around and regarded Hope as though she'd just sprouted another head. She batted her dark lashes and smiled coyly. "Ah assure you, sir, Ah mean ya no harm."

The trace of a grin tugged at sensuous lips as his assessing gaze raked her full length, twice. "You've got to be kidding me."

"Rotten Yankee," she muttered under her breath. Crossing her arms over her chest, she tapped out an aggravated rhythm with her toe. "How the hell do you expect me to leave when you've bolted the door and won't let me out through the window?"

"Locked the door," he corrected, slipping his hand into the front pocket of his trousers and extracting a key. He swung it teasingly beneath her nose. "Ah don't know where y'all are from," he said with a heavily satirical, and dreadfully bad, southern accent, "but 'round here, we'all call 'em locks."

She made a grab for the key but his lightning-quick reflexes easily snatched it away. She watched glumly as he tucked it back in his pocket, a cocky smile curling his lips.

"As for leaving," he shrugged. "You got in here all by yourself — you can leave the same way."

"The door wasn't *locked* when I came in," she reminded him, her gaze spitting fire as it settled on his smug countenance.

"It is now," he countered, just as coldly. "You're a smart girl. Figure it out."

If she thought it would have done any good, Hope would have lunged for his throat the second he turned his back on her and returned to his chair. There was nothing hurried in the way he lifted his feet and crossed his ankles atop the ivory comforter. Was his position supposed to be a mockery of her first true look at him, she wondered? Probably. The only difference was, where before his arms had rested on the wooden armrests, they were now crossed over the sinewy chest. From this viewpoint, she had ample opportunity to scrutinize each well-defined muscle that bulged from shoulder to elbow. The sight did nothing to bolster her rapidly dwindling confidence.

All right, she thought with a sigh of annoyance. If playing the rat's silly little game was what it took to get her out of this damn room, then fine, she would play it. But she would settle for nothing less than *winning.*

The lines were drawn, the battlefield mapped. If she wanted to leave, she was going to have to do it alone. No help would be offered from her stone-faced adversary.

The only two options that presented themselves were the obvious: the door and the window. The latter was forbidden, while the former was locked—not bolted, *locked.* That, however, was not an insurmountable obstacle. Every lock had a key, and this one's just happened to rest in a certain pocket. With the man sitting in that particular position, lifting the key off of him without his being aware of what she was doing was impossible, no doubt the reason he had chosen it.

Perhaps if she tried reasoning with him, or tried desperately pleading her case? No, she'd tried that already and it hadn't worked. The fool hadn't believed a word she'd said.

She scowled. Wait a minute. Hadn't her mother once told her that even the hardest of hearts could be swayed by the sight of a woman's tears? Yes, she had. But then, her mother had never met this particular man. A harder heart Hope doubted she'd find. Sighing, she closed her eyes and sent up a silent prayer. *For once, please God, let Mother be right about something!*

She decided to give the man one more chance before trying anything so desperate. "Sure you won't change your mind and unlock the door?" she asked sweetly as the man leaned over and plucked up his bottle of gin.

"Nope."

Okay, the matter was settled. Crying it was. Now, how did one go about forcing oneself into a fit of tears? Crying was not a weakness she liked to see displayed, in herself or others. Even now, it was hard to recall the last time she had allowed herself to indulge in self-pity of any kind. Or was it?

The memory came on her slowly, like the curling vapors of an early morning mist rolling over the water and onto the coast. Slowly, she walked over to the window and leaned against the wooden frame, the man behind her completely superseded by the memories clouding her mind.

They were unclear, fuzzy, fragmented in no discernible order. There was dark, then light. The face of her father, strained with fear as she had never seen it before. She saw her brother through the grimy glass, ten years old and fighting to rub the sleep from his eyes. There was smoke, everywhere there was smoke. She could smell the cloying odor now as surely as if it floated in the air. And pain. Gasping aloud, Hope flinched. Never would she forget the searing pain.

She hugged her arms tightly around her stomach. The tears streaming down her cheeks, the sobs shaking her body, were as genuine as the horrid piano music drifting up through the cracks in the floorboards.

The chair scraped against the floor. Muffled footsteps slowly approached from behind. She ignored the sounds as she sniffed and wiped her nose on her sleeve. The large hand that suddenly draped over her shoulder was not so easily ignored. The warmth of his palm penetrated the wool of her cloak and melted through the rosy muslin gown. It caressed the flesh beneath and made it tingle in a way no other touch had ever done.

"Whatever you're pulling, sunshine, I warn you it won't work." The ominous tone was touched with a trace of sympathy the man would rather not have felt.

She stiffened and jerked away. "Don't touch me, you bastard," she hissed, and with a quick sidestep slipped past him. Angrily, she wiped at the tears that streamed down her cheeks with balled fists, and inwardly flung a string of curses a mile long at the man behind her. It was *his* fault she had been forced to dredge up memories better left forgotten;

memories better left buried in the tiny cemetery in Clairmont, where the ashen remains of her mother's body lay. Of course, it never once occurred to Hope that it had been *her* idea to bring on those tears in the first place. No, far better to lay the blame at a stranger's doorstep rather than her own.

A sarcastic chuckle echoed through the air behind her as the man dragged his fingers through his hair. "Please, spare the theatrics. I've seen acting jobs in a bordello better than the one you just tried to pull off."

"You're despicable," she spat.

"Hmmm," the man breathed, neither agreeing nor disagreeing with her statement. "I've been called worse."

"Somehow that doesn't surprise me." Swallowing the lump in her throat, she willed her painful memories back into the shady corner of her mind where they belonged. Many years of practice made the task surprisingly simple.

His brows rose mockingly high, crinkling his sun-kissed forehead. "Do I detect a note of sarcasm? You know, if you're tired of my company, there *is* a way to leave. Just tell me who sent you to my room tonight and why. Then I'll be more than happy to unlock the door. In fact, I'll even escort you downstairs myself."

His voice had grown soft, cajoling. The change in timbre served to make her all the more leery. "Are we back to that again?" she asked with weary annoyance. "Lord, but I've never met a man as suspicious as you. How many times do I have to tell you? No-one-sent-me-here-I-stumbled-into-the-wrong-room!"

"About as many times as I have to tell you that I-don't-believe-you." His look darkened. "I want the truth."

He was sick in the head, plain and simple. What other explanation could there be? She *had* told him the truth. How many times now? Six? Seven? Did it matter? The man was no closer to believing her now than he had before. What more could she do to convince him? And why the hell did this have to be the first time in his life that Luke did what she'd told him to do!

"Look, mister, it's getting late and I'm tired. I still have a lot to do, and if you don't let me out of here pretty soon I'll—" *What? Break the door down?* She had already tried. The result had been the same as screaming her head off— fruitless. Spinning on her heel, she glared into that narrowed gaze. "All right, you want the truth? You *really* want the truth? Fine, I'll tell you. If you must know, the man who sent me is named Bart Bennett." Her hands rose, then fell and slapped her thighs helplessly. "There, does that make you happy?"

The golden brow knit in a frown as he ran a palm over the bristle of stubble coating his chin. All the while, he gazed at her thoughtfully. "Bart Bennett?" He squinted, shaking his head and searching his memory. "Never heard of him."

Hope sighed in disgust. "Somehow, that doesn't surprise me either, considering he sent me here to meet someone else. Now, I told you what you wanted to know and you agreed to unlock the door in return." She waited patiently, but the man made no attempt to move. "Well? Are you going to let me out of this dump or are we going to stand here and argue all night?"

"Who the hell is Bart Bennett?" he demanded, ignoring her last comment entirely.

"My father." She bit down hard on the inside of her cheek to keep from screaming. Good God, the man's skull was thick. At this rate she'd be lucky to get out of here before dawn! "Now will you please unlock the door?"

In one long stride, he closed the distance between them. Hope stiffened, refusing to be intimidated by that bullying glare, even when his fingers bit painfully into her shoulders.

"That does it," he barked angrily. "I want the truth and I want it now or so help me I'll—"

"Do what?" she taunted, lifting her chin with a courage she did not feel. "Take me over your knee? I'm a little too big

42

for that, don't you think?"

"No, I don't!"

The loudness of his voice echoing in her ears did nothing to alleviate the throbbing that was quickly returning to her temples. It did, however, intricately combine with the strength in his fingers and the anger shimmering in his eyes to effectively bring home the vulnerability of her position here. The man was quickly losing what little restraint he had. If he kept goading her, and she kept responding, God only knew what would happen.

I have to get out of here, she thought wildly, *and I have to get out of here quick!* Desperation made her act impulsively, in the only way Hope knew how. The man held her shoulders, but not her arms. Her lips curled into a cold smile as she did something she'd been longing to do since she had first opened her eyes. She didn't just slap that arrogant face, she balled up her fist, pooled all of her anger into her hand, and punched him as hard as she possibly could. The force of the blow made his head snap back. His hands instantly released her shoulders.

Skillfully, she lifted the key from the man's pocket before he could utter his first grunt of pain. By the time he had reached out a hand to steady his balance against the wall, shaking his head to clear it, she had the door unlocked.

Throwing it wide, she allowed herself a small, heady giggle of triumph. Her giggle turned into a full-fledged laugh when she saw the towering form of her brother standing with his hand poised in mid-knock.

If Luke Bennett had been a smaller man, he might have been sent tumbling backward at the force of his sister flinging herself into his arms. But he wasn't, and Luke didn't so much stagger as he accepted her weight and wrapped a large arm around her shoulder. Confused, he looked down at the top of his sister's head as it nestled into his shoulder, then let his gaze scan the room as he stroked the silky mane of chestnut hair.

The sight of the ugly bruise quickly beginning to swell on the blond man's jaw told Luke all he needed to know. His own deep, rumbling chuckle joined his sister's as he asked, "I guess he said no, huh?"

Chapter Three

Hope's arms dropped away from Luke's shoulders and she took a step back from her brother. "Who?" she asked, her voice as devoid of emotion as her face.

Luke grinned, nodding to the man who was gingerly exploring the bruise on his swollen jaw. "Him. Frazier. He said no, right?"

"Frazier?" She gulped, her head snapping to the side as she cast a quick glance at the half-naked blond. She turned beseechingly to her brother. "Him?" she asked, her voice a small, high-pitched squeak. "No. There must be a mistake." She shook her head, the wild disarray of chestnut curls swaying over her shoulders and back. "No, that's not—"

"Drake Frazier," her brother confirmed, wondering why his sister's cheeks had suddenly faded to such a deathly white, then just as quickly flooded crimson as her dark eyes widened with horror.

"Who the hell did you think I was?" a gruff voice called from behind, and Hope felt the knot in her stomach tighten as she turned toward the speaker.

Her shoulders stiffened as she sent him an indignant glare. "You never said who you were."

"Then why didn't you ask?" Luke phrased the question in such an innocently boyish way that Hope wanted to throttle him on the spot.

"I *did* ask," she informed her brother haughtily. An angry glare told Luke to keep his big mouth shut. Her next words were aimed directly at the man she now knew to be Drake Frazier. "He wouldn't tell me."

"Why the hell should I?" Frazier raged, wincing when his fingers found the center of the bruise on his chin. "You burst into my room in the middle of the night drunker than a skunk—and fully armed, I might add—collapse in my arms, then refuse to tell me who you are, why you came, or who sent you. What the hell did you expect me to think?"

Hope hadn't looked at it quite *that* way before, and she damn well wasn't about to waste time looking at it that way now. She raised her chin high, in what she hoped was a daunting manner. "I expected you to believe me when I said I had the wrong room," she replied tightly.

Frazier's gaze flickered between the two dark heads, eventually settling on Hope. If she had thought to see a measure of intimidation in those eyes when he noted her brother's towering size and girth, she was sorely disappointed. "Your friend here says you had the right room."

"And how was I supposed to know that?" she fairly screamed. Her temper was getting the better of her, but at that moment she didn't care. "You don't exactly fit the description I was given."

"Description?" Frazier's eyes narrowed to thin, sea-green slits as his voice hardened with caution. The hand that had been rubbing his jaw dropped to his side. "What description? Who gave it to you and why?"

She sighed in annoyance. All this bantering was getting them nowhere. She was no closer to obtaining his help now than she had been when she'd first set foot in this room. Although she was sorely tempted to push his anger to its limits, to feed his suspicions, whatever they were, she hesitated. His cooperation was needed desperately, and with a man as conceited, as arrogant, and as exceedingly suspicious as this one was proving to be, angering him would be

46

no incentive. Perhaps a different tactic was in order.

"Well?" His expression told her that he had no intention of letting either Bennett leave until he had the answers he wanted. "Who sent you?"

"My father," she said, holding her aggravation in check with a firm hand. "Didn't I already tell you that?"

"You did. And I still don't believe you."

"Listen, Frazier, my sister may be a lot of things, but she ain't no liar," Luke interceded. Wrapping a hulking arm around his sister's shoulders, he steered her away from the door. "Come on, Hope, let's go home. We don't need this guy's help anyway. I can handle things myself."

"No, you can't," she insisted, stopping her brother just as he was about to close the door. "If you could, I wouldn't be here. Oh, Luke, please don't look so sad," she pleaded, as her brother's crestfallen gaze dropped to the floor. Lord, but she hated it when her brother's lower lip trembled that way. It pulled at her heartstrings, and she had a feeling he knew it.

"You don't trust me," he pouted, his big foot drawing circles in the dust on the floorboards. "Why don't you just say it? You don't think I can beat the Swede, do you?"

"If you're talking about the Swedes who set up camp on the edge of town, then you'd better listen to her. She's right," a deep voice interjected from behind them. The two Bennetts turned to see Frazier regarding them thoughtfully. A trace of suspicion still lurked in his eyes, but it had lessened. "That *is* what this is all about, I take it?"

"Yes," she replied, deciding she might as well tell him the truth now that she knew who he was. At this point, the odds of getting this man to fight in her brother's place were almost as great as their chance of striking it rich in the mines which bordered this pitiful little town.

Drake nodded, and his expression took the form of a man busy fitting the last piece into a jigsaw puzzle. He rubbed his jaw again, his eyes never leaving Hope. "Tell your friend

47

to leave. He can go downstairs and fetch me a piece of beef to put on this bruise while you ask me what you came here for."

"Tell him yourself," she snapped, angry that he would treat her brother like the slab of meat he was referring to. "He isn't deaf."

But Frazier was no longer looking at her. He'd completely dismissed them as he bent to retrieve his glass from beside the recently vacated chair. The bottle of gin was scooped up from the floor.

Her gaze shifted between Frazier, as he splashed some of the clear liquid in the glass, and her brother, who was regarding the reputed gunslinger with open confusion. It was that innocent, guileless look in Luke's eyes that prompted her into a decision. "You heard him," she said to Luke, who stared at her as though viewing a total stranger. She nudged him in the direction of the stairs. "Go ahead," she prodded. "I'll be fine."

"I don't know," he stalled, obviously not pleased with the prospect of leaving his sister in such untrustworthy hands. He lowered his voice, nodding toward Frazier. "I don't trust him, Hope. What if he does us dirty? What if he takes our money, then doesn't come through?"

"He won't," she said firmly, "because I won't let him." She gave her brother another shove. "Now go on. Off with you, you big lug. And *don't* hurry back. It could take me a while to convince him."

"What if you can't?"

"That's my problem, and I'll deal with it when and *if* it comes up. You just go and get him the piece of beef. Hopefully, by the time you come back I'll have him convinced." She gave her brother's arm another shove. "Go on."

Squaring her shoulders, she stepped back into the room and closed the door. She could hear her brother's feet shuffling as he hesitated in the hall, and for a second she didn't think he would obey her any more now than he had in

48

the past. She was wrong. Like an obedient little boy's, his footsteps could soon be heard trailing down the hall.

"You'll have me convinced of what?" Frazier asked. He had moved to the window and was staring broodingly through the smudged pane as he nursed his drink. The bottle hung limply from his other hand as he unconsciously swirled the liquid inside.

So, Frazier was not as oblivious to their conversation as he would have liked her to think. Good. She let that knowledge sink in as she tried to overlook the fact that he hadn't bothered to turn toward her as he spoke. It was an annoying lack of manners, and to a strictly raised southerner, an insult of grave proportions.

Forcing a charming smile to her lips, she chose to ignore the man's disgraceful lack of courtesy. Keeping a strained note from the husky timbre of her voice was not as easily managed. "It would seem we've gotten off to a bad start, Mister Frazier. Shall we begin again?" With one hand behind her back, balled into a tight fist, she extended the other for a handshake.

He turned slowly, sparing the open palm a brief glance before concentrating on pouring himself another drink. That was progress, she thought. At least now he was *looking* at her.

Draining half the liquor, his gaze captured hers from over the rim of the glass. "Convince me of what?"

"Of fighting the Swedes on Saturday," she replied frankly, dropping her hand to her side. Her offer of friendship had been flatly refused. She resorted to bluntness, deciding intuitively it would be the best course of action when it came to handling a man like Drake Frazier.

Drake looked at Hope as though she were insane. Frowning, he tossed down the rest of his drink like it was water. "Why the hell would I do a thing like that?"

"Because I am willing to pay you generously for your—er—time."

49

She couldn't put her finger on it, but in some vague, indefinable way, his manner toward her had changed. She wasn't sure how, or what, had brought the change about, but it was definitely there. His guard dropped, his previous suspicion of her melted like snow under a hot sun once he discovered her reason for sneaking into his room. Or was the change only a trick of her imagination? She wasn't sure.

One blond eyebrow cocked as Frazier regarded her with a lazy smile. "How much?"

"Fifty dollars," she said, trying to hide her disgust for a man who could be bought so easily. Frazier only chuckled and turned back to the window. *So much for being easily bought,* she thought. "Seventy-five?" He seemed not to hear her. "All right," she sighed, taking a long, deep breath, "one hundred. But that's my final offer."

"Then take your money and buy someone else to fight in your pal's place. I'm not interested."

Her jaw hardened. "What do you mean you're not interested? I just offered you—"

"Less than I could make in one hand of poker," he cut her short. "What else have you got?"

"Else?" God, but she hated the way her voice squeaked that way. *Get a grip, Hope. Luke's life depends on it!* "What—" She stammered, clearing her throat. "What do you mean?"

He pulled his gaze from the window and let it trail slowly down her body. He assessed her in much the same way a man would contemplate a horse he was thinking of buying off the block. At any minute she expected him to ask her to open her mouth so he could inspect her teeth, or—she swallowed hard—worse.

"I mean," he said as his gaze ascended at a more leisurely rate, "that you'll have to sweeten the pot substantially if you want me even to consider it."

Scowling, she leaned back against the door. Her whole body felt weak. "I can't," she said flatly, her fingers nervously picking at the coarse wool of her cloak, plucking off an imaginary speck of lint. "It's all we have."

"We?" he asked, his voice a soft, sweet caress. Again she felt his suspicion perk. "Who, exactly, is we?"

Why had the timbre of his voice suddenly changed from harsh and demanding to calm and cajoling? And did it matter? She had a feeling that, yes, it did matter. Everything about this man mattered a great deal. She just wasn't sure why.

She sucked in a deep breath. "My father, my brother, and myself." She purposely made no mention of the rest of their little entourage. It would only complicate matters and warrant a fuller explanation. "We spent most of our savings on supplies. One hundred dollars is all we have left."

Drake nodded as he refilled his glass, then pushed himself away from the window. He approached her slowly, the way a leopard would its prey, and, to Hope's surprise, he offered the glass to her. She looked at the offering suspiciously, but made no move to take it.

"Go ahead," he insisted, pushing it into her suddenly limp hand. "I liked you better when you were drunk. You made more sense."

She sent him a nasty glare. She had no choice but to accept the glass, but she *did* have a choice about drinking the foul-smelling contents. She took a small sip, only to be polite. Drunk was the last thing she needed to be right now. Instinct told Hope she was going to need all her senses intact to match wits with this fellow.

But was matching wits all *Drake Frazier had in mind?* she wondered as he lifted the bottle in a silent toast. That thought alone was powerful enough to spur her into taking another drink, this one longer, as she watched him raise the neck of the bottle to his lips. Unlike the whiskey, the gin tasted bitter as it cut a path down her throat. The two did not mix well in her stomach. Still, there was no denying the nice warm, tingling after-effects. If nothing else, the liquor would help loosen her tongue.

"What if I said I didn't want your money?" he asked, as he wiped his mouth on the back of his hand, then set the bottle on the floor. "What if I said I wanted something else?"

"What else is there?" she countered with mock innocence. Her index finger trailed a nervous path around the rim of the glass. Knowing his lips had just touched the same smooth surface only seconds before did nothing to ease her tension.

A crooked smile played over his lips as his gaze resumed its bold exploration of her body. "Take a guess."

The insinuation was clear enough, and she could feel the hint of a blush kissing her cheek. Her skin felt as though his fingers were trailing hotly over her flesh instead of just his gaze. That the feeling *should* have bothered her, and *didn't*, was more than a little unnerving.

"Money is the only thing being offered here, gunslinger," she said, deciding it might be better to take her business elsewhere. With one hundred dollars, maybe she could buy someone else to fight in her brother's place. Not likely, but possible.

She pushed the half-empty glass at his chest. Her head, a little lighter for the gin, was filled with every intention of leaving.

It had been a mistake, offering him back the glass, but one she didn't realize until it was too late. His thick fingers wrapped around her hand as he reached for it, capturing the hand to his chest, glass and all. The touch was warm, electrifying. It shot through her body with an intensity she would never have thought possible. She tried to pull back, mentally as well as physically, from the feel of his warm skin beneath her knuckles, but his grip held fast. The pelt of curling hair on his chest, something she had been trying desperately to ignore, tickled the back of her hand. The sensations the touch aroused in her were shocking, exciting, and better left unexplored.

"I want more than just your money," he said softly. His

warm breath fanned her upturned face and smelled faintly of tobacco and gin. The scent mixed much too nicely with the aroma of freshly milled soap that clung to his sun-gold skin. "If I'm going to risk my neck, I damn well want to be sure the payment will be worth my while."

"I've already offered you—"

"Not nearly enough. Do you have any idea what could happen to me if I turned up to fight Saturday?"

"Yes," she said, gasping when the roughened tip of his index finger traced the delicate line of her jaw. "I—I know what will happen. The Swedes will be furious my brother won't be fighting. The easy win they'd planned won't be so easy after all." She pulled her head back. It was difficult trying to concentrate with the feel of his chest beneath her hand—and it was damn near impossible to think with his finger trailing freely over the lines of her face! "If they lose, by the camp's bylaws, the Swedes will be driven off our claim and forced to stake another somewhere else; one that might not show as much promise." Sighing, she tried to pull her hand away. His grip held firm and she didn't try again.

"If they lose, they are going to want revenge."

"I won't lie to you, Mr. Frazier. They're a hot-tempered lot of men, even if they aren't too bright. Yes, if they lose, they'll be thirsty for justice. And not just against us. They'll come here first. In their eyes, *you'll* be the one who robbed them of a potentially rich claim by stepping in for Luke." She shouldn't care about what would happen to Drake Frazier once the Swedes got hold of him. Shouldn't, but did. Much to her confusion and dismay, she found that not all of her misplaced concern could be attributed to the mixture of whiskey and gin.

She nibbled her bottom lip, completely unaware of how provocative the gesture appeared. "I haven't got anything else to offer," she whispered hoarsely. The second the words were out, she wished she could take them back. Damn, but it was hard to concentrate with the feel of his heart drumming right beneath her knuckles.

"Don't you?" Again his free hand rose, this time to cup her chin. The feel of his calloused fingers against her skin sent an entirely new shiver of delight coursing through her. "Think again. Even beneath that ugly cloak of yours, a blind man could see that you have one hell of a lot to offer a man."

Her large brown eyes widened. "Mr. Frazier, certainly you aren't suggesting . . ." His grin told her that, yes, that was exactly what he was suggesting. "Oh, no. If you think I'm going to . . ." Her words faded away, and she would have shaken her head to emphasize the protest had his hand not been holding her chin so firmly.

"Why not?" His gaze lingered on her softly parted lips. "Don't I appeal to you?" Her cheeks grew hot with a blush. The sight made his grin broaden. "Or would you rather have your brother go up against one of the Swedes? Funny, but I could have sworn you came here tonight to avoid that."

"I did," she answered miserably, then sighed in frustration. Oh what the hell, she might as well tell him the truth. He had probably already guessed it anyway. "Luke can't fight them. He isn't—he isn't right." The index finger of her free hand tapped her temple. "He's big. He has the strength to win, yes. He just doesn't have the intelligence to back it up. There was an accident when we were kids . . . Look, the reason doesn't matter. What *does* is that they'd make mincemeat out of him in less than a minute. I can't let that happen. He's my brother, for God's sake."

"So you'd rather see them make mincemeat out of me instead, is that it?"

"Yes—no!" She clenched her teeth and glared at him angrily. "Will you please let me go so I can think straight?"

"No."

"You aren't making this very easy, Mr. Frazier."

"That's your problem," he breathed as his thumb returned to caress the delicate line of her jaw. "And call me Drake. After all, we *are* going to be—ahem—*friends*."

"We aren't going to be *anything*," she insisted, trying to pull herself free. "And I'll be calling you a lot worse if you don't let me go." Her voice was rising in near panic, but she could no more control that than she could the frantic pounding of her heart as his fingertip brushed the corner of her mouth. She stiffened. "If you're tying to intimidate me, I might as well warn you it won't work."

But it is working, her mind screamed. *And it's working too damn well!*

Drake ignored her as he slipped the glass from her hand. Where it went, Hope didn't know. Her senses were spinning out of control. She felt his body shift, leaving her for the barest of seconds. The next thing she knew, his chest was pinning her against the door. It was more than the pressure of his body that made her suddenly gasp for air, although she would rather have died than admit it.

In a feeble attempt to free herself, she wedged her hands between their chest, trying to push him away. What a pitiful struggle *that* turned out to be! Her knees turned to jelly at the feel of his bare flesh beneath her splayed palms, and it was by willpower alone that she was able to keep herself from melting into the warm, solid length of Drake Frazier's body.

"Two hundred dollars?" she asked breathlessly. Her voice was nothing more than a throaty whisper as his lips captured her earlobe.

"You don't have that much," he reminded her softly. His breath was like a hot desert wind in her ear.

"I'll get it somewhere," she promised as she pushed at his shoulders.

He shook his head. "Sorry, not enough."

"Three?" she asked weakly. The flick of his tongue, moist and warm, teased the inner recesses of her ear. It was almost more than she could bear. "I have two pieces of gold that are worth—"

"If I wanted your gold I would have taken it when I stole

55

your bullets. Think of something else."

Why was she letting him do this to her? Why was she allowing him to awaken a passion inside her that she could never hope to quench? It was cruel, this sensual teasing, spiteful and cruel. His tender ministrations were stoking a desire in her that she had, long ago, learned she could never have. But, of course, Frazier had no way of knowing the truth.

"Damn it, Frazier, stop that!" she cried when his lips trailed a hot path down the sensitive taper of her neck.

Drake pulled his head up and sent her a look that pierced her to the core. "Why?" he asked dryly. "You wanted to buy me, didn't you? I'm naming my price. I think it's a pretty fair one, considering what you're asking me to risk."

"Name another one," she insisted breathlessly. "One that I can meet."

Although he doubted she was aware of it, the girl's eyes were round with an odd mixture of desperation and fear. Even a fool could see that the terror shimmering in that tearful gaze was genuine; and Drake Frazier was no fool. Reluctantly, he pushed her away.

Hope took a ragged gulp of air and leaned heavily against the door, all the while wondering why her body suddenly felt cold in the spots where his hand warmed it.

"That," he said as he retrieved the bottle and glass, "is my price. Meet it or not, it doesn't matter to me."

Her mind raced. Of course she couldn't meet his price, and for reasons other than the obvious, but she wasn't about to confess it to *him*. No, there had to be another way. Jenny Clarke was the first idea to spring to mind, and Hope pounced on it like a starving cat would a mouse. "What if I were to arrange a—um—*meeting* with someone else?" She rubbed her hands together nervously and tried to gauge his reaction. Damn it, but that face could be as emotionless as a stone! "Would that meet your—er—*needs?*"

Drake casually returned to the chair, stretching his lean

frame out and crossing his ankles beneath the bed. He polished off her unfinished drink, all the while eying her over the rim of the glass. "Depends. Who'd you have in mind?"

Lie, Hope, lie.

"A friend of mine," she answered evasively. Her mind was running in circles as she tried to think of a polite way to describe the brassy redhead, a girl who would lie with any miner who said please in the form of a sack of gold dust. "You'd like her," she rushed on when he sent her a skeptical glance. "She's very well endow—cute." Well, she *could* be, she reasoned, except for the abundance of color the girl caked on her face. "And she knows how to make a man happy." Ah, now that much was *definitely* true. Any prospector seen leaving Jenny Clarke's shanty sported a grin of satisfaction longer than the Ohio River. "Would that arrangement be suitable?"

Please, dear God let him say yes. Why is he shaking his head no?

"Why not?" she cried. She caught herself before she could stamp her foot in childish frustration, but the urge was still there.

His eyes were narrowed, his gaze warm and insinuating. "I've already stated my price. Now it's up to you to decide how much your brother's life is worth to you." His voice hardened. "Keep in mind, though, these fights can get messy."

"You think I don't know that?" she asked, shaking her head incredulously. Hugging her arms close to her chest, she sidestepped the chair and went to the window. It was too smeared with dirt to see much more than the inky black sky above. "I didn't just get off a ship in San Francisco yesterday, Mr. Frazier. My family and I have been in the mines for almost two years now. We've seen more than our fair share of fights over claims." She suppressed a shiver. The memories—one in particular—still had the power to make her blood run cold. The clink of glass meeting glass was followed

57

by the sound of gin splashing into his cup.

"I saw a Swede fight a guy once," she said when he held his peace. Her voice was soft, no stronger than the wind. "He was big, tall, blond. His poor opponents didn't stand a chance."

"Opponents? There was more than one?"

"Um-hmmm," she murmured, lost to the memory. "There were two, the guy originally chosen to fight, and the one who stepped in for him when his friend fell. Both were carted away in a burlap sack. Or, more correctly, what was left of them; neither lived to tell the tale." Slowly, her voice grew stronger as she turned and fixed Frazier with a cold glare. "You see, Mr. Frazier, the winner cheated. He used a knife to win the round. Not that it made any difference to the two dead men.

"To the miners' way of thinking, the Swede won the fight fair and square," she said, her voice filled with contempt. "Who knows? Maybe if the two men hadn't been so new to the mines they would have known that cheating is a way of life to most prospectors. But they *were* new, they didn't know. They fought a gentleman's fight with a man who was as much a gentleman as a cast iron skillet is a teapot; and they lost their lives in the bargain."

Shaking her head in disgust, she turned back to the window. "I still don't understand it. The Swede had size and strength on his side. He could have whipped his smaller opponents without even working up a sweat. He didn't. He cut them down instead. And all I could do was stand there and watch." She cleared her throat and wiped what looked suspiciously like a tear from her cheek. "The Swede passed by me, on his way to the saloon afterward. I heard a friend ask him why he'd bothered with the knife. 'I was winnin' the card game,' he said." She gave an emotionless chuckle. "He killed the two men quick so he could get back to a goddamn game of cards!" Her fist hit the window casing, and the force of the blow surprised even Hope. "Sometimes, in the middle of the night when I can't get to sleep, that voice still haunts me. I don't think I'll ever forget it." She turned to Frazier, who was watching her intently. Her dark brown gaze shimmered with desperation. "I can't let that happen to my brother. Not if I can stop it."

He lowered the glass from his lips. "Your brother is a big boy. I think he can take care of himself."

"No." She shook her head vigorously. "You don't understand. Luke will fight fair. He might be a bit slow with things, but he's a southerner born and bred. He'll fight like a gentleman and expect his opponent to do the same. He won't know what do to if the Swede pulls a knife, or tries some other dirty trick."

Drake eyed her long and hard, then turned his attention away. His voice, when it came, was hard and uncompromising. "Your devotion is admirable, but you're asking a hell of a lot from me. My price still stands, sunshine. You want my cooperation, you pay the price—*my* price."

She closed her eyes and took a deep, steadying breath as her heart plunged. Reluctantly, the words formed on her tongue, but she had to push them forcibly past her lips. "All right," she said, her voice shaking almost as badly as her hands. "I'll do it."

There, she had said it, she had agreed to the impossible. *So why don't I feel any better?* she wondered as she inched her way to the door. Why did she feel like a mouse cornered in a trap of its own making? Deep down, she knew why, but she pushed the answer away, banishing it to a hidden corner of her mind as her hand rested on the doorknob.

The feel of a hand on her cheek made her jump and spin around. She hadn't heard Frazier leave the chair, hadn't heard his silent tread as he crossed the floor. That he had done it so swiftly and stealthily was, of course, the reason for the sudden racing of her heart. Or so she told herself—repeatedly—as her lids flew open and her gaze was captured by intent, searching sea-green eyes.

59

Her throat constricted until she felt as though she would die of suffocation. Surely he wouldn't demand payment *now*. Yet, as his lips slowly descended toward her own, she found that prepayment was exactly what Frazier expected.

"No," she cried, turning her face away so that his lips landed harmlessly on her cheek. Well, not quite harmlessly. Her flesh was sizzling beneath the tender caress of his mouth.

"Don't play games with me, sunshine," a husky voice whispered in her ear as he buried his face in the sweet-smelling softness of her hair. The silky smooth tresses had the distinctively enticing aroma of blossoming lilac petals. A rare scent to be had in these parts to be sure, and one that Drake found he thoroughly enjoyed.

"I'm not playing games," she insisted, forcing her voice to sound calm, rational, everything that her insides were not. She pushed against his chest. Hadn't she learned by now that struggling with Frazier was worse than useless? "I'm not foolish enough to pay you before you do your job. You'll —" she hesitated, her mind racing as she was allowed space to pull slightly back, "you'll get paid Saturday night, after the fight. That is, *if* you show up."

"Oh, I'll show, alright," he replied, his voice a warm rush of breath in her ear, "with the right incentive."

His hands cupped her cheeks, and this time Hope had no opportunity to turn away as his lips claimed her own. Like the man, his kiss was hard and probing, demandingly insistent. She thought about pulling away. His fingers banished that thought as they traveled a slow, hot path over her cheeks, tickling the sensitive hollow behind her ears before his palms moved to support the back of her head. He pulled her closer than she had any right to be, but she was beyond trying to stop him.

His lips tasted of gin, but then, so did hers. The taste was not all that unpleasant. Indeed, just the opposite — it was wonderful, magnificent. Her knees felt suddenly weak, and it was against her will that she leaned against him, molding her body into the hard length of his.

The hands she had raised to ward him off were captured between their bodies, and the sensation of his bare flesh beneath her fingers assaulted her at the same time his tongue ran a flickering trail along her upper lip. A faint sigh floated on the air. It took a few seconds for Hope to realize the husky whisper, echoing over the off-key piano music, had emanated from her own throat.

The only things holding her up at that precise moment were the strong hands resting on the gentle curve of her waist. As his mouth teased her full, lower lip, his hands slipped around her. One cupped the small of her back while the other strayed to a point just below her shoulder blades. Both pulled her closer to that hard, lean frame, and both made the skin beneath her clothes feel as though it was smoldering.

She didn't realize she had allowed her own hands to stray higher until she felt the soft silk of his hair beneath her fingertips. The baby-fine curls that played at that thick nape wrapped around her fingers as she pulled him closer.

Pulled him closer? She hardly heard the strange, haunting echo of her mind. It was overridden by warm waves of eager anticipation, sensations that quickly flooded the rest of her body. It no longer mattered that she could never follow through on these feelings. What mattered was that she felt them, and they felt sinfully delicious!

The probing of his tongue became more insistent as he tested the place where her lips met, forging a path that let him invade the soft, moist recess and explore at leisure the perfect, even line of her teeth. Her own tongue ran frantic circles against the opposite side of the barrier, but she dared not surrender to the urge to remove the impediment for fear she would lose what little control remained of her badly tattered defenses.

I can't lose control, she reminded herself briskly, trying in vain to stem the liquid fire coursing through her veins. *Not with Drake Frazier, not with anybody.* But damn him! Why did he have to so expertly arouse the forbidden desires she had, in all her innocence, thought she could live without?

Drake took full advantage of her momentary lapse into thought. The second he felt her defenses slacken, he slipped his tongue into the honeyed sweetness of her mouth.

Stop this exquisite torture? Why would I want to? Restraint was only a dwindling memory as all form of protest left her mind.

She returned his kiss with a timid intimacy that grew bolder with each passing second. At first her tongue coyly flicked against his, darting and retreating, only to search again. But with each retreat, he sought her out, teasingly probing her into an awareness that was sweeping away her self-control at an alarming rate. She was vividly aware of every male inch that pressed tantalizingly against her.

The hands she'd wrapped around his neck now roved curiously over broad shoulders, glorying in the feel of muscles bunching tightly beneath her fingertips. His flesh seemed alive with the sinewy tendons beneath, tendons that seemed to be everywhere her inquisitive palms roamed. They were on his shoulders, his back, his upper arms. Even the thick cord of his neck was alive with movement as his mouth worked its sweet magic over hers. The curling golden hairs coating his chest tickled her palms and sent white-hot sparks of delight shooting up her arms, sparks that wrapped tightly around her heart and stole her breath. The taut line of his stomach was being thoroughly investigated just as his lips playfully encircled the timid exploration of her tongue, gently sucking it into his mouth.

Her fingers quickly surrendered themselves to the pleasures to be had. One of Frazier's hands, riding the curve of her back, pulled her closer. The other slid up her back and entwined itself in the cascade of shimmering chestnut satin. She ran her tongue along the line of his teeth, and her reward was a sweet, guttural moan released from somewhere deep in that muscular chest. The moan was soon joined by a soft sigh of her own.

There was another sound, too, one that Hope was becoming aware of in slow, languid degrees. It was the sound of knuckles rapping sharply on the door behind her. The noise, once it penetrated the foggy recess of her mind, served to jar her to her senses like no logic could have.

"Hope!" a frantic voice demanded as the knocking turned into an insistent pounding. The sound of a board splintering beneath a meaty fist cut the air, making her drop her hands as though she had just found them attached to the leathery hides of a crocodile.

He stiffened, his mouth leaving hers long enough to utter a string of muttered curses beneath a ragged breath. "Go away," he growled to the intruder, but it was already too late. The girl had pulled away from him and was regarding him with a look that was half passion, half terror. Even a fool could have seen her fear went far beyond virginal innocence.

"Hope, are you still in there?" The pounding grew more insistent, almost matching the frantic tempo of her heart as she took a weak step backward.

"Yes," she answered shakily. Her fingers were trembling badly as she raised them to her lips and sent the gunslinger a look filled with confusion, and a goodly portion of self-recrimination. "J-just a minute," she stammered, dropping her hand to her side the second she realized what she was doing. "I'll b-be right there."

"Hurry up," her brother barked testily, annoyed at being left alone in the hall.

She reached shakily behind her, wrapping her fingers around the doorknob as she sent Frazier a questioning glance. The feel of hard metal beneath her palm was oddly reassuring, as was the knowledge of Luke's presence just beyond the thick panel.

"You'll be there on Saturday?" she asked, her voice a

faint, husky whisper as she turned the knob.

The man looked long and hard into the beseeching, velvet brown gaze, and for a split second she expected him to refuse. Instead he nodded, turning away as he combed his fingers through wheat-gold hair and went in search of his infernal gin.

"I'll be there," he answered gruffly. He found the glass and drained it in one long gulp. He didn't bother to turn toward her as he asked, "And Saturday night, you'll be here?"

Hope was glad his back was to her, glad he could not see the flinch of self-hatred shimmering in her eyes as she slowly opened the door and backed out of the room.

Chapter Four

Saturday dawned hot and bright. Rumors of the fight between Luke Bennett and Oren Larzdon had spread faster than a brushfire. By mid-morning the sun was beating unmercifully on the miners' hat-covered heads as they left their diggin's and gathered at the outskirts of camp. The only relief from the heat was the cool southern breeze filtering down from the high Sierra Mountains. The gusts twisted in fluctuating waves through the rocky valley of Thirsty Gulch. The American River gurgled on, oblivious to those who continued to work it, ignoring the commotion.

Only two woman were present among the fifty or so men. Both were new to the camp. They'd arrived by muleback mid-week, and their presence caused a flurry of commotion amidst the women-hungry men. In less than two days the petite blonde widow had found herself an intended. The other, a plump, sandy-haired woman with five older children, was standing beside the husband she had traveled from the Northeast to join.

More than one covetous eye turned their way time and again. The women clung nervously to their men as they regarded the ragged faces around them with caution.

Hope slowed her burro as she rounded the path nature had crudely cut through the granite walls. Shielding her eyes from the sun, she squinted at the crowd. It was impossible to discern her men from the rest. They all looked alike: tattered clothes billowing clouds of dust with every movement, expectant faces so dark with dirt that the eyes and teeth looked stark white in comparison.

She nudged the burro on. The smell of sweat-soaked bodies and horse dung stung her nostrils. The former, of course, was due to the scorching fierceness of the day. No man would smell pretty after he'd just crawled out of a coyote hole. The shafts, dug deep in the ground to get at gold panning wouldn't reach, baked openly beneath the sun. The latter odor, ripe and pungent as it rippled through the air, was caused by the horses attached to the whims, large, hourglass-shaped drums used to hoist the miners from the coyote holes in round, crude wooden buckets.

In the distance, over the hum of conversation and the gentle whisper of the hot, dry wind and churning river, Hope could hear the grinding of the newly constructed stamp mill. Situated halfway between the town and the mines, the mill was in constant use. In the six days since their arrival, she had quickly grown used to hearing its annoying, crushing sound long into the night, as the newly dug gold was separated from the quartz.

The building's services were in such demand that another mill was under construction, this one wisely located closer to the diggin's. It was only a skeletal shell right now, but by the time winter set it, it would be in full swing. The new mill would rob no business from the old, but it would make the chore of loading and toting the heavy rock much easier for the miners.

"Hope!" A craggy, weathered voice called as she neared the outskirts of the gathering crowd. "Over here!"

She looked up to see a scrawny old man standing to the left of the sparse circle of men. He was waving his hat in the air to grab her attention. A worn leather vest draped his bony shoulders, covering the faded gray shirt beneath. A pair of limp, faded green trousers that had seen better years hung from his waist. Wispy pieces of a beard coated his pointed jaw. They were almost as scarce as the tufts of sun-whitened hair clinging to his well-seasoned scalp. His eyes, an indeterminate shade of hazel, were crooked. One bulged while the other narrowed into a permanent squint. That, in combination with a chin that jutted from his face at an unusual angle, as though he was always in the process of mid-chew, lent him a decidedly unfriendly appearance.

At Hope's smile and nod, Old Joe nudged the man beside him.

Bart Bennett was four inches shorter than his son Luke, and not nearly as thick. Unlike his old friend, his worn clothes fit his lanky frame well. He mumbled something to Old Joe before parting from the group. Eying his daughter warily, he approached the mule. His gait still held a trace of the swagger of a man used to roaming the rolling hills of his Virginia plantation.

"Thought I told you to stay put, missy," he said in the same thick southern drawl that had spun many a late night story. Though he wasn't large, Bart Bennett had the voice and carriage of a man twice his size.

"You did." Hope nodded, as she slipped from the burro's back, sending her father her most charming smile. As always, it melted the frosty demeanor Bart constantly strove to maintain with what he'd grown to regard as his sinfully wayward daughter.

"But you came anyway. Now, why aren't I surprised?" His sharp gaze scanned the crowd, noticing the men's hungry reaction to his daughter's presence.

Hope's smile weakened. She wasn't as oblivious to the stares as she pretended, however, they didn't bother her nearly as much as they bothered Bart. "Where's Luke?" she asked with forced cheerfulness. She watched, amused, as her father gauged the reactions of the men closest to them.

"Just sent Old Joe went to fetch him."

"And the twins?"

"Keeping an eye on the Swedes," Bart snorted as he glared at a young, tow-headed fellow who had the nerve to stare longingly at the high-buttoned neckline of his daughter's dress.

The thick cord of hair, caught at her nape with a peach ribbon, swayed at her waist as she followed her father's gaze. The young man in question was quick to turn his lecherous attention elsewhere. Hope anxiously scanned the crowd of eager, grubby faces. Her spirits dropped. Drake Frazier was not to be found.

Bart's gaze also followed suit. "Where is he?"

"He'll be here. Give him a chance."

"Hmph! We'll see about that, missy. We'll just see."

He will be here, she told herself, *he promised. Even a rat like Drake Frazier wouldn't go back on his word. Or would he?*

Unfortunately, her conscience chose that moment to remind her that she, too, had made a promise she never intended to honor. The memory of the pact did nothing to ease her tension. What if Frazier suspected her deception and decided not to fight because of it? No, he couldn't suspect. She'd given him no reason to think she wouldn't keep her end of the deal. But what if he *had—*?

Hope had no time to finish the thought as a murmur of approval rushed through the men. She turned to see Old Joe escorting Luke toward them. A few men reached out to pat the large back. One or two voices raised to call out a word of encouragement. Luke looked at them all as if they'd lost their minds. The look he sent his sister was filled with even more confusion. Hadn't Hope said he wouldn't be fighting today? Hadn't she said Frazier would be taking his place? Luke peered over the crowd with a scowl. The towering blond head was nowhere to be seen, and his sister looked more nervous than he'd ever seen her.

Old Joe opened his mouth to speak, then snapped it shut when Luke asked the very question he'd been about to voice.

"Where is he, Hope?" Luke asked as he joined them.

"How the hell should I know?" Puckering her lips, Hope turned her attention back to the crowd. For a split second, she saw a head whose coloring could rival that of the gunslinger's. When the man came into full view, she recognized the narrow shoulders and scrawny chest as belonging to Mac Snidley, the man whose coyote hole bordered theirs.

"You *are* the one who hired him." Bart's voice drew her attention back. "Didn't he say what time he'd be here?"

Her spirits dipped again as Hope nibbled her lower lip and frowned. "No, he didn't say," she lied, her throat constricting. Only now did she realize that, in her nervousness three nights ago, she had forgotten to tell Frazier what time the fight was. What if he thought it was to be in the afternoon? Worse still, what if he'd thought it was earlier this morning—and had already come and gone?

Bart's jaw tightened. "Well, missy, didn't you ask him?"

"Don't matter if she did or didn't." Old Joe's craggy voice saved her from answering. He nodded his fuzzy chin to a spot just beyond her shoulder. "He's comin' now."

Drake Frazier walked down the narrow dirt path with a gait that bespoke a man ready to win. His determination was reflected in each long stride as his boot heels crunched over the bits of dirt and gravel cluttering the trail. One by one, his commanding presence captured the miners' attention.

The gunslinger had come prepared to fight. Unlike the snug denims of three nights ago, the pants he wore now were loose-fitting, chocolate brown trousers. A cottony green plaid shirt billowed appealingly over the muscles in the broad shoulders and sinewy arms. The sleeves of the shirt were rolled to just below the elbows, exposing a good deal of bronze flesh and enticingly proportioned forearms. Since no hat graced his head, there was nothing to stop the light stirring of the breeze from blowing at the golden mane that framed the broad forehead and rugged cheekbones.

His confident, bordering on arrogant, stance set him

apart from the rest of the men. Hope noted that, as he reached the outskirts of the crowd, there was something about his mannerisms that showed him at ease with the others. He didn't openly greet the men surrounding him, yet he didn't peer down his nose at the prospectors, either. Instead, he joined the circle as though he belonged there, and, even though he towered above most of the others, he appeared oddly at home.

"I told you he'd be here," Hope informed her father with a proud smile. She watched, transfixed, as Frazier stopped to exchange greetings with a ragged miner.

"Hmph!" Bart snorted, then turned to Old Joe, but not before Hope could spot a hint of relief shimmering in his steely eyes. "For one hundred dollars, I didn't think he'd show."

Old Joe plucked off his hat and scratched vigorously at the weathered bald spot crowning his scalp before setting the worn leather back atop his head. His angular shoulders rose in a lazy shrug. "Some men'll do anythin' for a buck. Specially a fella like that 'un."

Money? Ha! If they only knew the half of it. She hadn't told them about the deal she'd struck with Frazier, and she didn't intend to. She hadn't even told Luke. There was no need, since she had no intention of honoring it.

Hope winced. Many times they had questioned Frazier's reasons for accepting a mere pittance for risking his life in going up against the Swedes. Never once did they question Hope's methods of getting him to do so. Their open trust ate at her conscience, such as it was. In securing her brother's life, her pride had taken a mortal blow. Never before had she given her word then reneged, and to do so now disturbed her more than she cared to admit.

"Think he can do it?" Luke asked Old Joe, as Frazier shook one miner's hand, then cheerfully clapped another on the back.

The old man jammed his fist in his pockets, cackling,

"He'd better. We already got a shaft dug. Hate like hell to leave it now." He nodded to the men gathering on the other side of the crowd. " 'Specially knowin' *they'd* be benefitin' from all our hard work."

Hope followed his gaze, her throat tightening. With the exception of one, all were tall, brawny men, almost equal to Luke in size and stature. Like the Bennetts, they'd traveled from camp to camp, looking to stake a rich claim. This time, they'd picked one already taken by the Bennetts. Things had turned nasty and then the Swedes came up with their idea. What could be simpler than having each group pick their biggest, strongest man to wage a fistfight, winner take claim? Hope, to her eternal regret, had somehow agreed. Since the idea didn't go against the town's bylaws, the agreement was considered settled.

Unfortunately, if Hope hadn't overlooked the most important aspect—who would fight. Old Joe was too old. So was her father. The Manchester twins weren't big enough to stand half a chance at winning. That left Luke. With his size and strength, he was the obvious candidate, and yet, because of his mental impairment, he couldn't be. The only flaw in an otherwise flawless plan, she belatedly mused.

"What if we lose?" Luke asked Old Joe. When he received no answer, he tapped his father's shoulder. "Does that mean we still have to pay Frazier, Pa? Even if he loses?"

"Dead men don't need money," Bart grumbled.

Drake Frazier emerged through the men to Hope's right and approached the group. A quick glance at the Swedes, who were eying them carefully, told her that this new development hadn't gone unnoticed. He didn't break stride as he latched onto Hope's arm and continued to move, with her in tow.

"A moment alone with your daughter, Bennett," was all the greeting he gave as he dragged a protesting Hope in his wake.

The shade of the granite boulder two feet away was a

welcome respite from the heat. Hope took no time to enjoy it. She swept a few chestnut wisps back from her brow and glared at him angrily. "What do you think you're doing?" she demanded when they stopped short, out of the crowd's hearing distance.

Although the hand was no longer pulling her, it was still painfully attached to her arm. She tried to shake it off, but like a pesky burr, it refused to leave.

"I'm upping the ante," Drake replied with a wry twist of his lips. His eyes shimmered in the rays of the late morning sun.

"Upping the—? What?! You can't do that!"

He chuckled sarcastically, running a roughened palm over his stubbled jaw. "Why not?" he shrugged. "I thought your offer over and realized that what you're offering is *not* worth risking my neck over. Now, either you make swallowing a few teeth worth my while, or your brother can do the fighting himself." He grinned wickedly, knowing damn well she wasn't in a position to refuse him. "Which will it be, sunshine?"

Hope's eyes narrowed and her stomach felt as though it had been tied in a strong, hard knot. What, exactly, did he want more of? "Isn't it a little late for this, Frazier?" she asked, her cheeks draining of color. "I told you before, one hundred dollars is all we have. Less now. What else is there?"

"What I want," he replied, his words slowed to prolong her agony, "is a cut of the take. If I win, I want part of the mine."

"Part of—but that's ridic—!" She snapped her mouth shut and took a few quick breaths to calm her temper. It didn't work. "What if you lose?" she asked tersely, as he dropped his hand from her arm. "What then?"

"I never lose." Drake caught and held her gaze, his smile outrageously confident.

Hope tore her attention away, sparing a glance at the tall, lusty, blond men. Which one would fight? It would have been tough to decide which of the four was the largest, the most foreboding. They all looked like they could easily tear the large boulder beside her out of the ground with their bare hands.

Frazier's gaze followed her own, but Hope noticed that it was entirely lacking in fear. Instead, every fiber of his body seemed rigidly self-assured. The man's ego was truly amazing.

"Let's suppose you *do* lose," she continued tightly, crossing her arms over her chest. "Whether you want to admit it or not, there *is* that chance. If we're going to make a deal here, I want to know exactly what I get out of it."

"Spoken like a true southern brat," he quipped sarcastically. "If I lose, Miss Bennett, you'll hardly win."

"As it stands right now, *Mr. Frazier*, if you lose, we move our camp. Obviously, no one will profit if that happens."

He smiled dryly. "Obviously. Any suggestions?"

"Yes, actually. On the off chance you do lose, I want all debts to be considered null and void." She averted her gaze to a pebble near her foot. "I think that's fair."

"Fair? It's fair only if you aren't the one bleeding in the dirt." He rubbed his jaw thoughtfully, his gaze focusing on the Swedes, then shook his head. "No. It was a good try, sunshine, but my original price stands. Even if I lose, I get the hundred dollars," he paused for the length of a heartbeat, "and the pleasure of your company for one night. If I win I get the same, plus a healthy cut of what comes out of your claim."

"But you won't work it," she sneered. "What's the matter, gunslinger? Afraid a little good, honest work might get your hands dirty? Or is it your reputation you're worried about?"

"The only thing I'm worried about right now is whether or not I can trust you," he growled.

His answer, shockingly honest, took Hope by surprise. She blushed fiercely when she realized his mistrust was well-founded.

"Of course I can be trusted," she lied, thrusting her chin up proudly as their gazes clashed. "No reason to think I can't be."

"Oh no? Look over there," he said, nodding to a point past her shoulder. "I can't believe all those men would let a woman — a supposedly decent one, mind you, not the ones at The Brass Button Tavern — roam the countryside unattached. Not when there are so many men and so few skirts. Logic says there's got to be a reason for that."

There was a reason, a good one. But Hope would be damned if she'd share it with the likes of this conniving rat! "Let's leave my personal life out of this, gunslinger. What I do, and who I do it with, is none of your goddamn business."

"It is if you'll be carrying anything contagious to my bed, lady." His attention returned to the men. "Miners aren't the cleanest of men. And they aren't known for being very particular about their women."

Hope contained the urge to slap the arrogant smirk from his face by balling up her hands into tight fists. The tips of her fingernails dug painful crescents into the fleshy part of her palms. She was blushing, she could feel it, and she hated the instinctive reaction. "I am no man's 'woman,' " she hissed indignantly, flexing her fingers and willing them to refrain from doing what they itched most to do.

Frazier's lazy smile made Hope's urge to whack him all the stronger. Containing her anger wasn't easy, but by using a healthy dose of Bennett determination, she managed.

Looking away for a diversion, she noticed the group behind her. The men shuffled restlessly, mumbling amongst themselves. Her father had stepped into what was now a circle of men, and was talking to one of the Swedes. The wild gestures of the burly blond suggested that whatever Bart Bennett was saying, it wasn't welcome news.

Her palms went suddenly moist and a surge of fear rushed through her veins. "It's time. Are you going to fight?"

"Depends. Do we have a deal?"

Hope sighed. There was no way out. He'd cornered her someplace between saving her pride and saving Luke's life. The latter easily won out. She forced the air from her lungs and drew in another ragged breath. "Yes," she said weakly, "we have a deal. I—I'll talk to my father and see what can be done about the mine."

"And tonight?" His voice was a soft, husky whisper as the tip of a calloused finger traced the smooth line of her jaw. "Don't tell me you forgot about tonight, sunshine?"

She swatted his hands away. "As if you'd let me!"

Frazier's deep, rumbling laughter was her only answer as he cupped her cheek, then dropped his hands to his side. His voice was still thick with humor as he said, "You know, I once read in a book—yes, I *can* read, don't look so surprised—that in medieval times, a lady fair would give her lover a token to take into battle. It was supposed to bring the fighter luck." All laughter was suddenly gone as his voice lowered to a throaty pitch. "Are you going to give me a token, Hope?"

"This isn't the Middle Ages," she replied tightly, hiding her surprise that a man like Drake Frazier would even know about such things. "And I am definitely *not* your lover."

"Yet," he dared to remind her. The single word coiled around Hope's spine. "A technicality that *will* be remedied. But I'd still like a token."

"Don't tell me you believe in that nonsense," she scoffed, gasping when he reached down and pulled a glistening, curved blade bowie knife from the top of his boot.

Before Hope could stop him, the sun-bronzed hands had reached out and sliced free a thick chestnut curl. His other hand returned the knife to its hidden sheath.

"A token," he stated, much too lightly for Hope's liking as her fingers automatically groped the place where the curl had been. She gaped, her mouth open wide in silent protest, as Frazier wound the thick lock of hair around his hand.

"Ready?" he asked, as he slipped the chestnut strand from

his knuckles and tucked it into his pants pocket.

He didn't wait for an answer as he strode by her, leaving nothing for Hope to do but follow in his wake. Not a pleasant prospect that, she soon realized as she was forced to face that broad back, and the swaggering stride of his lean hips.

Bart Bennett's gaze drifted from the brooding Swede to his daughter. Hope nodded tightly and took her place between Luke and Old Joe. Frazier stood a small distance from Luke. Although his gaze seemed to be drifting lazily about his surroundings, Hope doubted the sea-green eyes missed a thing.

"What's going on?" she asked Old Joe when her father and the Swede launched into another angry bout of conversation.

"Garth's madder'n a polecat in heat cause Luke won't be fightin'." Coughing in the back of his throat, he turned his head and spit in the dirt near his feet.

Luke puffed his chest proudly. "He's gonna be even madder when he finds out who's taking my place."

Watching Bart and Garth split apart, Hope had a feeling the Swede had just found out. Garth glared over his shoulder as Bart rejoined his group.

"Well?" Old Joe asked. "What'd he say?"

"What *could* he say?" Bart shrugged. "It wasn't in the rules that we couldn't get outside help. Nobody said outright that you were fighting, they just assumed it. Isn't our fault they jumped to the wrong conclusion."

"A conclusion we goaded them into," Hope chirped in.

"Maybe." Bart shrugged. "Maybe not. The point is, Luke's not fighting." He turned his attention to Drake, although his words were aimed at his daughter. "Your friend here is."

A flicker of unease washed over her as she watched the Swede Frazier would be fighting approach the other side of the circle.

76

Of course, Oren Larzdon turned out to be the biggest, brawniest man of the lot. His snowy blond head easily towered over the other men around him. His shoulders were wide, his arms muscular. There was a hardness in the bony face, and a flash of shrewdness in the pale blue eyes. Gut instinct told Hope that this man had no intention of fighting fair.

While her first impulse was to warn the gunslinger, the memory of his bowie knife was still fresh enough to stop her. Unlike Luke, Drake Frazier was prepared for any surprises. Her tension ebbed, but only slightly. She wouldn't feel completely at ease until the fight was over, no matter what the outcome.

"Ready?" Bart asked Drake, who nodded curtly. "Well then, let's get this over with. I got work to do."

Bart strode toward the circle's empty center. Garth and Oren approached from the other side. Frazier, however, did not fall into step behind her father. Instead, he took a sharp detour to the right, until he was standing barely a hands-breadth away from a startled Hope.

His eyes were intent as his gaze caressed her face. Was he trying to memorize her features, or, more likely, to remind her of their deal? She wondered, as she returned his gaze measure for measure.

Wordlessly, Drake's arm snaked out. It wrapped around her waist and back as he pulled her supple body roughly against him.

Hope was too stunned to protest as his lips crashed down on hers. His mouth was hard and demanding, yet at the same time sweetly draining, as it extracted from her a response she fought hard not to give.

In a heartbeat the kiss was over. Hope stumbled back a step when there was no longer a strong arm to support her trembling weight. Her fingers fluttered to her lips, her mouth still hot from the passionate kiss. Her eyes widened, confusion sparkling in their dark brown depths.

"Incentive." It was all the explanation Frazier offered before spinning on his heel and joining her father.

Her surprised gaze followed the arrogant strides. She tried hard to ignore the shocked stares of those around her. Had she looked, she would have seen the spark of realization twinkling in Old Joe's eyes.

Garth and Bart exchanged words. When they were through, Garth stepped over to the two contestants. Gripping the wrists of both men, he raised their hands in the air and turned his attention to the crowd. A murmur of approval echoed around Hope.

"Are yew ready?" he asked each man, his voice deep, penetrating, and thick with an odd European accent.

Both men nodded in turn. Garth dropped their hands, then stepped back. Bart had already retraced his steps to take a place at Old Joe's right.

The fight had begun.

The crowd grew quiet as the two opponents came face to face for the first time. Although both were tall, the Swede was taller. To the observant eye, both displayed equal amounts of strength and cunning.

Each combatant judged the other carefully, measuring up his strengths and weaknesses with a cold, calculating glance. The final outcome would rely heavily on these first, fleeting impressions.

The two men circled each other. Both crouched low, waiting for the other's attack. They had come almost full circle when Larzdon's meaty fist swung out in a direct path for Frazier's jaw.

Frazier ducked. The fist collided with empty air, missing his head by mere inches. Using the momentum of regaining his stance, he sank his fist deep in the Swede's stomach.

Oren grunted as the air rushed from his lungs. His body instinctively doubled at the waist. Drake sent the other fist crashing into his opponent's jaw before he'd completely pulled back from the first. The weight of the collision sent the Swede tumbling backward in the dirt. He landed with a thud and a cloud of dust, like a giant cedar being felled.

Although he'd gained the initiative, Frazier didn't launch another attack. Still crouched, he backed far enough away for Larzdon to regain his footing. He stayed close enough to imply the threat of danger.

Shaking his head, the Swede stumbled to his feet. Judging from the look on his face, he was as surprised as the rest of the men by Frazier's tactics.

"Come on, Frazier," a loud voice called out from the eerily silent crowd.

Larzdon balled his fists and brandished them in front of his wide chest. Unlike Frazier, who never stayed in the same spot for long, the Swede's feet were firmly rooted. He was going to make his opponent come to him.

"Got a bet on you," another yelled, never stating exactly *who* the bet was on.

Impatient to get on with it, Larzdon gave a feral growl and rushed. The thick muscle of his shoulder drove hard into Frazier's stomach. Both men were propelled backward. They landed in the dirt, the Swede on top, straddling Frazier's stomach as the other landed on his side. A fist drew back, and Hope flinched as it smashed into Drake's cheek. Hope felt the wave of pain as though it were her own.

The Swede pulled back to throw another punch. With lightning-quick reflexes, Frazier balled his fist and, cupping it with the other palm for leverage, jabbed his elbow into Larzdon's midsection. The elbow sank into the Swede's ribs, making Larzdon's aim go high. His fist barely grazed Frazier's temple. A roar of approval spread through the crowd as they made their favorite known.

With a quick thrust, Frazier toppled the man over and rolled to his feet. Larzdon landed on his side, his weight supported by his elbow while his free hand wrapped around his fractured rib.

Drake balanced himself on one foot, spinning on the ball

of his sole as he lashed out with the other. The heel of his boot crashed into the Swede's neck. With a strangled cry, Larzdon's back collided with the ground.

This time there was no chance for recovery. Drake was on him in an instant. His fist cracked into Larzdon's jaw, then delivered a second blow to the Swede's midsection.

Larzdon was at a disadvantage in this position and his eyes showed that he knew it. Unless he could wrestle himself free, the fight was over. Apparently not ready to surrender to defeat, his large fists flew, occasionally landing one lucky punch for every three of Drake's well-aimed blows.

By the time the Swede had regained his footing, both men were soaked with blood and sweat. Breathing hard, Larzdon resorted to his initial approach. Again Drake ducked. Oren was prepared for the move. His knee came up just in time to crack into Drake's chin.

Hope matched Drake groan for groan as she collapsed against her brother's arm and buried her face in his sleeve. The sound of fist hitting flesh rang clear on the late morning air and a small whimper of trepidation escaped her lips.

"Holy shit, he's got a knife!"

Old Joe's words caused icy fingers of fear to wrap around Hope's heart. Her head snapped up and her eyes once again focused on the fight.

Larzdon's lips drew back in a sinister smile, made even more evil by the gaping hole that had once been a front tooth. A steady stream of blood and saliva trickled down his chin. The blade of the knife was long, slightly arched as it shimmered in the sunlight. The redwood handle was nestled firmly in the Swede's sweaty palm.

Draw your knife! Hope screamed her thoughts to Drake. *Can't you see? He'll skin you alive if he can. Draw-your-knife!*

Drake lithely sidestepped Larzdon's sweeping hand. The movement was repeated. Oren thrusted. Frazier retreated far enough to avoid damage as his gaze flickered between the knife and his adversary. They reached the edge of the crowd, close enough for Hope to smell their sweat and to hear their ragged breaths. Her own was clogged somewhere in her throat, released in a gasp when Larzdon thrust again.

Luke's arm tightened around her waist as he stepped back with those around him, dragging her at his side.

The Swede's thrusts grew stronger, more confident with each swipe and retreat. He was playing with Drake, luring him toward a rock that would cause the gunslinger's footing to stumble. Then he'd be on him in a second.

Hope had a vision of the last fight she'd witnessed. She strained against the hindrance of Luke's arm as she lurched for the knife concealed in Drake's boot. If he wouldn't use it, she would!

As if sensing her intent, Drake stepped out of reach. Larzdon swung again, slicing a hole in the front of his opponent's shirt. His sinister chuckle hissed through the air.

Hope balled her hands into fists. *Her stupid, useless fists!* If Drake Frazier died, his blood would be on *her* hands. The thought was like a bucket of ice water splashing her face. With an insistent shove, she broke free of her brother's arms — only to be caught by Old Joe as she tried to bolt.

"Let me go," she demanded, lifting a foot and bringing it down hard on the old man's toe. He grunted in pain, but his grip held firm. For a man of his size and stature, he was strong. "I have to help. Let me go!"

"Why?" Old Joe barked in her ear, shifting her weight to prevent her from treading on him again. "So's you can get yerself killed too? Ha! Not a chance!"

A scream, hitch-pitched and eerily feminine, rippled over the hushed voices, stilling Hope in an instant. Her attention snapped to the combatants just as the sandy-haired woman collapsed into her husband's arms.

A smile spread over Frazier's face as he watched Larzdon's cheeks drain of color. The Swede's eyes were fixed on the long, curved steel of the bowie knife, and the hand that expertly wielded it. In comparison to the gunslinger's skill, his own attempts to end the fight looked clumsy and awkward.

The advantage had shifted so silently and swiftly that Larzdon seemed at a loss as to how it had happened. One second he was toying with the gunman, confident of victory; the next he was forced into a position that would take every ounce of his ability to survive.

Drake advanced, his stance low to balance any sudden attack. The Swede retreated. Again. The third time, obviously sensing defeat, Larzdon made a last-ditch attempt at victory. He lashed out with his knife, forcing all his weight behind the thrust. His aim was directed at Drake's heart. Hope gasped, straining against Old Joe's grasp. She opened her mouth to scream as she saw the point of the knife whip treacherously close to Drake's chest.

Drake's reaction was quick. He moved out of range before the deadly weapon could do more than graze his left shoulder.

Drake's aim was more accurate. As the Swede recovered from the failed attack, Drake made use of his own skills. Instead of lashing out with the blade, as Hope expected, he turned into a sidekick that smashed into Larzdon's arm. The knife was knocked out of the Swede's hand. It flew to the ground. Drake was sitting astride the other's waist, with the razor-sharp blade of his bowie knife pressed threateningly against Larzdon's throat before the Swede knew what hit him. Larzdon eyed his opponent carefully, then he raised his hands in defeat.

The fight was over. Hope's heart pounded with relief as a roar of approval filtered through the crowd.

A few of the men drifted forward, pulling Drake off Larzdon's stomach and patting him on the back. Another fetched the deserted knife from the dirt. Oren Larzdon, red-faced with defeat, slowly moved away from the buoyant crowd, rejoining his none too happy friends. Hope quickly lost sight of him.

"He did it, Hope," Luke cried gleefully, his eyes filled with childish merriment as he lifted his sister and swung her in the air. "Just like you said he would."

"Put me down, Luke," Hope giggled. Her spirits soared as she scanned the crowd. The peach-colored skirt billowed in rustling folds around her ankles as Luke set her back on her feet. "I can see who won. I do have eyes, you know." At Luke's pout, Hope grinned and softened her voice to a tone just above exasperation. Her palm cupped her brother's cheek. "You're just excited. I know." Standing on tiptoe, she planted a kiss on his craggy forehead. "But could you please stop tossing me around like a sack of potatoes?"

"Can't blame him fer bein' happy," Old Joe muttered as he pulled the hat from his head and smoothed back the wispy strands beneath. The sweat on his forehead helped to plaster the wayward strands to his scalp as he settled the hat back on. "The fight could a gone either way, as if you didn't know. Can't say there weren't a few seconds when I was perty sure we was gonna lose."

Using her palms to flatten the folds of her skirt, she sent the old man a victorious smile. "But we didn't," she reminded him lightly, "we won. We get to keep our claim."

"Fer now." Old Joe shrugged, turning his head to spit in the dirt. He sent a skeptical gaze with his bulging eye to Bart, who was heartily congratulating Drake Frazier.

Hope eyed Old Joe warily. With that crooked face of his, it was hard to tell what the old man was thinking. Had he guessed the price she was willing to pay to get Drake Frazier to fight? There was no way to tell. His lopsided gaze had shifted to the men who were slowly starting to drift back to their shafts.

Luke gave his sister's hand an impatient tug as Old Joe sent her a meaningful look, then slowly wandered off. "Come on, Hope. Let's go congratulate him."

"No," she cried, snatching her hand back. "I mean—" she hesitated, her gaze nervously searching the men. Frazier and her father were getting closer. "You go. I have to get back. I — I have laundry to finish."

"Finish it later. This is important."

"So is mending your shirt," she replied with feigned good cheer. She took a quick step toward the burro. *Too* quick, her mind told her as she forced her feet to a slower pace. It wouldn't do to have people see her rushing away as though she was being chased.

"Besides," she continued, taking another step, then another, "the candles will never harden in time if I put it off much longer." It didn't matter that she had hidden a dozen in reserve beneath the dresses in her trunk. Those were for an emergency. "And I still have more soap to mill." Half a dozen bars lay next to the candles. Even stretching her imagination to its fullest, she couldn't think of an emergency that involved soap. "You men use more in a day than the estate used in a week. I can barely keep up."

Luke scowled at his sister's curt, nervous laugh. "But —"

"And I have to start supper," she added, almost crying with relief when she felt the burro's coarse coat beneath her fingers. "It'll never get made if I stand around chatting all day." She swung on top of the coarse back and gestured impatiently to her brother. "Go on. Off with you. Send my congratulations to Frazier, then get back to work. The sooner we hit a vein and are out of this damn camp the better."

With a shaky smile, she turned the mule around, guiding the animal past the men who were slowly making their way back to town.

The fingers gripping the reins trembled, but Hope passed the involuntary shiver off as lack of breakfast. She was lying, of course, and she knew it. But lying was far better than admitting what was really troubling her.

Frazier would be coming for payment, and he would be coming for it soon. Hope couldn't let that happen, although she saw no way around it — yet. With a little time alone, maybe she could come up with a scheme that would free her from paying him his due. It was doubtful, true. In three days, she hadn't thought of one yet.

Her mind drifted to the strip of rippled flesh marring her back. Her spine stiffened as her heart took a nervous leap. She'd think of something. Dear Lord, she had to!

Chapter Five

Hope wrapped a thick cloth around the handle of the iron kettle and lifted it from the hearth. The muscles in her arms accepted the weight easily as she toted the heavy burden from the fireplace and set it down on the table with a thump. The hot, melted tallow swished against the kettle's gritty surface, clinging to the black iron sides and dripping slow, thick paths back down to the melted pool on the bottom. Fingers of steam curled in the air as she stirred the mixture with a wooden spoon, scenting the small room with the tallow's cloying aroma.

For the past two hours she'd gone about her chores in a daze, her mind concocting one farfetched plan after another, considering *anything* that could get her out of paying Drake Frazier. She'd tossed the majority of her crazy schemes aside — except that of telling him the truth. This was the one idea that returned over and over, annoying Hope to no end. She wouldn't tell him that, she rebuked herself, each time her mind toyed with the idea. She couldn't tell anyone that.

She was in the process of dipping the hardened candles for a second time when a prick of awareness tickled the nape of her neck. Suppressing a shudder, she draped the candles over a limb of the candle tree and spun on her heel.

Hope gasped when she saw Drake Frazier leaning casually against the door frame. He'd changed into a pair of snug-fitting denim trousers. As always, the Colt was strapped to his rock-hard thigh. A sky blue shirt stretched tightly over his broad shoulders, beneath a dull, cracked leather vest. His arms were crossed lazily over his chest, and his narrowed eyes were watching her every move. A slow smile of satisfaction spread over his lips as he reached up and pushed back the hat riding low on his brow.

Her heart skipped a beat as she nodded a greeting and turned back to her work. The normally easy task of lifting the second set of candles from their branch without allowing them to brush against the first became a difficult lesson in coordination. It didn't help to know that Frazier's eyes never left her. The heat of his gaze smoldered over her back as though tangible fingers stroked her flesh. While not a welcome feeling, Hope was surprised to find that the sensation was not nearly as unpleasant as she would have thought.

She ignored the sound of a match being struck as she dipped the wicks into the steaming tallow. By the time she had placed them on their branch, the room was heavy with the sulfurous odor of the match, intermingled with the scent of his cheroot. Hope recognized the distinctive aroma immediately, though where he had found one of those tiny cigars in this godforsaken place was anybody's guess. The scent brought unwilled memories of long summer days spent romping playfully on her grandparents' farm. Her grandfather had also appreciated the taste of a fine cigar.

Pushing the memory aside, Hope sent a disdainful glance over her shoulder. "If you have to smoke that thing, I'll thank you to do it somewhere else. Papa will be home soon and he can't stand the smell."

Drake kept his peace as he let the cheroot roll over his tongue, clamping it tightly between his teeth. He had no more intention of throwing the expensive, half-smoked cigar away than he had of leaving. He was having almost as much fun watching the color splash over high, regal cheekbones as he was eying Hope's suddenly rigid, self-conscious move-

87

ments.

Before she had noticed his presence, Drake had been treated to the gracefully fluid movement of enticingly long limbs. Watching the chestnut-haired beauty reminded him of watching a fragile leaf skimming the ground, wafted by an autumn breeze. Now that she had spotted him, though, her movements were tight, strained, and awkward. Knowing it was his presence that caused her discomfort brought a satisfied smile to his lips.

Drake took a puff of the cigar and released the smoke in a long, slow exhalation.

"Hello to you, too," he said, as his gaze raked her body.

Her fingers were long, he noticed as she turned to drape another candle to dry, the nails well-tended, although her hands were slightly red and work-roughened. For a woman with large bones, she had a nicely turned wrist, tapering into a creamy forearm. The tanned flesh there was exposed by the peach-colored sleeves she'd turned up to just below the elbows. His gaze narrowed on the gentle curve of her waist, and though he couldn't see her hips beneath the coarse folds of her dress, he imagined they would be lean, as would her legs, muscled from long hours of hard work.

Occasionally, she would send him a heated glance from the corner of those large, velvet brown eyes. The movement drew his gaze there, and to the rosy blush of her cheeks. She had a square face, with a short, pert nose that belied the hard set of her jaw. Her forehead was wide, but softened by the wispy chestnut curls that dared escape the thick, silky plait draping a broad shoulder.

With a ragged sigh, Drake threw the cheroot to the dirt and crushed it out with his heel. Pushing himself away from the door frame, he entered the cabin.

A fire crackled in the hearth, adding to the late afternoon heat. The air was thick with the scent of tobacco and laced with the odor of melted tallow, strong coffee, and freshly baked bread. Of them all, he found the last two aromas most welcoming.

Hope strove for an appearance of unruffled calm. Inside, she was trembling like a leaf. Her every move was followed by those daunting eyes, her every breath scrutinized by his piercing glance. She felt trapped in a cage, studied and examined like some rare breed of bird.

"Is there something I can do for you?" she asked in sudden annoyance. Drake had helped himself to the bench across from her, and the sound of wood scraping against the floor as he casually settled himself down did nothing to ease her tension.

"I think you already know the answer to that." He found a certain sense of satisfaction in the way her cheeks abruptly drained of color.

The candle she was taking from one of the branches slipped from her fingers and fell to the cloth. The fragile stick of half-hardened tallow broke like a twig snapped in two.

Hope picked up the broken candle and set it aside, reaching for the next. She tried hard to ignore the way her fingers were trembling, but it wasn't easy. It was even harder to meet his penetrating gaze, but she did that, too. "Do I?" she asked as she again dipped the thickening wick.

Drake looked at her long and hard, even after she had torn her gaze away. His intentions in coming here had, oddly enough, been honorable. He'd been drunk when they'd first made the deal, and he'd regretted his harsh words in the morning. Putting aside the way she'd rankled him before the fight, he'd come to tell Hope that, and to give her the chance to renege on a deal he had belatedly realized was unfair.

Doubt pierced his soul as he noted the girl's rigid stance. A suspicion nagged at the back of his mind, refusing to be denied.

She wasn't going to pay him, he realized suddenly. Worse, she had never had any *intention* of paying him. The bitch!

White hot anger churned through his blood. The intensity of the reaction surprised even Drake. It wasn't that she would have the audacity to go back on their deal that bothered him. Hadn't he come here to give her just that opportunity? No, it was the thought that she had been willing to let him think she'd go through with it that galled him no end.

He wouldn't let her get away with it, he decided abruptly, not stopping to question his decision. Two minutes ago he would have let her back out without a fight. But now that he'd discovered her deception, he decided he'd rather die first. Paying up was no more than the spoiled brat deserved! She'd regret playing him for a fool.

"What time can I expect you tonight?" Drake asked, his voice as deceptively smooth as a glass of carefully aged brandy.

She gasped, her trembling fingers hesitating as she pretended to let the melted liquid drip off a thickened wick and back into the kettle. It was nothing short of a miracle that the candles didn't slip from her suddenly cold, sweat-dampened fingers. Her teeth nibbled a full lower lip as she carefully draped the wick over a branch.

"I — I don't know. I hadn't thought about it." She didn't look at Drake. She didn't dare. He would see the lie mirrored in her eyes, Hope was sure of it.

"Think about it. I want to know what time to expect you."

"I — I don't know," she shrugged helplessly. "Sometime after supper, I guess."

She almost knocked over the candle tree as she reached out for another wick. Frazier's lightning-quick reflexes saved the labor of half a day's work.

"Make it before," he said, righting the wooden contraption and rising to his feet. With a fist still leaning against the tabletop to support his weight, he leaned forward and ran a fingertip suggestively down the smooth line of her jaw. The edge of his fingernail stroking her flesh sent a shiver curling

90

up Hope's spine. "And don't be late. I don't like to be kept waiting."

Every instinct she possessed screamed for her to pull away from the confusion of his touch, but the sea-green gaze was daring her to do just that. Swallowing hard, she gritted her teeth and endured the caress, putting all her indignation into a haughty glare. Drake's lips curled into a lazy smile as his hand dropped away.

She watched as he lifted one sinewy leg, then the other, over the dented oak bench. His arrogant stride carried him to the door, and Hope was sorely tempted to throw the kettle of scalding hot tallow at his retreating back. She couldn't do that, of course. She couldn't purposely put someone through the torturous healing of burned flesh—even someone like Drake Frazier—no matter how badly she wanted to. Still, the temptation was undeniably there.

Drake stopped when he reached the open door, gazing up into the clear, cloudless blue sky. To Hope's mounting frustration, he didn't bother to turn around when he curtly informed her, "Tell your father to find someone else to cook his breakfast in the morning. You won't be home until after dawn. Maybe later."

Pulling another cheroot from his pocket, he stuck it between his teeth, unlit, and rounded the corner. He was safely out of sight by the time a cast iron skillet crashed into the door frame.

It's suppertime, Hope's mind teased her as she toted the cleaned kettle, now filled with aromatic stew, to the table. Had Frazier realized she wasn't coming? she wondered.

The men eyed the kettle greedily, their hunger enhanced by a hard day's work and the tantalizing aroma of freshly baked bread. She had no more than set her burden down in the center of the table when all five men rose and reached for the ladle. Two hands reached the metal spoon first. Old

91

Joe met Kyle's angry glare over the pot.

"Will you two please stop?" Hope muttered in exasperation, as she took her seat beside her father. "I could have sworn I fed you this afternoon, yet here you're acting like a pack of starved wolves. There's enough for everyone, but no one's getting a drop if one of you doesn't put down the ladle."

Kyle, grudgingly bowing to age, sat down with a grunt and plucked up a slab of bread to slake his hunger. Smearing it with a glob of freshly churned butter, he chewed on it as he watched Old Joe heap his plate with the coveted stew.

Suppressing a smile, Hope reached for a slice of bread and cast a glance to the end of the table, at Kyle's twin. "Where were you two this morning? I would've thought a stampede of wild horses couldn't keep you away from a fight."

"We was there," Lyle replied. He pushed a strand of curling red hair from his brow and wrinkled his freckled nose. Although the twins were only a year younger than she in age, to Hope they looked hardly old enough to be out of short pants. "Bart wanted us to keep an eye on the Swedes."

Before anyone could beat him to it, Kyle stood and took the ladle Old Joe set next to the kettle. "Yeah, lot of fun *that* turned out to be. I was standin' behind Big Sal, and I couldn't see a thing."

"I did," his brother said, tapping his spoon against the table as he impatiently waited for the ladle to be passed his way.

Kyle scowled. " 'Course you did, you was on top of my shoulders. Prob'ly had the best view of anyone. 'Cept for him." He nodded to Luke, who was buttering himself three thick slices of the rapidly dwindling loaf of bread.

"I ain'—" Luke looked at his sister, who frowned. "I'm not complaining. I could see everything, not that there was much to see. The fight was over before it started."

"Good thing, too," Old Joe grumbled from around a mouthful of stew. The twinkle in his eye told Hope the meal was good. It was the only thing by way of a compliment she would get from him. "Lord knows where we'd be now if we'd lost."

Bart stood and ladled a healthy portion of the stew over the slices of bread that covered the bottom of his plate. "Upstream, probably," he said, as he passed the ladle to his daughter.

Hope handed the ladle to Lyle. As always, she'd wait until all of the men had helped themselves before dishing out her own smaller portion. It was silly, she knew. There was always plenty to go around, she saw to that, but old habits died hard.

"What on earth would we do upstream?" she scoffed, as she began spooning stew onto her plate. "We've already seen color here, and it looks rich. You said so yourself."

"A flake here or there doesn't amount to more than the food on this table," Bart drawled. The twins nodded in agreement, while Old Joe threw them all a speculative glance. "What we need to find is a vein. A good, thick vein. Then we'll *really* see some color."

"Maybe we'll get lucky, Pa," Luke replied. A drop of gravy trickled down his chin, and he wiped it away on the back of his sleeve. "You said we gotta have some luck sometime."

"Hmph!" Bart Bennett scowled darkly. It was going to take a whole lot more than luck to rebuild Lake's Edge. It was going to take cash, cold, hard cash. And if they didn't get some of it damn soon, then there wouldn't be any property back in Virginia to save. According to the letter he'd received the week before, the plantation was to be auctioned in less than three months. The last year had been a waste of time. Traipsing from camp to camp, always one step behind the rich claims, always settling for the ones that panned only enough flakes and dust to carry them to the next dead end. It would all be for nothing if Lake's Edge was auctioned off. All for nothing.

"Have you heard from Mr. Farley?" Hope asked, noticing

her father's sudden lack of appetite.

Bart sent his daughter a sharp glance, wondering how she knew, with such uncanny certainty, where his thoughts had drifted. "Now, why would I have heard from him?" he said evasively, taking a bite of the meal he suddenly had no taste for. "We've got no money to pay him. I'm sure he has better things to do with his time than draft a letter to this godforsaken place."

Hope put down her spoon and sent her father an even gaze. "Bradford Farley is more than our attorney, Papa. He's your friend. He would have written to tell you if Lake's Edge had been sold."

"Well, he hasn't." Bart wiped his mouth on the napkin he'd insisted his daughter make out of one of her old, mint green skirts, then slammed the square of cloth on the table beside his half-finished meal. His chair scraped the floor as he rose to his feet.

Hope watched in confusion as her father stamped to the door, while the others feigned acute interest in their food. Even Luke pretended not to notice their father's sudden, unwarranted anger.

"Where are you going?" she called as he wrenched open the door. It banged against the wall. What had she said to cause such hostility?

"Out," he barked. Grabbing his hat from the peg near the door, he jammed it on his head and sent his daughter a hot glance from over his shoulder. Turning to leave, he came an inch short of running headlong into Drake Frazier's rugged chest. "And what the hell do you want?" he growled. Not waiting for an answer, he sidestepped Frazier and disappeared into the shadows of dusk.

Hope's heart nearly stopped as she watched the gunslinger step into the cabin like a man who had frequented the place regularly. Conversation came to an abrupt halt as everyone turned, in unison, to cast their guest cautious glances. Old Joe's spoon stopped midway to his mouth as his bulging eye shifted from Hope to Drake, then back again. Of them all, he was the only one to notice the way the girl's cheeks drained of color, or the way the small vein in her throat throbbed frantically beneath the pale flesh.

The look Drake sent her made Hope swallow hard. The piece of bread she'd been chewing went down her throat with all the ease of a chunk of cotton, and with just as much taste.

"Frazier!" Luke cried with all the warmth of a long lost friend. He was the only one excited about their savior's presence. Hope could happily have kicked the daylights out of her brother's shin and had her feet not felt suddenly encased in lead she might have done just that. "Come on in and have a seat. There's lots of stew if you're hungry, and my sister makes a *great* stew. Best you've ever tasted, I'll bet." He preened, sending Hope an innocent smile. For the life of him, Luke couldn't figure out why his sister looked so mad.

"Yeah, Frazier," Old Joe grumbled, now that the invitation had been extended. "Come on in and pull up a seat."

Drake strutted to the table, and Hope noticed that this time no holster was attached to the black leather belt riding low on his hips. She was staring, she knew, but it couldn't be helped. Her gaze was perversely drawn to that sinewy thigh, and no amount of will could budge it, until Drake lazily slid onto the bench beside her.

"How you doing, Joe?"

"Not bad." The bulging eye scrutinized the gunslinger carefully.

"Been a long time. Two years?"

Old Joe nodded. "Yup, 'bout that."

Hope ignored the conversation. *Why did the only available spot have to be the one her father had just vacated?* her mind raged.

The twins' spoons clattered to their plates. Distaste shimmered in their matching hazel eyes as they focused on Drake. Kyle mumbled under his breath. The two stood and strode to the door, both retrieving their hats.

"We'll be at The Button," Lyle grumbled as they disappeared in Bart's wake, with Kyle slamming the door loudly behind them.

"Friendly guys," Drake said as he took Bart's plate and scraped the remains of her father's dinner onto what was left of Kyle's. Seemingly unfazed by the rude departure, he ladled a goodly portion of the stew onto the plate, then let his eyes settle on Hope.

A tingle of uneasiness rippled through her body, and no matter how she tried to ignore its presence, she was excruciatingly aware it was there. As though it were not bad enough to have his body within touching distance, the muscular length of his thigh was now pressing intimately against her own. All semblance of logical thought abandoned her.

Hope shifted her attention, and was immediately captured by his piercing gaze. *It's after suppertime,* those eyes were saying. Was it her imagination, or was there a flicker of frustration in those eyes as well?

"A spoon?" Drake said, his voice deep and cynically husky as his warm breath fanned her upturned cheek.

Hope pulled her gaze away and concentrated on pushing the stew around her plate, segregating the carrots and potatoes. She inclined her head toward the counter that held the utensils. "Get it yourself, you're not crippled." God, but she hated the way her voice came out as a throaty whisper!

"I'd rather you got it for me."

His voice was thick, dripping with hidden challenge. To Hope, that voice seemed to say, *"You didn't show up when I told you to. Now I intend to see you humiliated for keeping me waiting."*

Taking a deep breath to control her anger, Hope slammed down her spoon and climbed over the bench. Glaring angrily at Frazier, she found a clean spoon. It crashed onto the table next to his plate with enough force to make the handle of the kettle rattle.

Luke kept eating as though nothing had happened. He'd

seen his sister's anger before, and he wanted no part of it. Following the twins to The Brass Button was an idea that looked better by the minute, but he couldn't let Hope's stew go to waste; she'd never forgive him.

Old Joe was having a very different reaction to Drake Frazier's presence. In fact, his bulging eye stared at Hope quite peculiarly.

In all the time he'd been with the Bennetts, never once had he seen her fetch a spoon for one of the men — until now. She'd made it clear from the beginning that she was nobody's maid, and that if one of the men wanted something he'd best get it himself. Yet here she was fetching a spoon for Frazier like she was . . . well, like she was his woman. It wasn't right, he thought. It just wasn't right.

Hope glared at Frazier for a second, letting a string of curses run temptingly close to her tongue, then plucked the half-finished slice of bread from her plate and retreated to the rocking chair near the fire. The old wood groaned as she plopped onto it, but she barely heard it over the clank of Luke's spoon scraping up the last mouthfuls of stew from his plate.

Except for a curious glance over his shoulder, Luke ignored his sister's inexplicably sullen mood as he sent Drake a complimentary smile. "You fought good today," he said as he folded a slice of bread in half and stuffed the whole thing in his mouth.

Drake fingered the bruise swelling on his jaw, partially concealed beneath a coat of fresh stubble, and returned the big man's smile. The cut on his cheekbone had dried to a thin, jagged line that wasn't as easily hidden.

"You could have done it yourself," Drake replied, surprised at how easily the lie sprang to his lips. If it had been Luke fighting this morning, the boy would be dead right now. For some reason, the thought disturbed him.

"You think so?" he asked. "You really think I could'a whipped the Swede?" He leaned toward Drake, his voice dropping to a whisper. "I do too," he added with a wink, nodding over his shoulder. "I *told* her I could a done it, but she wouldn't believe me. Said I'd get myself hurt, maybe even killed. But you don't think I would of gotten killed, do you?"

Drake declined comment, his gaze drifting over the big man's shoulder to settle on Hope. She sat with her back ramrod straight, her long legs tucked beneath her. The large, velvet brown eyes were lost in the flickering light of the flames that bathed the girl in a shifting, crackling orange glow and made each copper highlight in her hair dance to life. The braid was still slung over her shoulder, much the way it had been that afternoon, but now more hair had escaped the tight plait. It was soft, that hair, shimmering with silky promise as the wavy tresses tickled the long, thin neck.

Feeling his stare, Hope looked up. A surge of color washed over her cheeks before she shifted her weight and turned her back to the table.

A slow smile pulled at Drake's lips. The girl might try to convey an air of disdain, but she wasn't as unaffected by his presence as she would like him to think, not by a long shot. And there was still the matter of payment to be discussed. Had she guessed that he wouldn't leave until the subject had been decided, he wondered? Yes, Drake thought. She knew it, and she wasn't at all pleased at the prospect. He turned his attention to the crooked old man at the end of the bench, realizing belatedly that Old Joe had been speaking to him, and that he had no idea what the man had said.

"Don't you think?" Old Joe insisted, knowing Frazier hadn't heard a word of it, and enjoying the man's discomfort. Nope, Drake Frazier hadn't changed a bit. His head could still be turned by a perty face. "Frazier?"

Drake shrugged, turning his attention to the rapidly cooling stew. To an observer, it would have looked as though he had responded to the question. Only Old Joe knew he hadn't.

"Come on, Frazier," Luke cried in innocent delight. The bench scraped in the roughly planked floor as he pushed himself to a stand. "It'll be fun. The twins're already there. Pa probably is too. You're coming, ain't you, Joe?"

The old man shook his head and waved the suggestion away with his spoon. "Gettin' too old for those kind a shenanigans. You two go, with my blessin's. Leave me outta it."

"They got girls," Luke teased. To Hope, he looked like a boy holding a bone just out of a hungry dog's reach as he anxiously rubbed his big, flat palms together. "Real live girls. How long's it been since you seen a real live girl, Joe? How long's it been since you *held* one?"

Old Joe stifled a groan. How long? *Too* long, that's how long!

Luke could see his old friend change his mind. The thought of "real live girls" could do that to a man, *any* man, stuck out here in the middle of nowhere with nary a skirt in sight. A body could get sick of seeing dusty trousers and sweat-soaked shirts real fast, especially when there wasn't a whole lot else to look at.

Old Joe wiped his mouth on the napkin, then set it aside and stood up. "You comin', pal?" he asked Frazier as he climbed over the bench. The bones in his knees cracked with age, but Old Joe hardly noticed. The thought of what was in store for him tonight was enough to take a good ten years off his face. Now, instead of looking ancient, he looked merely old.

Frazier shook his head as he dipped the spoon in his plate and brought it up heaped with vegetables and gravy. "Nope," he said flatly, his gaze meeting Old Joe's bulging eye head on. "The lady and I have some talking to do. Don't mind, do you?"

It wasn't a question, and Old Joe knew it. He wasn't sure leaving Hope alone with this guy was such a good idea after

99

all. But it was too late for second thoughts. If he tried to stay, he'd have to come up with a damned good reason for his sudden change of heart, and Old Joe wasn't that quick on his feet.

The larger eye narrowed until it was almost equal to the smaller one in size. He looked at Hope, who had suddenly gone deathly pale. She caught his gaze as it traveled from her to the sack of flour propped up in the corner near the counter. There was a pistol back there, his pistol, primed and ready to shoot.

Hope gave the barest of nods. She knew that, normally, leaving the gun behind would be risky. No man in his right mind walked the streets of Thirsty Gulch unarmed. But he had Luke to protect him. Most of the miners that trickled into Thirsty Gulch feared the big man, if only because they couldn't guess what he was or was not capable of. Old Joe and Luke would be safe without a gun, but Hope might need it to protect herself from Drake Frazier.

A smile curved her lips as the color returned to her cheeks. Just knowing the gun was there if she needed it was enough to bolster her pitifully floundering courage.

She nodded to the door. "You two go on. Have yourselves a good time." She sent them a stern look, much like a protective mother would cast on her precocious children. "And don't get in any trouble. Last time you went to The Button you—"

Old Joe groaned and shook his head as he plucked his hat, and Luke's from the rack. "I know, I know," he grumbled, tossing one to Luke before pulling the other on top of his own wispy head. "Don't need to go remindin' me." He looked like a hurt dog nursing his wounds. "I paid, didn't I?" he added as he pulled open the door and let Luke by. "And they *did* rebuild the place, didn't they?"

"Did they have a choice?" Hope countered.

He sent her a thoughtful glance, his wrinkled hand poised on the latch. "Nope. Guess they didn't at that." With a grin, he was gone.

"Come on, Joe, hurry it up," she heard her brother call impatiently as they rounded the corner of the shanty with a muffled crunch of dried leaves. "The good ones will all be gone by the time you—"

"Hold yer horses, young 'un. I's a comin'." The voice grew fainter. "I's a comin'."

Luke mumbled something, probably one of the curses Hope forbade him to use in the house, but they were too far away to hear. The words were lost on the cool night breeze.

Drake let his gaze settle on the girl in the rocking chair, noting that her attention had turned back to the fire. Although she pretended he'd left with the others, he recognized her preoccupation with the dancing flames for what it was.

Tension coiled in the room, so real it was almost palpable. If he reached up, Drake thought, he might actually feel the hostile currents hanging in the air like a thick, black cloud.

As Luke had promised, the stew was good, but not good enough to hold Drake's attention from the matters at hand. He pushed the plate away and stretched. The liquid motion caught Hope's attention from the corner of her eye.

She shifted her weight so she could no longer see him, but it did no good. She could *feel* him looking at her, *feel* his gaze raking over her body, missing nothing; her entire body tingled with the knowledge of his eyes. The emotions this kindled within made her limbs suddenly itchy and restless. Her fingers played with the peachy folds of her skirt, smudged with light patches of flour where the apron hadn't covered it. *That* nervous movement wasn't missed either. Forcing her grip to slacken, she raised a hand to her forehead and noticed her fingers were trembling.

Angry that a man's gaze—not his hands, *just his gaze*—could affect her so strongly, Hope sprang from the chair as though she'd just been struck by lightning. She wasn't pleased to find her knees shaking every bit as badly as her

101

fingers, but at least *they* were concealed beneath the billowing expanse of her skirt.

She walked to the table with what she hoped was a casual step, noticing as she did how more and more of her body began to tingle with each closing inch. By the time she reached the cracked oak tabletop, she could have collapsed onto the bench beside it in exhaustion.

Instead, she reached out and began plucking up the discarded plates one by one, scraping the remains of each into the near-empty kettle before adding them to the neat stack she'd created on the side.

It was difficult, but she found that with a great deal of effort she could almost forget Frazier's presence and carry on with her chores in the same manner she would have employed if he hadn't shown up at all. Almost.

The problem was, Drake Frazier had no intentions of being forgotten. "Put the plate down, Hope," he said, his voice hard, penetrating Hope's body as if he'd driven an icicle straight through her heart. She hesitated, but otherwise ignored him. "I said, put the plate down."

Hope did, but she put it in the stack and reached for another. "I don't have time for games, Mr. Frazier. I have work to do."

A hand snaked out and wrapped around her wrist as she reached for another plate. Hope froze. She wasn't surprised, she'd half expected it, but she was shocked that he'd done it so *fast*.

"I don't like games either, sunshine," he said through gritted teeth. Hope tried to pull away, afraid of the cold hostility in his voice. It was useless. His grip held painfully firm.

Even knowing a struggle was useless, she yanked again, almost dislocating her wrist for the effort. "Let me go!" she demanded, leaning back as he drew her up hard against the table. Her gaze flickered to the flour sack as she was forced to throw the other hand on top of the table to brace herself.

It did no good. With her elbows bent, drawing her body toward him until her torso was almost lying over the table was child's play.

"Let me go, you idiot, you're breaking my arm!" she hissed.

"I'll break more than that if you're trying to welch on our deal."

Drake dropped her arm. Hope, not expecting to be released, was forced back a step by the momentum of her struggle. Her arm ached from where his fingers had been. She rubbed the bruise that would probably be blue come morning, if not sooner. Her cheek stung from the memory of his breath.

"I was doing the dishes, Mr. Frazier," she replied tightly, her eyes averted to the sack of flour. "How was I supposed to know you'd be offended at the sight of a woman scraping plates? Besides," she let her gaze wander to the makeshift wooden counter as though searching for a weapon, "now that there are real women in town, I thought one of the girls at The Button would be more your style." There was a knife on the counter. A knife that still had a piece of carrot peel clinging to its dulled steel blade.

If there had been a back to this goddamned uncomfortable excuse for a bench, Drake would have leaned back and smiled. So, she thought she knew his style, did she? He'd see about that. Crossing his arms over his chest, he leaned his elbows on the table top, and sent Hope a piercing glare. "And how would you know anything about my—ahem—'style'?"

She flushed and looked away. "I've heard rumors." She shrugged, her gaze clashing with his. "I know what kind of man you are."

"Do you?" he drawled. The deep crease between his golden brows announced that he was not amused. "Do you really?"

"Yes," she answered, her voice as hard and flat as her

expression. "It doesn't take a genius to know what kind of man agrees to the kind of deal I offered you, at the price *you* set. That tells me more about you than any of the sordid rumors floating around Thirsty Gulch." She smiled, but the expression lacked sincerity. "You know, a southern gentleman would have agreed to the deal and declined payment. A northern gentleman would have agreed to the deal and taken the cash."

Drake chuckled when Hope paused for effect. "Which leaves me — ?"

"No gentleman," she finished, before he had the chance. His chuckle was snatched from the air as though it had never been.

The smile was back on his lips: cold, calculating, contemptuous. Hope suppressed a shiver, as well as the feeling that she might have pushed her luck too far this time. She'd made a mistake in speaking her mind without a weapon to back up her words. The error belatedly clicked in her mind with all the force of a hammer being cocked. She might have just made the biggest mistake of her life, and made it with the most ruthlessly dangerous man she'd ever met.

"Well, now, sunshine," he said on a sigh, the smile still in place, "you may be right. But a deal *is* a deal. And gentleman or not, I intend to see that this one's honored." He fingered the bruise on his cheek as his eyes narrowed on Hope. "I think I deserve it," he paused, "don't you?"

Yes, she thought, with a sinking feeling in the pit of her stomach, *he does*. Drake Frazier deserved to be paid for his services. It was a pity she couldn't pay him in quite the way she had promised.

Chapter Six

Dread quickly gave way to fear, and fear to panic, as she watched Drake slip each sinewy leg over the bench. His piercing eyes never leaving her, he reminded Hope of a bloodthirsty predator cornering its weaker prey. Would he toy with her, like a cat would a mouse? she wondered. Or would he skip the preliminaries and go straight for the jugular?

Drake rounded the table, his strides long and purposeful. It was the sound of his boot heels, a sharp thud on the scuffed plank floorboards, that finally prompted Hope into motion.

With a strangled cry, she hoisted her skirt and bolted around the opposite side of the table. She was farther from the gun, but closer to the knife. Her backup option just might pay off. The grin that tugged at Frazier's lips told her that he thought her move a foolish one. And why shouldn't he? With the exit at his back, and the only obvious weapon yet to be reached, he had every reason to be confident.

That confidence seeped into his voice, lacing his words with husky arrogance. "Where are you going to go, Hope? Even if you made it outside, I'd catch you before you cleared the woods."

"Maybe," Hope shrugged, nibbling at her lower lip as she fought the temptation to measure the distance between herself and the knife. The gunslinger was watching her too closely. If she risked so much as a glance in that direction he would glean her intent and stop her before she reached the counter.

"Definitely," he corrected with a cocky grin. "You can bet on it."

Instinct, goaded by the man's infernal arrogance, made her reach out and seize the top plate of the stack. It was heavy, that plate, molded out of good solid tin. She hurled it at Frazier's golden head without a second thought. Her eyes widened in disbelief as he sidestepped the flying projectile and snatched it from the air before it could hurt him. Hope waited, breathless, wondering if he was going to throw it back, knowing her reflexes were not that good.

Drake gauged the weight of the plate in his hand, his gaze flickering between an object that had the potential to be a deadly weapon, and the woman who had hurled it at him. "That wasn't very smart, sunshine," he admonished, setting the plate aside.

If Hope had planned for him to chase her around the other side of the table, she was sadly mistaken. First, Drake did not look like he was going to *chase* her anywhere, so much as he was going to stalk her like a dog sniffing out a wounded fox. Second, he was rounding the table on the side nearest the counter — *and the knife!*

He closed in another step. Two more and he would be around the table entirely. Already he had the advantage of distance, whereas Hope's only advantage was that of surprise. He would expect her to run away from him, not toward him. With any luck, the suddenness of her action would throw him off guard just long enough for her to reach the counter. A split-second pause, that was all she would need.

Taking in a deep gulp of air, she dug her fingers into the coarse fabric of her skirt, and ran for all she was worth.

The floor slapped at the booted soles of her feet and her braid bobbed against the small of her back. Her heart drummed so loudly in her ears that she could barely hear the muttered curse as it passed Drake Frazier's lips when he guessed her intent.

Swearing at his own stupidity for not having seen the knife before, Drake flew after her. As Hope had intended, she had taken him completely off guard. Unfortunately, his reaction time was not as slow as she would have liked.

Hope was quick, but Drake was quicker. She had no more felt the smooth wood of the counter top beneath her fingertips, before it was cruelly snatched away. An arm shot out from nowhere and wrapped itself tightly around her waist, pulling her back until she collided with the brick wall of his chest.

The air rushed from her lungs, and the tightness around her middle wouldn't let her draw more. She pulled at the arm, trying to loosen its hold. When that didn't work, she stretched out her arm and reached for the knife, at the same time pulling up her foot and sinking her heel deep into the shin behind her.

Drake grunted, a warm rush of air in her ear. His hold loosened but did not fall away. Hope stretched as far as she could and felt the knife's handle graze her fingertips. She was dragged back before her fingers could wrap around the handle.

"Let me go, you jackass!" she screamed, throwing a wild punch over her shoulder. The fist hit nothing but air. She threw another, this one over the other shoulder. She was rewarded with the feel of her knuckles smashing into Frazier's ear before her wrist was captured in his free hand. He forced her arm down so it crossed over the other, making them both useless.

Tears of frustration blurred her gaze, but Hope refused to give in to them. Nor would she give in to the infuriating power of the man behind her. With her hands pinned, she used the only thing left: her feet. Time and again her heel sank into a shin, a muscular calf, or when she was very lucky, a rock-hard thigh.

Her struggles seemed to have little effect. In fact, the more she fought, the tighter the arm around her waist became. Drawing breath became increasingly hard and it wasn't long before the room began to spin in sickening circles before her eyes. Blackness reared up from the floor, threatening to envelop her in its velvety folds. She resisted it, but only barely.

Reluctantly, she ceased her struggles and melted back against the gunslinger's chest. His hard shoulder pillowed her head and she could feel his heart drumming beneath the thick, rippled flesh of her shoulder blade. The sweet rush of his breath tickled her ear, fanning her cheek and neck. His grip had loosened enough to allow her deep, healing gulps of air.

"Are you done fighting?" he asked, his voice oddly gentle as his breath stirred the wisps of hair clinging to her jaw.

"No," she panted, her own voice trembling as she shook her head. She had expected to hear mockery in his tone, perhaps a sarcastic hint of victory as well. There was none, and the lack of it confused her. "Let me go, Drake," she pleaded, her words stronger now that the air had had a chance to work its magic. "Please? I'll pay you. I'll even have Papa increase your share in the mine. How does half of the profits sound? Three quarters? My God, you can have the whole damn thing, just let me go and forget our deal. *Pleeease* . . ."

The last was a ragged, broken whisper, filled with desperation — and something else. Drake scowled. Was it terror that shaped her words? It was the same tone he'd heard when she'd first come to him with the deal, when he'd suggested he preferred a different form of payment. He was again struck with the feeling that her reluctance went beyond virginal innocence. He couldn't help but remember how she'd acted with the other men. She laughed, she joked, she returned their stares. But not with him. With him she acted like a child who'd just woken up to find her worst nightmares come true.

With hands that were gentler than Drake ever dreamed they could be, he eased her around. Her shoulders were squared with pride, but she kept her eyes lowered. Cupping her chin, he tilted her head up so that she had no choice but to look at him.

"I don't want your money," he said softly, momentarily laying aside the irony of those words. He could feel Hope trying to pull away from him, but he refused to let her slip from the circle of his arm. Nor would he release her chin. Instead, he turned her head back when she would have looked away. "And I don't want your claim. Not all of it anyway."

"I know what you want," Hope replied flatly. Swallowing hard, she fought the urge to run. Where would she go? She couldn't run from this man, at least not very far. Hadn't he already proven that?

"What I want is an explanation," he continued as though she hadn't spoken. "First, I want to know why you would come to my room, solicit my help, and agree to a deal you had no intention of honoring." His voice lowered to a husky whisper. "Then I want to know why you can't honor it. Mind you, I want the truth — if you think you're capable of it."

Hope stiffened and her lips thinned into a tight, hard line. "I didn't have a choice," she said, tilting her chin away from his grasp as a spark of defiance flared in her eyes. "Believe me, if there had been another option, another man I thought could beat Larzdon, I would have taken my business somewhere else. Unfortunately, my father decided you were our best bet."

"So you decided to take a gamble and hope that the despicable Drake Frazier, that good-for-nothing gunslinger, would live up to his reputation, is that it?" Drake chuckled. It was a cold, mirthless sound. "I'm flattered."

"Don't be," she spat. Slapping his hand from her chin, she slipped from his grasp. She was surprised when he let her go so easily. "I didn't like the idea any more than you did. But, like I said, I had no choice." She took a deep breath and pushed on, determined to end this confrontation as soon as possible. "As for 'payment,' well *my* offer was for one hundred dollars. *You're* the one who insisted on more."

"And *you're* the one who agreed to it," he reminded her coldly. Reaching out, he let the tip of his finger stroke the smooth line of her jaw.

Hope pulled back, more from the odd, tingling sensation the touch evoked than from the contact itself. "Not by choice!"

"Ah, so you *were* forced then," he nodded, crossing one arm over his chest. That muscular forearm pillowed the elbow of the other arm as he lazily stroked his chin with the tips of his index finger and thumb.

He was mocking her, she realized, though she didn't call him on it. She didn't dare.

"And where did they hide the gun, sunshine?" he asked, a sly grin pulling at one corner of his mouth. "In your underdrawers?"

"That's pretty low, Frazier. Even for you. What do you think, that they threatened my life and forced me to come to you that night?" she demanded tightly. Her eyes narrowed angrily as her hands balled into useless fists at her sides. "My own father? My brother? My friends? Think again. Your life may be ruled by the wrong end of a rifle, but not mine." She tapped an index finger against her

110

temple. "Unlike most of the women in Thirsty, I happen to have a brain in here. And what's more, I know how to use it. What they suggested that night made perfect sense. Everything would have been fine if you'd taken my first offer. *You're* the one who complicated things by not taking the money."

"Did it ever occur to you that there might be a *reason* you were the one chosen to deliver that message, Hope Bennett?" Drake asked, his voice low and deadly serious. "Of all the people in this little band of yours, why you? Why not one of the twins? Or that big hulking brother of yours? Isn't the old man trustworthy enough to carry a message? Is your father too sick to be walking the streets alone at night? *Why you?*"

Hope tipped her head to one side, her gaze wary as a shiver of apprehension curled up her spine. He was trying to trick her, she thought. Trying to make her think that her family would sell her virtue for services rendered. He was wrong, of course. They wouldn't do that to her, not her family, her friends. She knew it.

This time it was Drake's finger that tapped her temple. "Think about it, sunshine," he said, that infuriatingly lop-sided grin slipping back into place. "You have a brain in there. Use it."

"Oh, no," Hope insisted, shaking her head as she brushed a stray chestnut curl from her brow. "If you're trying to tell me they sent me to . . . to . . . you're wrong. I was chosen because I'm the only cool-headed one of the lot. And they thought you'd listen to a woman."

"Listen? You're sure about that?"

"Yes, I'm sure," Hope defended staunchly. She wasn't lying, was she? Good Lord, he managed to make her doubt her own family! She was lost. "What other reason could there be?"

"I don't believe you. I think they picked you for another

111

reason, and if you can't see that then you're a goddamn fool."

"Get out," she hissed, her brown eyes shimmering with anger. To Hope's surprise, Drake made no attempt to stop her as she briskly stamped to the door. Flinging the flimsy thing wide, she jerked her thumb into the cool, dark night. "Just get the hell out."

"What, and solve all of your problems?" Drake asked as he slowly advanced on her. Again, she was struck with the impression of a wolf cornering its prey. "My leaving would solve all of your problems, wouldn't it, Hope?" Drake pulled her away from the door and closed it. His fingers did not drop from her arms, however. "Sorry, sunshine. You got yourself into this mess and you're going to have to get yourself out. I can't help you there."

"Can't? Or won't? There's a big difference. *Can't* help means you couldn't release me from our deal even if you wanted to. But we both know that isn't true, don't we?"

"All right," he conceded, pursing his lips and giving a brisk nod of his golden head. "I *won't* help you then. Better?" His palms were tracing slow, tantalizingly hot paths down the outside of her arms, over her elbows, down to her wrists, then back up again. A shiver trembled through the tendons beneath his fingertips, and the feel made Drake smile. While her sharp tongue could deny the physical attraction crackling between them, her body was powerless to deny it. That faint trembling and the becoming flush that kissed her cheeks, coupled with the pulse throbbing frantically in the creamy base of her throat, told him quite a different story.

Hope's tongue darted over her suddenly parched lips as she tried to ignore the shiver of delight Frazier's more than casual touch inspired. "What did—" She hesitated, looked away, then continued faintly, "What did you mean before, when you said I'd been sent to your room for a reason?

112

Why did you *really* mean?"

"Exactly what you thought I meant," he replied, his features melting to stark seriousness. "That they sent you because they thought my head would be more easily turned by a lifted skirt then by a gap-toothed smile. Have to admit, their reasoning was pretty sound. It did work, didn't it?"

"You don't expect me to believe the deciding factor in your fighting today was whether or not I would—um—" Hope flushed clear down to her toes, "*compensate* for your time."

"Why not?" he asked dryly. "It's the truth."

"And if we'd sent my brother, or Old Joe instead?" she asked. Her heart was pounding a mile a minute and her palms were suddenly cold and damp with nervous anticipation. "What then?"

Drake chuckled. "First, I think they would have had the good sense *not* to show up in my room half-drunk," he replied, causing Hope's flush to deepen. "Second, I don't think their fainting in my arms would have had quite the same effect." This was said with a sly, knowing wink. "Third, and last, I would have sent them packing the second they made the offer—an offer, I might add, that they could not have sweetened the same way you did."

"But you didn't send *me* packing. Why not? Why them and not me?" Hope's voice was soft, breathless, the direct result of the hand that had slipped around her waist and now gently stroked the small of her back.

Drake pulled Hope against him, surprised at the pleasure the feel of her lithe body against his incited. "Let's just say the opportunity to get to know you better was more than I could resist."

The words were whispered hoarsely against her ear, rustling through the chestnut waves, caressing her cheek like a warm summer breeze caresses a soft forest leaf. Her breath lodged in her throat and she tilted her chin up only to be caught again by that brilliant, piercing gaze.

"Don't," she breathed softly. Her hands splayed helplessly atop the sinewy chest, as she watched the sensuously carved mouth dip with lazy confidence. Her tongue tingled with the savored memory of his taste, and Hope sucked in a ragged gasp when she felt her body spark to keen awareness. Eager anticipation shot through her blood as she unconsciously craned her neck to meet the kiss.

His lips were soft and tender, gently coaxing the fire that kindled in her veins. The sweet, lingering warmth of his touch ignited the first fragile sparks of passion.

With a whispered sigh of resignation, Hope lost herself to the taste of his lips, to the pleasant, spicy aroma that seemed to both surround and engulf her at once. Combined with the sweet magic of his kiss, her wall of resistance was knocked down as though it were built of porcelain.

Drake sensed her surrender with a surge of satisfaction. In his hotel room, she had begun to return his ardor, only to overcome the weakness and pull away. Though the passion had been fleeting, it had been enough to hint at a churning jumble of desires, carefully guarded beneath her defiant pose; a revelation that served only to whet his appetite for her.

The hands at her waist grew bolder, and though Hope would normally have called a quick halt to such intimate contact, she was suddenly too gloriously diverted by the first insistent probing of a warm, moist tongue flickering over her lips. She found herself slipping her hands up over the broad shoulders, entwining her arms around the thick cord of Drake's neck, burying her fingers deep in the flaxen smoothness of his hair. The strands felt deliciously like raw silk beneath her fingertips.

Since she had already molded her body into his, there was no need to hold her still. Drake put his hands to better use. The gentle curve of her hips fit the cup of his palm to perfection. He let his hands linger there, inwardly amazed at how the feel of warm, vibrant flesh beneath the smooth muslin made his fingers itch to remove the barrier. His imagination was quick to conjure up the image of soft, creamy flesh. The thought brought a rumbled groan to the back of his throat.

Hope blossomed beneath the demanding exploration of Drake's tongue. The kiss deepened, intensifying to an incredible pitch. Denial was wiped away, leaving not a trace in the wake of an all-consuming passion that burst through Hope's body.

In unison, the hands that stroked her hips turned inward, trailing over the quivering, taut flesh of her stomach. They gained momentum as they reached the swell of her breasts. The palms lingered there, savoring the feel of the firmly upthrust buds straining against the thin fabric, before continuing up and settling on the table of her shoulders.

He couldn't slip his hands over her shoulders to trail down the curve of her back, as he would have liked, without breaking the circle of her arms. The exquisite feel of her hands caressing his neck, tickling the underside of his earlobe, was too pleasurable a sensation to surrender.

Instead, Drake contented himself on another downward stroke. This time, his fingers didn't just hesitate, they stopped completely when they reached the curve of her breasts. Like her hips, each one nestled perfectly in the center of his palm. Before there had been only a deep, insistent desire to remove the annoying barrier separating hand from flesh. Now there was a burning, aching *need* to do so.

The playful antics of Drake's teeth trying to nibble at the tip of her darting tongue distracted Hope long enough for him to free the first three buttons at the nape of her neck.

115

Two more slipped from their holes in the time it took for realization to begin nipping at the back of Hope's mind. By the time the seventh button slipped free, she was shockingly aware of what was going on. Her heart skipped a beat, then began pounding furiously.

Hot fingertips seared across the rippled strip of flesh on her back a split second before a strangled cry of terror escaped her lips. Frantically, she pushed against the wall of his chest. Surprised, Drake let her go, and she slipped easily from the circle of his arms.

She wasted no time. The gut-wrenching fear pumping through her veins had the same effect as a bucket of ice water being thrown over a sleeping drunk. Terror served to drive away any remnants of passion that might have remained.

A quick look at the confusion on Drake's hardening features convinced Hope not to wait for the rest of his reaction. Hoisting her skirts, she bolted for the sack of flour. The skirt slipped from her fingers only once. It wrapped itself around her ankles, trying to trip her, but she reached out and steadied herself on the side of the table before any damage could be done. Snatching up the peachy folds, she plunged on. Another mistake like that and Frazier would be on her before she could reach the gun.

Two footsteps thudded on the planks behind her in the time it took her to reach the lumpy sack. Skidding to a stop, and coming treacherously close to slamming into the wall, she crouched low and grabbed the pistol. Her calves sent a weak protest to her mind as, still in a half-squat, she spun on her heel and leveled the barrel smack at the middle of Frazier's chest.

Drake had been on the other end of a gun barrel enough times to know when to stop. He came to an abrupt halt in the middle of the floor, and to Hope he looked remarkably like a charging bull brought up short by a barbed wire fence.

"Come any closer and I'll take your head off," she warned, her voice a breathless mixture of exertion, fear, and dread. She punctuated the threat by pulling the hammer back with her thumb. The metallic click of the rotating chambers echoed, loud and ominous in the ensuing silence.

Working under the assumption that the gun was loaded—and only a fool would be stupid enough to assume that it wasn't—Drake assessed Hope's skill and decided there was little doubt she had enough to use the gun. But *would* she? One glance told him the girl was petrified, and, like a frightened, cornered animal, her actions couldn't be predicted.

Drake was right, Hope was scared to death. However, he'd surprisingly overestimated her prowess with a firearm. She made no effort to correct the mistaken assumption. If Frazier thought she could do something besides load, point, and fire the pistol, then all the better. *She* certainly wasn't about to admit that her lessons had stopped just shy of teaching her how to aim the damn thing.

A lazy grin twisted Drake's lips as his gaze flickered between the gun and Hope. Only the leery glitter in his eyes gave hint to the trepidation coursing inside.

"Well, sunshine, are you going to shoot me with that thing or am I going to have to wrestle it away from you?" he drawled with an easy shrug, as he settled his hands on his hips. The gaze took on a decidedly wicked twinkle. "Personally, I prefer the latter."

She tilted her chin proudly, meeting his gaze head on. "Try it," she spat, trying to ignore the trickle of admiration that seeped into her blood at the man's apparent immunity to fear. That he could be so calm in the face of adversity, while *she* held the upper hand and *still* sat trembling like a leaf, annoyed Hope to no end. "Go ahead and try it, Frazier. But you'd better move fast because . . ." she

117

paused, angling the gun until the barrel was aimed directly at the space between his golden brows, "so help me God, it'll be the last thing you ever do."

Her words seemed to have no impact. Casually, Frazier took a seat on the crudely built bench. Leaning back, he rested his back against the table's edge and lazily stretched his legs out before him. He crossed his arms over his chest, his booted legs at the ankles. To Hope, he looked for all the world like an old friend come to chat.

"You know," Drake said as he stared thoughtfully into the dwindling fire, "you're going to have a tough time explaining my dead body to the rest of your little gang when they return." His gaze swept the room, then settled on Hope accusingly. "What are you going to tell them? That when I came to collect payment, you, having changed your mind, shot me instead? Don't think the miners' court'll go easy on you with that one."

Now that he was sitting, and no longer an immediate threat, Hope felt secure enough in shifting her weight until she was sitting on the hard, cold floor. Her aching calves sighed in relief. "They won't convict me," she replied with a shrug, surprised at the confidence that rang clear in her voice. "Not when I tell them I shot you in self-defense. After all, a girl does have to defend her honor. Especially in a place like this."

A throaty chuckle rumbled in Drake's chest, a humor that was not reflected in the eyes that never left her. "Is that what you're going to tell them? That I tried to steal your virtue? Not very original, sunshine. I'd have thought you'd come up with something a little more dramatic."

Again, she shrugged. "It doesn't have to be original, or dramatic, just good enough so it sounds like the truth." Her thumb rubbed the cold band of metal that separated the sides of the pistol's carved ivory handle. "They'll believe it. I'd bet my life on it."

"You *will* be, if shooting me's what you decide to do." His gaze shifted to her mouth and Hope felt a sudden warmth there. It was as if he'd run his index finger over the smooth flesh, not just his gaze. "Are you willing to take that chance?" Drake asked, his voice softly probing. "Are the consequences really that bad?"

"If you'd just leave peacefully there wouldn't *be* any consequences," she spat, resting her forearms on drawn-up knees. She was careful never to let the barrel of the gun waver, a sign of weakness that this man would be quick to take full advantage of.

"I can't do that."

"Why not?" she fairly screamed. "Don't force me to shoot you, Frazier. I will if I have to, we both know it, but I don't think it's what either of us wants."

Drake fingered the jagged cut on his cheek, then let his thumb trail over the blush swelling on his stubbly jaw. The look he sent her was one of unconcealed desire and determination. "I know what I want," he replied slowly, poignantly. "And I think I know what you want, too."

"How convenient. Is there anything you *don't* know?" she quipped sarcastically, rearranging her position so the buttons of her dress didn't cut into her back quite so sharply.

"As a matter of fact . . ." Drake's voice trailed away and he sent her that arrogantly confident smile again, the one Hope would gladly have shot right off his face. "I haven't quite figured out why you're fighting me so hard. Why would you offer me compensation you had no intention of giving? And why won't you give it?" He shrugged. "Can't figure that one out. I don't suppose you'd care to enlighten me?"

"Hardly."

"Of course, there's always the chance—" his brow furrowed into a scowl. "You're not married, are you?"

He would have heard if she was, Drake told himself. In

119

Thirsty Gulch, there wasn't too much about a person that one *didn't* hear about. The husband of a girl in her marital prime, especially a girl who was as attractive as this one, couldn't be kept a secret, now could it? Hope Bennett had a sour disposition, true, but men in these parts didn't give a fig for disposition. So long as she kept the bed warm and the meals on the table, mended the shirts and took care of the menial tasks, she could have any disposition she wanted to.

With such thoughts answering his own question, Drake wasn't surprised to see Hope shake her head with almost laughable disbelief. Her thoughts must have traveled the same path.

"Hmmm," Drake sighed thoughtfully. His frown deepened as he rubbed a palm down his jaw. "Guess that brings us to question number two, sunshine. Why aren't you married?"

Drake thought he must have hit a sore spot, for Hope flinched as though she had been slapped across the face, before carefully schooling her features back to rigid self-composure. *When did she pull away from me?* he found himself wondering. *Not when I kissed her. No, she returned that affection quite nicely, thank you very much. But the buttons on her dress—*

"That's none of your business," she hissed, her brown eyes narrow and glistening bright with indignation. He was hitting too close to home, she thought with a sense of panic. Much too close to home. "And stop calling me that. Why do you keep calling me that?"

Drake smiled, but his gaze remained thoughtful. "Oh, I don't know. Your winning disposition, I suppose," he replied flippantly, adding a sarcastic chuckle.

"Don't toy with me, Frazier," Hope warned, her voice low and angry as she gestured toward his chest with the gun. "I don't enjoy being played with any more than I like being made to look a fool."

120

"And *I* don't like being held at the receiving end of a pistol," he countered, just as hotly. His eyes narrowed to angry, sea-green slits. "Guess that makes us just about even, *sunshine.*"

Holding her anger in check was not something Hope had much practice at, or much use for. And now, she didn't even try. Sneering, she jutted her chin at the door. "If you don't like the company, feel free to leave. Nobody's stopping you. God knows, I'm not using this thing to *keep* you here."

Drake shook his head as though she had just offered him a cup of coffee, and he'd politely declined it. "Nah," he said, sliding a little lower in the bench. "Thanks for the offer, but I think I'd rather wait around until you're ready to pay me." A derisive smile tugged at the corner of his lips. "Or shoot me. Whichever comes first."

"Then make yourself comfortable, gunslinger, because I'm not going to shoot you unless you ask for it." There was no need to elaborate. The look on Frazier's face said he'd drawn the right conclusion.

Drake sent Hope a quick look from the corner of his eye as he pretended to turn his attention back to the fire. His calculating gaze assessed the dark shadows etched beneath the lower lashes and the drooping of her eyelids. He watched as she stifled a yawn with the back of her hand, thinking he hadn't seen. The barrel of the gun dipped until it was pointed at a place somewhere between his ankle and his calf. Her guard had lowered, if only momentarily.

The time to move was here, and Drake seized it with every ounce of energy he possessed. It took barely a second for his muscles to tighten from lazy relaxation to rigid awareness.

Hope was alert at once, the yawn caught in her throat as she trained the gun on his sculpted profile. Except for a slight change in position he seemed to have totally dismissed her. His gaze was still trained on the dying flames in the hearth. Odd, but his eyes seemed more alert now, more purposeful. His arms were no longer crossed atop his chest. Instead, his hands were cushioned there, the fingers apparently relaxed and linked atop the tight stomach. His ankles were no longer crossed either. Now his feet were spread apart, both boots firmly planted on the floor.

Recognition dawned a split second too late. By the time Hope realized what Frazier was about, he had lithely uncoiled from his lazy pose and hurled himself at her, full force.

Hope had barely enough time to swallow a gasp before the weight of his body came smashing down on top of her. Air rushed from her lungs at the same time the bullet left the gun with an earsplitting explosion. The bone-jarring impact of his body prevented any aim she might have taken, and the shot went harmlessly high and wide. The bullet lodged in one of the beams that crisscrossed the ceiling, splintering the wood with a crackling sound that might have been made by a log on the fire, or by the snapping of her ribs.

A hand snaked out of nowhere, closing around her wrist in a viselike grip that made the blood, trapped in the fingers coiled around the gun throb with each frantic beat of her heart. Hope tried to move her thumb, tried to make it reach the cold metal hammer that would buy her another shot. Her hand wouldn't respond. It took all her strength, and most of her self-control, just to keep hold of the carved ivory handle.

Frazier must have sensed her intent. His grip tightened by painful degrees until she was convinced the bones in her arm would snap from the pressure. He shifted his weight enough to allow her air, and Hope took deep gulps of it. She watched, horrified, while her unresponsive fingers drained from pale white to ice cold blue. One by one they uncurled from the handle like the petals of a blossoming

122

rosebud, until the pistol lay nestled in the darkening flesh of her palm.

In one fluid motion, Drake released her hand and snatched up the weapon. With an angry growl, he flung it to the other side of the room. It smashed into the wall, scarring the unstained wood, before clattering harmlessly to the floor.

Her hand tingled with pain, and Hope gasped as her circulation returned. She managed to lift her hand an inch off the floor, but it promptly fell back. Though she would have loved nothing better than to smack that look of arrogant self-satisfaction off Drake Frazier's face, that chore would have to wait. Her other hand was pinned helplessly between their chests, and it would probably be quite a while before Frazier trusted her enough to free it.

"What are you going to do now, gunslinger? Force me?" Hope taunted breathlessly. Her voice was filled with loathing as she tilted her chin up to meet his gaze. The large, slanted brown eyes sparkled with anger, and there wasn't a trace of defeat to be found in her hard, square features.

"Maybe," he replied, his voice a husky whisper. His gaze dropped to her softly parted lips and Hope's breath caught as she felt his warm breath wash over her cheeks and neck. "Maybe not." He nodded over his shoulder. "That thing have any more bullets in it?"

Her lips curled into a sly grin and her eyes narrowed in challenge. "Go check."

"Ha! Not a chance. I'm comfortable right where I am."

"That makes one of us," Hope muttered. She squirmed, trying to free the hand caught between their bodies. The strength had finally returned to her other hand, and Hope balled it into a fist and pushed impatiently against his shoulder. It was like trying to move God. "Will you please get off me? I can't breathe."

"Not until you tell me why you pulled a gun on me."

"Isn't it obvious?"

"I want the real reason, sunshine, not the 'obvious' one."

Hope flushed and lowered her gaze to his lips. Sensuous, enticingly molded lips. Hot color flooded her cheeks as she renewed her struggles. This time, as she pushed and strained against him, she noticed a spark of emotion flicker in those fathomless green eyes. Desire? Admiration? Disgust? What had it been? She didn't know. It came and went so fast that, before she knew it, she was once again staring into a gaze that was hard and indecipherable.

"Tell me, Hope," Drake whispered. His prodding was so soft that, for an instant, Hope was tempted to tell him what he wanted to know.

The same hand that, just moments before, had been ready to twist her arm into pieces, now tenderly brushed a sweat-dampened curl from her brow. At first she flinched from the touch, but his fingers were so warm, so exquisitely gentle, that she found herself relaxing against them. It was a mistake, she knew, but one that she had no control over. Her body was responding to his nearness with alarming speed, and the result was a breathless sense of anticipation that both confused and frightened her.

"Drake," Hope sighed, giving another feeble push at his shoulder. Odd, but his name tasted like nectar to her lips. Against her will, she found herself thoroughly enchanted. "Let me up," she pleaded weakly.

She had to get away from him, Hope realized suddenly. She had to get away from his spicy scent, his warm touch, his tender words. The combined attack on her senses was wreaking havoc, weakening her self-control with dismaying ease. Already she could feel her resolve fading. Another few minutes of this exquisite torture and her traitorous body would be melting against him, as it so badly wanted to do now. And if she let that happen, everything would be lost.

"Let me up," she cried suddenly. She pushed against him

with all her might, as though by turning Frazier away she could also push her deepest, darkest fears back into the far closet of her mind where they belonged, under lock and key. "Let me up and then leave. Don't . . . please, don't make me—" her voice cracked as she swallowed a sob. *I won't cry. I won't cry. I WON'T CRY!* she chanted to herself as a tear slipped down her cheek.

Damn it! Hope turned her head away, praying that Frazier hadn't seen. She should have known better. Those eagle eyes never missed a thing.

Drake lifted her chin with the crook of his index finger and turned her to him. Her eyes, large and round, reminded him of a doe his grandfather had forced him to hunt and trap. Even then, he hadn't been able to fire the bullet that would bring the deer down.

And now? he wondered, as he peered into a pair of wide, innocent, velvet brown eyes, the pupils of which were encircled with a golden band to match the glistening flecks in the irises.

He should have been able to pull the trigger without compunction. Past and present had combined to make Drake the hard, bitter shell of a man that he was, but still there was something about those innocent eyes that reminded him of the frightened doe. The reminder scratched painfully close to the tender feelings he'd buried long ago. He'd actually forgotten they existed.

With a muffled curse, Drake threw himself from her as though her dress had just reached a degree past boiling.

Hope felt a waft of cold air brush over her body as he pulled away. An inexplicable emptiness welled in the pit of her stomach, and confusion shimmered in her eyes as she sat up. She watched him run his fingers through his hair as he angrily stalked toward the gun. Wiping away the dampness on her cheek with the back of her hand, she tried to ignore her sudden panic.

Is he going to shoot me? she wondered frantically. She pushed her back hard against the wall and tucked her knees as close to her chest as she could get them. *And am I just going to sit here and let him do it without putting up a fight? Hell, no!*

Fueled by indignation, she pushed herself to her feet and staggered to the counter. She ached from the cramped position, from having borne the weight of Drake's body on hers. Hope ignored her muscles' scream of protest as her fingers wrapped around the knife's wooden handle. Behind her echoed the familiar click and roll of the pistol's tumblers.

Hope spun on her heel. A frown wrinkled her brow as she watched Drake inspect the gun's chambers curiously.

"Hmph!" he snorted, snapping the metal door shut. To her aggravation, he addressed her without bothering to turn her way as he tested the weight of the pistol. "The knife's not going to do you much good, sunshine," he said, with a devilish grin, as he twirled the gun on his index finger and let it slap neatly into his palm. "Or did you forget that there were five more shells in this beauty?"

Hope stiffened. "I didn't forget," she lied. Actually, she'd had no way of knowing how many bullets Old Joe kept in the gun. "I figured I might need them all in case you tried anything nasty."

Drake shrugged. In two steps he reached the table, where he placed the pistol next to the pile of neatly stacked dishes. "Keep it then, if it makes you feel better, but you won't be needing it. I've decided to—" he scowled, then sent her a cold grin, "postpone payment for the time being."

"Postpone?" Now what was he up to? Her eyes narrowed as she regarded him with open suspicion. "Not that I'm complaining, mind you, but why? What brought about this sudden change of heart? I thought you were anxious to get—um—*paid.*"

"Don't push it," Drake warned, his voice hard, cold, and as devoid of emotion as his eyes. "Keep arguing and I just might change my mind. And you wouldn't want me to do that, would you, sunshine?"

"No!" she cried, much too quickly.

Drake nodded, her sudden, frightened reaction again raising the question he held in the back of his mind. "That's what I thought."

He sent Hope a long, hard look, then headed for the door. The cold night air rushed past him, scattering a few dried leaves on the floor. They rustled loudly as they skipped across the bare, flat planks.

Drake stopped short, and for a second Hope feared he had changed his mind. Her heart did a crazy flip-flop in her chest, and her palms grew damp as she rubbed them briskly together. Whether the reaction was caused by fear or anticipation, she was never really sure.

A sun-kissed hand reached out and plucked his hat from the rack. He settled the worn leather on top of his golden head. His voice, when it came, was so soft it might have been made by the wind; Hope knew better. "I'll be back, sunshine. You can bet on it."

By the time he had closed the door behind his rugged back, Hope was leaning weakly against the table, trembling far more than the fragile leaves scattering the floor.

Chapter Seven

Though he did not make it his sleeping quarters, Drake Frazier might as well have taken up permanent residence in the Bennett household. Everywhere Hope turned, Drake was there. If the tinny sound of his harmonica didn't accompany her to bed, chuckles over the wondrous things he'd said during the day did. Everywhere she turned, she either met with his smiling green eyes or with the clinging, smoky scent of his infernal cheroots — an odor her father, atypically, abided without complaint. Even after he'd left their cabin for his hotel room, she could smell that pungent scent, and the aroma haunted her dreams.

Except for Old Joe, everyone had taken to the gunslinger as though he was a part of the family. Essentially, she supposed, he was. Her alliance with Frazier had opened up a line of friendship between him and the others that even a sharply honed axe couldn't break. Though her father remained cautious, even he had grown accustomed to seeing Drake's eagle-sharp features over his supper plate. That the gunslinger didn't work in the mine, yet unflinchingly drained a percentage of the take, seemed to matter only to Hope.

Using the back of her arm, Hope wiped the sweat from her brow and looked down at the pile of apple slices. Cut into perfect little wedges, they would soon be baking in a flaky crust for an after-dinner treat.

She was molding the thin dough into a pie plate when Luke trudged through the door. A sparkling of rain moistened his crop of chestnut curls.

"It's startin' to rain. Pa said we could call it a day."

Hope looked over her brother's shoulder and scowled. "So where is everybody?"

"Pa sent the twins into Sutter's Fort for supplies. Him and Old Joe'll be up shortly. They're puttin' stuff away." He licked his sun-parched lips as his gaze settled on the raw pies.

"They aren't cooked so don't even think about it," she warned him as she wiped her hands. Since it never occurred to Luke to offer help, Hope herself was in the process of tucking the pies into the alcove inside the brick hearth when the door opened again.

"Damn, but if'n he ain't right." Old Joe shook off the rain that clung to him like a dog shook off his bath. Crystal droplets splattered the floor and table as Bart and Drake Frazier did the same.

"There's better money in hydraulics, sure," Drake conceded grudgingly. Hope watched as he plucked the hat from his head and hung it on what was quickly becoming "his" hook on the rack. "But it's an expensive thing to start. You'd have to buy more equipment and hire more men, and there's no guarantee it'd pay off. The mine could run dry."

"But it's still something to think about," Bart said as, with a flick of his wrist, he flipped his hat on a curved wood hook. When had her father started seeking out Drake Frazier's opinion or approval? she wondered.

Drake nodded, his eyes lighting on Hope. "Yup, it's something to think about."

For a split second, she thought he was speaking to her, then blushed furiously when she realized he was talking to her father. No, that was wrong. His lips might be talking to Bart, but he gazed at her alone. *You haven't paid me, sunshine,* those eyes accused.

She turned away and tossed the towel onto the counter. The cloth landed in a crumpled heap on top of a pile of browning apple peels.

"I don't know," Old Joe said, shaking his head as he scratched his chin. Noticing where Frazier's gaze rested, the narrow eye widened until it was almost the same size as the one that bugged. "Try askin' Hope. The gal's got a right good head on her shoulders. Perty one, too," he added, with a wink. " 'Course, right now she looks like hell. What's a matter with you, girl?" he added, noting the dark circles etched beneath her bloodshot eyes.

"Nothing. I'm fine, just a little tired," she lied, badly. She dearly wished she could blame her lumpy mattress for her recent restless nights, instead of the piercing sea-green gaze that haunted her, which even now was directed at her intently. "Ask me what?"

Drake shrugged. "Bart's thinking about investing in hydraulics. Joe doesn't like the idea."

"And your opinion?" she asked cautiously, settling her hands on her hips. "Or don't you have one?"

"He's keepin' it to himself," Old Joe told her, glancing between the two. "Fer now."

"It's not my decision." Drake's tone lacked the defensiveness his words suggested. "Well, sunshine, what do you think?"

"You saw what hydraulics did to the land in Comstock County, Papa," she replied as she untied the apron from behind her back and pulled it off. That, too, was banished to the counter. "As I recall, you were just as shocked as the rest of us. The hoses and forced water ravaged the land until there was nothing left but crevasses and muddy gulches. Didn't you say what they did was disgusting?" Her gaze narrowed accusingly. "I can't believe you'd even suggest it."

"See?" Old Joe preened as he perched on the bench. "Told ya she had a good head."

"Gotta do something, missy," Bart grumbled. He lowered himself carefully onto the bench, massaging his aching back. "As it is, we're only pulling out enough dust to buy necessaries. What's going to happen when winter sets in? We don't have nearly enough money to buy the supplies it'll take us to weather a winter in Thirsty Gulch."

If they didn't have the money to buy supplies, it went without saying there would be none left over to pay the taxes on Lake's Edge. Time was running short. If they didn't strike pay dirt soon, it would be too late to save the plantation. *And then what?* Hope thought. Lake's Edge was the only thing that kept her father going—that, and the dream that one day, with a little luck, he could restore it to its former glory. Without that dream to cling to, the same dream that had brought them to California in the first place, Bart Bennett would crumple and die as surely as a dry leaf withered and fell from a late autumn maple tree.

Hope ran her palms down the front of her homespun skirt and sighed. "Maybe hydraulics are the answer. I don't know," she shrugged, ignoring Old Joe's look of horror. "It doesn't matter, it's too late in the year to start now anyway. Like he said," she nodded to Drake, grudgingly admitting he was right, "starting up would mean adding expensive equipment. We don't have the money for it any more than we have the money to hire on more men. Maybe in the spring."

Bart lowered his face into his hands. "Time is one luxury we don't have, missy."

The hopeless look in her father's eyes told Hope what she had suspected all along. Either the mine paid off—and paid off quick—or Lake's Edge was lost. Suddenly it was crystal clear, the reasons behind her father's tight-lipped, evasive answers whenever she dared to inquire about matters back home.

Old Joe launched into a lecture on his somewhat dated opinion of hydraulics. Hope didn't hear a word as her gaze shifted to Frazier. He was listening to the exchange between Bart and Old Joe with apparent interest, but occasionally she caught his gaze straying to her.

Her eyes narrowed, her mind racing. What little profit the mine churned out was being drained away by the gunslinger's cut. Her mouth went dry. Could Frazier be convinced to abandon his share of the profits? And did she have a right to ask him to? No, she didn't. She had already welched on half of their deal, as Frazier took every opportunity to remind her of, so how, in all good conscience, could she ask him to forget the rest?

She had no choice. Time was running short, if the look on her father's face was anything to go by. Better by far to get rid of Frazier's cut of the profits, and risk his wrath, than to lose Lake's Edge.

While the men were deep in conversation, Hope slipped quietly to the gunslinger's side.

"I seen a few Chinamen driftin' 'round town with not much to do. We could hire them perty cheap."

"Yeah, probably, but . . ."

The rest of her father's answer was lost as she placed a hand on Drake Frazier's shoulder. A shiver of delight coursed up her arm as her gaze was captured by his.

"I need to talk to you," she said, her words soft enough for only him to hear. One golden eyebrow cocked in question. "In private," she added, her gaze insistent, "please. It's — it's important."

Drake nodded. "I'll get your cloak," he said, uncoiling his lean frame from the hard bench. Hope caught a whiff of his soapy scent as he strode to the rack and retrieved his hat.

Setting it atop the silky mane of hair, he reached out with the other hand to retrieve the black cloak.

He tossed it to Hope, and she caught it in midair, flinging the coarse wool over her shoulders. It billowed around her legs, settling like an ebony cloud around her ankles.

"Where's you two off to?" Old Joe asked, his large eye bulging with suspicion. Bart might not see what was going on between his daughter and the gunslinger, but Old Joe wasn't so blind. He'd caught more than one secretive glance pass between the two when they both thought no one was looking. And he caught the looks Drake sent Hope when she wasn't looking. It didn't help that he knew Frazier from way back, and knew him well enough not to trust him for a minute.

"I promised Fra—Drake I'd show him the hens Mrs. Magrew sold Luke yesterday," Hope said weakly, as she tied a poorly shaped bow beneath her chin. Her fingers were trembling as she pulled the hood into place.

"Don't stay out long, missy," Bart said, seemingly unfazed at the prospect of his daughter leaving with Frazier. "It's only drizzling out now, but it's going to be raining fierce soon." He massaged the base of his spine. "This back never lies."

"I won't be long," she assured him, heading for the back door. Drake followed close behind. She could feel the heat of his body melting through the layers of her clothes, caressing the skin beneath as she stepped into the rain.

Drake pulled the door closed behind them, then fell into step behind Hope as she bypassed the lopsided coop. It had taken Luke the better part of yesterday afternoon to nail together a crude little shelter for the three scraggly hens. The trio of gaunt, feathery birds ran about in the barbed wire run, cackling wildly as raindrops pounded against their beaks.

133

The previous week Luke had built a shed for tools, and it was to this Hope now headed. She stopped in front of the door, then, on impulse, reached back and took his hand. Opening the door, she gave his arm a tug.

Stumbling in the mud, Drake came treacherously close to falling. "Wait a minute," he muttered. "Where are we going?"

"In the shed, fool." She swung the door wide, sparing him a brief glance. The only concession he'd made to the foul weather was his cracked leather vest, and the collar he'd turned up high. "Or didn't you notice it's raining out here? Duck," she said as she crouched and entered the shed, "Luke made the door too low."

The scent of sawdust was strong in the large, as yet vacant room. But the dirt floor was dry and the walls cut the chill, moist breeze. Dreary gray sunlight filtered in through the single window and the slats in the walls, streaking the floor.

"You call those things hens?" he chuckled sarcastically as he nodded to the door. "I've seen fatter pigeons."

"Laugh all you want, but you won't think it's so funny when you sit down to a proper breakfast of poached eggs," Hope scoffed defensively. She brushed the hood back from her head and let it hang limply over her shoulder as she sent him a crooked grin. "Or doesn't the thought of a dish of custard at the end of a long day appeal to you?"

"I don't think you brought me out in the rain to talk about custard, sunshine," Drake said as he stuffed his hands into the pocket of his tight denim trousers. It was either that or surrender to the temptation of reaching out to caress one of the silky chestnut curls brushing against a flawlessly ivory cheek. "Get to the point."

Crossing her arms over her chest, she averted her gaze to a ray of sun that flickered over the hem of her skirt. Where were all the words she had carefully rehearsed as they'd crossed the yard? she wondered. Shaking her head, Hope tried to pull them back to mind, but they were gone. Her mind was frighteningly blank.

Drake's hand reached from out of nowhere to cup her chin, gently pulling her attention back to him. The caress of his rough fingers was warm against the coolness of her rain-damp skin. His gaze was dark, searching, and totally unnerving.

"I never paid you." To her embarrassment, she spilled out the first words to enter her mind. The comment brought a spark of emotion to Drake's eyes. Or was it a trick of light? She couldn't tell. Whatever it was, it disappeared too quickly.

"I know that." His voice rang a pitch lower than normal as his thumb traced the delicate line of her jaw. She shivered, but didn't pull away from the touch. Drake wondered why.

"No, you don't understand. I never . . . never—"

"I know." Turning his hand, he savored the feel of satiny flesh beneath his palm. She felt good, he thought, as he caught the sweet scent of lilac petals clinging to her skin. The fragrance, though fleeting, overrode the smell of sawdust, of dirt, of everything. Did she know how much emotion her doe eyes revealed? No, he didn't think she did. Otherwise she would have turned away.

Hope swallowed hard. The tip of her tongue darted out to moisten her lips. She tried to focus her attention on forming the words that came awkwardly to her tongue, but it was difficult to think with the feel of his palm searing her cheek.

"You—you know I haven't paid you," she conceded, her voice husky with pent-up emotion. Her gaze dropped to the pulse throbbing at the base of the thick cord of his neck. "You don't know why."

"Then tell me."

135

Hope looked long and hard into that penetrating gaze, then nodded. She dropped to the floor of the shed as though her knees could no longer support her weight. Drake hunkered down beside her. To Hope's relief, he made no move to touch her. She didn't think she'd be able to concentrate with that roughened hand caressing away her thoughts.

"I never intended to pay you," she admitted, finally. The words were torn from somewhere deep in her soul. "I—I really thought I could—" She sucked in a ragged sigh. "That I could— Oh, I don't know what I thought."

"You thought you could hire me to fight for your brother and that afterward, with any amount of luck, I'd find myself on the wrong end of a Winchester come dusk on Saturday night."

She chuckled despite herself. "No, I've never had that kind of luck." She ran her fingers through the sawdust which powdered the dirt. Her expression turned serious. "I should never have promised you something I couldn't give. My father's a good man. He brought his kids up better than that. He told me to never make a promise I couldn't keep, and until now I never have. But Luke's life was at stake and I had to do something. I couldn't let him fight Larzdon. He would have been killed. I know it as sure as I'm sitting here—and so do you."

The urge to touch one of the chestnut waves spilling over her shoulder was too great to resist. Drake reached out and captured one of the curls between his fingers, marveling at its softness and the way it wrapped around his finger. "So you came to me."

"Damn it, Drake," her open palm slapped her lap, "you were supposed to take the money. You weren't supposed to—"

"Take you?"

Sea-green clashed with brown velvet. Hope's gaze

dropped to the lips that were slowly lowering toward her. A heartbeat passed, more than enough time to stop him if she tried. She didn't try.

This was not at all like the hard, punishing kiss he'd left her with that night in his hotel room. His lips were soft, surprisingly gentle, and when he urged her back, Hope went without complaint. It was enticing, the feel of the hard floor against her back, and the feel of the hard man against her front. Her arms circled his neck.

He drank deeply of the honeyed sweetness being offered. There was no stiffness in the body beneath him, only soft, generous curves begging to be explored. His palm slowly ascended the small taper of her waist, brushed lightly against the outer swell of her breast, then ran a tantalizing path down the sensitive inner column of her arm. He marveled at the way her breath fanned his cheek, igniting a burning fire there that quickly seeped into his blood. A groan escaped his lips as her body curved into his own with bittersweet perfection.

The aroma of fresh sawdust mixed with the tender scent of lilacs. It rekindled the fire that had been burning in Drake since the first minute he'd laid eyes on the chestnut-haired beauty. Her hair spread around them like a pillow of glistening silk, soft and inviting. His lips left hers to trail a path of fiery kisses across her cheek, fluttering over her brow, and finally tasting the salty tang of tears clinging to her eyelids.

Grudgingly, he pulled away, resting his weight on an elbow as he looked down at the delicately carved face, and the stream of tears that moistened her cheeks. Mesmerized, he reached out to capture a tear on the tip of his index finger. It glistened for a second in the shadowy light before he rubbed it into the calloused finger with his thumb.

"I don't understand," he said, his voice a harsh whisper against the backdrop of squawking wet hens outside. She was crying now, but she *had* responded to him, damn it! It wasn't his imagination, not this time.

"I know," she sputtered weakly. With a clenched fist, she wiped away her tears. "You can't understand. You don't know."

"Know what?" Drake tried to keep his impatience from creeping into his words, and failed miserably. "I'll receive payment from you now, or I'll have the reason why."

"Damn it, Frazier! You don't understand anything."

Taking a deep breath, Drake struggled to restrain his raging emotions. Fear had crept into Hope's eyes, and it pierced him to the core. "Maybe not. But one thing I know for sure, sunshine. You can't tease a man with promises, then expect him to turn away." His finger trailed a feather-light line over her trembling lower lip. "Life doesn't work like that. *I* don't work like that."

"I didn't mean to tease you. I would never do that."

Her doe eyes pleaded with him to believe her. Instinctively, he did. "But you won't pay me either. You're talking in circles, Hope. Either you want me or you don't."

She released a trembling sigh and turned her gaze away, only to have him drag it back. "The situation isn't that easy. I—I'm not like other girls. I—I can't *do* what they can, no matter how much I might want to."

Drake strove to read some meaning into her words, knowing that whatever she was trying to convey bothered her deeply. Yet, no matter how he tried, his mind circled back to one thing. He couldn't understand how she could kiss him with such unabashed passion one minute, then tell him she couldn't physically love him the next.

He scowled as he reached out and cupped an ivory cheek. The tingling sensation her cool skin caused his palm made coherent thought impossible. He wanted her, God! he wanted her, like no other woman he'd known before. And she wanted him, too. The fire in her kiss told him that. So why did she insist on building this wall between them? Didn't she know that he would tear it down, brick by brick, if that's what it took to possess her, body and soul?

Hope watched the emotions flickering across Drake's face. For once they were not concealed. For once he had dropped his guard long enough to reveal the inner workings of his mind. He was confused, and he had every right to be. She had made promises she hadn't kept. But how could she explain her reason for entering into their arrangement under false pretenses, and explain it in a way that didn't sound foolish and contrived?

The words formed on her tongue, then stubbornly refused to spill from her lips. Her gaze misted over, settling on the sensuous line of his lips, afraid to look higher. She couldn't stand to see the recrimination that must be floating in his eyes.

She swallowed hard. Her heart told her it was time Drake knew the truth. She would have no more lies between them.

Chapter Eight

Hope's fingers flickered over the hand that caressed her cheek before she nudged Drake away. Thankfully, he eased back far enough for her to turn and sit cross-legged, her back facing him.

She took a deep breath, then pulled the ties beneath her chin. The cloak floated around her shoulders, landing atop the floor like a blanket. She barely noticed. She was too busy concentrating on her trembling fingers as she slipped free the line of tiny buttons holding the bodice of her dress in place. She could feel Drake's gaze through the coarse blue homespun, grazing the flesh beneath. She was glad her back was to him. She had no desire to see the disgust in his eyes when she showed him in action what her voice refused to say.

With the last button free, she pushed the ivory lace collar down over her shoulders and freed her arms from the tight-fitting sleeves. The fabric sagged, wrinkling around her waist. Now the thick curtain of her hair and the nearly transparent cotton of her chemise were the only barriers between her naked back and Drake Frazier.

A hen squawked in the distance as she worked the laces of her chemise. The white cotton joined the dress, gathering in a belt-like circle of material around her waist. She closed her eyes tight, hating the salty tear that dripped over her cheek, splashing on her bare forearm. With the last of her energy, she reached up and swept the lush chestnut waves over her shoulder, exposing her back.

Drake squinted, at first thinking the rippled stretch of flesh a trick of light and shadows. He was wrong. The scar, as long as it was wide, ran from the left side of her waist, across the delicate spine, and disappeared just above her right shoulder blade. Thicker than the rest of her skin, it had the puckered appearance of water into which a stone had just been thrown, except there was no distinct pattern to these ripples. Leaning closer, he noticed the flesh edging the scar was a faded pink that gradually shaded into a more healthy peach as it neared the middle.

His heart tightened as though clenched by an iron fist. She had been burned, and burned badly. She was lucky to be alive. He had seen men die of lesser burns, whether from the trauma itself or from infection setting in after the healing process had begun. There was no risk of that happening to Hope. This was not a recent injury, and new flesh had grown to cover the sensitive tissue and muscle beneath.

Physically, she appeared to have survived the ordeal with few repercussions. What the scar had done to her mind and soul was another matter.

Instinctively, he reached out and caressed the scarred strip of flesh. Her back stiffened beneath his palm, every muscle growing rigid with morbid anticipation. A small gasp escaped her lips at the feel of his fingers, and the sound tugged at Drake's heart with a force he would never have thought possible.

"No," she cried, her voice a desperate, strangled whisper as strong hands tried to turn her around. "Let me go. You've seen why I can't pay you. There's no reason for you to stay." She hugged her arms close to her chest, rocking back and forth as tears flowed freely down her cheeks. She hated those tears. She hated them almost as much as she hated the scar that crossed her back and the painful memories it accompanied.

"You're wrong. There's every reason for me to stay." His voice came out as a growl filled with raw emotion, as he succeeded in turning her to face him. "You've avoided me long enough, Hope Bennett. I won't let you push me away again."

"But—" She lifted her tear-streaked face, letting his warm breath caress her moist cheeks as he captured her gaze. There was no disgust in those sea-green eyes, no repulsion, no glint of pity. Only compassion shimmered there, and— could it be? Yes. His eyes were aglow with a deep, burning desire that was mirrored in her soul.

Slipping a hand beneath her chin, Drake's mouth captured her lips. The salty taste of her tears was strong on his tongue as he slowly lowered her atop the cloak blanketing the dirt.

"You should have told me sooner," he whispered against her lips, as his hand slid down her side to the gentle indentation of her waist. Her skin felt like spun satin beneath his fingertips. "Do you know how badly I've wanted you?"

"No," she confessed in a husky, awe-filled whisper as his lips trailed down the slender column of her throat. "But I know how much I've wanted you."

Her arms wrapped around the thick cord of his neck as she pulled his lips to hers. She kissed him deeply, clinging to his warmth like a drowning woman clutches her rescuer. His hair was silken beneath her fingertips, the curls at his nape, still damp with rain, tickled her palms. She was lost, lost to everything except the feel of his lips, the smell of his skin, and the gentle rush of his breath in her ear. Any protest she might have made withered like a desert rose beneath the hot magic of his kiss.

142

A throaty moan echoed in her ears as she tipped her chin, allowing him better access to the sensitive hollow of her throat. His tongue flickered over the soft skin, a moist caress against her hot flesh. Her fingers entwined themselves in the thick golden mane, but she neither pulled him away nor guided him as his kisses trailed lower.

With feather-light fingers, he pushed away the chestnut waves hiding her beauty from view. His gaze feasted on flawless perfection before his lips lowered to tease a shell-pink nipple.

Hope sighed and instinctively arched into his long, hard length. He felt wonderful, more wonderful than she had imagined in her dreams. She could feel his need pulsing against her thigh, and she shyly launched an investigation.

Delicate fingers slipped beneath the collar of his shirt, and Hope savored the feel of him as her hands slipped over his shoulders and back. His flesh was hard, firm, deliciously enticing, every muscle she encountered alive with motion.

The buttons of his shirt slipped free with amazing ease, and soon she found more pleasures to be explored. The taut stomach tightened then relaxed as she let her hands rove over that sun-kissed stretch of flesh. The back of her fingers strayed over the side of his ribs, slipping beneath his arms until she was again free to explore the sinewy back.

And that neck! How could she resist such an inviting cord of flesh? His skin was deliciously warm beneath her lips, and tasted of fresh rainwater. Her tongue flickered over the sensitive ear, playfully nibbling on the soft lobe before shifting her exploration to its inner recesses.

Drake moaned softly and buried his face in the luxurious blanket of her hair. No sooner had his lips left her than his hand took up the investigation, his palm cupping a delicate mound of flesh. Sparks of delight twisted up Hope's spine as she arched against him. Her fingers clung to the sun-kissed back as she tried to melt her body into his.

The rock-solid weight of him covered half her body, pushing her against the hard earth. The sensation ignited new sparks of awareness. A tug at the clothes around her waist made her lift her hips enough for the dress and chemise to be peeled away. In a matter of seconds, he had stripped away their clothes and tossed them to a crumpled heap by her feet.

The cool afternoon air washed over her body. Shivering, she curled into Drake, seeking and receiving his warmth.

"You're beautiful," he whispered into her hair, as he pulled her close against his side.

For the first time in her life, Hope believed it. In his arms, she felt beautiful.

His hand slipped down her back, over the scarred flesh, settling on her hip. He let his tongue slide in a hot, moist path down the column of her throat, hesitating on the hollow where her pulse beat out a frantic tempo, then slipping lower. The soft curves pressing against him were enough to drive Drake to distraction, but he held his fervent passion in check, slow and steady, as his lips settled on a rosy bud.

Hope tangled her fingers in his hair. A throaty moan escaped her softly parted lips as she closed her eyes and surrendered herself fully to the warm, throbbing need that pooled in her stomach and spread lower at an alarming rate.

One foot slipped up the back of his calf. The coarse golden curls that clung to the skin there tickled the delicate arch of her sole. Her foot rose higher, gliding over a firm thigh before she wrapped her leg around lean hips. A tremor passed through him, and she savored the provocative realization that her effect on him was equal to the tantalizing effect he had on her. The knowledge was heady. It fed her determination to return the pleasure his caresses brought, tenfold.

Coyly at first, she extended her range of exploration. The feel of his skin gliding beneath her palm brought forth a tingling sensation all its own. It was enough encouragement for her timid strokes to grow bolder. The firm path of his side passed beneath her hand, as did a sinewy hip and the back of an upper thigh.

She gloried in the feel of his weathered flesh, the clean rainwater scent of him. His fingers forged a trail of their own, and she quivered wherever he touched her. His strokes seared a torrid path between the sensitive flesh of her inner thighs. She opened to him without restraint, arching against his hand.

Skillfully, he kindled her passion until Hope thought she would go crazy with want. Shifting his weight, his hands retreated, gripping the sides of her hips. His mouth caught her gasp of surprised ecstasy as he slipped between her thighs, plunging into the warm, moist recesses of her soul.

Hope stiffened. Bitter disappointment formed crystal tears in her eyes, as the sharp pain pierced her. What cruel trick of nature was this?

Drake shifted so his weight was supported by the elbows flanking her shoulders. He lifted his head and lost himself to the tear-filled, brown velvet gaze. Once he was sure the pain had subsided, he began carefully moving inside her. His heart plunged, then rose to the highest peak when he saw the betrayal leave her eyes, replaced by a hooded passion that made her gaze come alive once more.

A tempo older than time was struck, and she met each thrust with a frantic desire. Every beat of his heart led her higher, pulling her into a spiral of ecstasy that promised eternal gratification with each glorious thrust and retreat.

They topped the clouds as one, soaring together, their passion simultaneously exploding into pulsating bursts of rapture.

Hope clung to the wondrous sensations as long as she could, reluctant to abandon the waves of satisfaction that washed over her body. Her body basked in the aftermath of the deliciously erotic sensations, and when Drake groaned and collapsed atop her, spent, she accepted his weight without complaint. Never in her life had she felt anything as wonderful as the male hardness pressing against her.

Wrapping her arms around his back, she hugged him close. She was afraid to let go, afraid she would wake to find their love had been nothing more than a dream.

"No," she cried when he started to pull away. Her voice was still low, still husky from newly quenched passion. "Please, don't leave me. Not yet."

Every muscle in his body tightened as he withdrew from her softness. Relaxation returned only after he had stretched out on the cloak of black wool and pulled the soft body that glowed with the contentment of their lovemaking hard against his side.

"I'm not going anywhere, sunshine," he whispered, his breath in her ear as he nuzzled her neck.

Hope snuggled against him, provocatively draping a leg over his thighs as she pulled the edge of her cloak over the lower half of their bodies. There wasn't enough free material to cover them completely. It didn't matter. The feel of his warm arms around her, and the drumming of his heart beneath her ear was all she needed. The air around them could have registered thirty degrees below zero, and still Hope doubted the blood pumping through her veins would have acknowledged the cold.

"Keep wiggling around like that and Luke will have to build another shed. We won't be leaving," he teased, his voice still thick with passion.

Hope grinned. Her teeth nipped playfully at a hard male nipple as she reached across him and plucked up a stalk of hay. Slowly, she ran it over the rich pelt of hair lining his

146

chest.

Drake closed his eyes and sucked in a ragged breath, groaning as the piece of hay traveled the taut line of his stomach; and lower still.

Her wrist was snatched in a steely grip. In one lithe motion she was tossed onto her back, with Drake's eagle-sharp face looming above.

Instead of fear, her gaze twinkled with mischief. "Why, Mistah Fraziah, whatever are ya doin'?" She batted the thick fringe of lashes as her dark brows rose in feigned innocence. "Surely y'all wouldn't think a takin' advantage of a sweet little gal like mahself?"

"That's exactly what I'm thinking. Come here," he growled, snatching the stalk of hay from her fingers and lowering his lips to hers.

She giggled as she surrendered herself to the searing demand of his kiss, and his own sensuous form of revenge.

Sitting with his back propped against the sturdy trunk of a maple, Tubbs pulled one knee up and rested his elbow atop it. A half-smoked cigar dangled from his fingers and a cloud of smoke poured from his lips, floating up to join the gray thunderclouds marring the sky.

An occasional drop of rain threaded its way through the branches overhead, but for the most part the lush ceiling of leaves kept him dry, if not warm. It didn't matter. Wet or dry, warm or cold, his job was almost at an end. By tomorrow he'd be aboard a ship set for Boston, eager to claim the second portion of his fee, money for a job well done. And by tomorrow, his job *would* be done.

Sighing, Tubbs took another drag off the cigar. It was a cheap brand of tobacco that left a bitter taste on his tongue. Today it was all he could afford, but tomorrow would be different. Tomorrow he'd have the money to indulge in a

147

box of the richest cigars San Francisco had to offer. It would be his first order of business, after he'd booked passage on the elegant clipper ship slotted to set sail at noon.

Tomorrow, Tubbs thought. Exhaling, he tossed the distasteful cigar into a puddle. He watched as the glowing tip sizzled out.

Glancing over his shoulder, his gaze narrowed on the largest in the long row of grubby cabins. Smoke curled in wisps from the stone chimney, carrying with it the tangy scent of baking pie. A rare delicacy, to be sure. Too bad they wouldn't have the chance to enjoy it. An evil smile curled over his lips as he tapped a finger against the jug by his side.

As on the nights before, Frazier had returned with the rest of the men; they'd come home earlier tonight because of the foul weather. He'd been in there almost half an hour now. These days the gunslinger took the majority of his meals with the Bennetts. Chances were, he wouldn't be out soon. But Tyrone Tubbs wasn't a man who took chances. Especially life-threatening ones. He'd learned *that* lesson weeks ago.

Taking potshots at the gunslinger from a hotel window as the man was riding out to the mines hadn't been one of Tubbs's most brilliant ideas. At the time, it had been an opportunity too good to pass up. Now he could see it for the stupid move it was. Luck was the only thing that had kept Frazier from seeing and recognizing him — luck and distance. Tubbs wouldn't stretch his luck a second time.

Two weeks, that mistake had cost him. Two weeks of lying low, waiting for Frazier to make a mistake. Two weeks of skulking in alleys and spending his money gaming and whoring in The Brass Button Tavern while he marked Frazier's comings and goings. Looking back, he had to admit the time had paid off. He now knew Drake Frazier's schedule better than the gunslinger knew it himself. And he knew Frazier's weakness.

His eyes glistened when he thought of the arrogant woman who'd gypped him out of four hundred bucks worth of nuggets. His fingers itched over the cloth he'd stuck in the glass jug's neck. He wouldn't be sorry to see the last of that little bitch. His only regret was that he wouldn't get the payment he deserved for getting rid of her as well.

Tubbs chuckled as he stuck a piece of grass between his teeth. A drop of rain fell off a leaf, splashing on the worn leather of his hat. No, he wouldn't get a thing for taking her out. He'd just have to drown his regret at that slight with the money he'd earn for ridding the world of Drake Frazier.

Fifteen minutes. He'd give the gunslinger fifteen minutes to show his ugly face. If he wasn't out by then, it was a safe enough bet the guy wouldn't leave the cabin until well into the night.

Again, Tubbs chuckled. The ominous sound rivaled the nervous whicker of the horses he'd tethered behind the granite boulder. They were workhorses, each one as poor an excuse for horseflesh as ever he'd seen. But they had been cheap, he reminded himself as he spit out the grass. They might be old nags ready for slaughter, but they'd do the job just fine.

He pulled another stale cigar from his pocket and stuck it in his mouth, rolling it over his tongue before clamping it between his teeth. Yup, fifteen minutes and Drake Frazier wouldn't be going anywhere.

"I didn't bring you out here for this," Hope said, her voice a tentative whisper, as she let her fingers trace a path down his breastbone. Her fingertip stopped just short of his navel and she chanced a glance at him from beneath hooded lashes.

"You brought me out here to show off those wretched hens," he reminded her lightly. Snatching up her hand, he brought the fingers to his lips. Their gazes met, and when Drake saw the serious glint in her dark eyes, his expression sobered. "Why did you bring me out here, sunshine?"

The newborn honesty between them felt right, too fragile to tamper with. She rested her chin atop the hand pillowed on his chest as she sent him a small half-smile. "I wanted to tell you I planned to welch on the rest of our deal."

One golden eyebrow cocked high in that broad forehead and she couldn't resist the temptation to reach up and brush the tousled hair from his brow. "Our deal," he said, his tone low and guarded. "It always comes back to that, doesn't it?"

Hope felt his thoughts as though they were her own. The hand on his brow turned to caress his cheek, her eyes softly searching. "Don't get defensive on me now, Drake. I'm here because here is where I want to be. I want to be in your arms. I—" Her voice cracked and she turned her face away. "I just never thought you—that *any* man would ever want me. I'm . . . I'm not—"

"You're beautiful," he whispered huskily, covering her hand with his own. He planted a soft kiss in her palm. "Every single inch of you."

Hope swallowed hard, her smile waning. "When you say that, I can almost let myself believe it."

"Believe it. I don't lie."

"But—"

"I said I don't lie."

As he spoke, his fingers trailed a path down her back. Hope's breath caught as she waited for his reaction. There was none. His expression didn't change, the intense emotion reflected in his eyes remained. Was it possible her scars truly meant nothing to him? There was a way to find out,

150

though she was reluctant to try it.

Sighing, Hope dropped her head back to his chest. His flesh felt warm beneath her cheek. She savored the bittersweet sensation. She tried to memorize the sound of his heart drumming its gentle rhythm beneath her ear, terrified this might be the last time she would ever feel his body pressed intimately against her own. *Say it and get it over with, Hope,* she told herself. *It's the only way you'll ever know for sure.*

Fifteen minutes turned into twenty; twenty into thirty.

Tubbs fingered the jug, his eyes bright with cruelty. The tip of a fresh cigar glowed as he pushed himself to his feet. He stretched the tightness out of muscles that were stiff from his cramped position.

Anticipation pumped through his veins as he leaned over and picked up the jug. The contents sloshed against the glass, soaking into the cloth that corked the bottle. Peeking around the tree, he assured himself that there were no witnesses to his presence before he stepped from his hiding place.

He'd waited an extra ten minutes hoping the drizzle would subside. Instead, the light shower had turned into a downpour. It didn't matter. There was enough kerosene in the jug to set most of Thirsty Gulch on fire. Another two-bit mining town burning to the ground wasn't unusual in the Mother Lode. It wouldn't draw much attention. And if it did, who cared? By the time the first question was asked, Tubbs would be rounding the Horn, halfway to Boston.

The sharp point of a rock worked its way through a crack in the sole of his boot as he stealthily approached the cabin. He took perverse pleasure in the slight pain.

A rumble of voices echoed through the walls of the cabin as Tubbs slipped soundlessly through the shadows. He pressed his back hard against the rough-hewn sides, waiting

151

for the cry of alarm that would warn him his presence had been noticed.

The seconds stretched out for what seemed like an eternity, and no cry of warning came. Confident, he pulled the cork of cloth from the jug. The pungent odor of the kerosene hit him at once. He'd have to be quick before the stench worked its way inside.

Spurned by that thought, Tubbs started pouring a line of the foul-smelling liquid around the cabin. It took only a few short minutes to round all four sides. The jug was still half-full. He poured most of what remained on the front step. Creeping to the back, he dumped the rest at the foot of the back door. The hens squawked in the barbed wire run as they saw him dart around the far side of the house, heading for the trees.

Running now, he ripped the cigar from his mouth and threw it at the back door. The kerosene there burst into flames, working around the sides of the cabin in simultaneous lines of fire.

He reached the trees just as the first cry of alarm rang out behind him. His breath was coming in long, hard gasps as he plucked up the rifle from where it leaned against a thick maple trunk. He'd tethered the horses so that the leather straps were freed with a quick flick of the wrist.

Lifting the rifle to his shoulder, he took swift aim at the back hooves of one of his horses. Skittish already, they needed no more prompting to bolt toward the row of cabins.

His arm still ached from the sharp recoil as he primed the weapon again and released the shot at the clouds.

"Indians!" a woman screamed, as she ran from a cabin whose roof had caught fire from one of the many sparks dancing through the sky. "Help! We're being attacked by Indians!"

Tubbs grinned as he reloaded the rifle one last time and

trained the barrel on the panic-stricken woman. *Indians!
Sure wish I'd thought of it,* he chuckled derisively as he pulled
the trigger and watched her fall into a clump of bloodied
calico.

Taking a deep breath, Hope shifted, looking up until she
was captured by his questioning gaze. "The debt's been
paid," she said finally. The words came out as a ragged
sigh. "What happens now?"

Slowly, Drake's lips curled into a rakish grin. "Are you
trying to get rid of me, sunshine?" His timbre hardened,
but his eyes remained softly teasing. "If that's what you're
up to, I might as well warn you it won't be easy. Or did you
forget I still own a piece of your claim?"

Hope stiffened and pulled away from him. The movement was so quick he had no time to stop her as she sat up.
"I didn't forget. But I was hoping you had."

A hen squawked outside. Hope ignored it. Reaching for
her chemise, she pulled it from underneath her wrinkled
dress and slipped it over her head. It floated to her hips like
a white cloud. She pulled the tangled mane of hair from
beneath the cotton in one angry motion and was in the
process of reaching for the crumpled remains of her dress
when she was stopped by the steely grip that wrapped
around her forearm like a snake.

"Don't do this, Hope. It isn't fair to either one of us."

"What isn't fair?" she asked through a fog of tears. Good
God, for a woman who hated crying, she'd sure done a lot
of it since she'd met this man! She tried to pull away, but
Drake refused to let go. She glared at him. "I'm paying my
debts," she spat, as she wiped the hair away from her face.
"You saved my brother's life and now you've been paid for
it. What's so unfair about that? Isn't that what all this is
about? Paying debts?"

"There's more than that between us, Hope Bennett, and you damn well know it," he barked.

"Do I?" She turned toward him, angrily brushing away a tear as it fell off her cheek. *Goddamn worthless tears!* "Then prove it, Drake. Prove it! Call off the rest of the deal. We're so close to making it now, just give us a chance, for God's sake!"

Scowling, Drake dropped her arm, accepting her into his embrace when she collapsed against him. He stroked the long satin strands of chestnut hair, and as her tears soaked into his skin he whispered comfort in her ear.

"I don't want your money, Hope," he said, when her sobs had finally subsided. "I don't need it and I don't want it." She pulled away from him, her eyes half filled with the need to believe him, and half filled with doubt. "Haven't you figured that out by now?"

"What do you mean?" she asked cautiously. "I thought the money was the reason you agreed to fight in the first place. And why are you looking at me like that? What's so funny?"

Smiling, Drake tapped his index finger against her frowning brow. "Think, sunshine. You said you have a brain in there, *use* it. What was my first demand? Before a cut in the take, before the money."

"You wanted—" Her frown deepened and she shook her head in confusion. "But I thought—"

"Wrong. You thought wrong." Tipping her chin up with the crook of his finger, he lowered his mouth to hers. "I think I like you best when you don't think at all," he whispered seductively against her lips.

A shiver coursed through her, but it was one completely devoid of passion. "Drake!" she cried, her voice cracking with panic as she pulled away and reached for her dress. "Do you smell it? It's—oh my God, *noooo!*"

"Smell wh—?"

154

Two gunshots cut the early evening air, stopping his words cold. Drake was tugging on his trousers as the third rang out, followed immediately by the frantic shriek of a woman outside.

Hope stumbled outside, her knees weak with fear as she watched the flames greedily devouring the cabin. Smoke burned her eyes, stinging her nostrils as she tripped over her own feet and almost landed in the mud. Drake's strong hand steadied her, but all too soon it was gone.

Bare-chested, he ran into the yard, scooping up the wooden bucket as his feet propelled him forward in one smooth movement. Muscles rippled in his shoulders and upper arms, the rain-damp skin glistening in the vibrant glow of crackling firelight.

One of the walls had burst into flames by the time Hope joined Drake at the pump. Her hair was plastered to her cheeks and neck. Her eyes were wide, the pupils dilated from pure terror as she groped for his arm.

"Help them, Drake," she pleaded. The words were raw, torn from her lungs, thick and cracking with emotion. "Please God, my family is in there!"

Shaking off her arm, Drake ran with the now full bucket and splashed the contents on the rapidly spreading flames. The pungent odor of kerosene was strong here, and Drake's nostrils flared with the scent of it as he spun on a bare heel and ran back to refill the bucket.

A movement at the corner of his eye caught his attention, and Drake turned in time to see a darkly clad figure disappearing behind the line of bordering trees. Not breaking stride, he continued running for the pump. But the memory remained planted in the back of his mind as he thrust the bucket beneath the rusty spout.

Hope forced the lever up and down in frantic motions. The water splashed into the wooden bucket in rhythmic gushes as she screamed to terrified neighbors who had left

155

their own cabins to bring her more pails.

Except for the ones who had their own fires to fight, most complied in an astoundingly short time. In less than five minutes, they had formed an assembly line, with Hope on one end, frantically pumping water into empty pails, and Drake on the other, trying in vain to douse the fire.

As she worked the pump, Hope's eyes eagerly sought each bedraggled face, praying to catch a glimpse of one of her own. She doggedly questioned any new man who arrived, asking if they'd seen any of her family alive.

Although it seemed like hours, in reality it took less than ten minutes for all four walls to catch in white-hot flames. She kept pumping, glaring at those who shook their heads sadly, passed on the bucket, then turned away. The assembly line shortened. People drifted back to their own cabins—the cabins the rain had saved. Hope hurled angry accusations at their retreating backs and kept on pumping.

Exactly when she began to refill buckets that were already full, she didn't know. Numbly, she kept working the pump. When people drifted away, she picked up their pails and threw water onto the roaring flames herself. The heat of the fire seared her cheeks as she turned to run for more.

She picked up empty buckets as she ran back for the pump, sliding in the mud more times than not. She filled two, sometimes three pails at a time, carrying them all at once. The rain pouring down from the heavens helped, but not a lot. The cabin continued to burn with alarming speed.

"Stop it, Hope," Drake growled. He reached out an arm, catching her around the waist in mid-stride.

She kicked and screamed like a wild woman at the unwelcome restraint. "Let me go! I have to get them out!"

"It's too late, Hope. You did all you could, but it's too late."

"No!" She shook her head vigorously, her wet hair slap-

156

ping his cheek like the tail of a whip. Frantically, she lashed out at the golden head with an empty bucket. Her voice trembled with a sob as one of the walls gave a mournful groan. "It isn't too late. It isn't! *Help me, God damn you!*"

She tried to break away from his grip. Drake held strong.

Another shot ripped through the night, and Drake heard the bullet whistle close to his ear. "Son of a bitch!"

Without a second thought, he scooped a squirming Hope under his arm, carrying her as he reached out to grab the reins of a bolting horse. The move would have sent a lesser man toppling to the ground. As it was, Drake had his hands full between balancing them both and yanking the skittish horse to a stop.

He set her down but gave her no time to pull away as he hugged her close to his naked chest and swung them onto the saddle.

"No!" she screamed, fighting the steely grip around her waist in an attempt to slide off the animal's back. "Stop! Let me down! I have to save my family!"

"It's too late to save them, Hope," he bellowed in her ear as he urged the horse in the direction of the cabins that still stood. "You have to save yourself."

The reality of his words hit Hope so hard she felt like she'd just been punched in the gut. "No," she sobbed weakly, collapsing against his rain-slickened chest. "No."

Another shot rang out. Hope felt pain explode in her heart a split second before it exploded in her shoulder. Fingers of black velvet reached up to claim her. The numbness was a relief, and she surrendered to the painless, yawning gap.

Chapter Nine

I want to die!

Through all the pain, through all the muffled voices and bone-jarring movement, that was the one thought that remained constant.

Twice Hope had come close to losing herself to the all-consuming, blissfully painless darkness. Both times, a husky voice and a sea of green had penetrated the agony that enveloped her, forcefully pulling her back when she would rather have slipped quietly away.

Her mood shifted between numbness and pure terror. She dreamed of her father, and Luke. When the nightmares came, she tried to run from them, tried to hide. But she never went far before a firm arm would pull her back, and a husky voice would demand she stop fighting. Eventually, she gave up and slipped back into the dark, healing oblivion.

Drake reached out and fingered a chestnut curl that clung to Hope's sweat-dampened forehead. The fever still raged, and her skin felt close to boiling as his hand brushed against her moist brow.

Sighing, he let the strand of hair fall back into place as he took a rag from a bowl of rainwater. Squeezing the moisture from it, he ran the cloth over her forehead, her cheeks, the long taper of her neck. He took special care to be gentle as he passed the lump of bandage wrapped around her shoulder. After he had finished sponging the alabaster skin on her front, he carefully rolled her on her side and did the same to her back.

Once the chore was completed, the rag was tossed back into the bowl. He rubbed her skin dry with another strip of cloth. A soft moan escaped parted lips as he tenderly covered her body with a tattered old comforter.

There was no chair on which to sit in the close confines of the wagon, so Drake scrunched down in what little space was free on the floor. His legs were drawn up to his chest, his elbows pillowed atop his knees as his hands dangled helplessly between his calves. His backrest was a fifty pound sack of flour.

She was quiet again, he thought as he watched the thick fringe of ebony lashes flicker against a deathly pale cheek. For now. Who knew when she'd call out again, when she'd throw the comforter to the floor and try to run from the wagon, as she had just now?

He'd been lucky. So far Hope's fits, as he'd begun to call them, were confined mostly to the night hours. That gave Drake time during the day to drive the ox and wagon he'd bought. Considering the circumstances, he'd made good time. In the two weeks since the fire, he'd put the worst of the journey behind them. The Mother Lode was nothing more than a memory, a ragged outline of jutting mountains in the distant horizon. Ahead stretched the dry, flat plains.

Drake let his chin sag to his chest. Driving the ox and caring for Hope by day, coupled with snatching a few catnaps between fighting her fits at night, was taking its toll. Even his teeth felt tired.

Not for the first time did he wonder at his reasons for

bringing Hope along. At the time it seemed a rational thing to do. Now, however, when he had one foot in the waking, and one foot in the sleeping world, he wasn't so sure.

He could never have left her in the dirt to bleed to death. That decision went without question. But why had he brought her up on the horse with him in the first place? He'd recognized Tubbs immediately, and he knew the vile creature's bullets were meant for himself, not Hope. On the ground she would have been safe. He could just as easily have mounted the horse alone and ridden for safety without her.

But he hadn't. He'd scooped her unwilling body up in the saddle with him, and had gotten her shot in the process. If she died from the infection that raged through her body, it would be his fault, no one else's.

Except Tubbs, his mind insisted. Tubbs! He'd kill the scrawny little reptile if he ever had the misfortune to meet up with him again. And if Hope died . . .

His hands tightened into fists. If Hope died, he'd make finding Tubbs his life's goal. And after he'd squashed the life out of him, Drake would turn his sights on his brother. Surely any man who employed a man like Tubbs to do his dirty work deserved no better than to die the same agonizing death as his hireling.

Again, Drake's thoughts turned to Hope.

I should have left her behind, where she was safe. Why didn't I? As his eyelids wearily blinked shut and his head rolled back to be cushioned by the sack of flour, Drake found he was no closer to an answer now than he had been two weeks ago.

Hope's mouth felt like the inside of a boll of cotton, her stomach like a yawning, empty pit. Her eyes stung as she slowly opened them.

160

She tried to lift her arms, to wipe the sleep from her eyes, but the pain that shot through her shoulder stopped her cold. Relaxing, she squinted and took her first real look at her surroundings.

On closer examination, what she had first thought to be a murky gray sky turned out to be canvas stretched taut over the arched, skeletal ribs of a wagon. The interior was cramped, the pegs on its sideboards holding everything from a rifle to a skillet. Sacks of nameless foodstuffs were strewn wherever space allowed. Beside the straw mattress on which she lay was a table made of three pieces of wood, crudely nailed together. The top of it was dark with water stains. The shelf-like fixture was nailed to the floor and the bottom was crammed with half-filled jugs of water, a few rags, an empty bowl, and a pile of white cloth that had been cut into strips, then neatly folded and stacked.

The wagon wasn't moving, and it took Hope a few seconds to realize that the pale orange light surrounding her was not a product of the sun, but the glow of the lamp swinging from a hook attached to the center beam overhead.

Closing her eyes, she let the sights wash through her mind as her hearing tuned in to the sounds of the night.

Outside she could hear the gentle whicker of a horse, maybe two. A hoot owl's call drifted on the cool night air, accompanied by the annoyed trill of a bird. In the distance, if she listened close, was an occasional gurgle of water. A campfire crackled nearby. The aroma of fresh biscuits and the sizzle of frying bacon alerted her to the hunger that gnawed within.

Her tongue felt thick, like it was coated with fur, as she tried to moisten her dry, cracked lips. Her stomach voiced a complaint, but Hope ignored it as she tried to focus her thoughts on where the ache seeping though her body originated. Her shoulder. No, her arm. No, somewhere just in between. Yes, that was it, she decided as she felt the wagon sway with a sudden weight. Opening her eyes this time was not nearly as difficult.

Using one hand to steady his balance, and the other to hold on to his plate, Drake pushed himself into the wagon. He didn't notice her, and Hope remained still, doing nothing to indicate she was alert. She watched as he hunched beneath the lamp, taking a seat on the hard wood floor. He was so close she could feel the heat of his body, and smell the masculine scent of his flesh. The fragrance mingled with the tantalizing aroma of his meal.

Her hand itched to reach out and feel that muscular shoulder bunch beneath her palm. She cursed the weakness in her limbs that forbade her to give in to the wicked temptation.

Drake must have sensed her perusal. As his fingers brought the piping hot biscuit to his lips, his gaze hesitantly lifted to Hope's. His expression did not change, but the hand stopped, poised in midair.

"Hope?" The voice cracked as the biscuit was lowered. The plate was quickly set atop the table beside the mattress, and just as quickly forgotten as he knelt beside her.

She tried to smile, but it was a weak gesture at best. "Where have you brought me, gunslinger? Never mind." She averted her gaze to the half-filled jugs. "Is that water? I'm dying of thirst."

Drake fumbled with a jug, and Hope let him lift her head and raise the neck of it to her lips. The water was stale, but it tasted good nonetheless. "Small sips," he directed, eying her carefully as she let the soothing liquid trickle down her throat.

"Just a little more," she pleaded when he pulled the jug away and tucked it back under the shelf.

Drake shook his head. "You've had plenty. In fact, I probably shouldn't have given you that much. You've been pretty sick."

"So I gathered." She picked up a hand and forced it to her forehead. The movement sapped what little strength she had. Her flesh, she was relieved to find, was cool, but the dampness of her hair told her how recently her fever had broken. Her gaze shifted from his frown of concern to the biscuit that wafted tendrils of steam in the air. "I don't suppose you'd be willing to share your food, would you?"

"You're hungry? Already?" Drake gulped. Henry Mead, the doctor they'd passed a week back on another train heading west, had told him what to do about the fever. But the man hadn't given instructions for when she woke up. Drake hadn't thought to ask. He'd harbored his doubts as to whether that moment would ever come.

"Of course I'm hungry," she smiled weakly. "What did you expect? How long has it been since I've had anything to eat?"

The reality that she was awake, and speaking, was only now beginning to register, in slowly building waves of elation. The extent of that relief as it swept through his blood shocked Drake. "I gave you some broth at noon." He grinned. "You gave it right back."

"Sorry," she murmured. Her cheeks flooded with color as she averted her gaze to the lamp swinging overhead.

"Don't be. You were sick; it couldn't be helped." Taking the biscuit from his plate, he broke it in half and handed the larger chunk to Hope.

Her embarrassment subsided long enough for her to accept the warm piece of bread. She took a small, hesitant bite. Although her gaze rested elsewhere, she could feel the heat of Drake's eyes watching her carefully. The biscuit slipped down her throat with apparent ease. The next bite

163

was bigger. And the next.

"Is that bacon?" she asked, a grin curling her lips as she eyed the plate hungrily. *"Real* bacon?"

Drake returned the grin. Satisfied that she wasn't going to be sick again, he pulled the plate from the shelf. "Real? As opposed to what?"

"Don't get fresh with me, Frazier. I've been sick."

The bacon was still warm from the cooking fire. To Hope, it tasted richer than any apple pie she'd ever baked. She licked the grease from her fingers as she eyed the other strip.

"I think I liked you better when you were senseless," he griped good-naturedly as he handed over the plate. "At least then you didn't eat all my supper."

"Where are you going?" she asked around a mouthful of food as she watched him make his way to the end of the wagon.

"For more food," he replied over his shoulder.

Pulling back the curtain he'd hung over the canvas opening to keep out the cool night air, he disappeared. In less than a minute, he returned with another plate of food, this one heaped with more than enough for two.

"I had a feeling you'd wake up tonight," he said, as he leaned over her and dropped some of the contents onto her almost empty plate.

"You can't be too comfortable down there." She raised a fresh biscuit to her lips and watched him settle back onto the hard wood floor. There was barely enough room to sit, though she had to admit he made good use of the accommodations. Slipping his long legs beneath the low platform on which she reclined, Drake settled the plate on the firm pillow of his thighs and began to eat with a vengeance.

They finished the meal in silence, though both eyed the other when they thought they weren't being watched. For the first time, Hope noticed the dark circles beneath Drake's eyes, and the pronounced hollows under his cheeks. His hands were dirty and his hair was shaggy and rumpled. He looked like he hadn't seen a bar of soap in weeks.

With his hunger slaked, Drake wearily settled his empty plate on top of the shelf. His questioning glance flickered over her half-finished food, and she handed over her own plate. "Guess I felt hungrier than I really was," she apologized.

Drake settled back on the floor. His thoughts drifted to the pot of coffee sitting close enough to the fire to stay warm, but not close enough to burn. The strong brew would've done him good right about now. Too bad he didn't have the energy to go and fetch it.

"Drake?"

Hope's soft voice penetrated the tired cloud that had settled over him. One eye opened and regarded her skeptically. "Hmmm?"

"You can't sleep down there."

Funny, but she hadn't stopped to wonder where he'd been sleeping while she was sick. "I'm fine, Hope," he mumbled wearily. Pulling his hat from the floor, he placed it over the upper portion of his face and rested back against the sack of flour. "Go to sleep. The doctor said you needed plenty of rest."

Doctor? What doctor? It didn't matter, she decided. She'd ask him about it in the morning. Right now, she had to get him off the floor. He couldn't sleep down there, and even with all her strength intact she wasn't strong enough to pick him up!

"Drake?" He grumbled, shifting but not answering. Sighing, she lifted the comforter invitingly. The cool night air wafted over her naked body, and pain shot through her shoulder as she huddled back against the wall, stealing the

165

focus of her concentration. "Come on, gunslinger, there's room enough for two."

Without conscious thought, Drake whipped the hat from his head, uncoiled his legs from beneath the platform, blew out the lamp, then climbed tiredly onto the mattress. He mumbled something about saving the dishes until morning as Hope flipped the blanket over them both, then rolled onto her right side. She kept her back to him for fear of putting any undo pressure on her wound. But that didn't stop her from snuggling into the warmth his body offered. The hand that draped her hip was a heavy, thoroughly welcome presence.

"We should talk," he murmured into her hair. "There are things you have to know about—"

"No." She reached around her waist with her right hand and let it rest atop the one that possessively rode her hip. Her reaction to pain was fast and sure from years of practice. "I remember what happened. That's enough. Talking about it won't change it."

Hope felt Drake stiffen, as though he meant to challenge the words. But sleep won out in the end. As they lay there, bathed in silence and the pale glow of moonlight, she could feel his body gradually relaxing. The breath that warmed her ear and neck eased into a deep rhythm.

Stifling a yawn, Hope basked in the feel of his body snuggled against her, and in the wave of sensations that feeling evoked. It wasn't long before she joined him in sleep.

Hope awoke to find Drake working free the buttons of his sleep-wrinkled shirt. She was not unmindful of the way he kept his back to her as he slipped the shirt from his shoulders. She was treated to a fine display of a rippling

166

back, and muscular shoulders before a clean shirt was shaken loose from a wooden crate and the sleeves slipped up over his arms.

"What doctor?" she asked, stifling a yawn.

He glanced over his shoulder, and the surprise that flickered in his eyes soon melted to warmth. "Morning, sunshine," he said with that infernal, lopsided grin. "And aren't we talkative today? You must be feeling better."

"I am, thank you," she answered with light sarcasm. She shifted on the mattress, and winced at the pain that shot down her arm. "And what doctor? Where is he?"

"Probably in California by now. We passed another wagon last week." He pulled the collar around his neck and worked the buttons closed. "Damn good thing we did too," he added, his hand poised over a fresh pair of trousers. Apparently he thought better of changing his pants in front of her, for he left the clean ones in place and unbuttoned the ones that hugged his lean hips. "As luck would have it, there was a doctor with them. You wouldn't have made it if it weren't for Henry Mead, not that we'll ever see him again for you to thank."

Tucking the tails of the red flannel shirt inside the waistband of his denim trousers, he worked the buttons shut then turned to face Hope. She was sending him an accusingly skeptical glare as he slipped a leather vest over his shoulders, then reached for a plain red bandanna. The latter was tied around his neck with supple fingers.

Hope scowled. "A week? I was sick for that long?"

"Longer." Drake reached for the gunbelt. He buckled it around his waist and tied the holster straps around a sinewy thigh. "We've been on the trail for almost three."

"Trail? Three weeks!" She struggled to sit, but the pain in her shoulder drove her back to the mattress. "Now wait just a cotton picking minute. Where the hell do you think

167

you're taking me? I have a claim to work, Drake. I don't have time to be traipsing around the country in a wagon."

Drake's expression darkened, and to Hope it looked like thunderclouds blocking out the sun. "Don't be a fool. I'm sure Oren Larzdon and his band of merry misfits were all over that claim before the ink on your father's death certificate dried." Hope winced at his bluntness, and Drake's tone softened. "I'm sorry, sunshine, but it's the truth. You're going to have to face it sooner or later. It might as well be now."

The familiar ache tugged at her heart with icy fingers. Hope resolutely pushed it away. "You saw them take the claim, then?" she asked, her voice as flat and lifeless as her expression.

"In case you didn't notice, there was a man shooting at us back there," he informed her briskly, his look guarded. "Once we got on that horse, I didn't think stopping was in either of our best interests." A glint of cynicism touched his eyes. "For some crazy reason I thought getting you patched up was more important than sticking around to fight for a claim that wasn't paying dirt."

"It would have paid," she replied tightly. Her cheeks, already pale, lost whatever color had returned. Her hands clutched the comforter beneath her chin in a death-grip. "It showed more color than all the other mines combined. It *would* have paid. I know it."

"Maybe," he shrugged, running a palm along his stubbled jaw, "maybe not. That's something we'll never know." Drake kept his tone neutral. He was treading on thin ice and he knew it. While he didn't want to upset Hope any more than she already was, he was having a devil of a time keeping his anger in check. Goddamn, but she was the most unpredictable woman he'd ever met! He wouldn't put it past her to pull some hot-headed stunt that would pop the

168

stitches that doctor had so carefully sewn into her shoulder. And all for want of a claim that wasn't paying enough to survive!

Drake cleared his throat, and tried to clear his mind as well. He had to keep her calm, even if it meant kicking the daylights out of the wagon wheel later, to vent his frustration. If he allowed her to get too upset, he risked jeopardizing her recovery. Drake didn't need a doctor to tell him that Hope's recovery was still too new to jeopardize.

"I'm going back."

Her words fell over him like a dark cloud. His eyes narrowed angrily as he growled, "Over my dead body."

Hope's eyes glistened with raw challenge. "If that's what it takes."

"Don't try it, sunshine," he replied, holding a firm hand over his mounting annoyance. "I don't care if I have to hogtie you to the bed, you're not going anywhere."

"Get out your rope then, Frazier," she taunted, her gaze boldly holding his, "because as soon as I'm well enough, I'm going back to work my claim."

A cold smile played on Drake's lips; a smile that was not mirrored in his eyes. "Sunshine, by the time you're well enough, I'll probably be more than happy to see you go."

She opened her mouth to retaliate, but he had already stalked from the wagon.

Balling up a fist, she slammed it into the sideboard. The force of the blow sent a bolt of pain ricocheting through her shoulder, slicing down her other arm. Hope gasped, inwardly swearing at the injury that forced her to lie immobile, unable to do anything but listen to Drake Frazier's threats.

But I won't be immobile forever, she swore beneath her breath, determined to teach the damn gunslinger a sorely needed lesson just as soon as she regained her strength.

Chapter Ten

Thick smoke curled around her legs like dense fog. It stung her eyes and clogged her lungs until she could barely breathe. What little air she was able to draw was filled with the thick, acrid scent of charred wood.

Hope opened her mouth to scream. No sound escaped her lips. Her throat burned and felt like it had been briskly rubbed with sandpaper.

She ran. There was no seeing through the sheet of smoke, yet she ran anyway. Her chest rose and fell in wheezing gasps. The toe of her foot caught on something small and hard, throwing her off balance. This time the scream tore from her lungs in an agonizing cry as she crashed to the ground.

The crackle of flames scorching brick and devouring wood grew louder as she scrambled to her feet. The smoke was too thick to see from which direction the noise came.

Hope ran to the left, guided by instinct. Gasping, she broke through the cloud of smoke. Tears streamed down her cheeks as she leaned against a towering oak tree. The bark cut into her cheek as she pressed against it, inhaling deeply of the crisp night air. The only trace left of the burning wood was the scent of it clinging to her hair.

She waited until her breathing slowed to normal before

pushing away from the tree. Small stones bit into the soles of her bare feet as she staggered down the gravel drive. She hardly noticed them. Her attention was focused entirely on the sight slowly rising over the incline as she walked up it.

Lake's Edge in all its glory. The familiar view stirred her heart, bringing a smile of remembrance to her lips.

The house was magnificent, its red brick complemented by towering white columns and white trim. Oil lamps burned in all but one of the windows, illuminating the lush grass sprawling out from all sides. Carried on the breeze was a hint of honeysuckle, and the notes of a Bagatelle in A minor by Beethoven. Hope recognized the melody immediately, and her fingers flexed in response. Many times, her fingers had flown over the same keys, trying in vain to master the work.

Slowly, she drew closer to the house. The music seemed to increase its momentum with each step. The sound of voices and laughter drifted out from open windows where curtains billowed softly with the breeze.

Hope passed the last towering oak lining the drive, and ran for the front door. The tempo of the music increased until it sounded like the player within was no longer trickling over the notes but punching each ivory key with unnecessary force. A surge of laughter — *Luke's laughter* — rippled through the air as she neared the front door. Her feet flew over the steps sandwiched between long white columns. As the laughter subsided, the sound of a woman's chatter and the insistent chirp of crickets prevailed.

The music softened as Hope hesitated on the porch, her ears alerted to the voices coming from inside. *Mama.* That was her mother's voice, Hope was sure of it. Her father's voice was there as well, and Old Joe's.

Pain tightened around Hope's heart as she reached for

171

the doorknob that glistened in the moonlight. A sob escaped her lips as she grasped the metal and started to turn it.

Pain shot up her arm, surging from the hand wrapped around the door knob. She pulled away with a gasp, looking down in horror at the flesh of her palm. It was black and bubbled, burned beyond recognition.

The music stopped abruptly as Hope's scream cut the night.

Hope? Hope, wake up.

"No! Let me go! I have to help them!"

Stop it, Hope. You keep fighting like this and you'll rip those stitches wide open. Neither of us needs that. Now wake up, dammit!

The voice was stern. It echoed from the inky black sky and not from the man who had forcefully carried her away from the certain death of a fiery inferno.

"Go away!" she yelled, thrashing out. Her fist collided with something solid and warm. Something that grunted.

Hope awoke from the nightmare with a blood-curdling scream. Her lungs burned, as though the misty smoke of her dreams had really cut her throat. Her fingers were trembling. Slowly, she willed herself to focus, and found herself looking into Drake's face. Her eyes were still wide with horror.

"Let me go!" she demanded, trying to turn from the steely grip encircling her upper arms as she lashed out with a fist. It collided with his jaw, and the stubble there scratched the back of her hand. "Let me go! I have to help them!"

"Killing yourself isn't going to help anyone." Drake forced her back to the mattress. She arched against him,

172

tears pouring down her cheeks. "Stop it, Hope. There's no one to help. Listen to me! There's no one to help anymore but yourself."

"No!" She shook her head vigorously, straining against the weight that crossed her waist, pinning her to the bed. "No, I don't believe you. I want Luke. Where's Lu—?"

The words caught in her throat as pain shot through her like a knife. The fire. Papa, Luke, even Old Joe. They were dead now, and Drake was right. She couldn't help them anymore.

With a sob, she collapsed back on the mattress. Drake's body still weighed her down, but she no longer pushed him away.

"It was so real," she whimpered. Instinctively, her hands reached up around Drake's back, clutching his shirt. She bunched the smooth cloth in her fists and pulled him closer. Her nose filled with the scent of sweat and trail dirt.

"I know," he whispered soothingly in her ear, as his fingers stroked her tear-dampened cheek. "It was only a dream, Hope, a nightmare. It wasn't real."

"But it was!" she cried. Burying her face in his shoulder, she let the soft flannel soak up the tears that refused to stop. "It *was* real. I could see the house, and—"

"Shhh." Drake's breath was like a warm caress against her cheek. "You don't have to talk about it."

Hope nodded and swallowed hard. Her throat still felt rough and scratchy, but the pain had eased. The agony that sliced through her heart, however, had not. Her tears continued to fall. She clutched his back, his shoulder muffling her heart-wrenching sobs.

Drake comforted her as best he could. He wasn't used to hysterical women, though, and his words and actions were stiff and stilted.

Carefully, he rolled his weight to the inside of the mattress, bringing Hope's trembling body along with him. His movements were gentle so as not to put any pressure on her injured shoulder. Instinctively, she burrowed against his side, her sobs muffled by his shoulder. Drake rested his cheek against the top of her head. One hand stroked her upper arm while the other ran soothingly down the dampness of her cheek. She smelled fresh and soapy, an enticing aroma that lingered from her noontime bath.

He let her cry, feeling no repulsion as her tears soaked into his shirt. She clung to him desperately at first, giving free rein to the emotions the dream had evoked.

To Drake, it was the sound of bittersweet music. He had worried when she seemed to accept her family's death so easily. The emotions such pain brought had been buried, and buried well. Now, at long last, they were being resurrected. Although he died a little with each ragged sob that escaped her lips, he knew the pain was necessary. It was the only way for her to come to terms with the tragedy.

What he couldn't understand was why her pain sliced through his heart like a knife, why he felt her loss as though it was his own. What was it about her tears that twisted unmercifully at his gut?

In slow degrees, her grip loosened. Eventually, all that remained of her panic-stricken cries and demanding clinging were ragged gasps of breath and a gentle caress against his torso.

As Hope relaxed, so did Drake. And as the sobs ceased to rack her body, he became more aware of the gentle curves pressing intimately against him.

The skin that glided beneath his palms felt like a bolt of rich satin. His thoughts were inundated with the wonderfully fresh scent clinging to the chestnut tresses that tickled his cheek and neck. Earlier, he'd helped her into a clean

174

chemise, but the crisp cotton was now a barrier between his flesh and hers. For that matter, the thickness of his flannel shirt and tough denim trousers might as well have been cast aside along with the comforter she had thrust from her body during the nightmare. His memory served him well enough to know how perfectly the generous curves would fit against his naked side.

Without thinking, he turned his head until his lips were nestled in the shimmering softness of her hair. She shifted, leaning against him still more. The movement of her leg being thrown across his middle made him groan. His body burst with rigid awakening, excruciatingly aware of every soft inch that pressed against him. They stayed like that for what seemed to Drake like tormentingly long hours.

"Hope?" His voice was a low, throaty whisper. "Are you asleep?"

A second moan escaped his lips as she shifted her weight, moving against him in a way that was both provocative and innocent. Diligently, he stifled the sound as he willed away the flaming stiffness in his body. Did she know the effect she was having on him? Did she care?

Hope wiped her eyes dry on his shirt, then tipped her chin up. She was instantly captured by his hooded gaze. Frowning in confusion, she pillowed her chin on the hand that lay on his chest. The feel of his heart beating steadily beneath her palm was unnerving in an exciting sort of way.

"No," she said finally, sniffling. Of its own accord her hand reached out and cupped his cheek. The stubble of whiskers scratched her palm.

His brow knit in concern. "Are you all right?"

"Fine."

Her voice was thick with conviction, and Drake wondered if she was trying to convince him, or herself. "You're sure?"

She nodded, then snuggled her head in his shoulder. "I—I'm sorry about . . . I didn't mean to lose control that way."

"Nothing to be sorry about." He pulled her fingers to his lips, his tongue tasting the tips of each one. "If anyone has a right to cry, it's you. Tears are nothing to be ashamed of."

A shiver curled up her spine as she became aware of his tongue against her skin. "I don't like to cry," she said simply. She couldn't say more. It was growing too difficult to think. She waited until her heart had stopped its wild throbbing and her breathing returned to normal, then said, "I've been thinking of how nice you've been to me." Her eyes narrowed in confusion. "I've been thinking about how you tended me all by yourself. Why didn't you ask the doctor to stay on?"

"He had places to go." Drake sighed, as though his efforts toward her recovery were minor. "And I don't trust doctors."

"And now?" she pressed. "Why are you here now?"

Drake scowled. "I heard you screaming. You were making an awful ruckus, sunshine, and I . . ." His mind went blank.

"You could've waited. The dream would've passed."

He shrugged and she felt a twitch of pain in her shoulder. "I suppose I could have, although I don't see what good it would have done. I wasn't about to just sit around twiddling my thumbs and listening to you scream. I had to do something." He gave her shoulders a gentle squeeze. "You're my responsibility, Hope, and gentleman or not, I don't take my responsibilities lightly."

Her voice hardened. "I'm my own responsibility, Drake. No one else's."

"Fine," he snapped, his tone equally as cold. Now why had her words angered him so much? They were defensively spoken, yet they grated. "Let's say tomorrow you start assuming some of that responsibility by riding as scout. And when you're not doing that, you can fix the meals and scrape dishes. I'm sure I've got some shirts and trousers that need washing and mending. You can do that in your spare time — if you have any. There, does that make you feel better? More independent?"

"If you don't think I can do it, think again." Lifting up, Hope met his angry glare. "My mother always said one woman could do as much as any man — and twice as fast — all she had to do was put her mind to it."

"Is that a fact?" he chuckled sarcastically. "Well, you introduce me to her sometime and I'll gladly set her straight."

Hope's expression fell as she collapsed against the solid chest. The pain in her heart sliced deep. "I can't. She died five years ago."

"Oh, damn. Look, I'm sorry, sunshine, I—"

"Sorry?" she asked tightly. "What are you sorry for? You just all but said you wouldn't have liked my mother even if you'd met her."

"That isn't fair, Hope."

"Isn't it? Why not? It's the truth."

Ignoring the dull throbbing in her shoulder, she pushed away from him. She lay on the mattress, her eyes staring sightlessly at the dark outline of the wagon's canvas hood. She would have given anything for the strength to climb out of the wagonbed and seek the solitary company of the dusk. Instead, she lay in the quickly diminishing light of day, constantly aware of the warm virility of the man stretched lazily beside her.

The mattress shifted as Drake rolled to his side. Raising

177

himself up, he propped his weight on one elbow. His palm itched to reach out and stroke the creamy cheek playing hide and seek with the shadows. He didn't dare. "You act as if you are the only person in the world who ever lost someone they loved. Hasn't it ever occurred to you that I might have lost someone, too?" His words were soft, his meaning was not.

Hope turned toward him, squinting into the shadows that sculpted his features. It was almost dark now. "No," she said frankly, a frown marring her brow. "It never has. I guess I just thought . . . oh, I don't know what I thought." She turned away, then turned back again and continued the thought without being asked. "I never thought men like you *had* any family to lose."

"Did you ever stop to think that losing a family might be what it took to *make* a man like me?"

The question was direct and to the point. She answered it with the same bluntness. "Did it?"

He shrugged. "In an indirect way, yeah, I suppose you could say that."

He didn't offer any more information, but Hope couldn't let the matter rest there. Of its own accord, her hand reached up, the palm drawing slowly down the hard, bristling line of his jaw. The muscles beneath her fingertips stiffened, and to her surprise, instead of trying to pull away, he turned his face so his lips grazed her wrist.

"Tell me who you lost, Drake." Her drawl thickened and her voice deepening to a pitch huskier than normal. Her hand continued to caress his cheek, drinking of its warmth.

"Everyone."

The single word, so solemnly spoken, settled around Hope like a thick, dark cloak. Her gaze softened as she stared at his silhouette, but she doubted there was enough

178

daylight left for him to see the emotion swimming in her eyes. The hand caressing his cheek slipped past his ear. Her fingers buried themselves in the silky curls clinging to his nape as she pulled his head down and pillowed it atop her right shoulder. His hair tickled her cheek and his warm breath seared through the thin cotton chemise, washing over the sensitive flesh beneath.

"You have no family then?" she asked softly, her fingers stroking his temple.

Drake stiffened, his tone hard and unyielding. "I have a brother in Boston, and, I would imagine by now, a sister-in-law. However, the three of us are not . . . friendly."

Hope swallowed hard. A brother. God, what she wouldn't give to have hers back! "Your brother and his wife, do they have any children?"

"When I left, Charles and Angelique weren't even married. If there's a God, the two will never procreate."

"You don't like him very much, do you?" she asked softly. The tightening in his shoulders told Hope all she needed to know.

"I hate him. Almost more than I hate his wife."

His unconcealed anger took her by surprise. "But he's your brother, Drake," she persisted warily. "Surely any differences between you can be smoothed over. After all, his children will be your nieces or nephews. You can't hold his sins against innocent children."

"Keep out of this, sunshine. You don't know what you're talking about."

"Maybe not, but I *do* know what it's like to have a brother." Her voice cracked. "Until recently I had one myself. Luke and I had our differences, but I loved him. And I would have loved any children he had."

"And what if your precious brother had stolen the heart of the only woman you ever loved?" he growled. "How

179

would you have felt about him then?"

She gasped. That his brother's wife had been the only woman to capture his heart hurt her more than she would admit. "Angelique?" she asked, her voice a throaty whisper.

Drake relaxed, his tone forcibly light. "It doesn't matter. It happened a long time ago. It's in the past now, where it belongs."

"But—"

"Leave it alone, sunshine. It doesn't concern you." Reaching up, he cupped his hand over hers. Turning it over, he placed small kisses on the tips of her fingers, her knuckles, the center of her palm. His tongue darted out to taste the hollow in her wrist, running a moist path over the pulse throbbing there.

There was no denying her body's immediate response to his touch. The shock of her reaction rippled down Hope's arm in a way that was breathtakingly spontaneous and irresistible.

A blatant form of wildly sinful torture, she thought, as warm kisses trailed up the column of her arm. His lips had reached her upper arm, and she bent her elbow and let her fingers sink into the golden mane of hair.

"You're avoiding my questions, gunslinger," she whispered, her voice a husky sigh.

"Are you complaining?" he countered, nuzzling her shoulder. His fingers pushed aside the white cotton chemise and his breath kissed her skin. He tasted the flesh there only briefly as thoughts of her healing wound cut through his mind. Good God, he didn't want to hurt her!

"I know I should be, but no, I'm not complaining."

"Good." He shifted, planting a leisurely kiss on her brow before he made to leave the bed. His palms burned where they had touched her warm flesh. "Save that thought for later. Right now you need your rest and you need your strength. And I need a bath."

The mattress sagged as he reluctantly slipped his long legs over the side. Hope reached out and grabbed his arm before he could stand. "Where are you going?"

"To fix us some supper."

"Now?" A pout turned her lips as she settled against the mattress. Although she knew he was right, she couldn't help feeling cheated. She wanted him back on the mattress with her. Maybe she shouldn't, and maybe she hadn't healed enough for such antics, but that was what she wanted — it was what her heart and body screamed for. He hadn't moved, but sat there staring at her. She regarded him through a shield of lashes, a sly grin turning her lips.

"Well," she sighed heavily, "I suppose if you *must* go I shouldn't stop you . . ." The lashes lifted and her gaze clashed with his. She drowned in those sea-green pools. "There is one thing, though."

A slow grin spread over Drake's lips as he leaned toward her. He pushed a chestnut curl from her temple, his fingers lingering on her cool brow. "And what's that, sunshine?"

The grin blossomed into a wicked smile, and her eyes sparkled with mischief as she reached up and cupped his cheeks in her palms. "Incentive." She breathed the single word with tantalizing slowness as she pulled his lips down to hers.

A groan tickled the back of Drake's throat as he grudgingly pulled his lips from Hope's. "Your shoulder —"

"Is fine. Believe me for once, gunslinger."

His gaze darkened as it roved her face, then cleared with relief and a goodly portion of desire. "In that case I suppose supper could wait. Nah, you must be starving . . . so maybe I should . . ."

Hope fixed Drake with a stern look.

"Ah, hell." He could resist the temptation no longer. With a growl, his mouth crashed down on hers. "Payment," he whispered hoarsely against her lips as he devoured her honeyed softness.

She lost herself to his kiss. Unconsciously, she slipped her hand beneath the neck of his shirt, letting her fingers glide over the smooth muscles rippling in his shoulders. Trail dirt still clung to his skin but Hope didn't care. She was enticed by the feel of his flesh gliding beneath her hands, and the magic of his deepening kiss.

Slowly, Drake lowered himself to her side, careful not to let his weight or hands brush against her wounded shoulder. The risk of what he was doing was lost to the scent of her hair, the feel of her hand on his back, the sweet, buttery taste of her tongue. A small corner of his mind remained alert to any sign of pain as he let his hand trail down her arm. His index finger drew a slow circle on her palm before sliding over to the gentle curve of her hip. With a moan, he stroked the white cotton that covered her skin. Lying down on the mattress, he pulled her hard against him and arched into her side.

A moan of pleasure rumbled in her throat. She drank fully of him, her tongue matching his in the game they played, while her hand strayed to the collar of his shirt. One by one she slipped free the buttons, exposing the golden hair that matted his chest in a widening vee. When she reached the bottom, she spread the shirt wide and slipped it with delicious slowness over a broad, sun-kissed shoulder.

His skin tightened as her palm roamed up the taut line of his stomach, teasing the golden curls and the hard nipples buried there. White-hot desire surged through him as her hand slid over the quivering flesh covering his rib cage. He trapped it against his side with his arm, halting her torturous investigation to launch a counteroffensive of his own.

His mouth shifted from her lips to her neck. His teeth nibbled the slender throat, teasing the sensitive place where neck met shoulder. When she groaned aloud, he knew he had found his spot. Nestling down on the mattress, he pushed away the cumbersome tresses and buried his face in her neck. His tongue teased the sensitive flesh, and each hot breath that washed over her skin made Hope tighten with pleasure.

With exquisite slowness, his fingers trailed down the outer stretch of her thigh, catching on the hem of the chemise where it had bunched around her knees. An inch lower and his hand had found its way beneath the hem. His fingers tickled the back of her knees before beginning a breathtaking ascent.

Hope's breath caught in her throat as his fingers grazed the inside of her thigh. His mouth kissed the frantically pulsating hollow in her throat. A large palm brushed aside a nest of chestnut curls. He teased that spot for less than a heartbeat, then ascended higher.

Hope moistened suddenly parched lips as he passed over her waist, drew a line over several ribs, then closed tenderly over a creamy breast. A wave of new sensations crashed over her, razor-sharp sensations expertly honed beneath his hand. And, oh, what he did to her neck and shoulder was almost indecent!

Dragging the back of her fingers down his side, she slipped her fingertips beneath his waistband. The boldness of her actions surprised them both, and for the space of a sigh, neither moved. But her curiosity was whetted, and passion goaded her on.

Undoing the buttons of his snug-fitting trousers without

ripping open her stitches proved to be a lesson in coordination. Once she almost gave up, but the feel of a curiously solid pressure down there doubled her determination. When the last button finally slipped free, she gave a throaty giggle of victory. An added victory was to be had, it would seem. The second Drake felt her hand struggling with the buttons of his trousers, he'd stopped nibbling on her neck, and the hand that had been gliding over her ribs stopped abruptly on her abdomen.

She didn't immediately seize the advantage of her conquest. No, she had some well-deserved teasing of her own to do first. Dipping a finger just beneath the parted waistband, she drew her finger up in a long, straight line. What started out as a thin mass of golden curls beneath her inquisitive fingertip noticeably thickened the higher she went. Her lips curled into a smile as she heard Drake's breath deepen to a thick, ragged gulp.

Her fingertip teased each small nipple in turn before straying down the same slow path it had just ascended. His stomach muscles contracted as she passed, and a pent-up sigh whispered through the air as her hand disappeared in the open trousers and her fingers curled around him.

"I hope you know what you're doing, sunshine," he growled in her ear, as his hand parted the creamy thighs and slipped between.

"And if I don't?" she asked huskily, draping a leg across his hip. "What happens then?"

"You learn."

Gently, she found herself pressed back against the mattress. Her hands were again free, and she used them to run a smooth path over his arm and shoulders as he slipped the rest of his shirt free and tossed it aside. His trousers were quick to follow, as was her chemise.

Even cloaked in shadows, Hope thought, he looked

magnificent, what with his broad shoulders, lean hips, and various other enticing commodities. Every muscle flexed with life. Her palms itched to reach out and caress each sinewy tissue, but there wasn't time. Drake, having divested them of their clothes, had returned to her side.

His thumb traced the cloth wrapped around her shoulder. "I don't want to hurt you," he said, his voice serious.

Hope caressed his cheek, his neck, his shoulder. "You won't," she assured him, then reached up and pulled him down on top of her.

Drake took full advantage of the invitation. As his lips sought her mouth, his knee worked its way between her thighs. She moaned with pleasure, opening to him fully, the way the dewy petals of a rose open to the first kiss of a morning sun.

No further enticement was necessary. Keeping as much weight off Hope as was possible, Drake buried himself in her sweetness.

His movements were sure and firm, igniting a fire from what had, only seconds before, been a slow, exquisite kindling. She matched him thrust for thrust, wrapping her legs around his rock-hard thighs and urging him deeper. Like a tidal wave, their pleasure increased, driving them closer and closer to the fulfillment their bodies feverishly craved.

What had begun as a gentle, insistent throbbing grew to a pulsating demand met with each thrust and retreat. Higher and higher they climbed until, finally, Hope reached the shattering peak of ecstasy. With a cry of pure delight, she clutched Drake's sides, glorying in the feel of each delicious plunge of magnificent satisfaction.

The feel of Hope tightening around him tore Drake apart. With a groan, he buried his face against the sensuous taper of her throat. Filling her completely, he surrendered to the shuddering, white-hot satisfaction.

Slowly, Hope relaxed. When Drake rolled off her and dragged her against his side, she went without complaint. His breathing was harsh and ragged as it grazed the top of her head. To Hope, it was the sweetest caress, matched only by the sound of his heart pounding beneath her ear. She nuzzled closer. Never in her life could she remember feeling anything as wonderful as the arm encircling her shoulders.

"No regrets?" he asked, tossing the comforter over their naked bodies.

The yawn she had been about to stifle died in her throat. Her heart tightened and she couldn't seem to stop the instinctive response that ripped through her. "No," she whispered hoarsely. "No regrets."

Closing her eyes, she blinked back tears. Her contentment evaporated quicker than steam off boiling water. She shouldn't feel disappointment, but she did, and felt it deeply. She'd asked nothing from Drake Frazier, and nothing was exactly what she'd received.

Silly fool! she chided herself angrily. *What did you expect, sweet words of love? And from a gunslinger no less!*

"Hope?"

Closing her eyes, she pretended to be on the verge of sleep. She could feel Drake watching her, but she didn't have the courage to face him; not yet. She was too disappointed, too angry with herself for expecting something she could never have.

"Hope, are you awake?"

She forced her breathing to go slow and even.

Goddamn it, Hope! she mentally screamed at herself. *Didn't you learn long ago that love is for other people, not you? Why should this time be any different?* Because Drake had accepted her scars. *So? Why wouldn't he? It would be an awful*

186

dull ride without someone to dally with. And no one else is available.

That he had made love to her before today didn't matter in the least. She knew his motives for what they were now. At least, she thought she did.

Chapter Eleven

Six days saw Hope well enough to sit by the campfire for the evening meals. She felt guilty at having to let Drake run fetch-and-tow for her, but her strength hadn't returned enough to let her do much by herself yet.

Yet, Hope thought as she sat huddled beneath a warm wool blanket. She stared vacantly into the dancing flames that would cook their dinner as soon as Drake brought it back. The sky above was black as ink, with a layer of clouds covering all but a handful of twinkling stars from view. The moon could be distinguished only by the silver glow it radiated from behind its fluffy white covering. The Platte River gurgled as it twisted over the ground at her right, like a gigantic snake. Somewhere, a wolf bayed at the moon.

Most nights, the low notes of Drake's harmonica rivaled the pleasant sound of trickling water. Tonight, he was out hunting game, and Hope found she missed the music almost as much as she missed the man. Even knowing he would be back soon didn't settle her unusually alert nerves.

Her hair was still damp from a recent bath. She combed the snarls out with her fingers, letting the crackling warmth of the campfire dry the hair in glistening curls around her face and shoulders, then tied the thick chestnut strands back at her nape with the thin strip of leather she had found among Drake's belongings. A twinge shot through her shoulder and her hand dropped to her lap. The baggy denim trousers he had bought her felt rough against her skin.

Wrinkling her nose, she glanced down at her shirt — Drake's shirt. The plaid material hung from her shoulders, the shoulder seams falling halfway to her elbows. In compensation, she'd rolled the too long sleeves up over her wrists, halfway between forearm and elbow. The tail was purposely not tucked in, her sole attempt to conceal the indecency of her male attire — not that anyone would see to care. But she still had some pride!

Sighing, her thoughts turned to Drake. Perhaps it was the spicy scent that still clung to the flannel enveloping her shoulders that brought on the thoughts she had, until now, so steadfastly avoided. Or perhaps, more likely, it was the emptiness she felt with him gone.

She shouldn't miss him, she told herself. Shouldn't, but did. All week he'd been the epitome of kindness. With ease, he thawed the cold wall she had constructed. When she needed the hairbrush, he was there to fetch it. When she was thirsty, he was there with a sip from his canteen. And the nights!

Hope blushed to the tips of her toes when she thought of the long, hot nights spent enfolded in his embrace. Her vow that she would never let him touch her again had melted when she'd felt his lips on hers. And she wasn't sorry. Convinced though she was that the attention couldn't last, she'd enjoyed every second. No words of love were spoken, and she quickly stopped waiting for them. He didn't love her, he probably never would, but for now she would greedily take what he gave without asking for more.

These nights would be remembered, as would the gentle

189

way he had nursed her. When she was alone again, she would think of this time fondly, without regret. But she did not look forward to seeing "civilization" again.

A frog croaked from a place downstream. Hope smiled at the pleasant sound as she picked up a rock and tossed it into the water. It landed with a loud splash. The sound masked the frog's throaty croaks, as well as the crunch of dirt made by footsteps slowly creeping up from behind.

The fire was nothing more than smoldering embers by the time Drake returned to camp. The wolf continued to bay in the distance. It was a dark, ominous sound. The half-wild mustang beneath him snorted as the two dead rabbits he'd slung over the saddle horn slapped the horse's shoulder.

Scowling, Drake dismounted. The prickle of apprehension that had hit him from out of the blue nearly an hour before was still pulling at his gut. Try though he might, he couldn't seem to rid himself of it, though he could think of no logical reason for the feeling of intense foreboding.

Running a palm over the back of his aching neck, he surveyed the camp. The smell of charred mesquite was still thick in air that was sweet with coming rain. Hope was nowhere to be seen. Nothing wrong there. He hadn't expected her to be awake and waiting for him. She was still recuperating, she needed her rest; no matter how good it would have felt to look into her smiling face right now.

A vision of dark hair and bewitchingly large eyes floated at the forefront of his mind as Drake guided the horse toward the wagon. Another surge of morbid anticipation rushed through him.

Goddamn it, what was wrong with him? Nothing was the matter. Everything here was fine, perfectly normal.

190

Perhaps too normal.

Temporarily looping the horse's reins around the spokes of the wagon wheel, he decided to check on Hope before he led the horse to the river.

Pushing the canvas curtain aside, he entered the wagon. The wooden joints groaned as the floorboard accepted his weight, the wagon imperceptibly swaying as he moved toward the mattress. With the small interior steeped in shadows, it was impossible to tell whether she was asleep on the bed or not.

Drake's ears told him what his eyes did not. There was no soft rush of breathing to counter the frog croaking in the river, no shifting of the mattress to absorb the sound of his footsteps.

Like a man walking to the gallows, he approached the mattress. His fists were gripped tightly by his sides as his eyes focused on the shadow-encased bed.

Empty.

Drake tried not to notice the way his heart constricted with each frantic beat. Tried not to, but did.

"Hope?" he called desperately. He hadn't expected an answer, and he didn't get one.

Turning on his heel he stalked from the wagon. His breath lodged painfully in his throat as he scanned the dirt. A winter spent with Dakota Indians had taught him how to decipher prints better than most trackers. He used that knowledge now — reading the grounds as though his life depended on it. And it did.

Hope's footsteps were easy to spot, as were his own. It was the third set — a man's footprints — and those of a horse, that made his blood run cold and his hands clench into iron fists. She'd been gone no more than a couple of hours. The prints were too fresh for it to be longer.

"Dammit!" he growled as he thrust himself to his feet.

As though the horse could feel his agitation, the black mustang danced to the right as Drake passed it and entered the wagon. Two minutes later he emerged with a sack of supplies. Tearing the dead rabbits off the saddle horn, he attached the sack to it, then, with a feral growl, spun toward the fidgety horse. He didn't notice that his palms were laced with sweat until he grabbed the reins. Only then did the magnitude of what was happening hit him like a brick being thrust at his stomach.

Hope had been kidnapped, and Drake had an uncanny feeling he knew who'd taken her. Where and why was another story.

His mind whirled with unanswered questions as Drake swung into the saddle. His former weariness was gone, replaced by stark terror. Digging his heel into the mustang's flanks, he set the horse in motion. It bolted forward, and Drake leaned closer to the sinewy back to give his mount speed.

The air whipped at his face, the ragged ends of his hair stung his cheeks and brow. He loosened his grip on the reins, giving the horse its head.

She's alive! his mind screamed over and over, in time to the stallion's pounding treads. He wasn't sure if he was stating a fact or stating a prayer.

Fear, unlike any he had known before, gripped his heart in cold, tight fingers as he rode hard into the night, fast in the direction the hoofprints had led.

Hope sat erect in the saddle, willing her tired, aching body not to slump against the scrawny chest at her back. Try though she did to ignore him, she could feel the man there. Her nostrils stung with the odor of his perspiration and her ears echoed with each rush of his breath. His body, moving in rhythm with the horse's gentle canter, was as real as the black drizzle that fell from the midnight sky.

Her once clean clothes were now streaked with dirt from her feeble struggle at the riverbank. The rain plastered the shirt to her body. The shoulder seam had ripped during the scuffle and was now torn and frayed, the delicate skin beneath exposed to the cold, damp air. Three buttons at the collar had popped free, leaving the rapid pulse at her throat equally as bare.

"Almost there, sweet thing."

The man's voice from over her shoulder made Hope stiffen. She hadn't been able to get a good look at him at the river, and since then she hadn't dared to try. Still, there was something in his tone that struck a familiar chord within her. Something in his condescending manner made her think the man hadn't stumbled upon her by accident.

"Where's 'there'?" she asked suddenly, her accent thickening as her tongue tripped over the question.

The man chuckled, and the mirthless sound curled up her spine. "You'll see soon enough."

The rain started to fall faster, causing the man to kick the horse to a quicker pace. Hope was forced to grip the slippery saddle horn with both hands and dig her knees deep in the horse's side to keep from sliding off. Rain trickled down her cheeks in cool rivulets, slipping down her throat and pooling in the hollow between her breasts. She shivered, lowering her head to the moist air that whipped her cheeks as she leaned closer to the horse's back.

Her backside brushed against the man's thigh, and she immediately sat forward again. The quiver of revulsion that coursed through her was as tangible as the rain soaking through her clothes.

In the distance, the shape of a small, deserted way station could be distinguished from the shadows. She squinted in that direction, her spirits momentarily soaring at the thought of a clean floor and a warm fire.

No lights glowed in the shack's windows. The darkness of the structure made it appear more than a little foreboding. It seemed to rise up out of the night from nowhere.

The man guided the horse beneath the dilapidated lean-to propped against the side wall. Close up, the shack appeared to be in an even greater state of disrepair.

At the man's nudge, Hope dismounted. Her feet slipped in the mud, and she had to quickly grab for the saddle horn to avoid falling into the muck. All thoughts of running for freedom were swiftly cast aside as the man dropped with a thump to her side.

As at the river, the barrel of his gun was pressed hard against her waist. It was a sure means of squelching any further thoughts of escape.

The man wrapped his hand around her upper arm and she found herself being dragged toward the decrepit way station. A bolt of lightning streaked across the clouded sky, illuminating the ground below. In the brief, flickering light, Hope glanced back and gained her first true glance at her captor.

"You!" Swallowing hard, she tried to keep the scream that lodged in her throat from spilling over her lips. A breathless gasp escaped her, as the door was thrown open wide and she was brusquely shoved into the shack's stuffy interior.

Reluctantly, Drake reined the horse in and guided it to the river's edge. Though he would rather have pushed on, the stallion's sides were starting to heave and a fine lather was coating the silky flesh beneath his knees. If he didn't stop now, he wouldn't have a mount to ride.

Swinging off the saddle, he looped the reins over the powerful neck. The mustang dipped his nose in the cool, flowing water and, kneeling on the bank, Drake did the same.

Twice, he plunged his head into the icy depths. The flesh on his neck prickled with the water's chill as he came up gasping. Trickles of moisture poured down his chest and back. The wetness mixed with the sweat coating his body to turn the trail dust embedded inside his clothes to an itchy paste.

Swiping the dripping hair from his brow, he glanced up at the sky. Dawn was still hours away, and until the sun broke free of the midnight sky, he would have to keep stopping to make sure he was still following the same tracks. He'd wasted precious time doing that, but it couldn't be helped. The sooner he found Hope, the better. He wouldn't wait until daylight and risk Tubbs hurting her — or worse — before he could reach her.

The thought of Tubbs's greasy hands anywhere on Hope's body sent a bolt of rage shooting through Drake's blood. He'd rip the man to shreds with his bare hands if he found the bastard had so much as bruised Hope's little finger. As it was, he thought he'd have a hard time not killing Tubbs for having taken her in the first place.

He grabbed the hat he'd carelessly tossed aside and crammed it on his still-wet head. Tubbs! How the hell had the bastard found them? Drake had purposely avoided taking a ship from San Francisco, knowing that to be the first place Tubbs would look. And he hadn't wired ahead to Boston, suspecting that Tubbs would have hired no-good thugs like himself to watch the depots and trading posts. So how had he found them? And why had he taken

Hope?!

With a ragged curse, he grabbed the reins and pulled the horse's nose from the water. In one lithe motion he'd swung into the saddle and kicked the horse on. The clouds in the sky were darkening, and the first drops of rain splattered the top of his hat and his bare forearms. Soon, it would be coming down in sheets, washing away the tracks. If that happened, he'd never find Hope.

Swallowing past a sudden lump in his throat, he spurred the horse on. The tired stallion grunted in protest. Drake felt a momentary pang of guilt. He'd never ridden a horse so hard. But then, he'd never had a reason to charge through the night as though demons were biting at his heels. He hoped to God he never would again!

"So you remember me, do you?" Tyrone Tubbs asked sarcastically, as another bolt of lightning shot through the sky. "I was wondering how long it would take."

Hope chafed the flesh prickling on her forearms. "Did you think I'd forget someone who tried to steal my gold?"

Although she couldn't see his face, she could feel his anger. "Steal?! Funny, the way I remember it, you were just itching to give those little nuggets to the first man who'd lead you to Drake Frazier. Standing in my shoes, you owe me big for making me look like a fool in front of my friends."

Hope stared incredulously into the darkness. She winced when the gun barrel jabbed her ribs. "Is that what this is all about? You followed us into God knows where and kidnapped me just because you think I made a fool out of you? Don't you think that's a bit extreme?"

"Don't flatter yourself, sweet thing," he snarled. "If I'd wanted to get back at you that bad, I could have done it in

Thirsty Gulch. Lord knows, I had plenty of opportunity."

She shivered as his tone took on a whole new, sinister air. "I don't understand. Why else would you—"

"Definitely not for you. Tempting though you seem to think you are, you're just an added bonus. Frazier's the one I'm after, and you're the one who's going to get him here for me. This time, I'm not leaving anything to chance."

Hope could have laughed at the irony of it all. Could anything be farther from the truth? Lord, it would be more likely that the gunslinger would get down on his hands and knees and thank his lucky stars she was gone, out of his hair for good.

"You think Drake's going to come for me?" she scoffed. "Think again, Tinks, Tudd, or whatever the hell your name is. He won't come. He has better things to do with his time than traipse all over the countryside looking for me."

"Wanna bet?"

A shuffle of footsteps told Hope he had neared her side. Her gaze flickered between her abductor and the door. The sky chose the moment to deliver another lightning bolt. The indecision in her eyes was painfully obvious in the flickering, white-yellow light.

Again, the pistol was shoved into her wet side. "I wouldn't try it, sweet thing. My patience with you is already wearing thin. If you're smart, you won't push me."

Lifting her chin high, she dismissed the threat. "What do you want with Frazier, Tinks? Did he make a fool out of you, too? Seems to be a popular pastime these days."

She gasped as his fingers bit into her upper arm and she was brought up hard against his wet chest. The urge to yank away was strong, but she squashed it, as a rumble of thunder echoed in the distance. Rain sliced at the window pane. His breath fanned her face and Hope tried not to gag on the rancid stench.

"I told you not to push me. You'd better start listening to what I say, woman, or you're going to find yourself in the corner, trussed up like a chicken with a gag stuffed down your throat. How does *that* thought appeal to you?"

Hope's blood ran cold. She didn't doubt he possessed the audacity to make good on the threat. That she would allow him to do so without a fight, however, was questionable.

He didn't wait for an answer as he reached in front of her and grabbed something off the table to her left. The gritty sound of a match being struck was followed by a sudden flare of light. She blinked quickly to adjust her eyes to the unexpected brightness.

"There," he said, as he set the globeless lamp back in place atop the rickety table, "now I'll see it if you try to pull anything stupid."

He ran the tip of his finger down the smooth line of her jaw, and it took every ounce of willpower she possessed not to turn her head and sink her teeth into his flesh. Instead, she pulled back, straining away from the repugnant touch as far as she dared.

"What do you want with Frazier?" she asked again, her tone dry, her glare angry and dark.

"What do you think I want with him, sweet thing?"

"If I knew that, I wouldn't be asking you."

Her head snapped back under the force of his slap. With a startled cry, she covered her stinging cheek and glared at him angrily. She bit down hard on her lower lip to keep a furious retort at bay. The taste of blood on her tongue increased her fury.

"What are you doing?" she demanded when he crossed to the saddlebag dropped carelessly in the corner.

She watched him crouch, his hands rifling through the

worn leather pouch before emerging with a strong piece of rope and a rag. A smug smile of satisfaction spread over his thin lips as he straightened and turned back toward her. Her heart skipped a beat with every step that brought him closer. Swallowing hard, her gaze flickered between the contemptible strip of rope and the sinister glint in those fathomless, coal black eyes.

"I told you I wouldn't take any more of your flak," he sneered. Grabbing her wrist, he wrapped the cord tightly around her tender flesh. She flinched, but steadfastly refused to cry out. "I'm not like your lover, sweet thing. When I say I'm going to do something, I *do* it. Maybe next time you'll listen when I tell you to watch your tongue." His beady gaze met hers. "If there is a next time."

His fingers felt cold and clammy as they brushed against her skin. The pungent smell of his sweat gave a new meaning to the word repulsive. Trying to ignore the churning in her stomach, Hope waited until he dipped his head to secure the rope in a knot at the base of her thumbs, then made her move.

Chapter Twelve

With dexterity, Hope pulled her knee up and slammed it painfully into Tubbs's groin. A whoosh of air rushed from his lungs as he instinctively doubled over.

Again, her knee ascended. This time it crashed into his jaw. He was propelled backward, collapsing onto the dust-strewn floor with a resounding *thud*.

Hope wasted no time in bolting for the door. As she ran, she pried free the rope and let it drop to the floor. Throwing open the door, she dashed into the cold, wet night. She could hear him following, but his pursuit was slow.

Her feet squished in the mud as she rounded the corner of the shack, skidding to a stop in front of the dappled gray. She had just pulled free the reins and thrown them over the horse's neck when her captor came bounding around the corner. In his haste to catch her, she noticed, he'd left his gun behind.

Hope vaulted atop the gray's back, wincing as pain jolted through her shoulder. A hand closed around her ankle as she grabbed the rain-slick leather in her trembling fingers.

Looking down, she was captured by his sinister glare. His thin lips curled back in an ominous smile that made a shiver of dread ripple over her shoulders.

"Let me go!" She tried to jerk her leg free, but his brutal grasp held firm.

"Nice try, sweet thing," he groused, "but you aren't going anywhere."

"The hell I'm not!" She pulled her hand back and delivered a resounding blow to his temple.

He staggered backward, but his fingers stayed painfully molded to her ankle. It was all Hope could do to keep her seat. The horse snorted nervously, sidestepping the man at its side. One lethal hoof pounded the dirt.

In a last-ditch attempt at freedom, she grabbed the leather crop from behind the saddle and brought it down across his leering face. The man grunted as he fell back. This time he was successful in bringing her down with him.

Hope toppled from the horse's back and landed on her side in the mud, the riding crop still tightly clutched in her hand. The pain that exploded in her shoulder made her world go treacherously dark. Groaning, she willed her surroundings to stop their nauseating spinning. Desperately, she tried to scramble to her feet, but the mud made the ground too slippery. With his weight pinning her legs to the ground, getting up proved an insurmountable task.

She raised the switch to strike again. He knocked it from her hand. The crop splattered in a puddle, too far away for any hope of getting it back again.

In an instant, he was on top of her, his weight pinning her to the ground. The knees that tightened around her ribs made even the smallest breath impossible.

"No!" she screamed as his eyes settled on the mud-caked length of her neck. The last of her breath left her. A feral smile curled his lips as his fingers quickly followed his gaze.

"Told you my patience with you was thin, woman. You

201

should've listened." His fingers tightened around her throat. His smile turned into an evil leer when a strangled croak escaped her lips. "Too bad you didn't, because now you're going to have to pay the price for disobedience. I don't tolerate disobedience, sweet thing. Not from anybody."

Hope struggled, her fingers clawing at the hands that were squeezing the life from her throat. He seemed completely unaffected by her struggles.

"Don't think I need to keep you around to get to Frazier. He knows I've got you. He'll come, whether you're alive or dead. No way he's going to know which you are. Not that it matters, since he'll be buried by your side soon enough."

Oh my God, he's going to kill Drake. The thought ripped through Hope's mind with all the force of the lightning bolt that cut through the sky.

Frantically, she reached out and seized a handful of mud. She flung it at his face, and it hit his skin with a sickening slap. Thunder crackled overhead, overriding the man's cry of surprise when the muck embedded itself in his eyes.

His hold weakened enough for Hope to push him back. His hands released her throat as he tried to rub the mud from his stinging eyes.

Gasping for breath, she attempted to squirm out from under him. In her struggles, her foot smashed into the horse's rear leg. Already skittish from the storm, the contact made the gray rear up on its hind legs. Another streak of lightning illuminated the magnificent stance of the horse pawing the air.

Its front hooves hit the dirt with a crash. Again, the gray bucked, its back hooves shooting out to catch Tubbs in the temple. Just as he was reaching for Hope he toppled lifelessly into the mud.

With a cry, she shoved the body away. She was shaking badly as she raised herself to her feet. She had taken no more than a step when her legs buckled beneath her.

Her knees hit the ground in a bone-jarring collision that made her eyes water. Her hands were buried up to the wrists in mud. In her mind, the sight of Tubbs being struck by the deadly hooves played over and over again.

Hugging her arms around her stomach, she leaned forward as nausea racked her stomach. When she was done, she numbly collapsed atop the cold, wet mud.

How long she stayed like that, she didn't know. It seemed that for an eternity the rain lashed at her face and neck, soaking her already wet clothes, but it might actually have been only a few minutes. She'd lost all track of time.

At the feel of a hand on her shoulder, she screamed. So convinced had she been it was Tubbs, come back from the dead to seek his revenge, that she almost wept with relief to find herself staring into a pair of familiar sea-green eyes.

Without thinking, Hope threw herself headlong into his outstretched arms. "Drake! I—I didn't think you'd come," she sobbed into his shoulder. The tears that had been building now burst from her. Desperately, she clung to the warm strength pressing against her.

"Shhh. I'm here, Hope. I'm here." Drake wrapped his arms around her back and cradled her against his shoulder. His hands stroked the mud-streaked hair that limply hung to the small of her back.

"He tr-tried to kill me, D-Drake," she whispered against his throat, her voice trembling almost as much as her body. "He tried to strangle me. I couldn't st-stop him."

"Hush, sunshine," Drake murmured in her ear as he hugged her close. "You don't have to talk about it. It's all over now. He can't hurt you anymore."

With a ragged sigh, she nodded. Instinctively, her arms tightened around his neck when his weight shifted.

"Come on. Let's get you inside where it's warm." Instead of leading her, as she had expected, Drake bent and swept her up into his arms, offering a harbor of safety unlike any she had known before.

Drake turned toward the deserted shack, rainwater pouring down his harshly chiseled face. His arms supported her weight easily, as though he was carrying nothing larger than a small child. His boots squished in the mud with each long stride until he stopped at the shack's door. He had only to nudge it with his foot to send it flying open.

He stepped into the center of the room and tenderly lowered her to her feet. The feel of his wet, sinewy body slipping against hers made her tingle.

Hope shivered. She was soaked to the skin, her clothes thoroughly drenched. The pieces of hair that insistently escaped the leather thong at her neck were etched with dirt and plastered to her face. She pushed the filthy tresses from her brow as she returned his appraising glance.

He guided her over to the single chair beneath the window and pushed her down onto the cane seat. Like a lifeless puppet, she complied.

"I'll be back in a minute," he promised. His eyes were dark, their expression unreadable, as he reached down to caress her muddy cheek. The touch was wonderful and much too fleeting as he sighed, pulled away, then turned for the door.

Hope sat, shivering with emotion as much as cold, waiting expectantly for the gunslinger's return. It wasn't long before, true to his word, he was back, almost as quickly as he'd gone. A saddlebag was tucked beneath one arm, a faded bedroll beneath the other.

"Are you all right?" he asked, as he dropped his burden

onto the dirty floor. A cloud of dust billowed up from the floor.

Hope nodded, her smile weak. Now that Drake was near, her strength was slowly beginning to return. "Yes. I just — I just need you to hold me."

Drake plucked the wet hat from his head and tossed it into a dusty corner. All traces of concern were suddenly gone from both his voice and his expression, replaced by an inexplicable warmth. Insistent fingers wrapped around Hope's wrist. Before she knew what he was doing, he had tugged her into his tight embrace.

Hope savored the contact. She could feel the furious beat of his heart beneath her cheek. His clothes were as wet and dirty as her own, but she didn't mind. The warmth of his body made up for it.

"I thought I'd lost you, sunshine," he whispered in her hair, his voice so soft she had to strain to hear him. "I don't think I've ever been so scared in my life."

A nervous laugh escaped her. "I was scared to death myself. That man was going to kill me — then you. I still don't know why." Her voice was strong compared to the weakness that invaded her knees. Instinctively, her arms tightened around him. Drake's body responded in kind and she was rewarded with a deep whiff of his thoroughly masculine scent.

"Tubbs was a sick man," Drake said, his tone serious. "His depravity was topped only by the man who hired him."

"Hired him?" she gasped, pulling slightly away to stare into his eyes. "Someone hired him to kidnap me and then kill us? Why? Who would do such a thing?"

"My brother," he replied solemnly.

Hope shook her head, her eyes wide. "No. No, it can't be true. Nobody would do something like that to his own brother, I tell you."

His gaze hardened. "You've never met Charles, Hope. You have no idea what the man is capable of. Murder would be a small enough price for him to pay to have me out of his life for good."

"But how can you be sure? Maybe —"

The finger he slanted across her lips stifled Hope's words. She glanced up at him, her gaze wide-eyed and innocent.

"It was Charles. I recognized his henchman back in Thirsty Gulch. Tubbs was the one who started the fire in your cabin." His fingertip brushed her wounded shoulder. "He also did this."

Her cheeks drained of color as a shudder trembled across her shoulder. "He was going to kill you, Drake," she said, her voice flat. "He said so. He said he took me so you'd follow him. I —" she averted her suddenly moist gaze to the rain-drenched window, "I told him he was wrong. I told him you wouldn't come, that you didn't care enough to try and find me."

"Come here." Drake pulled her up hard against his chest and buried his face in her hair. The gentle rush of his breath whispered in her ear.

The guilt of her admission ate at her. She hadn't believed he would come for her, *yet he had*. He'd risked his life tracking them down, and she'd just repaid him by slapping him in the face with her doubts.

Hope shivered as she tried to pull away. Drake refused to let her go as his lips nuzzled her ear. All sense of fear and humiliation vanished like steam under the feel of his lips brushing against her flesh.

"Let me go, Drake," she argued weakly, trying to twist from his grasp again. His hold tightened and she became excruciatingly aware of every virile inch that pressed so

206

intimately against her. "Let me go. There's something I have to do."

"Whatever it is, it can wait," he murmured huskily, as he lowered his head to taste the delicate line of her jaw. Her skin tasted of rainwater.

A tremor that had nothing to do with fear coursed through her veins. "No," she replied, her voice a hoarse, ragged breath, "it can't. I don't know about you, but I'm soaking wet and freezing. I want dry clothes and a fire."

"What do you think I'm trying to build here?" he countered teasingly, as his mouth worked tiny kisses up the line of her neck, over her jaw. Cupping her cheeks, he pulled her face up to his. With the tip of his thumb, he wiped away the tears that trailed down her cheeks unchecked. "I need you, Hope, even more than I realized. The whole time I was searching for you, I feared I would never see you again. Now that I've found you, I don't want to let you go. I want to take you in my arms and love you the way you were meant to be loved." His eyes darkened until they glistened like emeralds in the lamplight. "Let me, Hope. Let me love you."

Drake didn't wait for an answer as his mouth sought its own response, a response Hope was helpless to deny. With each tantalizing stroke of his tongue, she lost a little more of her rapidly dwindling self-control.

She needed this man, she realized suddenly. She needed to feel his tender lovemaking wipe away all the bitter memories this night had held. By the time his tongue had touched the honeyed sweetness of her own, she no longer had the power to deny their hungry bodies the release both so eagerly craved.

Pushing all doubts aside, she surrendered to the urgency of his kiss. The sheer intensity of desire that coursed through her blood still frightened her, but the sweetness of

Drake's skilled, urgent caresses quickly blotted out her fear.

"Ah, Hope," he whispered huskily against her lips. His breath was a hot caress against her moist flesh as she tangled her fingers in the damp thickness of his hair. "My sweet, beautiful, Hope. Tell me you need me as much as I need you. *Tell me, sunshine.*"

"Yes," she sighed, straining into the hard promise of his body. She had no control over the passionate fire raging through her blood, over the wild beating of her heart. Her thick lashes flickered shut as she allowed Drake to lower her to the floor. "Ooohhh, yeessss . . ."

"What are you doing?" she asked sleepily. Rain splattered noisily against the window and a rumble of thunder echoed in the distance. With a contented sigh, she smoothed the wrinkles from the bedroll Drake had placed over her naked body.

"Your wish is my command, m'lady," he replied as he knelt next to the cold, empty hearth and began piling it high with sticks and twigs. From over his shoulder, he sent her his most charming smile. "I'm building you a fire."

Drake had put on his trousers to fetch the wood. Hope pushed up on one elbow and watched him, fascinated by the way the rain glistened against his bare torso, aroused by the way the snug denim stretched over his lean hips. His damp hair shimmered in the pale glow of moonlight.

"Isn't it a little late for that, gunslinger?" she asked, a teasing lilt to her voice. Her smile came easily now that she basked in the sweet afterglow of their lovemaking.

"It's never too late." Drake shot her a glance of pure deviltry as he touched the match to the wood. The sticks caught and the small room was quickly filled with flickering orange shadows. Still holding Hope's gaze, he raised the burning match and blew it out. A waft of smoke curled in the air around his head as he tossed the match aside. "Come here, wench."

"Wench, is it now?" Hope giggled. Clutching the blanket to her chest, she wiggled out of his reach. "Wherever did you pick up these words? Hasn't anyone ever told you that gamblers and rogues don't talk that way?"

"I'm not a rogue." One golden brow rose in mock offense as he tossed a log into the fire then lurched for her. He pinned her squirming body beneath his. "Gambler? Unquestionably. Rogue? Not a chance."

His mouth swooped down to steal a fleeting kiss. She smiled, wrapping her arms around his neck and pulling him closer. The golden curls at his sunkissed nape were damp as they tickled her bare forearms.

"You are a rogue," she murmured against his lips, her eyelids heavy with satiation. "And a conceited one at that. Now get under this blanket before you catch a chill."

With a playful shove, Hope pushed Drake off her. He slipped beneath the blanket when she lifted it invitingly.

"Hmmm, you're right, this is much better." He sighed with contentment as he scooped her to his side.

Hope nestled her head on the hard pillow of his shoulder. His heart beat a rhythmic tempo in her ear as the fire warmed her cheek and brow. "Where did you learn those things, Drake?" she asked, as her fingers teased the golden pelt of hair on his chest.

"What things?"

The memory of the fight flashed through her mind, as did the lock of hair he'd stolen from her on that day. "Oh, I don't know." She shrugged. "Ladies fair, jousting knights, wenches — that sort of thing. Not exactly the kind of stuff you expect to find in your average gunslinger's repertoire."

A chuckle rippled deep in the back of his throat. "I'm

209

not your average gunslinger, sunshine."

Hope slapped his chest playfully. She placed her hands on his chest, one atop the other, cushioning her chin on her knuckles as she glanced up at him through hooded lashes. Each exhalation of his breath fanned her face, setting her skin alive with liquid fire. *That* I'd already guessed! But you still haven't answered my question. Why won't you tell me about yourself? I know you had a life before you came to California. You mentioned your brother and his wife, the problems there, and you said something about Boston. But you didn't give details. Why not?"

"Probably for the same reason you refuse to talk about your family. Some things aren't worth rehashing."

Hope stiffened. She tried to pull away, but the arm encircling her shoulders wouldn't let her. "That's different," she replied flatly, firmly squelching her tumultous emotions. "You already know about my family. I don't know anything about yours."

"Not much to tell," he shrugged. "The ones I cared about are dead. The ones I don't give a damn about, aren't. Isn't that the way life usually works?"

"Charles and Angelique," Hope muttered miserably. Suddenly, she was sorry she'd broached the subject. Already, she could feel Drake pulling away from her. Maybe not physically, but mentally he was withdrawing, throwing up his all-too-familiar wall of defense. "Look, if you'd rather not talk about—"

"What do you want to know, Hope?" he asked, his voice as devoid of sincerity as his suddenly leery gaze.

"Whatever you want to tell me."

Drake was quiet for so long that, at first, she thought he'd fallen asleep. The rise and fall of his chest beneath her palms was slow and even. Long golden lashes flickered

210

against his tanned cheek.

"My grandfather was a champion of medieval history," he said finally, his emotionless voice and his words taking her by surprise. "He had an entire library of books devoted to the subject, as well as an authentic suit of armor gracing the main hall, and hand-worked tapestries on the wall. He was also a master with a lute. In the summer, to celebrate my birthday, he would stage a miniature jousting match on our front lawn. I think it'd be impossible to be reared in a house with a fanatic like Thomas Frazier and not have some of his interests rub off."

"You lived with your grandparents, then?" She frowned. "Hmmm. What about your parents? Did they live there, too?"

"They died when Chuck and I were small. I barely remember them. As for my grandmother, well, I never knew her at all. She died when my mother was heavy with me. I heard she was a good woman, though. Well liked, well respected."

Hope averted her gaze to the fire. A pang of guilt pricked at her heart as she remembered her accusation that a man like Drake Frazier had never known what it was like to lose someone he loved. He *had* loved, and he had lost. Perhaps they were not so different after all.

"I'm sorry," she whispered softly. "I didn't know." She ran her fingers lightly over the stubble shadowing his jaw. Gently, his fingers wrapped around her wrist, drawing her arm up until the inside of her forearm brushed against his cheek.

"Nothing to be sorry about." He turned his face to the side and planted a kiss on the pulse that throbbed in her wrist. "When I think about it, I'd have to say that I'm glad my parents died when they did. This way, they were spared the heartbreak of seeing the monster their son

211

became."

Hope's fingers twisted in his hair as she turned his head forcefully toward her. "Open your eyes and look at me, gunslinger." The thick fringe of golden lashes flickered up and she was instantly captured by his sea-green gaze. Hope thought that she would gladly drown in those haunting pools. "Don't be so hard on yourself, Drake. You're not so bad."

A rush of air left his nostrils. It might have been a derisive chuckle. Then again, it might not. "I wasn't referring to myself, sunshine. I was talking about Charles."

"You really hate him, don't you?"

"Yeah," he replied wearily, "I have him. Obviously, the feeling is mutual. Tubbs is proof enough of that."

When Drake didn't elaborate further, Hope deemed it wise not to push the subject. Instead, she changed it. Slipping her arm from his hand she asked, "Why'd you come to California? I mean, Thirsty Gulch seems like a long way to go just to get away from your brother."

"Gold," he answered simply. Although his eyelids had snapped shut again, one light eyebrow was cocked high in his sun-kissed brow. "What brought you?"

"Gold." She lapsed into thoughtful silence as her gaze strayed to the raindrops lapping at the window. A shiver touched her shoulders, and Drake's arm instinctively pulled her closer. Sighing, she let her gaze rove his profile. "Drake? *Drake*. Don't you dare fall asleep on me now. I have a question to ask you. Wake up, damn it."

"Hmmm?" he murmured, stifling a yawn.

"You never said where we're heading," she said, shaking his shoulder before he could fall asleep again. "Tell me. I want to know where you're taking me."

"Boston," he answered, his voice slurred with exhaustion. "We're going to Boston."

212

Her eyes widened in alarm. "Boston?! I don't want to go to Boston! I want to go to Virginia." She gave his shoulder another shake. "Did you hear me, Frazier? I said I want to go to Virginia. I want to go home."

"The horses probably heard you, Hope." He heaved a heavy sigh and slowly pried his eyelids open. "Aren't you the one who insisted on returning to the gold mines? What happened? You seemed pretty determined."

"That was weeks ago, and I changed my mind. I want to go home."

"Fine," he muttered with a shake of his head. "But it'll have to wait. I have business to take care of in Boston first. I promise, when everything's been taken care of there, I'll take you wherever you want to go. Virginia, London, hell, I'll even take you to Russia if you want."

"I don't want to go to Russia," she replied absently, as her thumb grazed the prickly softness of his jaw. "Drake, now that Tubbs is dead, what are you going to do about Charles?" she asked cautiously. Her hand slipped down his neck, over the throbbing hollow in his throat, and down to the firm pillow of his chest. She tugged at a few wispy chest hairs to keep him awake.

Drake swatted her hand away. His green eyes narrowed as he looked at her. He opened his mouth to say something, then quickly snapped it shut again. Frowning, he took a deep breath, pursed his lips, and said finally, "That depends on you."

"Me? Why? I haven't got anything to do with this."

"It's a long, complicated story, sunshine," he sighed, raking back the golden curls falling over his brow. He'd been hoping she would simply agree to help, no matter what the terms. He should have known Hope Bennett's intense curiosity would never allow that.

Hope squinted into the flickering shadows, lingering on

213

his tired profile. She wavered between the urge to reach out and stroke that sharp cheek, and the need to know as much about this man as he was willing to confide. In the end, the latter won out. "We've got all night. God knows, I'm not going anywhere."

Drake nodded. His eyes clouded with thought as he averted his gaze to the fire. "You know, there was a time not too long ago when the only thing that kept me going from one mining town to the next was knowing that, one day, I'd get back everything that was rightfully mine. At the time, I wasn't sure how I'd go about it. California gave me the answer."

She gave in to the temptation in her fingers and reached out to caress that hardened cheek. When Drake seemed not to notice the contact, she let her hand drop back to his chest. "I don't know, it seems to me like a long way to go for revenge."

He shrugged. "Maybe, but Boston was too close. I was too well known, and everyone for miles knew how my grandfather had overlooked me in his will, leaving everything to Chuck. So I left. I didn't know where I'd end up and I didn't care." His voice thickened with bitter memories. "As long as I had a bottle in front of me, I was happy. After six months, ten gunfights, and innumerable hangovers, I realized that about the only thing constant inebriation was going to get me was an early grave. It damn well wasn't going to get my business back. I'd worked my way to somewhere in Ohio, I think, when I started hearing rumors about gold. In one of my more lucid moments I thought, 'What the hell, California would be as good a place to pick up my life as any.' At least I still had enough sense to know I couldn't be worse off than I already was."

Hope scowled. "So you traipsed all the way across the

country for gold, but had no intention of staking a claim? I don't see how you thought that would win your business back."

"I planned to work the mines," he said, placing his warm palm over hers. She could feel his heart drumming steadily beneath her fingertips. "I went with the same aspirations every other young man traveling to the gold mines had. The lure of a quick fortune is heady stuff, sunshine. Not many men can resist it. My resolve got me to San Francisco, but the second my feet hit the dirt, I stumbled into the first saloon I found. It didn't take long to find out I could make more money off the gambling prospectors than I could plying a pick or swirling a pan." He shifted, his eyes darkening thoughtfully as he met her gaze. "Think about it, Hope. I would have been damn foolish to trade in my deck of cards for a canvas tent and shovel. In one day, I could haul in twice what the miners dug from the ground, with only half the effort." A crooked grin twisted his lips. "I like to think of it as utilizing the abilities I have, but since you worked a pan yourself, I'm sure you think I took the lazy man's way out."

"I didn't say that," she hedged. Sighing, she looked guiltily away. "I just don't see where gambling and shooting could be less dangerous than mining the land."

"Gambling," Drake corrected gently. "The only time I used my gun in California was to save my miserable hide." The sly, lopsided grin twisted his lips. "That was one nice thing about my drunken trek from coast to coast. My reputation may have been exaggerated, but it was well earned. Most men with a half a grain of sense were smart enough to steer clear. They'd meet me across a gaming table, maybe share a glass or two, but that was *all* they'd have to do with me."

"Sounds lonely," Hope mused, tracing her fingertip down

215

the thick pelt of curling hairs on his chest, over the rippling flesh of his tight stomach.

The brazenly inquisitive fingers made Drake suck in his breath. He had slipped his hand over hers and pulled her fingers to his mouth. His lips were warm, his breath hot against her flesh. The stubble of whiskers coating his jaw scratched her open palm. The sensation held its own form of sensual appeal. With a ragged sigh, he plopped the hand back on his chest. While even that simple touch was distracting, his reaction to the contact wasn't nearly as dramatic as when she was boldly stroking his flesh.

"My solitude was self-imposed," he continued, his voice a little more hoarse than before. "If anything, I enjoyed it. When I wasn't playing cards, I had plenty of time to plot my revenge against Charles and Angelique. By then, two and a half years had slipped by. I suppose my desire for vengeance should have tapered off, mellowed, but it didn't; it grew. Their betrayal ate at me night and day, like a festering wound that refused to heal. I couldn't rest. Not until they'd paid for their deception, and I'd gotten back the company before my brother's squandering ways ran it into the ground. Before I knew it, I not only had a plan, but I also had enough money to back it."

"And then?" she asked softly.

"And then I met you." The arm around her shoulder tightened. "I'm close now, sunshine. So close I can taste it."

Hope squirmed, and Drake immediately loosened his grip. "I don't see what any of this has to do with me. I have no influential friends in Boston, or anywhere else for that matter. And no money. I'm afraid I wouldn't be too much help."

"Not in that way, true," he said, scratching his jaw thoughtfully. "But you have grace, elegance, and a beauty most women only dream of."

Hope wasn't entirely sure she believed his sweet words, but she let it pass. A dark eyebrow cocked high in her forehead. "So?"

His fingertips tapped the pert turn of her nose. "So, I have a proposition for you."

"A proposition?" She stiffened, her dark eyes shimmering with suspicion. "What kind of proposition?"

"How much money would it take to pay the back taxes on your place in Virginia and rebuild your house?"

"I don't know," she stated flatly, her eyes narrow and cautious, "but it would be a lot. The house was completely destroyed, and no matter how hard I worked, it would take more than myself to get the fields cultivated again. All the servants we had were sold to pay what we could. A few stayed after we left, but I guess they've probably moved on by now."

"How much?"

She settled on the most outrageous sum that sprang to mind. "Ten thousand dollars."

Drake gave a low whistle and pulled a reluctant Hope back to his side when she tried to move away. "And what would you be willing to do to get your land back, sunshine? How far would you be willing to go?"

"I wouldn't do anything illegal, if that's what you mean," she said tersely. "I'd rather work and earn the money. At least that way I'd have the satisfaction of knowing I rebuilt everything myself."

A low, mirthless chuckle rumbled in his throat. "Do you have any idea how long it would take you to earn that kind of money? Don't forget, you'd have to pay your living expenses while you're working. That in itself can mean major expenditures. Even if you could get a job that pays — and there aren't too many around for a woman — it could take you damn near the rest of your life to save ten thousand dollars."

"I know that. What are you getting at?"

"You hired me once. Now I want to hire you. It's a job, strictly business, of course."

Hope clutched the bedroll to her chest and sat up. Suddenly, the feel of his warm, supple flesh pressing intimately against her was a distraction she couldn't afford. "To do what?"

"To be my wife."

"You want to marry me?" she gasped, her dark eyes widening in surprise.

"No," he said, his voice completely devoid of emotion. He was watching her closely, gauging each emotion as it flickered across her finely honed features. "I want to hire you to *pretend* you're my wife. I want you to come with me to Boston and play the part of the devoted wife to the hilt. If you do your job well, when I'm done with my brother and his wife I'll personally return you to Virginia and buy back your estate, lock, stock and barrel." His gaze darkened. "What you do with the rest of your life is your concern. I won't interfere."

He wants to buy my favors, use me, then cast me aside like a piece of rubbish!

Humiliation boiled in Hope's blood. Never could she remember feeling so insulted. The urge to slap his arrogant face was second only to the urge to grab his Colt from where he'd carelessly tossed it to the floor, and shoot him straight through the heart—if he had one! As for her own heart, it felt as though it were being brutally wrenched in two. She might have expected callous treatment from this man, but to have the reality of it so carelessly flung in her face was ten times worse than the nagging doubts she'd harbored before.

She gritted her teeth and glared at him with an intensity

218

that went far beyond loathing. "If I agree, what proof do I have that you'll keep your end of the bargain?" she asked tightly, refusing to look at him.

"I showed up at your damn fight in Thirsty Gulch, didn't I?" he countered dryly. "That should prove I'm a man of my word." His expression hardened. "I'll pay you. Never doubt it. I may be a gunslinger and a rogue in your eyes, but I'm no liar."

Hope nodded briskly. If this was the only way she was going to get back her land, she might as well bite her tongue and do it. At least she'd have something to call her own when all this was over. Small compensation, true, but it wasn't as though she had much choice.

"All right," she agreed through thin, tight lips. "I don't like it, but I'll do it." Glaring at Drake, she inched away, bringing the bedroll with her and adding, "I'm warning you, cross me on this and whatever you have in mind for your brother and his wife will seem like child's play compared to what I'll do to you when I find you. And I *will* find you, gunslinger. I'll hunt you down like a dog if I have to, but I'll see that you pay me."

"Do your job and it'll never come to that."

It was the last thing he said before rolling onto his side, leaving Hope to brood in silence.

The urge to lash out was strong, but suppressed. With steely Bennett determination, she resolved to see this nasty job through to its end. And when it was over, when she had the money to buy back Lake's Edge, she'd never have to lay eyes on Drake Frazier again.

Good riddance, she thought as she plopped to the floor and clutched the blanket beneath her chin. Now, if she could just convince her heart to believe what her head was telling her . . . not an easy feat when her soul felt severed in two.

219

A tear trickled down her cheek, splashing on the floor and mixing with the dust there. Gritting her teeth, she swiped it away, determined not to cry. She wouldn't give Drake Frazier the satisfaction of seeing just how badly he'd hurt her. Instead, she concentrated on willing her body to relax. As a distraction, she focused on the gentle rhythm of Drake's breaths. He seemed to fall asleep immediately. Soon, his soft, familiar snores filled the air.

Hope tossed and turned, toying with the idea of waking Drake up, just for spite. But she couldn't face him yet, she needed time for his startling "proposition" to sink in. Time to mull it all over and somehow come to terms with the idea of pretending to be this cold-hearted gunslinger's wife. Her thoughts churned as she struggled to put her warring emotions into perspective. While she was hurt that he could use her so callously, she also felt a traitorous shiver of delight at the prospect of being so close to him. This latter feeling was quickly squelched.

With a restless sigh, she rolled onto her back. The floor made a hard bed; it was even more uncomfortable without Drake's warmth. Hope was used to the feel of him snuggling against her in the night, used to his soft snores stirring the curls that framed her brow. But as much as she missed the reassurance of his flesh against hers, she didn't seek him out. She had her pride!

The firelight danced across the grimy ceiling beams. It was as good a place to focus her concentration as any. And that was when she heard it.

"Angelique?" The voice was sleep-softened and muffled, almost lost to the rain pelting against the window.

She tensed, the muscles in her body coiling tight, although she didn't move. Her breathing slowed and weakened as she strained to hear every whisper of sound. Above the rain, wind, and the crackling flames in the hearth, there was nothing. A pang of doubt ran through her. Had she heard him call out Angelique's name in his sleep, or was her tortured imagination playing cruel tricks on her?

Her hands fisted the bedroll as her gaze snapped to the side, in time to see Drake roll onto his back. One sun-kissed arm was flung lazily over his eyes.

"Angelique!" This time, there was no mistaking Drake's voice, or the name he called out.

Hope sucked in a quick breath and tried to ignore the stab of betrayal that knifed through her. But the pain ran too deep, its intensity was too stunning to deny. Swallowing hard, she buried her face beneath the bedroll.

I thought I'd lost you, sunshine. I don't think I've ever been so scared in my life. With the memory of those words came the first sliver of rage. Instead of pushing the feeling away, Hope clung to the thread of anger. It wasn't easy, but by applying a little Bennett determination, she managed to funnel her pain into boiling fury. It helped.

Her jaw hardened as she lowered the bedroll to glare at the handsome, sleeping face of the man beside her.

The rotten bastard! She had believed him. No, she hadn't just believed him, she'd welcomed his admission with open arms. But it hadn't been an admission of affection, Hope fumed, it had been his way of securing an agreement from her—an agreement that would see her *pretending* to be his wife. For some reason Drake needed her to get back at Charles and Angelique, and he would stop at nothing to secure her loyalty, even if it meant hinting at an affection he didn't feel. An affection he reserved for "the only woman he could ever love."

Damn him! No matter what Angelique had done, Drake still loved her. Why else would he call out her name in his sleep? Why else would he *hire* a woman to play his wife?

221

Of course he didn't want to marry Hope. He wanted to be free for Angelique once Charles was ruined!

Stunned by the thoughts churning though her head, Hope rolled to a sit. The blanket fell in lumpy folds to her waist. She didn't retrieve it.

I'll go with him to Boston, she decided abruptly, firmly. Whatever it took to get Drake's precious business back and ruin his brother, she would do. Then, when this whole damn mess was over, she'd take the money he'd promised, *with interest,* and go home to Lake's Edge, where it was safe, leaving Drake to his precious Angelique. They deserved each other!

With that decided, she pulled the bedroll high, crept as far away from Drake's sleeping form as she could and still keep warm, then plopped back down on the floor. But she didn't sleep. Not for a long, long time.

222

Chapter Thirteen

The robin's egg blue sky was cloudless, broken only by the golden ball of sun that warmed the hard-packed ground. Up ahead, wide open plains stretched as far as the eye could see, an unwelcome, barren expanse, interrupted sporadically by clumps of thick prairie grass and an occasional gnarled mesquite tree. To the right was the Platte River, a long, winding ribbon that had the look and taste of gurgling mud.

The California Trail twisted toward a hill which spanned the distant horizon. The hill looked to be rich, cast iron blue. With the dappled gray moving beneath her, Hope attributed that illusion to the position of the late afternoon sun, coupled with distance.

As had been the case for the last week, the widely traveled stretch was littered with graves. Ahead and behind, old gravesites blended with new, the total too numerous to count. The tally increased wherever a cholera epidemic had run rampant through a wagon train, then decreased as the disease tapered off. In a vicious circle, the course would repeat itself every few miles.

Hope had long since abandoned the habit of reading the crudely chiseled crosses or carefully etched stones used as markers for some of the fresher mounds. Her heart went out to the families who, upon reaching their destination of

223

California or the Oregon Territory, came back to reclaim the remains of their kin. The chance of finding any specific grave among so many was slim. As Drake had curtly pointed out scarcely two days before, such luck was the exception, not the rule.

She repressed a shudder as his words lingered hauntingly in her mind. "If the Indians don't dig up the bodies, the wild coyotes will. Some of the ones buried under rocks stand a chance of surviving. A *minimal* chance. The coyotes'll probably leave them alone. The Indians aren't so easily fooled."

With each passing mile, Hope began to think the term "coyote hole" would be more appropriate here than in the mines she'd left behind. In three weeks' time they had passed more clawed out holes in the ground than she cared to remember. Most were empty, although a few still bore the scattered remains of sun-bleached bones. It was a grim sight, one made even more heartrending when the marker declared the body inside the pit as that of a child.

Hope swallowed hard and pushed the depressing thoughts aside. The dappled gray swayed beneath her and she leaned low over its sinewy back. Her heels nudged the mare forward, but the horse's gait barely increased. Lazy easily earned the nickname she'd been given, Hope thought derisively, as she willed the gray to a swifter pace. Her attempt to outstrip Frazier's darker, more accomplished mount was almost comical.

The mare took her own sweet time, but eventually Lazy responded to the insistent prodding, as though she could actually hear the words that were silently screamed at her. Gradually, the pace quickened. The distance between Hope and Drake shortened, but even the gray's best was not enough. The second Drake had seen what she was about, he'd urged his own mount faster. The distance widened until it was too great for Lazy's sluggish sprint to close.

Raising her hand in good-natured defeat, Hope slowed the horse to a canter, then reined Lazy in. The horse whickered, shaking her speckled head from side to side. "Easy, girl," she crooned. Holding the reins firm in one hand, she patted the silky mane with the other.

Drake drew up along side the gray. Grudgingly, Hope had to admit to how perfectly he held his seat atop the jet black mustang, back rigid, head straight, knees tightly gripping the winded stallion's sinewy ribs. A boyish grin split his face, and the shock of the expression made it all the more endearing. The green eyes sparkled with delight beneath the shadows of his hat as the large hands expertly reined the horse in.

Since the morning they had buried Tubbs behind the deserted shack, nearly six weeks before, she had rarely seen him crack a smile, aside from a derisive chuckle or sarcastic grin. But this reaction was instinctive, putting to good use the tiny lines that shot from his eyes; lines that indicated a man who had at one time been given to laughter. In spite of herself, she enjoyed the sight.

"Giving up so soon, sunshine?" he asked, as he pushed back his hat and mopped the sweat from his brow. "Or did you want to race best out of three?"

"Trade horses with me and then we'll see who gives up," she countered contritely. But she couldn't help the grin that tugged at her lips. Her dark eyes shimmered with challenge as her gaze touched on the pitch black animal beneath him. "What's the matter, gunslinger, afraid you'll lose?"

Chuckling, he pushed the hat low on his brow, once again casting the upper portion of his face in enticingly vague shadows. "I'm afraid you'll kill yourself."

"I've ridden mounts that would make that nag of yours look like a plow horse." She nodded to the half-wild mustang. "Back in Virginia we had an entire stable full of them."

"Is that a fact?" Drake's glance was filled with barely concealed amusement.

"That's a fact."

The smirk was back in place as he dragged a hand over the stubbly line of his cheek. "If I didn't know better, I'd think you don't like poor old Lazy here." He reached out and patted the gray's sweat-lathered side.

She fingered the reins as her horse sidestepped the black. She eyed Drake's mount. "Lazy's fine," she evaded, "if you're on your way to the market. Raven has more speed. Even an untrained eye could see that."

The saddle squeaked as she shifted her weight. Cupping her hand over her eyes to shield out the blinding sun, she looked back over the rough terrain stretching endlessly behind them. The scattered imprints of horses' hooves were the only indication that they had passed. Soon, the light, warm breeze would cover even those.

"How far do you think we've come?" she asked wistfully, her attention averting to Drake. "And how much further do we have to go?"

"Not far. Another week, maybe two, and we should be in Missouri. From there, we'll head due north and catch the first train going to Boston. With luck, we'll reach the coast before the first snow flies."

"And if we can't?"

Drake shrugged, a heartbreaking smile curling his lips. "Then we get wet. Won't be the first time."

Hope nodded absently. She hesitated, nibbling her lower lip in indecision. "I—I know you don't want to talk about it, but I'd like to know what you plan to do once we get to Boston. Are you going to bring formal charges up against your brother?"

Drake's good humor faded as quickly as it had come. His jaw hardened, his expression melting until it was perfectly blank. "Do you think I should?"

She hesitated, then shook her head. "No. No matter what he is, no matter what awful things he's done, he's still your brother, Drake. You can't forget that."

"Shouldn't you be lecturing Charles on the loyalty due 'family'?" he drawled sarcastically. "Or have you forgotten that it was my dear, sweet brother who hired Tubbs to hunt me down and kill me in the first place?"

"I haven't forgotten, but you can't be positive your brother was behind that. Who's to say Tubbs didn't lose some money to you in a card game, then hunt you down to take the losses out of your hide?"

Drake's fingers snaked out and wrapped around her wrist. With a quick tug, he pulled her close, until their faces were barely a handsbreadth apart. It was all she could do to keep from tumbling out of the saddle as Lazy sidestepped the black with growing agitation.

"*I'm* to say," he growled angrily, his breath kissing her upturned face. "If Tubbs had played hands across a table from me, I'd remember it. I'm not stupid enough to think it was mere coincidence that he traveled all the way from Boston and just happened to show up in the same mining town I was in — *three times*. It seems awful peculiar that shots were taken at my head the second that man showed his ugly face. He followed me from camp to camp. I sat back and watched him. Why the hell do you think I was so suspicious of you the night you showed up drunk in my room? I thought you were in cahoots with him, and I wasn't letting you out until I was damn sure you weren't. No, it wasn't coincidence that it was Tubbs's bullet that landed in *your* shoulder, even though it was meant for me. And you'd be a damn fool to think it was." He laughed a derisive, merciless sound. "How can you sit here and *defend* the man who almost killed you?"

"I'm not defending Tubbs," she argued, pulling away from him. "I'm defending family. I may not have one anymore, but I can still remember what it was like when my family was alive. No one would do such a thing to his own brother!"

"I'll say it again: you don't know Charles, you don't know what he is and isn't capable of."

She brushed back the wisps of chestnut curls from her brow. "No, maybe not. But I knew Luke. I knew what it was like to—"

"Don't compare the two, Hope. It isn't the same."

Drake watched the delicate jaw harden. He recognized the gesture for what it was, a sign that she had no intention of surrendering the fight. Not yet, anyway. Sighing, he rested his hands on the saddle horn and turned his eyes to the horizon. When he looked back, Hope's lower lip was thrust out in an enticing pout.

"You never said what you plan to do to Charles," she reminded him tersely. "Did you forget to answer the question, or don't you trust me?"

"Trust has nothing to do with it. But as long as we're on the subject . . ." he grumbled, his voice trailing suggestively away. The sea-green gaze captured hers, and he watched as her back went rigid. Her chin automatically rose at a proud angle, and the gesture made the long taper of her neck appear almost swan-like as it rose from the collar of his flannel shirt.

Hope eyed Drake suspiciously. "What are you getting at, Frazier?"

"What I'm 'getting at' is that there seems to be a lack of that commodity when it comes to us." His eyes narrowed shrewdly as he raked her form. "Or have you forgotten that morning in the way station?"

Hope looked guiltily away. If her eyes didn't give away her feelings, the color that splashed over her cheeks most certainly would. "That has nothing to do with this. Leave it alone."

"It has everything to do with this." The crook of his finger cupped her chin, bringing her gaze back to his. "You've been acting like there's nothing at all between us for the last six weeks. You avoid me at every turn, and talk to me only when you have no choice. I think it's about time you told me why."

"There's nothing to tell." She pulled back, breaking the disturbing contact. What should she tell him? That his inability to verbally express any feelings for her left her raw? That she was petrified he would resume his relationship with Angelique once they returned to Boston? She could always mention the demeaning "job" he'd hired her for. Or perhaps he wanted to hear her confess that she knew, deep down in her heart, that no man could ever love a woman as hideously scarred as herself.

Hope confided nothing of the kind. Instead she rested back in the saddle and studied the toe of her boot, peeking out from the rolled-up hem of her dusty trousers. "There's nothing to tell, because there is nothing going on between us."

"Oh really?"

In an instant, Drake had slipped from the saddle, dragging a reluctant Hope along with him. Was it intentional, she wondered, the way her body was forced to slide slowly down the length of his before she was set on her feet?

"Let me go," she ordered breathlessly. Every inch pressing against him was excruciatingly aware of the muscular male flesh lying dormant beneath trail-dusty clothes. "There's still enough daylight to make at least five more miles," she was quick to point out. She was not relieved to note the way her tone bordered on desperation. "If we keep stopping like this we'll never get to Missouri."

"We'll get there," he drawled huskily. "We'll just be five hours late." One hand reached up, the backside drawn leisurely down the soft expanse of her cheek. Hope trem-

229

bled. "Tell me something. Can you honestly say that all of the time we've spent together means absolutely nothing to you?"

"Nothing," she echoed. Swallowing hard, she looked away.

Drake was quick to pull her back, his green eyes darkening. "Don't lie to me, sunshine. And don't lie to yourself. You know damn well that whatever your lips say, your body has a mind all its own. That's one thing that *never* lies."

"And what about you, Drake?" she countered without thinking. "As long as we're being honest, can *you* honestly say that Angelique really means nothing to you anymore?"

"Angelique?!" Drake stared incredulously into the hauntingly large, velvet brown eyes. The arm around her waist tightened, and he refused to let her go when she struggled to break free. He was determined to get at the bottom of this, even if it meant spending the rest of their damn lives in the wilderness, alone. He'd find out what had been eating Hope for the past six weeks, or he'd die trying!

"All right," he said, gripping both her arms and forcing her to return his gaze when she would have looked away. He could tell from her tight expression that she hadn't meant to reveal so much. "I want to know what you think Angelique has to do with this and I want to know now. The truth, please."

Hope bit her tongue and refused to answer. For a split second, she thought Drake would throttle a reply out of her. He didn't, although the black look that remained on his face said that he was giving the matter serious thought.

"She has nothing to do with you and me, sunshine. *Nothing.* That part of my life is over. It has been for years."

"If you say so," she replied. She tried to shrug, but his hands, pinning her arms to her side, made it impossible. She continued with feigned lightness, "Honestly, I don't know why I brought the subject up in the first place. It was foolish of me. Can we go now?"

Although Drake dropped his hands to his side, he continued to block her path to the horse. Hope tried to step around him, but somehow Drake always ended up in front of her, thwarting every attempt. His intent, no doubt. "No, we can't. Not until you tell me what you meant by my feelings for Angelique—or lack thereof."

"Lack?!" All the hurt and anguish she had bottled up for the last six weeks exploded in the single word. Although she tried to hold them back, bitter tears stung her eyes. She wiped them angrily away. "How dare you lie to me, Drake Frazier? Especially after insisting *I* be honest with *you.*"

Drake scowled darkly. "My feelings for Angelique have been dead for years. I'm not lying to you about that."

"No?" she demanded hotly, her hands instinctively balling into tight fists at her side. "Then I must be hearing things, gunslinger, because that night in the cabin it was *her* name you called out in your sleep. *Angelique's—not mine!*"

Spinning on her heel, she stalked around him. Drake was too busy trying to take in what she'd just said to stop her. His initial instinct was to go after her, but the blow she had just dealt him kept his feet firmly rooted to the ground. Only at the rumble of hoofbeats did he finally look up.

She reined the black stallion around and dug the heels of her boots firmly into the mustang's flanks. The black bolted, and a lesser rider would have lost her seat. Hope held firm, and in no time the two were running as one.

The wind whipped at her hair and caressed the trail of salty tears that fell from her eyes. The sobs that tore from her lungs were heard only by the gnarled tree she passed.

. . . *it was her name you called out in your sleep.*

She urged the horse faster, but no matter how quickly the ground passed beneath the stallion's hooves, the truth of her words kept coming back to haunt her.

* * *

231

It had taken Drake the rest of the day, and a goodly portion of the night, to find Hope's camp. Without the benefit of sunlight to illuminate her tracks, or a campfire to divulge her whereabouts, he had been just about ready to call off his search for the night.

But luck was with him. As he made ready to break and prepare his own camp, he had stumbled on Hope's. She was fast asleep, tucked snugly in the bedroll, her gentle snores echoing through the night. The gritty dirt was her only pillow, and her chestnut hair spread over it like a bolt of rich, dark silk.

While Drake had presumed that fear of him finding her had been Hope's reason for not lighting a campfire, he soon found out exhaustion had played a bigger part in it. Now, as he sat back and watched her sleep, stretched out near the crackling fire he'd made, he toyed with the idea of waking her up and fixing them dinner.

The idea was just as quickly abandoned. Considering the angry terms they'd parted on, it might be better if they both got a decent night's sleep before coming face to face again.

Head to head would be more like it, he silently corrected himself as he downed the cup of coffee he'd fixed over an hour before. The foul-tasting brew had long since grown cold, but he drank it without complaint. What good would complaining do when there was no one to listen?

From the corner of his eye, Drake could see Hope bent at the waist, curled beneath the bedroll. The blanket was not so thick that he could miss the outline of her perfectly shaped backside, or the soft indentation where calf tapered into thigh. Even completely dressed and covered chin to foot in a lumpy bedroll, he could feel his body's response to her nearness. Knowing full well what satiny delights lay concealed beneath that coarse blanket did nothing to ease the desire spreading through his blood with the force of a

232

rapidly burning brushfire.

Scowling darkly, he fought the surge of confusion that swelled in his chest and tore his gaze away. His encounter with Hope that afternoon was still fresh enough in his mind to make him blanch when he thought of it.

He'd called out Angelique's name in his sleep? He still couldn't believe he'd been so foolish—as though he had any control over it! Was it any wonder Hope had treated him like a walking case of cholera for the past six weeks? He couldn't blame her for feeling betrayed and hurt. How would he have felt had the situation been reversed?

It was a stupid question. He knew damn well how he'd feel. Even now his chest tightened with the intensity of an emotion that could be nothing short of raw, hard jealousy.

Again, his eyes settled on Hope's sleeping form. She looked like a child, he thought, as he watched her shift restlessly. Her brow was smooth, her expression serenely peaceful. A thick fringe of dark, red-tipped lashes concealed the bitterness that constantly swam in those velvet brown eyes.

Innocent eyes, he thought. *The eyes of one who has lived through a tragedy that could scar a man's, or woman's, very soul.* The pain was always there in that haunting gaze. You had only to look to see it. Now there was more pain, and this time Drake knew he had been the one to put it there.

Clenching his hands into fists, he vividly remembered the feel of her flesh beneath his palm, and the rippled strip of skin that ran the stretch of her back. He felt the pain the scar signified to Hope—both mentally and physically—as though it were his own. The strong surge of emotion shook him to the core, leaving shock in its wake, and still more confusion.

Although Drake hungered to wake Hope up and reassure her, over and over, that Angelique meant nothing to him, he didn't. To do so would be to open up speculation on

233

exactly what he *did* feel for his ex-fiancée. It would also force him to confront the feelings he harbored for Hope.

He couldn't do that; not yet — not now — maybe not ever.

Combing tired fingers through his hair, Drake pulled his gaze from the sleeping woman. Stubbornly, it was drawn back time and again. With a resigned sigh, he strode past his own bedroll, kicking it as he passed, and slipped into the one covering Hope. Pulling her soft body next to his, he was rewarded with a soft sigh as she cuddled against him in sleep. With the feel of soft curves pressing against him, he slept.

Chapter Fourteen

Elbert Sneyd pushed his wire-rimmed half-spectacles up until they sat atop the bump in the middle of his long, narrow nose. Clearing his throat, he nervously peered over the top rim and sent his client an inquisitive glance. His voice was high, femininely so. "You're sure about this?"

Lacing his fingers across his chest, Drake relaxed against the plush burgundy cushion of the Hepplewhite-style chair. "Quite sure."

"Very well, then." Reluctantly, Elbert nodded, his lips tight as his narrow gaze focused on Drake.

In appearance, Drake had changed greatly since the time he had left Boston for parts unknown. He was bigger now, more muscular, and his face was weathered a healthy shade of bronze from long hours spent traveling beneath a scorching sun that had bleached his once brown hair a golden blond.

But one thing about Drake had not changed. The determined glint still shimmered in those piercing green eyes. Elbert recognized righteous determination when he saw it, and he was looking at an abundance of it now. No, thinking again he realized some things about Drake Frazier hadn't changed a bit; they had only strengthened.

Withdrawing a small key from his vest pocket, the lawyer leaned to the right and unlocked the bottom drawer. A folder was withdrawn, then set on the desk that, except for a small brass mantel clock ticking away the time and an ornately carved pen holder, was meticulously bare. A steel pen protruded from the latter, and Drake thought it looked every bit as long and thin as its owner.

Unlike himself, the only change time had brought to the proper Boston attorney was a hairline that receded back almost to the crown of his smooth white scalp. That, and a noticeable lessening of his nervous lisp. But that was all. Even decked out in an expensively tailored suit, Elbert remained the anxious, gaunt little boy Drake had befriended as a child. The same boy that Drake had taught to climb trees, who had fished by his side as a youngster.

The drawer slid shut, the lock clicking into place before the key was again tucked safely into the lawyer's breast pocket. The papers in his bony hands crinkled loudly in the ensuing silence as Elbert leafed through the crisp sheets with a grip that shook incessantly. He pulled over a dozen pages from the file, then pushed the folder aside. "It's all here, as per your request." He slid the papers across the desk's polished surface and nervously cleared his throat. "I beg you to think hard before you act on this. It could be most damaging."

Drake eyed the incriminating pages, but made no move to take them. His gaze shifted to the lawyer. Physically, the man had the appearance of a rat minus the whiskers. But his reputation for being the best damn attorney Boston had to offer stood, regardless. Despite his looks, Drake trusted the man implicitly. "Don't worry, Elbert, there isn't much else I *have* thought about for the past three years."

The watery, steel blue eyes behind the spectacles narrowed. "I can take that to mean you've decided to go through with this, then? Are you sure?"

"Do I have any other choice? Charles is running the company into the ground. In a year, maybe less, Frazier & Sons will be bankrupt. I can't just sit back and watch my brother bleed the company dry. Not after all the work I put into it myself." Shaking his head, he dragged his fingers through tousled golden hair. "No, I can't just do nothing. And in my heart, I don't think my grandfather or my father would want me to. Do you?"

The barest trace of a smile came to Elbert's thin lips. The mention of the two men brought back long-forgotten memories. "Your grandfather was a complex man, I cannot deny that. He worked hard to get his company off the ground, and harder still to keep it going." Entwining his bony fingers, he rested his elbows atop the desk. Two trembling index fingers pointed straight up, forming a shaky perch on which he rested his chin. "Unfortunately, I am inclined to agree with you. Thomas Frazier would definitely not approve of the goings on at Frazier & Sons. Had he been more aware of what was happening around him, I doubt he would have signed the company over to your brother." He scowled, his lips puckering. "However, as I said before you left—and as I still believe now—there are better ways to handle this situation. Your measures are a little too extreme for my tastes."

Drake chuckled derisively. "Ah, yes, I remember now. You wanted to take the case to court. Contest the will. That sort of thing."

"I still believe in that. It *is* the wisest decision."

"It's also the longer one. Contesting the will would take time—time that I don't have. I can't be running in and out of court at the beck and call of every judge from here to Cambridge. That could take months, even years. You said so yourself."

"I know what I said," Elbert sputtered as he leaned back in his chair. The wood groaned with the suddenness of the movement. "And I recall informing you at the time that any matter of this importance would make for a lengthy process in court. But—"

"*But*, how much time will *this* take in comparison?" Drake cut him short. Leaning over the desk, he scooped up the papers and held them out to the lawyer. "If you've done your job right, there should be enough incriminating evidence in here to ruin Charles for good. *Ruin him!*" His fist slammed onto the mahogany desk top and the papers wrinkled in his fist. "Do you have any idea how hard I've worked for this? Do you know how *long* I have waited for this moment? You claim to be my friend, but your defense of him condones what my brother did! My grandfather wouldn't have wanted things to end all tied up in legal bureaucracy. I know it. And I may not have known my father as well as I would have liked, but I *do* know that if he was anything like his father, Maurice Frazier would have expected more from his son than what Charles has given him."

Reluctantly, Elbert nodded. His trembling fingers nervously played with the buttons of his navy blue waistcoat. "I remember very little of your father, Drake, but I have heard my father speak of him. And from what I can recall, your father was cut from the same cloth as your grandfather. He would have expected nothing short of perfection, and settled for nothing less."

"And you think Charles has lived up to those expectations?" he demanded angrily. Standing now, Drake leaned ominously against the desk. His hands, balled into tight fists, rested atop the polished surface, bracing his weight. His face was hard, his eyes glistening in the waning light with rigid determination. "Charles stole what was rightfully mine, Elbert. While I was busy running the family business, my brother was busy stealing it—as well as my fiancée—out from under my nose. Until now, there wasn't anything I could do about it. Now I can, and I assure you, I *won't* let him get away with it. It's long past time Charles was called to answer for what he's done."

Elbert licked his lips, his eyes straying to the closed door leading to the outer office. His voice lowered until it was just shy of a whisper. "I can understand your anger, Drake, and . . ." another glance at the door to be sure it was still closed, "I agree with you. Your hatred for your brother is well founded. I cannot honestly say I would feel differently were I in your shoes. But *you* must understand that it is my *job* to direct my clients through the proper legal channels. While I cannot condone blackmail professionally," his gaze met Drake's with unconcealed meaning, "what I condone personally is my own affair."

Drake eyed the lawyer cautiously. "Then you'll help me?"

The lawyer's gaze shifted to the papers still clutched in Drake's angry grasp. Slowly, the veneer of the "proper Bostonian attorney" was chipping away. "My dear friend, I already have. You hired me to anonymously collect as many debtor's notes against Charles Frazier as the money you forwarded me would allow, then secretly invest them in the company. If you would sit down and take a moment to look at those papers, you would see how well your misadventures in the gold mines paid off. Your timing was so extraordinary it was almost eerie. Every time Charles gambled away more of his inheritance, I would receive enough money from you to purchase his notes. Secretly purchasing the shares was difficult, I won't lie to you there, but not impossible. You did a fine job of furnishing me with more than enough funds to complete the task."

"I did? You mean I really had enough to buy him out?" Drake dropped the pages on the desk and sat back in the chair as though he'd had the wind knocked out of him. The magnitude of what his friend was saying washed over him. Elation was only one of the many emotions sparkling in the sea-green eyes.

Elbert grinned as he peered over the top of his spectacles. "And then some. You are now in possession of the controlling interest in Frazier & Sons. And, since you could not be reached in California, I took the liberty of bringing in an accountant to invest the excess funds — again, anonymously — in other business pursuits. The accountant's name, his credentials, and the calculations of each transaction, are detailed in those papers." He nodded his nearly nonexistent chin at the crumpled papers on his desk. "What you choose to do with all of this is no longer a concern of mine. My job is done." He sent Drake a poignant glance. "Yours, I am afraid, is just beginning."

Drake looked up sharply. His eyes narrowed and a scowl marred his brow. "What do you mean? Did Charles guess I'm the anonymous buyer? Did he?"

"Good heavens, no." Elbert chuckled, waving away Drake's concern as though it were nothing more than a pesky fly. "Your request was for total anonymity, and anonymity is what I provided. I must say, though, the identity of the buyer — or buyers, since no one knows how many there are — who have been purchasing up so many shares of Frazier & Sons has caused quite a bit of conjecture in these parts. As for your brother," he shrugged, again eying the closed door. He leaned over the desk toward Drake, his watery blue eyes sparkling with conspiracy. "For some reason, Charles has been operating under the assumption that you died in California over four months ago. Personally, I would love to be a fly on the wall when he first sets eyes on you. No doubt he will be quite surprised to find you alive and well."

"No doubt," Drake agreed dryly, his scowl deepening. Pulling a long, thin cheroot from his pocket, he ran it through his fingers, his expression thoughtful. The vision of Tyrone Tubbs, his face lit by the glow of dancing orange flames, touched his memory. If he'd harbored any doubts as to the man's employer before, those doubts were now gone. Accepting a light from the lawyer, as well as a cut crystal ashtray, Drake settled back in the chair. He inhaled deeply, releasing the smoke from his lungs in a slow, steady stream. "Who told Charles I was dead?"

The lawyer scowled, shaking his head. "I have no idea. At

first the news was just idle gossip trickling around town, and we all know how distorted *that* can be. As I recall, I had just heard from you the week before, so I paid no attention to it. Of course, no one knew that." He reclined back in his chair, squinting thoughtfully as he entwined trembling fingers over his wiry chest. "Imagine my surprise when Charles, out of the blue, publicly confirmed the rumors. I don't need to tell you how nervous I was until you finally wired me from St. Louis. Had I not been almost ninety-eight percent sure you were alive, I might have believed him. The boy was convincing. He had poor Angelique falling into a swoon at his feet when he made the announcement. I hear she took to her bed for weeks afterward."

Drake crushed his barely smoked cigar out in the crystal ashtray, then set it aside and rose from the chair. Like a caged animal, he paced the room. His back was rigid, his jaw a hard, uncompromising line. "I understand your telling me about Charles, but why do I get the feeling you're trying to feel me out about something else here? If you have something to say, man, just say it and get it over with."

"I wish things were that easy," Elbert sighed. Again he pushed the spectacles up on a nose that was now moist with nervous perspiration. Clasping his trembling hands together on the desk top, he cleared his throat. His normally soft voice sounded even softer. "This is different. Normally I would never ask a client such a—ahem—personal question. But, you've been my friend for as many years as I can remember, so I feel justified in asking you—"

"Get to the point."

Elbert pushed his glasses back up his nose as he watched Drake lean an elbow against the engraved marble mantel. The penetrating gaze was hooded, trained on the flames crackling inside the hearth. "I need to know if you still have feelings for her. Are you still in love with Angelique?"

The smell of charred wood was strong. The scent brought with it the bittersweet memory of a newly constructed shed, nestled in the California gold mines. Unconsciously, Drake's hand strayed into the pocket of his trousers. Thoughtfully, he rubbed the silky lock of braided chestnut hair between his thumb and index finger. The jagged edge of the key strung through it grazed against his palm. He'd waited a long time to use that key.

Drake shifted his gaze. He studied his friend long and hard. His answer, when it came, was cold and filled with loathing. "Angelique Rutland killed any feelings I had the day she agreed to marry my brother. Disgust is about the only thing I feel for her now."

"I know I should have never asked, but . . ." Elbert paused as he massaged the twitch in the corner of his left eye with quaking fingertips. "You must understand, Theodore Rutland is a practicing lawyer in this city. While we rarely see each other socially, he is still a business associate. I am concerned that your revenge against Charles, well-founded though it may be, could also cause repercussions for Rutland's daughter. I would rather see Angelique left out of this."

Drake pushed away from the fireplace and retrieved the worn leather hat hanging on the hook beside the door. He turned back to the lawyer as he settled the hat atop his head. "She's his wife, Elbert. If Charles falls—no, *when* Charles falls, she goes down with him. It's inevitable."

"I realized hurting Charles is inevitable. But is there no way to avoid hurting Angelique?" Sighing, he dragged his palm over the bald top of his head as he raised the other hand in a shaky plea for attention. "Please, Drake, let me explain. I can imagine how much it must have hurt when Angelique married Charles. Since I know firsthand how cold and manipulative the woman can be, I will not defend her on that score—or any other." The door to the outer office opened a crack. Both men heard the barely perceptible squeak of hinges. Neither acknowledged it. Elbert paused, pursuing his lips and choosing his words with shrewd precision. "However, I would not feel I had fulfilled my duty to my *business associate* if I did not try, in some *smaaall* way, to dissuade you. Do you understand what I am trying to say, Mr. Fredrickson?"

Drake stifled a chuckle, carefully lowering his voice so their eavesdropper couldn't hear. "Fredrickson?"

Elbert muttered under his breath, "I never worked well under pressure. You know that."

Drake grinned and pulled the brim of his hat low on his brow. His voice rose enough for every juicy word to be caught by the prying ears. "Very well, Mr. Sneyd. I understand your concern and I will take it into consideration. I do want to assure you, however, that the innocent will remained unharmed." His grin broadened. "Does that put your mind at rest?"

Elbert pushed up the spectacles and returned the grin. Picking the papers up off his desk, he held them out to Drake. "Yes, sir, it most certainly does. I thank you for your understanding. You have most definitely put my mind at rest."

Drake took the papers and tucked them under his arm. "Notify the accountant I'll be in touch with him before the end of the week. Good day, Mr. Sneyd." From the corner of his eye, Drake saw the door swing shut. *Where the hell is Hope?* he wondered as he turned for the door. And why was she letting Sneyd's secretary spy on his private conversations? Or was she the one doing the spying? The thought did not sit well.

"Good day, Mr. —" Elbert's gaze shifted to the door. Seeing it was shut, his staunchly professional demeanor thawed. "Good-bye, Drake. It's good to have you back."

"Feel's good to be back, Elbert." He stopped, his hand poised over the doorknob as he looked back at his friend. He fingered the papers tucked beneath his arm. "I'll be in touch."

"You won't have to," Elbert said as he plucked up Drake's

folder. He dug long fingers into his breast pocket in search of the desk key. "Charles and Angelique are throwing a charity ball at the house tonight. I've been invited. No doubt, we'll see each other there."

"*Charity* ball? *Charles?* You've got to be kidding me. The man has no more interest in charity functions than I have in fashion plates. What's he up to now?"

Elbert shook his head thoughtfully. "I'm not sure, though I'm curious to find out. The benefits are to go to the Bradfield-Stillwell Home. Do the names sound familiar?"

Drake's expression darkened. "Yeah," he spat through gritted teeth, "very familiar."

"I thought they would. Like I said, I don't know what he's up to, but I do know this whole charity ball is suspicious. Of course, I have no proof. However, your brother's sudden interest in procuring funds for a home for wayward boys seems particularly suspicious since the party's conception coincides, to the day, with the date his inheritance ran dry. Now, I'm not suggesting he is doing anything illegal, but if you should happen to stumble on any information about this Bradfield-Stillwell Home, I'd be most interested in seeing it."

He nodded slowly, his lips tight. "I'll see what I can do."

"Oh, Drake, one more thing," Elbert stopped his friend, whose hand was poised on the knob. "That matter you wired me about from St. Louis. It's all been taken care of. The receipt is somewhere in those papers, in case you need it."

He nodded once more to his old friend, then opened the door and stepped into the outer office.

The question of who had been eavesdropping was abruptly answered. The secretary, a kid that couldn't possibly over the age of seventeen, was sitting behind a small desk. Bent forward, he'd rested his elbows on the desk top and cushioned his pointed chin atop entwined fingers. His beady gaze was rigidly trained on the bench running against the wall to Drake's immediate right — and the woman who slept on it.

With its high, slated back posts and narrow, curved armrests, the hard wooden bench looked like an uncomfortable bed. Hope shifted. Her cheek was pillowed on her forearms, her knees drawn up almost to her chest as she huddled in the folds of one of Drake's shirts. The hat she'd been wearing when they'd entered the office had fallen off. It now rested on the dark brown carpet near one of the bench's spindled legs. The ends of the thick plait of hair curving over her shoulder dragged the floor, scarcely an inch away from the hat. Her deep, rhythmic breaths told Drake she had been asleep for some time.

A sudden stab of guilt at ever having suspected her of spying on him made Drake pull the door closed with more force than was necessary. He regarded the secretary with a suspicious glare. "How long has she been asleep?"

"About an hour, Mr. Fredrickson," the secretary answered distractedly as he continued to scrutinize Hope. "How long has she been a *she?*" His eyes widened when he realized the impact of what he had just said. He fidgeted uncomfortably, the beady gaze flickered between the Colt strapped to the rugged man's thigh and the anger that shimmered in those piercing green eyes. His confidence burst and he stammered, "I . . . I m-mean . . . that is — er — you both . . . I mean, I would have s-sworn when you came in that you were b-both men."

"And I know for a fact that when I came in, I didn't give you my name," he growled angrily.

Drake dropped the papers to the floor and approached the small desk in much the same way a lion would stalk his prey. In one lithe movement, he reached across the desk and grabbed a fistful of the young man's coat. He included enough skin in his grasp to make his point painfully clear as he dragged the dark-haired fellow halfway across the desk. They were nose to nose, and Drake almost gagged on the rancid odor of the young man's breath. "Tell me how you learned my name and tell me fast. I'm not known for my patience — and I don't like snoops."

"I didn't snoop," the man defended, his voice seriously lacking in truthfulness. He licked his fleshy lips, his gaze darting over Drake's shoulder and resting on the woman asleep on the bench. He nodded in Hope's direction. "Sh-she told me."

"Like hell she did," Drake snarled, pushing the kid back into his chair with a brutal shove. The wooden backrest banged against the wall as he pulled the pistol from his holster. "You should try to remember your lies, pal. Two minutes ago you told me the lady's been asleep an hour. Good trick. We've only been here forty-five minutes. Now," he flipped open the cylinder, giving the kid ample opportunity to see the six fresh bullets nestled snugly in the gun's chamber, and continued, "my Colt says you're going to tell me the truth."

"I did," the kid whined miserably, his eyes never leaving the deadly pistol.

"Is that a fact?" With a flick of his wrist, Drake snapped the chamber shut. The sound of metal grinding against metal echoed loudly as he glared at the red-faced secretary. "What's your name, kid?"

"M-Mason," was the hoarse answer as he huddled further down in the chair. "D-Daniel Mason."

"How long have you been working for Mr. Sneyd, Daniel Mason?"

"About s-six months."

Drake grinned. The expression was not mirrored in his eyes. "Tell me something, Danny boy, have you ever met an Indian?" The kid's eyes rounded, his cheeks draining of color as he shook his head. "I have. In fact, I spent an entire winter with the Dakota tribe. Ever heard of'em?" Again, the boy shook his head. This time it was a weak, fearful gesture. "They're a Plains tribe, cousins to the Apache. The

Dakotas are known for two things: being very fierce and very strict. They don't like liars." His gaze narrowed on the boy whose complexion had gone past white, and was now a deathly shade of gray. Slowly, he pulled the hammer back on the gun. "How would you like to find out firsthand what the Dakotas do to people who lie to them, Danny boy?"

The boy's eyes were so wide they appeared to be bulging from their sockets. "I was listening at the door," he blurted in a rush. His trembling fingers loosened the stiffly starched cravat at his throat. "The lady didn't tell me your name, I overheard you and Mr. Sneyd talking. But I wasn't snooping. It was an accident. I was—er—polishing the doorknob. Yes, I was polishing the doorknob and the door slipped open. It was an accident. It could have happened to anybody." He looked down the unwavering barrel of the gun and swallowed hard.

"An accident that will never be repeated. Just like my name and my presence here today won't ever be repeated. Am I right?"

"Oh, y-yes, sir. Definitely. It won't happen again."

Drake nodded curtly. "Smart boy," he said as he lowered the hammer back into place and slipped the gun into the holster. "Get back to work. Mr. Sneyd doesn't pay you to sit and stare at his clients."

"Yes, sir," Danny boy said, his voice brimming with enthusiasm as he delved into the stack of files cluttering his desk. Grabbing the top one, he muttered something about making a delivery, then ran out the door leading outside. His coat remained on the peg near the door, alongside his hat and scarf.

Drake shook his head in disgust as he approached the narrow bench. Hunkering down beside it, he gave Hope's broad shoulder a gentle shake. "Wake up, sunshine, we have to go."

Hope murmured something unintelligible in response. Her brow crinkled with annoyance as she batted his hand away.

"Come on, Hope, wake up." Sighing, he leaned close to her ear and whispered, "If you wake up right now, I promise you can have a real bed to sleep in tonight."

The dark lashes fluttered up. "A real bed?" she asked suspiciously, stifling a yawn with the back of her hand. "Did I hear you say something about a *real* bed?"

"Thought that would grab your attention," he said with a warm grin. For a split second, when she smiled at him like that, he could almost believe there was nothing wrong between them. Almost. "And yes, that's exactly what I said. After a few months of sleeping on the cold, hard ground, a nice soft mattress and pillow sounds pretty good to me, too."

"Well, what are we waiting for?" she asked, all signs of tiredness suddenly gone. Leaning forward, she scooped the hat off the carpet and pushed herself to a sit. Long months on the trail had taught her how to ignore the soreness in her muscles from the cramped position she'd slept in. "You promised me a real bed, gunslinger, and I intend to see you keep your word."

One golden eyebrow rose high in his forehead. "Is that a fact?"

"Uh-hum." Her eyes shimmered with a teasing glint as she sent Drake a provocative glance from beneath her lashes. One hand settled the hat on her head; the other lifted the gun from his holster before Drake could even guess what she'd done—until he heard the hammer cock. She lowered the barrel until it was in direct line with his chest. "You ever meet a gold prospector?" she mimicked his earlier words with a wicked grin. "Well, I have. In fact, I spent an entire winter in the Mother Lode. Now, how would you like to find out firsthand what we miners do to people who don't keep their promises, gunslinger?"

Drake's expression hardened, but his eyes danced with laughter. "You little witch. You weren't asleep at all, were you?"

"No," she said with an impish shrug. She lowered the hammer into place, then handed the gun back to Drake, handle first. "I just got sick of that beady little man staring at me."

Drake took the gun and slipped it back in the holster. "Where did you learn how to do that?" he asked as he snapped the strap into place.

Hope batted her lashes with feigned innocence. "Fake sleep? Nowhere. I guess it just comes natural."

"Hooope?" Drake's voice lowered sternly. "You know what I'm talking about, now answer me. Who taught you how to lift a man's gun like that?"

Hope lowered her gaze and tried her best to look chastised. It didn't work. The thought of a real bed, soft and fluffy, had put her in an incredibly good mood. Though the mood didn't seem to be infectious, she couldn't help the teasing sparkle in her eyes as she asked, "And if I don't make a full confession? What are you going to do, beat me into submission?"

"Now that sounds like the best idea I've heard all day."

"Careful, Frazier, I just might like that." As she spoke, Hope ran the tip of her index finger down his jaw. Her finger paused at the slight indentation of his chin before slipping up to trace the line of his lower lip. She raised her gaze to his. It was the first time she'd touched him in almost two months, and the contact rippled up her arm like a path of white-hot fire. "Then where would we be?" she asked, her voice a pitch huskier than normal.

"I don't know," he answered, his voice a throaty whisper as he turned his lips into her palm, "but I'd sure as hell like to find out." Enclosing her hand in his, he slipped her arm around his neck and stole a slow, tender kiss.

Hope tingled with awareness. She returned the kiss, and at the same time attempted to fight off the insistent sensations that coursed through her blood. It was a losing battle, she realized miserably, thinking it would have been better to never have touched him at all. It was too late, of course, her body was already demanding a release that was long overdue.

"Where did you say that bed was?" she asked against his lips.

"I didn't."

Reluctantly, Drake pulled away. It was either that or risk molesting the witch in the office of one of Boston's finest — and busiest — attorneys. He collected the papers, folded them in half, then stuck them in the pocket of his brown leather vest. "Come on," he said tightly. Grabbing her hand, he pulled her off the bench. "If we hurry we can be there in less than an hour."

Hope stumbled, clutching Drake's arm to keep from falling flat on her face. "Wait a minute, where are we going?"

"Home." The single word held no warmth.

A shiver that had nothing to do with the cold curled down Hope's spine as they stepped into the chilly night air.

Chapter Fifteen

The streets of Boston were as crowded when Hope and Drake left the lawyer's office as they'd been when they had arrived. It was only the character of the people lining the streets that had changed dramatically.

Drake slammed the door and descended the stone stairs in Hope's wake. Her shoulders trembled in the cool night air, and though he was tempted to reach out and offer some of his warmth, he didn't dare. Her good humor in Sneyd's outer office had been too rare, too fleeting to last. Now that she'd had time to come to her senses, he thought she would rather accept warmth from a pit viper than from himself. The dirty look she shot him confirmed that thought.

Hope shivered and pulled Drake's hat low. She could feel the warmth of his eyes boring holes into her back as she focused her attention on the people and carts darting this way and that about the street. The smell of leather, dirt, and cloying perfume was strong and, while not oppressive, she couldn't help but long for the clean freshness of the open range and prairies. The soft, peaceful sounds of the trail—air rushing past her ear, broken by the occasional squawk of a bird—were replaced by voices yelling from all quarters, horses whickering, men laughing, dogs yapping, doors slamming, and a host of other, equally annoying, sounds. The ruckus grew to a deafening pitch the closer they came to the road.

The clothes that had served her so well on the trail now earned her stares of contempt. More than one elegantly attired couple out for an evening stroll stopped to gape at the masculine attire cloaking the obviously female form.

In her naivete, Hope had assumed she would pass for an overgrown youth—until she looked down and caught a glimpse of the flannel as it was caught by the cool breeze and molded to the curve of her breasts. She reached up and yanked Drake's hat still lower. While the murky shadows beneath the brim could disguise the feminine turn of cheek and jaw, there was nothing to disguise the curve of womanly hips beneath the baggy trousers, or the nipped waist around which they were tied. As if that weren't bad enough, the chestnut plait bobbing to her hips was a concrete proof of her gender.

Blushing hotly, she looked down and concentrated on placing one booted foot in front of the other. For every step that *clop-thumped* on the boardwalk, she counted off a day— one for each day it would take her to see this mess through and get back home to Virginia.

And *what* had she been thinking to joke and tease Drake Frazier in the lawyer's outer office? Hope wondered as she wove her way through passersby.. Had she lost her mind? For the last few weeks she had acknowledged the gunslinger's presence only when absolutely necessary, and even then she'd done so grudgingly. *But with good reason!* she was quick to remind herself. Still, all that had been forgotten as she stood in that dreary office and exchanged words with the miserable rat as though they were the best of friends. And then some!

It was his touch that had confused her so badly, she thought, completely dismissing the fact that *she* had been the one to make the first contact, not Drake. Suppressing her feelings and urges these last weeks had been hard. While she'd striven to remain coolly distant, it wasn't easy.

When the nights had grown too cold to sleep comfortably, she'd agreed to share Drake's bedroll—for warmth, of course, no other reason. The true meaning of torture became crystal clear beneath the twinkling stars and pale moon, when she could feel the hard fibers of his body snuggled against her, awakening a response that grew harder and harder to deny.

She'd gotten herself through those agonizing weeks by repeating over and over to herself that it was Angelique's name he had whispered that night, not hers. She had to keep remembering that if she was going to finish this job, collect her money, and return to Virginia, where she could forget this part of her life had ever even happened. Unfortunately, forgetting Drake Frazier wouldn't be that easy, she thought, as she swung onto Lazy's back and gently kicked the mare on. In fact, it would be damn near impossible.

With a ragged sigh, she guided the horse into the street, following the gunslinger's rugged back. The sinewy beast beneath him moved in time with each sensual sway of his body. Try though she did not to notice it, her gaze kept straying to the spot where horse and rider touched.

"Almost there," Drake called over his shoulder after they'd been in the saddle an hour, maybe more. Hope didn't answer.

The city had slowly given way to the gentle swell of a country landscape. She looked on the new surroundings with a relief that bordered on jubilation. She'd been away from civilization too long, she decided, if she preferred a tree-lined back road to a city boardwalk. But like it more she did, as they turned onto a narrow street edged by sturdy maple and spruce trees. Hope drank deeply of the clean, fresh scent. Brittle red, orange, and gold leaves scattered the dirt road, crackling beneath the horses' hooves.

Another side street slipped past, followed by another, and another. Eventually, the soft strum of a violin began to fight the soft night sounds for prominence. The haunting notes increased, accompanied by the sound of voices and laughter, as they rounded a bend and a large white Georgian manor came into view.

The twisting drive was lined with inky black carriages. A woman, resplendent in a minty crinoline ball gown, strolled the lush green lawn.

Holding up a hand, Drake reined in his horse and indicated that Hope should do the same. Scowling, she obeyed, but the second the woman had rounded the corner she shot out a question.

"What are we doing here? I thought we were going to *your* house," she said tersely. "You promised me a real bed."

As he'd expected, her attitude toward him had again changed. Her voice was colder, more demanding. A dry smile tugged at Drake's lips, though his eyes never left the house. "I did, and you'll get it," he replied, distracted. "You'll just have to wait a bit."

"But—"

He shook his head, lifting his head and dragging impatient fingers through the wind-tousled golden mane. "No buts." He turned to her then, his eyes filled with an emotion Hope had never seen there before.

She couldn't see enough of his face in the hazy light to discern his feelings, and suddenly she didn't want to. Her spine stiffened. "We aren't going in there," she gasped. "Drake, we can't. Look at us. We'd never make it past the front door."

"Oh, we're going in all right, sunshine. This is one party I don't intend to miss." Turning, he slapped the horse's rump and helped Raven pick a path through the trees to their right. The grin he sent over his broad shoulder made his sea-green eyes twinkle with deviltry and reminded Hope more of the Drake she'd known in their earlier days on the trail. Instinctively, her heart twisted.

She wasn't going in, no matter what he said to convince her otherwise. Still, she had a gnawing curiosity to see what the gunslinger was about, and so she followed.

"No, I won't do it." Hope shook her head, her jaw hardening with determination. She crossed her arms over her chest and glared at Drake in the flickering moonlight. Her gaze shifted between him and the downstairs window he was threatening to shimmy through. Her toe tapped a furious rhythm on the hard-packed earth, but otherwise she refused to move.

"What happens if someone sees us?" she demanded angrily, wondering all the while why she should even care. "It sounds like there are at least two hundred people in there. We're bound to get caught. Besides, they have laws against scampering into other people's houses in the middle of the night, and while they may not abide by those laws in California, they certainly do in Virginia. I'd think Boston would be even worse."

"It is," Drake agreed with a smile that made her swallow hard and lean against the house for balance. Crouching down, he cupped his hands to make a step. "Will it help if I guarantee you a jury of your peers?"

"No. And it won't change my mind either."

Drake straightened, and resisted the urge to throttle her stubborn neck on the spot. "Hope, you said yourself we'd never make it through the front door dressed like this."

"And I meant it," she agreed tersely. "But I don't see where crawling in through the window is going to do any good, either. I don't even see why you want to get into this house."

"Because it's my house."

Hope's eyes widened. She blinked a couple of times, opened her mouth to say something, then snapped it shut again. She scowled, glancing from the window to Drake. Her gaze eventually settled on the latter. "What do we do once we get in?"

"Get dressed, of course." He reached out and took the threadbare collar of her flannel between his thumb and forefinger. His eyes were dark, penetrating. "What would you say to trading this in for a bit of silk or satin? You said once that you used to wear them all the time."

"I did," she replied, her voice cracking as her resolve weakened. Silk? Satin? Lord, the temptation was too great to resist. She looked down at the heavy boots encasing her feet, at the cuffs of the trousers rolled up to her ankles, and added, "You'll have a hard time finding a gown for me, gunslinger. Most dresses don't fit, and I don't like people ogling my ankles. In case you haven't noticed, I'm a little taller than most girls."

"I've noticed. In fact, there isn't a whole lot I haven't noticed about you, sunshine." His eyes darkened as he ran a tantalizing finger over her jaw, her lower lip, her cheek. "I'm not complaining."

Hope shifted uncomfortably when his hand traveled to the first button of her shirt. The fingers against her flesh were hot, and extremely distracting. She swatted his hand and tried to pull away. The house pressing into her back stopped that.

She eyed him suspiciously. "Suppose we get inside, and by some miracle of God you find clothes that actually fit us—"

"I will."

She ignored the interruption. "Then what? Join the party? If so, how long do you think it'll be before someone recognizes you?" Her expression grew suddenly guarded. "Are Charles and Angelique inside? What happens if they see us? And then—"

The hand Drake clamped over her mouth stopped her barrage of questions. "The only way you're going to get any answers is to climb through that window." He nodded to the whitewashed wall over her head. "Now, I'm going to take my hand away, and I'm going to offer to boost you up—one

256

more time. Refuse, and you'll be spending the rest of the night in the stable. I won't come back for you once I'm inside."

The hand, which had blocked off half her supply of air, was removed. She took a deep breath as he hunched over and cupped his hands into a makeshift stair. He glanced up expectantly.

"Well?" he asked, a single golden brow cocked high in his sunkissed forehead. "Which will it be? A nice, soft, feather tick bed or a prickly, lumpy, pile of straw?"

Hope pursed her lips and glanced down at his hands with open disdain. There was no doubt in her mind that he'd carry through on his threat and leave her to pass the night in the stable—wherever *that* was.

"Hoooope?"

Her gaze drifted to the expensive carriages lining the cobblestone drive. *Someone* had driven them here. It wouldn't surprise her to find all the liverymen gathered in the stable Drake had threatened her with, having their own party.

"I don't like this," she said finally, testing her foot on the step of his entwined knuckles. His palms closed around her boot, making it impossible to pull away.

"You don't have to. Just hurry up and get inside. It's getting cold out here."

"It's supposed to be cold. That's why they call it winter."

"It isn't cold inside. It's nice and toasty warm. And there are real beds in there."

"I suppose you think you can bribe me now?" she replied. He hoisted her and she started to scramble up the wall, cursing all the while at what a perfectly stupid thing she was doing. "Well, maybe you can," she continued, clinging to the scratchy wall. Her fingers brushed against the window sill and she made a grab of it, giggling when her hand closed around the whitewashed wood.

Drake grunted as he shoved her through the window he'd

pried open with a tree branch. Hope shimmied through the opening. He heard a thump as her body tumbled over the window sill, crashing to the floor. He prayed the sound would be masked by the lively cotillion the orchestra chose to strike up at that moment.

Hope peeked out the window and sent him a mocking glare. "Well? Are you coming, or would you rather wait until one of the guests stumbles in here and finds me? They'll probably think I'm a thief, come to snatch the silverware." She chuckled despite herself when she glanced down at her tattered clothing. "Can't say I'd blame them."

"I can't go anywhere until you move, sunshine."

She backed away from the window to give him room to maneuver, and when she looked up it was to see Drake springing lithely to the floor. Her breath caught in her throat. He looked undeniably handsome, what with the moonlight flickering in behind him, silhouetting his body and casting his muscular frame in enticingly vague shadows. Though his clothes were in as bad a state as her own, he looked oddly at home against the softly painted wall and plush Chippendale furnishings.

She was reminded of the day of the fight between him and the Swede, and the way his towering presence had immediately gained the respect of those around him. The memory fled the second Drake grabbed her arm and propelled her toward the door.

He lifted a finger to his lips as a surge of laughter echoed down the hall. Footsteps approached, then receded in the other direction. The last strains of the cotillion echoed away, replaced by the easy notes of a Czechoslovakian gallop.

Drake eased the door open an inch and, with his back pressed to the wall, scanned the passageway. She could tell by the way his tense features relaxed that it was now empty.

"Come on," he said. Reaching down, he grabbed her hand and pulled her into the hall.

Wordlessly, she allowed herself to be dragged through the

oddly decorated house—a mixture of regal antiquities, medieval wall hangings, and other centuries-old paraphernalia. She was yanked briskly from room to room, and once she was forced to press against Drake in a stuffy closet, when one guest chose to drift through the same room they were sneaking through. They climbed stairs that were too narrow and plain to be for anyone but servants. The upstairs hall was deserted.

Hope half-walked, half-ran down the carpeted hallway, trying to keep up with Drake's long strides. When they reached the end, he opened the door to their right and pushed her inside an inky black room.

"Wait here. And don't light the lamp," he hissed in the darkness before slipping back to the hall.

Though Hope was tempted to disobey him just for spite, she didn't. She didn't want to be caught—alone in this crowded house, looking like she did—and forced to explain her presence. So she waited in the darkness, not daring to move for fear of tripping, and enjoyed the music that drifted up through the floorboards. Her eyes were just beginning to adjust to the scant light when the doorknob turned and the door squeaked open. Drake slipped inside.

"Here, get dressed."

Something that rustled nicely was pushed into her arms before Drake crossed to the other side of the room. Although it was dark, especially in comparison to the hall from which he'd come, his feet never stumbled.

Hope fingered the smooth material in her hands and tried to ignore the sounds of Drake undressing. The smell of crushed roses drifted to her as she lifted the soft fabric to her nose. It smelled even more wonderful than it felt as she stroked it against her cheek. She held the gown to her front, running her hand down the smooth satin, and was surprised to find that the hem fell to the floor. Where had he found a dress that was long enough, she wondered?

It had been more years than she cared to remember since

she had worn a dress that felt as exquisite as this one. Even in the dark, she knew it would be breathtaking. What she didn't know was how she was expected to put it on with no light to tell front from back. Drake, she knew from the sounds emanating from his corner, was having no such problem.

With a resigned sigh, she moved away from the moonlight streaming in through the window, and set about dressing.

Luckily, some things were not easily forgotten. She needed no light to work free the hooks running up the dress's back, her fingers did it from memory. She set the dress on the floor and used the same skill to distinguish the right and wrong side of the underclothes, as well as the petticoats Drake had provided. Those too were set aside, ready and waiting. Since there were no slippers, she decided to go barefoot and hope no one peeked beneath the hem.

"Are you sure this is going to fit?" she asked skeptically. She slipped the flannel over her shoulders then reached for the rope that secured the trousers around her waist. "I really don't like to show my ankles. I wasn't joking about that."

"It'll fit," he replied in the darkness.

She worked the pants down her hips, dearly wished for a good hot bath, and reached for the chemise. The white linen was like a glowing beacon in the darkness. It wasn't until the crisp fabric was sliding down her naked body that Hope noticed the lack of noise in Drake's corner of the room.

She pulled the neckband over her head and settled it around her shoulders, her eyes scanning the room. She couldn't see Drake in the darkness, but then, she didn't have to. Her skin tingled with the feel of his hungry gaze.

Turning her back on where she imagined him to be, she reached for the petticoats, then the gown. Her fingers were trembling badly. Scooping her long plait of hair from the neckline, she draped it over a shoulder and reached for the hooks. She was able to secure the lower ones, and a few at the top, but the rest remained stubbornly out of reach.

Hope gritted her teeth in frustration, and toyed with the idea of asking for help. The thought of his fingers touching the flesh on her back, even through the layers of under-clothes, made her breath catch. She wasn't entirely sure her tired, frazzled nerves could withstand such sensual torment.

"If you're not going to ask, I suppose I'll have to offer."

Drake's voice came from directly over her shoulder, so close she could feel the warmth of his breath kissing her neck. She didn't protest when his fingers began joining hook and eye.

"I could have done it myself," she said, squirming at the feel of his strong fingers against her back.

"We don't have all night, sunshine." His hands hesitated as they brushed against the healed wound on her shoulder. "There," he said. Dropping his hands to his side, he took a quick step back. "Ready to face your admirers?"

"I won't have any if I can't think of something to do with my hair." Her fingers self-consciously strayed to the plait draping her shoulder. The ball gown might be exquisite — that had yet to be seen — but a droopy braid of scattered hair would swiftly shatter that illusion.

Drake moved in the darkness. A drawer was opened, then closed. Another. His footsteps came back and a cold metal comb was pushed into her fingers. "Think you can do it in the dark?" he asked, his voice heavily suggestive.

Hope ignored the sarcasm as she worked her hair free of the braid. She pulled the comb through her hair, nearly ripping the tangled strands from her scalp. When she was done, she let the glossy chestnut tresses hang in thick waves to her back. The style might not be fashionable, but there was no help for it. She had no ornamental combs or pins to secure it, and she didn't waste her time wishing for any. She'd lived without them before, she'd do so again.

"Ready." She shoved the comb into his chest and marched

for the door.

"Not so fast."

She stopped, her hand poised on the knob, and turned back. Drake was a towering, black shadow in the moonlight. Two long strides and he was beside her, his calloused palm stroking her cheek. The ripple of anticipation that curled her toes was not easily ignored. His breath was hot against her cheek, and for a moment Hope thought he was going to kiss her.

Would I stop him if he tried? she wondered as her chin lifted, and her eyes automatically began to close.

"You're working for me now, sunshine," he said dryly, his hand closing over hers on the doorknob. "If you want to earn your keep, see that you don't forget it."

"Bastard," she spat, angrily shoving his hand away. The sound of her palm hitting his arrogant jaw was loud, countered only by the clatter of the door as she wrenched it open and let it crash into the wall.

She stepped into the lamplit hall, her palm stinging from the blow as she balled her fingers into a fist and hid them in the voluminous folds of her skirt—all the while struggling to swallow her fury. She heard Drake behind her, but refused to look back. If he wanted to beat her for her obstinance, so be it, she couldn't stop him. But one thing was for certain, she wouldn't sit idly by while he humiliated her. She'd die first!

"I hope you got your anger out back there," he said as he tightly grabbed her upper arm and started dragging her down the hall, "because in a few minutes you're going to be introduced as my devoted wife. I expect you to play the part—to the hilt."

"I said I would, didn't—" She stopped abruptly as her gaze flickered to Drake, and she was awarded with her first real look at him since he'd changed. Her bare feet tripped over thin air and she collided weakly against his arm.

This was *not* the Drake Frazier she'd met that night so

262

many months ago in The Brass Button Tavern. It couldn't be! Except for the white silk cravat knotted perfectly at his throat, and the matching ruffle that peeked from his cuffs, he was dressed head to toe in midnight black. An expensively tailored waistcoat strained over the broad shoulders, emphasizing their appealing width. Hope's cheeks flooded crimson as she noted the matching breeches, so tight they were indecent, hugging each muscular curve of calf and thigh. The lean hips, tight and firm, were as flagrantly displayed. Her blush deepened as she tore her gaze away from that particular spot and fixed her shock-filled stare at the handprint reddening his cheek. It was the only safe place she could find to look.

In his tightly clinging denims and flannels, he'd looked dangerously handsome, sensually appealing. Now, he looked absolutely magnificent.

"Pleasantly surprised, I hope," he said, a mocking grin twisting his lips as his gaze ran down her front. His good humor quickly evaporated.

So in awe had she been of Drake's transformation, Hope hadn't taken her own into account. Made curious by his sudden silence, she glanced down. Her gasp of surprise hissed down the empty hall.

As Drake had promised, the gown was satin. Soft, shimmering, rose-colored satin that, he was pleased to find, complemented the healthy glow in her cheeks to perfection and abruptly reminded Drake of the gown he had first seen her in. Except for the color, the resemblance ended there. The neckline was becomingly low, draping her shoulders and exposing a good deal of tempting, creamy flesh. The wonderfully low neckline and short, puffed sleeves were accented with shimmering gold ribbons that enhanced the sparkling amber flecks in her eyes. More ribbons were woven in a zigzag pattern on the full skirt that draped gracefully from her hips. With no crinoline to destroy the elegant line of skirt, it fell gracefully to the carpeted floor.

Slowly, his gaze ascended the appealingly curved form. He clenched his fists tightly at his side and resisted the urge to reach out and touch the waves of chestnut that floated to her waist like a velvet cloud.

"Pleasantly surprised, I hope," she mimicked, inclining her head in his general direction. She was shocked — and more than a little pleased — by his sudden discomfort. It wasn't often she found the gunslinger at a loss for words, and she fully intended to enjoy it.

Hope dipped a curtsey fit for the queen of England herself, then swiped the train of her skirt behind her and turned down the hall.

A gaping Drake was quick to follow, but not before he had indulged in the pleasure of watching those tempting hips sway.

A few elegantly dressed couples in silks and satins lined the plushly carpeted stairs. Alive with animated chatter, their conversation came to an abrupt halt as, one by one, their attention was drawn to the striking pair standing in repose at the top of the landing. More people stopped in mid-conversation, watching the two as they descended the staircase with unspoken elegance.

Hope felt the stares of curiosity that passed over herself and Drake, and instinctively tucked her hand in the warm crook of his arm. She half expected him to pull away, but instead he merely placed his palm over her fingers and continued to the bottom. His golden head occasionally nodded at the guests they passed, but the friendly gesture was rarely returned.

"They don't seem to recognize you," she leaned toward Drake and whispered, as they proceeded toward the doors from which the music flowed.

He looked down at Hope and sent her a smile that nearly stopped her heart from beating. The gesture may have been made for their audience, but for a split second the sight of his laughing, almost loving eyes, made her forget where she was and what she'd come here for. Drake, ever the antagonist, was quick to remind her.

"They're staring at my lovely wife," he murmured huskily. Dropping her hand, he reached out to cup the handful of chestnut waves cascading over her creamy shoulder. His eyes darkened as his hooded gaze returned to her face. "I think I've been overshadowed."

Hope blushed under the compliment and looked away. Her attention settled on a pair of youthfully pretty girls standing near a suit of armor positioned in the foyer near the main door. They twittered excitedly behind their fluttering fans. Girlish giggles filled the air. Their eyes never left Drake, making it excruciatingly clear who amongst the gathering had brought that dreamy sparkle to their eyes.

"Look over there." A half-grin tugged at her lips as she directed Drake's attention to his youthful admirers. "Now who's being overshadowed?"

The girls gasped and looked away, pretending not to notice his speculative gaze. When he glanced back at Hope, his eyes were alive with deviltry. "Judging from the reaction we're getting," he shrugged, "I'd say damn near everyone. Shall we?"

Hope blamed the sparkle that touched her eyes on the excitement of those around them. For whatever reason, her spirits were considerably lighter as she slipped her hand under his elbow and allowed him to guide her to the ballroom.

On each side of the open doorway stood a tall, garishly dressed servant. Both men were approximately of the same age, size, and stature, and both displayed somber-to-the-point-of-bored expressions. They glanced at each guest traveling in or out with only a passing interest, saving their attention for the more attractive female guests.

The two pairs of eyes lit on Drake and Hope as they approached the door. The men snapped to attention, but whether the reaction was born of recognition or intimidation, Hope was never really sure.

"Would you care to be announced, sir?" the man on the left, no more than a boy really, asked. The one on the right opened his mouth, presumably to ask the same question, then snapped it shut. His eyes were riveted to the woman clinging to the rugged man's arm, and his youthful attention refused to waver.

"Yes," Drake replied, his hand tightening over Hope's fingers. "Wait thirty seconds, then announce Mr. and Mrs. Drake Phillip Frazier."

Drake glanced down at Hope, missing the look the two young men exchanged. "Are you ready?"

Her gaze drifted through the door, over the crush of well-dressed guests who danced, strolled, and mingled with their peers.

"Yes," she said with a brisk nod. "As ready as I'll ever be, I suppose."

The polished pine dance floor was sunken from the ground floor by four steps. Her grip on Drake's arm tightened and she wondered if her knees would sustain her long enough to reach the bottom. Already their presence had attracted the attention of those closest to the door.

The servant on the left stepped inside the doorway as the music drew to an end. Clearing his throat, he attracted only a small amount of attention. The handsome couple behind him, however, silenced any tongues that continued to wag.

"Introducing Mr. and Mrs. Drake Phillip Frazier."

Cutting a half-bow, the young boy with the intimidatingly loud voice swept away. All too quickly, there was nothing to block Drake and Hope from the sea of curious eyes that greedily devoured them.

Chapter Sixteen

Rage shot through Charles Frazier's blood. Angry fingers raked through his dark blond curls as his steel blue gaze narrowed on the man introduced as his brother. The fingers encircling the stem of a crystal snifter grew white-knuckled from strain.

Drake had changed severely in the last three years, but not so severely that his finely honed features were unrecognizable. The shoulders were broader, the stance more rigidly self-assured, the hair lighter. But there was no denying the sculpted cheekbones that matched Charles's own, or the long, straight nose that branded him a Frazier.

Charles downed the rest of the brandy in one fiery gulp, then reached for another glass. He could feel the crowd's attention shifting anxiously between himself and his brother, its curiosity tangible. With dogged determination, he commanded his features to remain impassive, but that did nothing to alleviate the anger festering within him.

Drake was supposed to be dead. Tubbs had wired him from some godforsaken town in California telling him the unsavory job had been completed. Charles had even included a bonus in the money he'd wired Tubbs, for a job well done!

But the bastard wasn't dead, Charles thought as he tossed back the second brandy. The liquor seared down his throat, settling in his stomach to mix with his ever-increasing ire.

He turned to place the glass on a tray, and scowled when there was none to be found. "Damn!" he muttered as his eyes encountered the orchestra leader's. He sent the man a curt nod, and the air was quickly filled with the gay notes of a waltz. No one danced.

The ice blue eyes watched as Drake leaned close to the woman by his side and whispered something in the fetching creature's ear. She gave a vibrant smile and nodded. Together, the two moved as one to the dance floor. Like the Red Sea, the gathering parted to let them pass.

The rustle of skirts reached Charles's ears a split second before an insistent hand tugged at his sleeve. Turning, Charles found himself looking into the narrow brown gaze of his wife. A shimmer of distaste flickered in his eyes, as he unconsciously summed up a comparison between the woman at his side and the one at his brother's. Again, Drake had won the prize. Angelique, though beautiful, paled in comparison to the woman who danced so gracefully in the circle of Drake's arms.

"I was strolling in the garden when I heard—" Angelique stopped abruptly when a servant passed close by her side. She grabbed a glass of fruited wine off his tray and downed the contents, all the while holding on to the lackey's arm. With trembling fingers, she replaced the goblet, took another, then waved the astonished servant away. "Is it true?" she hissed in her husband's ear.

Her breath reeked of liquor. Charles wrinkled his nose in distaste and nodded to the dance floor. There was small satisfaction to be had in the way his wife's face drained of all color. The grip on his arm became painfully tight as she struggled to remain upright.

"Oh my God," Angelique sighed, careful to keep her voice lowered in case anyone close by heard. She leaned weakly against Charles, her shocked gaze searching the intense blue eyes she had long ago learned to despise. The color was slowly returning to her cheeks. "You told me Drake was dead," she spat. "You said he died in an accident in," she shivered delicately, "California."

"So I was told," Charles growled throatily. His eyes glistened like hard, cold slivers of ice beneath his sardonically arched brows. "Apparently, my informant was mistaken."

"Mistaken?" she gasped. She pulled away from his side as though his sleeve had just burst into flames. Her features were pinched with fury. "Is that all you can say? Good Lord, Charles, how could you be so stupid? The man is hardly dead. Even a fool like yourself can see that."

Through no fault of my own, he thought, but did not say. His hand snaked out and grabbed her arm. His fingers bit into her flesh as he drew Angelique hard against his side. Her yelp of surprise brought more than a few inquisitive glances.

"Watch your tongue, wife," he hissed in her face, "or you'll find yourself lacking it come morning."

Her lips turned up in a smile that had no foundation in humor. "Do not threaten me, Charles. Drake is back now, where he belongs. He won't appreciate you threatening the woman he was once engaged to marry."

Charles's face tightened into a mask of pure rage. The powerful grip he had on her arm came threateningly close to snapping the bones in two. "Three years ago, *wife*. A lot has changed since then. You married *me*," he paused, his nostril flaring with contempt, "and *he* married *her*. Not the act of a man who pines for another."

Angelique's jaw hardened as she averted her gaze to the dancing couple. The two seemed as oblivious to the people milling around them as they were to the curious mumbling their presence created. Their self-absorption pierced her heart.

Shaking off his hand, she glanced back at her husband. No attempt was made to conceal the hatred she felt. "He may have married the chit, but he loves me. Just look at her," she scoffed, sipping thoughtfully on the fruited wine as Charles snatched another glass of brandy. "I find the reason Drake married her glaringly apparent, even if you do not. Her coloring, her bone structure. Why, she could pass for my sister! Yes," she stated with conviction, "the woman is a substitute for me — and as a substitute she will be easily overshadowed."

"You are deluding yourself again, dear wife. Drake won't care to have you back after the reckless way you treated him. As much as I hate him, even I cannot blame him for that."

A cold, calculating glint entered Angelique's eyes as she pressed the chilly rim of her glass against pursed lips. "Would you care to wager on it, *husband*?"

"Let me put it another way." His eyes darkened to a rich, vibrant shade of turquoise as he drew a finger across the long taper of her neck. To an observant onlooker, the gesture might be mistaken for a loving caress. To Angelique, it was anything but. "Deceive me once, with my brother or any other man, and I will slit this lovely throat."

"Is that supposed to frighten me?" she countered with a mocking grin. "Come now, Charles, we both know there is no love lost in this poor excuse for a marriage. You've never cared who shared my bed before, so why pretend to care now?" She sent him a bitter glance. "Or are you finally beginning to realize just how pitiful a specimen you are when compared to your brother?"

His hand curled into a claw that threatened to close around her slender neck. Angelique took a quick step back. She knew Charles would not initiate a scene. To do so would only double the attention his brother's spectacular entrance had attracted.

"Your threats mean nothing to me," she hissed, shoving her half-empty glass into his solid chest. "I will have Drake back. *You* cannot stop me."

"I rarely waste my time making idle threats, Angelique.

I'd as soon kill you both before allowing you to humiliate me the way we humiliated him."

Her lips tightened as her gaze raked his hatefully muscular form. Rugged, but not nearly as appealing as his brother's, she thought as she reached out and straightened his blue silk cravat. "Sharpen your blade then, *husband*. You'll be needing it soon."

With a rustle of her silk skirt, Angelique pivoted and strolled regally away. Her bearing was straight and proud, as though she hadn't a care in the world.

The glass splintered in his hand, slicing his palm as Charles watched his wife maneuver herself through the crowd. Trickles of blood dripped down his fingertips, spotting the polished floorboards. He noticed neither that nor the stinging pain of the alcohol as it seeped into the cuts.

"I do not make idle threats, witch," he spat darkly, stalking in her wake.

She might have been floating on air for all the ground Hope felt beneath her feet. The soft linen brushing against her calves was a luxury in itself. But it was nothing in comparison to the tingling sensations evoked by the strong arms around her waist, and the solid chest that grazed her breasts.

Dancing with no slippers to protect her feet could have been a fatal mistake — were she waltzing with anyone but Drake Frazier. She needn't have worried. Not once were her fragile toes trod upon as he swept her into his arms and guided her with precision across the empty dance floor.

Who would have guessed that the hardened gunslinger who had taken on Oren Larzdon without blinking would be so familiar with the intricate steps of the dance? Certainly not she. But then, there was a lot she didn't know about this man. And his list of mysterious attributes was multiplying by the minute.

"What are you thinking?"

The husky voice caused Hope to glance up in surprise. "I was wondering which one of these men is your brother," she lied, not at all liking the direction her thoughts had taken. It was growing more and more difficult to remind herself she really should hate this man. "Do you see him anywhere?"

The sea-green eyes scanned the room as the dance made an elaborate turn. When his gaze darkened, and his arms tightened, she knew he had found Charles.

"Brace yourself, sunshine, we're about to run straight into a storm." He glanced down at her, his face expressionless. "Or more correctly, it is about to run into us. Charles and Angelique are heading this way."

A strangled "Oh!" was about all she could manage through the sudden dryness in her throat. Although Drake's attention focused exclusively on her, Hope knew he was aware of every step his brother took. He seemed not to notice her grip tightening with alarm on his shoulder and hand.

Drake waited until Charles and Angelique reached the border of the crowd, then drew a startled Hope hard against his chest. She blushed furiously at the intimate contact and he couldn't help but smile.

"Kiss me," he demanded throatily, his lips cutting a hot path to her own as his eyes darkened with passion. "And make it good—your job depends on it."

Hope didn't have to make it anything. The first touch of his warm lips against her and she was lost. Her hands crept up around his neck, her fingers instinctively tangling in the rich mane of his hair as she opened up to him like flower petals open to the kiss of the morning sun.

It seemed like an eternity had passed since the last time she had felt his body pressing insistently into hers, his mouth demanding a passion she could not hide. She clung weakly to his broad shoulders, forgetting for the moment

272

where they were, forgetting as well the captivated audience their mutual passion ensnared.

Her fingers ached to peel back the expensive shirt, to feel once again his rippling flesh beneath her hungry fingertips. The fine clothes could not disguise the smell of leather and sweat clinging to his body. It was a familiar scent that warmed Hope to the core, and she drank of it deeply as she surrendered herself to the consuming fire of his kiss.

All too soon, he pulled away. "Sorry," he murmured, his eyes saying he was anything but. "I don't think the old biddies huddled in the corner over there would appreciate our showing them what they've been missing all these years. Do you?"

She glanced up, her eyelids still heavy with unquenched passion. "Oh, I don't know. I think they might enjoy it." She paused, a mischievous grin tugging her lips. "It would certainly give them something to discuss at the next Church Social."

"Incorrigible," Drake chuckled. Clucking his tongue he shook his head. "Absolutely incorrigible. You should be ashamed of yourself, Miss Bennett."

"Mrs. Frazier," she corrected stiffly. "And I'm not ashamed in the least. Why should I be? I doubt we're the only people who ever felt this way." To her surprise, she found she wasn't lying. She truly wasn't ashamed of the passion she felt for this man—although she knew by all rights she should be.

His eyes sparkled. "Maybe not," he agreed with a shrug, slowing his steps as the music drew to an end. "But I'd bet my life we're the only ones who display it so openly. This room will never be the same again."

Neither will I, Hope thought as she dipped a curtsey to his neatly cut bow. *Neither will I.*

"Hello, Drake." The voice, remarkably like the purr of a contented feline, flowed over his shoulder with a satisfied sigh.

Drake straightened and all semblance of lightness left his body like steam floating up from a kettle. He took Hope's suddenly cold hand and tucked it into the crook of his elbow.

By the time Drake had turned toward his brother and sister-in-law, the transformation was complete. The smile he sent to the tall, dark haired woman was filled with warmth. Only Hope seemed to notice that the warmth did not touch his eyes. Angelique was too busy preening to recognize the falseness, and Charles merely stood gripping a blood-stained white linen handkerchief around his hand as he glowered at them all.

"Angelique," Drake greeted, ignoring the outraged look that crossed his brother's face. He inclined his head to the woman, untangling Hope's fingers from his arm before stepping from her side. Angelique's victorious smile lit up the room. Hope's heart tightened.

"I should be quite angry with you," Angelique murmured, accepting the fleeting kiss Drake placed on her flushed porcelain cheek. "The least you could have done was send word. We've thought you dead for these past months, you know."

"And did the thought upset you?" he asked candidly, running the back of his hand over her jaw. Hope shivered, remembering all too well the feel of his weathered knuckles grazing her own eager flesh.

"It upset some of us," Charles interjected hotly, before Angelique had a chance to answer. A muscle twitched beneath his left eye, reminding Hope of Drake when he was angered. "Some of us did not mind so much." He turned his attention to a flustered Hope, and she found herself pinned under his steel blue gaze. "And who might this lovely creature be?" he asked coldly. "I heard her introduced as your wife, but perhaps I heard wrong?"

"You heard right," Drake replied casually, his eyes never leaving Angelique, who preened like a contented cat under the unwavering attention. He offered no more information, but continued to pierce Angelique with his stare.

Charles gave a snort of disgust as he extended his hand to Hope. "I'll presume you have a name, but my brother is too unmannerly to give it. Charles Frazier," he introduced himself, taking her damp hand in his and pumping it lightly. "Yourself?"

"Hope Benn — Frazier," she corrected quickly, through suddenly parched lips. She snatched her hand back as soon as politeness allowed, not at all liking the feel of his soft palm beneath her fingers. As inconspicuously as possible, she wiped the feel of him off on her skirt. No, Hope thought, *Angelique's* skirt — for it was abruptly apparent from whose closet the gown had been borrowed.

Angelique tore her gaze from Drake's, and regarded Hope head to toe with a glance just shy of loathing. "Hope?" she purred, a false smile turning her lips. Her nostrils flared with distaste. "How . . . quaint." She looked back at Drake, dismissing Hope as though she were of no consequence. Slipping her hand beneath his elbow, she rubbed the breasts that threatened to spill free of the daringly low décolletage of her gown against Drake's upper arm. "I am simply *dying* to hear all the details of your trip, darling. You've been gone so long." The thick lashes lowered coyly. "And we've so much time to make up for."

Hope gritted her teeth and tried not to scream. Always an intelligent man, Drake Frazier suddenly seemed not to possess a logical bone in his body. Perhaps it was the feel of soft flesh rubbing suggestively against his sleeve that was robbing him of all form of common sense? She hid her clenched fists in her skirt. Or perhaps it was finally being reunited with the true object of his affection — instead of a poorly built substitute?

Whatever the reasons for his bizarre behavior, Hope thought that if she was forced to stand here and watch this disgusting display for one more minute, she would surely be ill.

Angelique leaned close to Drake and whispered something in his ear that brought a smile to his lips. *He never smiled that way at me*, Hope thought as the orchestra began the first strains of another waltz.

Thrusting her chin up high, Hope turned to Charles. Her accent thickened considerably, and there was a glint of determination sparkling in her eyes. "Mr. Frazier," she said with a coquettish grin that put Angelique to shame, "if your dance card isn't filled, and you think it not too forward of me, I would be honored if you would lead me through the next dance."

How easy it was to slip back into the role of genteel southern belle, Hope thought, as Charles regarded her with veiled surprise.

Inclining his head, he held out his arm for her to take. "Why, Mrs. Frazier, I'd be delighted," he replied smoothly. His arrogant smile showed he was quite pleased with this unexpected turn of events. "More so if you would do me the honor of calling me Charles. After all, we are *family* now," he added, patting her hand. "That in itself should allow us to be more familiar. Wouldn't you agree?"

Swallowing her revulsion, she placed her hand on his sleeve and nodded. "Charles it is," she said, meeting Drake's stormy glare. Her gaze shifted to an amused Angelique, then back to Drake. "You don't mind, of course, if I dance with your brother?"

Although phrased as a question, it was anything but. Drake gave a brisk nod, his attention distracted by her connivance. Reluctantly, he tore his gaze away from Hope as Charles led her to the center of the dance floor. Against his will, it returned time and again.

"Mr. Frazier—Charles," Hope said as she placed one hand on a shoulder almost as broad as Drake's. The other was captured inside the curled fingers of his wounded hand. The linen handkerchief scraped against her palm. "You do dance well, I hope. I mean, you aren't given to treading on toes?"

"Toes?" he asked. With effort, he wrenched his gaze from his brother's back as Drake and Angelique disappeared through the open french doors leading to the veranda. He led into the first steps of the dance, turning his full attention to the curious creature in his arms. "Why do you ask?"

With an impish grin, she glanced down at the bare feet peeking from beneath her hem. Charles followed her gaze, his eyes widening when he saw the shell-pink toes. "What happened to your slippers?"

"Your wife's wardrobe wasn't that generous," she replied, as though she were telling him how much a wagon load of corn would fetch in a market booth.

To her surprise, he tipped back his head and let loose a laugh that rumbled from somewhere deep in his broad chest. The crystal blue eyes sparkled. "I thought the gown looked familiar," he said as he swept her through a half-circle. "I just couldn't place it. How on earth did *you* get it?"

"Stolen," she replied in a clandestine whisper. "As, I'm sure, are my husband's clothes." Her gaze raked his form, noting how close his build was to Drake's. Not quite as rugged, nor as broad, but close all the same. "Yours?"

"Ah, now those I recognized," he nodded. "And yes, they are mine." His gaze hardened, a little.

"You have a wonderful tailor," she said, thinking that she liked Drake far better in a pair of tight denims, a threadbare flannel, and a worn leather vest and stetson. "Tell me something," she said lightly, her skirts rustling around her ankles as she was propelled away from, then back into, his arms. "Does it bother you that my husband has abducted your wife? And that, as we speak, they are probably strolling some secluded spot in the garden, catching up on old times?"

Hope wasn't disappointed. The arm encircling her waist tightened and the blue eyes clouded with anger. It was

277

exactly the reaction she had expected. He had been too charming, too careless in his reaction to the entire situation. Now she could see the truth. Charles Frazier was more disturbed with the way the evening was progressing than he cared to let on.

And what other feelings is he hiding? she wondered.

"Should it bother me?" he said finally, his voice tight. "After all, you might say I am doing the same with *his* wife."

"But it isn't the same," she corrected shrewdly. "Those two go way back—or so I'm told—whereas we don't have any old times to catch up on."

"Yet," he conceded, with a nod and a calculating smile.

"Yet," she repeated cautiously, feeling as though she'd been caught between a rock and a hungry wolf. This man had stolen Drake's fiancée out from under his nose. Hope didn't know why, but instinctively she knew that he was going to try and do the same thing with her.

Should I let him? she wondered as they lapped into an uneasy silence. She remembered all too clearly how Drake had hung on every word that flowed from Angelique's lips. A stab of jealousy pierced her heart. While she harbored nothing but disgust for this caricature of Drake, she was also finding it difficult not to throw Drake's callous treatment of her back in his face.

It would serve the gunslinger right to see that someone else could actually be attracted to her, Hope thought with a satisfied grin. It didn't matter that Charles was forcing himself to feign attraction. The means would suit the end.

A few more couples drifted onto the dance floor. She eyed them warily, noticing how each one looked quickly away whenever her gaze met theirs.

"Is it stuffy in here?" she asked suddenly. The cloying smell of flowery perfume and spicy male cologne seemed to be pressing in on her from all sides.

"I hadn't noticed." The crystal blue eyes narrowed on her, and she could see that Charles wasn't fooled for a minute.

He was also more than willing to play the game. "Would you care to step outside for a bit of air? The garden is quite lovely this time of year. The roses died with the first frost, but it's still filled with delectable surprises. You really should see it."

Hope nodded, letting herself be guided from the dance floor. She wasn't entirely sure she'd made the right decision in indicating a wish to see the gardens. But of one thing she was sure — she couldn't stand another moment of twirling through the stilted steps of a dance with a man she abhorred, all the while wondering what Drake and Angelique were doing!

Chapter Seventeen

Charles was right. Although a goodly portion of the flowers had faded with the passing of autumn, the leafy shrubs so artfully arranged were really quite beautiful. The air snapped with the beginnings of a winter chill as the light of a crescent moon glittered over the winding paths. By the time Hope had seen her fiftieth bare rosebush, her twentieth petunia stalk, and her thirtieth withered violet, she was ready to pluck each shrub where they stood. Drake and Angelique were nowhere to be seen.

Charles hesitated beside a whitewashed, wrought iron bench buried amidst leafy ivy. His hands were clasped behind his broad back, and his dark blond hair shimmered in the pale moonlight. For a second, he looked remarkably like his brother. Then he turned. One glance at his cold blue eyes dispelled the image.

He seemed to have forgotten there were no slippers on her feet to protect them from the branches and stones littering the paths. Hope's stinging soles had not. For the last half hour she had dogged this man's footsteps, the whole time wondering if his elaborately roundabout route was not purposely devised to keep her away from whatever area he presumed his brother and wife to be in. Now she was sure that was his motive. His easy acceptance of the pair's absence was exactly that—too easy.

"It appears they've wandered father than the gardens," he said, eloquently stating the obvious as he gestured Hope toward the bench. His liquor-soaked breath fogged the air. "Shall we sit and enjoy the quiet awhile before returning?"

"No, thank you," she declined with a forced smile. She eyed the bench, but staunchly refused to approach it. Though the seat was a tempting respite for her aching feet, it wasn't tempting enough to risk spending any more time alone in Charles Frazier's company than was necessary. "Shouldn't you be getting back to your guests?"

"They can wait," he scoffed with a casual wave of his hand. His icy gaze settled on her creamy flesh where it swelled beneath the rosy satin neckline. "It isn't often I'm honored by moonlight, and a beautiful woman," he added suggestively.

Hope shivered, ignoring the compliment, as well as the insinuation. "You forget, I've met your wife," she countered pointedly. The muscle returned to twitch beneath his eye. "I'd think you were used to both by now."

Again the hands were clasped behind his suddenly rigid back. "Ah, very good, Hope. Spoken like a true jealous wife. Perhaps I underestimated your feelings for my brother."

And perhaps not, Hope added to herself. "That's none of your business," she snapped, dearly wishing she hadn't given in to her curiosity and taken Charles up on his offer to stroll the moonswept gardens. "Unless you can find a more congenial topic, I'll be forced to return inside."

Her heart skipped a beat, then pounded frantically when a cold, malicious sneer curled his lips. Belatedly, she realized her mistake. His words, uttered in a tone close to boredom, confirmed it. "I do hope you can pick your way back alone then, dearest sister-in-law. I fear I'm enjoying the fresh air and moonlight too much to return just yet."

Frantically, her thoughts circled back over the many twisting paths that had led them this far. Not only couldn't she recall which path led where, but she was also becoming aware of the chirping crickets, croaking bull frogs — and total absence of music. If the strains of the orchestra could not reach them here, then it stood to reason that her screams of panic would not reach the house. But she *wouldn't* panic, Hope commanded herself. To do so would be a fatal mistake.

"You're enjoying this, aren't you?" she jeered. Crossing her arms over her chest, she glared angrily into the glint of satisfaction shimmering in his eyes. "What was your plan in luring me out here, Charles Frazier? To keep me away long enough for Drake to suspect — ? It doesn't matter." She tapped her toe on the dry leaves in aggravation. Her thoughts drifted to the scar lining her back and she wondered what this man's reaction to it would be. Instinctively, she knew it would be disgust. "Whatever your plan, it won't work. He knows me well enough to know my morals aren't that loose."

"He thought the same about Angelique," Charles took great pleasure in reminding her as he took a threatening step forward, "and look what happened there."

"I'm not Angelique," she countered, with a quick step back. She was ready to bolt back into the thick of the garden. "My head isn't turned by sugary words and false attention."

"No?" Half the distance between them was closed in one long stride. "Then what would it take to turn that pretty little head?"

"Your brother."

He reached out and clamped a fierce hand on her shoulder as she turned to flee. Abruptly, Hope was swung back to face him.

"Afraid you're twenty years too late for that," he said, his tone light. Too light, she thought. "Angelique set her sights on Drake when she was eight. Having him has been her single-minded pursuit in life, a pursuit that was delayed a bit when we married. In all the years I've known her, I've yet to see my wife denied anything she wants. She would never tolerate it." The fingers tightened, biting painfully into her shoulder. "Have no doubts, *Mrs. Frazier*. If Angelique wants your husband back, she *will* get him. There's nothing you can do to stop her."

She tried to shake off his hand. It didn't work. "I won't have to. I have faith in my husband, sir, and because of that faith, I think he'll see her manipulations for what they are. Drake's no fool. He won't be so easily duped a second time."

"No?" Charles asked slyly. "I don't agree. My wife can be very persuasive. By now she probably has your husband convinced I *forced* her to marry me. It wouldn't surprise me to find them locked in a lover's embrace beneath one of these rosebushes."

One dark brow rose in challenge as Hope finally succeeded in pushing his hand away. "And did you?" she countered. "Force her to marry you? It's the only reason I can think of for a woman to leave a man like Drake for a man like you. And if you really think they are low enough to be rolling beneath rosebushes, I say we should take a look around and see. Or doesn't your confidence extend that far?"

"I can think of far more pleasurable things to do in a moonlit garden," he growled, the sardonic brows furrowing together in undisguised fury. He reached out and pulled her hard against him.

The air left Hope's lungs in a rush. Feebly, she struggled against him. Her bare toes collided with his shin. Although the contact caused pain to shoot through her foot, it seemed to have no effect on Charles. His grip merely tightened until it was all she could do to draw breath.

"Your heartfelt defense of my brother is touching, but misplaced." His wounded hand captured her waist as, without warning, the fingers of the other entwined in her hair and yanked. "Unfortunately for you, you'll have to settle for

283

second best. You'll have to settle for me."

Hope gasped as her chin snapped up, her scalp stinging with the abuse. Their gazes clashed before his angry mouth crashed down on hers.

The kiss was hard and punishing, its purpose no doubt. By the time Charles pulled away, her lips were swollen and bruised, her humiliation complete.

"There now," he said smugly, his hands dropping from her as he straightened his crooked cravat. "That wasn't so bad, was it? Given a little time, I've no doubt you'll grow used to my attention. Eventually, you'll probably prefer it to Drake's. Most women do."

"I'd rather die!" she spat, literally, in his face. The spittle trickled in moist droplets down his cheek and chin.

She didn't wait for his reaction. Hoisting the skirt above her knees, she turned and bolted down the path. Rocks and sticks bit at her tender feet, tripping her at every turn. Ignoring the pain, she plunged on, her flight becoming frantic when she heard the heavy tread that signaled a quick pursuit.

One path melted into the next. She followed them in no discernible order as sharp branches reached out to rip at her hair and arms. Lithely, she dodged those she could, and bore the stinging pain of the ones seen too late.

When she could run no more, she stopped and leaned heavily against the rough bark of a maple tree. Her breath was coming in long, searing gasps that rivaled the frantic pounding of her heart for prominence.

Dry leaves crunched on the path stretching to her right. Hope made ready to flee again. Before she had taken the first step, a figure emerged. Her breath caught in her throat at the sight of broad shoulders, tapered hips, and light hair that glistened to a rich shade of silver in the pale moonlight.

"Hope?" The sea-green eyes raked her tattered form, finally settling on her kiss-swollen lips. "What the hell—?"

"Drake!" Without thinking, she catapulted herself into the

safety of his arms, burying her face in the warm hollow of his shoulder. Desperately, she clung to him, drawing from his strength.

"Hope," Drake murmured, his voice struggling to remain calm. His palm stroked the length of her hair in time to each ragged breath. "What are you doing out here? And what happened to your dress?"

Mutely, she shook her head. Words of explanation died on her tongue, unspoken. It didn't matter. None of it mattered anymore. Her encounter with Charles, her suspicions of Angelique. All that mattered was that Drake was here, holding her, soothing her, comforting her in a way that only he could. Little by little she felt her anxiety melt away, replaced by a different, more complex sensation, a sensation only Drake Frazier was able to stir within her.

"Hold me," she whispered hoarsely against his neck. "Right now, I just need you to hold me."

Drake's arms tightened around her protectively. "Oh, sunshine, what did he do to you?" he groaned, resting his cheek atop her head. "It was Charles, wasn't it?"

It was a statement, not a question, but Hope nodded anyway. "Yes," she said, her voice cracking. "It was Charles."

Although he didn't let go, Drake pulled slightly away. The tip of his thumb trailed over her bruised, quivering lower lip. Damn! He should have known Charles would take his fury out on Hope. Why hadn't the thought occurred to him *before* it was too late to stop his vengeful brother?! "And this?" he asked roughly. Again she nodded and his gaze hardened dangerously. "What else did he do to you? He didn't — ?"

"No!" Hope shivered in disgust. God Lord, she couldn't even bear the *thought* of that! "I was lucky enough to get away before things got out of hand. As far as I know, he's still searching the garden trying to find me."

Drake raked his fingers through his hair and gave a brisk nod of satisfaction. "You shouldn't have come out here. You should have stayed inside where it was safe."

"I thought it *was* safe. I didn't think he would—I mean, I thought *you* were out here!"

The arms encircling her shoulders and waist dropped abruptly to his side. Hope shivered with cold when he took a step away. "With Angelique?" he inquired from over his shoulder.

She frowned. What had she said to bring about such a sudden shift in moods? "Yes," she repeated impatiently, "with Angelique. As I recall, you *did* leave with her." Stiffening, she scanned the path in both directions. Except for broken branches, dry leaves, and crickets, they were alone. She turned her curious gaze on Drake. "Speaking of Angelique . . ."

"We went back inside for punch," he explained with a shrug. "When I saw you were missing, I left her there."

Should I be grateful? she thought sarcastically. Did the thought of leaving Angelique's side hold no appeal for Drake? The hard set of his jaw made her wonder if he didn't have better things to do with his night than rescuing her from the clutches of his overly eager brother.

Swallowing past the sudden tightness in her throat, she swept the skirt aside and turned down the path. "I'm sorry to spoil your evening. Please, don't let me keep you."

With each step, she waited for Drake to stop her. He didn't. She could feel his eyes boring holes in her rigid back as she rounded the corner and came into full view of the back of the house, but that was all. No footsteps followed her and no hand shot out to stop her progress.

Her heart tightened with bitter disappointment and regret as she lifted the torn skirt and ascended the veranda's chiseled stone steps. The sight of Angelique's preening face at the top of the stairs made Hope hesitate. Blinking back tears, she tilted her chin at a haughty angle and swept past the manipulative woman. Ignoring the contented smile tugging Angelique's lips was not as easy, but Hope managed it.

"Have no doubts, Mrs. Frazier. If Angelique wants your husband back, she will get him. There's nothing you can do to stop her." Charles's words haunted Hope as she dashed the moistness from her eyes, then swept into the crowded ballroom.

"Mrs. Frazier, retiring so soon?"

Hope was turning the knob of what she presumed to be Drake's bedroom door when Charles's hatefully familiar voice stopped her cold. Dropping the hand to her side, she turned to see him leaning lazily against the wall near the stairwell.

"It's been a long day," she murmured noncommittally. When he continued to stare at her, she pursed her lips and glared at him in annoyance. "Is there something I can do for you?"

His head shook in slow, thoughtful sways. "Not directly. However, I think there is something I can do for you."

"Dear Lord, why me?" she sighed, wearily resting her shoulder against the door. Louder, she added, "If you have something to say, say it. It's been a long day and I'm tired. I'd rather enjoy a nice soft bed than spend the rest of the night playing stupid little guessing games with you."

His lips tightened angrily. "I've devised a way for you to keep a ring around your finger, woman," he snapped, shoving his hands deep inside his trouser pockets. "The least you can do is be grateful."

"Me?" she scoffed in disgust. "I don't think so, sir. You're too selfish to be wasting time racking your brain to think of ways for me to keep my husband."

"Perhaps," he countered shrewdly. "But I would rack my brain thinking of ways to keep my wife. I see no reason we can't both profit from my ingenuity."

"I do. I've had enough of you tonight to last a lifetime." She reached for the doorknob with trembling fingers and turned. "Whatever plan you've concocted, I want no part of it."

"Even if it means losing my brother?"

Hope's gaze returned to him slowly. Her dark eyes sparkled with conviction. To think that once she had actually defended this weasel to Drake! What had she been thinking of? Comparing this swine to Luke and what she'd shared with him was like comparing night to day.

"Even then," she said, finally. "You see, Mr. Frazier, if Angelique is successful in stealing Drake away from me, then that would mean I never really had him to begin with. All the fighting in the world wouldn't keep him at my side if it's Angelique he wants to be with. I believe you said words to that effect in the garden tonight."

"So you'd just give up?" he asked incredulously. Pushing away from the wall, he approached her. Hope, remembering all too well her previous encounter with him, flinched. "Without a fight? I don't believe it!"

"Believe whatever you want. Right now I'm too tired to care. Now if you will excuse me—"

"I most certainly will not!" Before she could stop him, he reached out and slammed the door shut. "You may be willing to let them make a fool out of you, but I'm not so generous."

"What do you mean?" she demanded. The smell of brandy on his breath was strong, and she instinctively retreated a step. There was small comfort in knowing the houseful of guests below would hinder any further physical attempts he might make.

Charles hesitated, his crystal blue eyes shimmering with disgust as he leaned against the closed door. "Do you know where your husband is right now, madame? Or my wife?"

"The last time I saw Drake, he was in the garden—alone."

That she had seen Drake since her encounter with himself seemed to surprise Charles, but he recovered quickly. He fixed her with a glance just shy of recrimination. "Perhaps for the moment he was alone," he conceded coldly, "but how long do you think Angelique will allow him to stay that way?"

"I don't know," she replied tersely, "and I don't care."

It was a lie. She cared — so much so that the thought of Drake slipping off into the night with Angelique brought a stab of pain to her heart the likes of which she hadn't felt since learning her family had perished in the fire in Thirsty Gulch. But she'd rather rot in hell before letting this man see, and play on, her pain.

Of course, Charles saw through the veneer of haughty disdain only too well. His lazy smile attested to that. "Don't you?" He reached out and brushed his cloth-covered knuckles against her suddenly warm cheek. Hope swatted his hand away, but the damage had been done. "Then why do you flush very time I mention your husband and my wife together?" he argued. "And why do your eyes shimmer with betrayal?"

"I haven't been betrayed."

"Yet," he conceded with a brisk nod. "But how long will that last? How long before they submit to the treacherous passions of their bodies? A passion that has been too long denied?" He watched as the tip of her shell-pink tongue darted out to lick suddenly parched lips. When the moment was ripe, he pounced. "And what do you do, madame, while your husband is out romancing another?" Charles scoffed derisively. "When we first met, I would have sworn you'd shown a touch of spirit. I must have been wrong. Only a complete fool would give full blessings to her husband's blatant indiscretions by welcoming him back into her bed." His eyes drifted to the closed door, and the long, thin fingers that tightly gripped the latch. "Yet it would seem that is exactly what you are about to do."

Hope faltered. Her hand came off the knob as though it had just metamorphosed into a snake. "This is the only room I know, and I — I have to sleep somewhere," she replied, hating the way her voice cracked, and her heart throbbed deafeningly in her ears.

His mirthless laugh echoed down the hall as he shoved himself away from the door. His large hand swept the paneled hall, indicating the other closed doors. "This is not Bethlehem, madame," he said with a sardonic leer. "We do have room at the inn. Pick a room and I will see it is readied for you. If you wish, I'll see to it that Drake is not told where you've gone."

"Why?" she demanded softly, clenching her fists in the tattered remains of her skirt. "Why would you do that?"

"Entirely selfish reason, I assure you," he said with a mock bow. "I happen to think that a night spent alone, away from his lovely wife's company, will show Drake what he stands to miss should he decide to pursue my wife. No matter what you say, you are not the only one who would like to see your marriage work, Mrs. Frazier."

"But he may not spend the night alone," she reminded him coldly. Charles's gaze darkened, but it was the only evidence her words had struck close to his heart — if, indeed, he had one.

His lips drew into a fine, tight line. "My wife is many things, but she is no fool. Even Angelique would not be so stupid as to visit another man's bed while under my roof. Especially my brother's."

Hope kept her opinions about Angelique's intelligence to herself. Seeds of doubt — doubt that this man had insidiously planted — tickled the back of her mind.

Charles's reasons were, as he admitted, selfish. But was he right? Would a night alone cause Drake to appreciate her more, or would it serve only to make him suspect her "marital" fidelity?

She didn't know, but her feminine pride screamed for her to find out. Slowly, she nodded. "All right," she said finally. Her brows knit in a frown as she tapped an index finger against pursed lips. Was she making a mistake? Would

Drake truly miss her? Time would tell. "I accept. Fix one of your rooms. I don't care which."

Charles, seemingly unable to believe his good fortune, smiled happily and beat a hasty retreat. He returned quickly, two servants in tow. Hope leaned wearily against the door, keeping a sharp eye on the hall in case Drake should unexpectedly appear. The servants, a mousy woman and a gaunt, haggard man, disappeared into a room across the hall.

Charles's gravelly voice boomed orders for what seemed like an eternity before the three emerged. The servants scurried down the hall, the woman's arms laden with bed-linen, as they disappeared down the stairwell.

"M'lady, your bedchamber awaits."

Hope tossed restlessly atop the big, cold, empty bed. Sleep, that ever elusive state, avoided her, as it had done the better part of the night. She wanted to believe that her restlessness was caused by fear of the nightmares that had renewed themselves after her last encounter with Tyrone Tubbs, but she was honest enough to recognize that as a lie. There were other reasons for her insomnia, reasons she avoided contemplating.

The music below had stopped hours ago and the silence was deafening. Her ears missed the soft snores Drake usually made in the bedroll beside her, and her body missed the warmth she was so used to curling into. Instead of the spicy scent of sweat, her nostrils were greeted with the smell of freshly laundered sheets. And, while her cheek might be cushioned by a soft, feather tick pillow, it was a muscular chest she wished to feel beneath her cheek.

Drake! her mind screamed against her throbbing temples. Was he in his own room, she wondered painfully, or was he with Angelique? And did she really want to know the answer?

Angelique's name, not yours, her mind rudely reminded her. Her heart tightened with the bitter memory.

"Fresh air," she murmured in frustration, eying the closed windows on the far wall.

Yes, that's it. I just need a little air and then I'll be able to sleep, she thought, as she threw off the heavy covers and crept to the window nearest the bed. She was used to sleeping beneath the stars, with the cool, sweet breeze wafting over her cheek. This room, although twice the size of the cabin in Thirsty Gulch, was too small, too stuffy. She felt trapped.

Kneeling on the window seat, she unlatched the shutters and threw them wide. Her relief was immediate. She took a long, deep breath of the cool breeze that, heavy with the scent of coming rain, made the lace curtains by her side dance. In the distance was the playful chirp of birds and the faint rustling of tree leaves. The sound was like sweet music to her ears.

The knots of frustration tightening her stomach slowly began to ease. She lowered herself onto the window seat and sat cross-legged, her back cushioned against the window sill. She closed her eyes against the first fragile fingers of dawn streaking the sky, and could almost imagine the wide open prairie stretching endlessly around her, and Lazy's slow, steady gait rocking between her thighs.

Yes, I just needed some fresh air, she thought again, relieved. She scooted down on the seat until her head was cushioned against the hard wood.

Stifling a yawn, she savored the feel of the cool breeze against her bare calves and thighs. The white cotton chemise had bunched up to her hips, but she didn't right it. She enjoyed the feel too much, and unconsciously imagined it to be a pair of calloused palms stroking over her flesh.

Sighing, she closed her eyes and surrounded herself in darkness—only to have her eyelids snap back up in shock.

Imagined calloused palms? God lord, those *were* calloused palms! They were on her calves, tenderly stroking the back of her knee, slipping briefly between her thighs before drifting up to linger on the quivering expanse of her stomach.

Hope sat bolt upright. Her head missed colliding with Drake's by mere inches.

"How long have you been here? And what the hell are you doing?" she gasped as his hand boldly ascended. She glared angrily into his decidedly lecherous grin and, with trembling fingers, tried to push the chemise into place. He swatted her hand away, refusing to allow it.

"Surprised? Didn't you think I'd find you?" he queried lazily. Again, his fingers slipped beneath the skirt's hem, this time to tease her navel while his warm breath teased her upper chest and neck. His eyes were dark with a mixture of passion and victory. "You can't hide from me, sunshine. You can try, but I'll find you." His lips lowered to taste the creamy hollow of her throat and he whispered against her tingling flesh, "I'll always find you."

"I—I don't want you to find me," she countered weakly. Her hands pushed desperately against his shoulders even as her body arched into his chest and hips. "And—my God, the window's open, Drake. Someone will see."

"That's the least of your worries, but it is a damn good reason for you not to struggle." His lips nuzzled and nibbled at her neck. A white-hôt spark of desire rushed through her. "I'd hate to see you tumble to your death at such an inopportune moment."

Hope went limp at the thought of falling through the window. At least, that was the reason she gave herself. She refused to believe her sudden stillness had anything to do with the shivers of desire his expert hand was eliciting.

"Let me go," she whispered huskily, even as her hands crept around his neck and her fingers buried themselves in the silky softness of his hair. She was leaning against the window sill now, and the hard wood was as firm and inflexible against her back as the male chest pressing intimately against her breasts. "I — I don't want this to happen."

He lifted his head, his gaze dark and penetrating as it searched her face. "Do you have a choice? Do you have the strength to stop it, even if you want to? God knows, I don't."

The sensual timbre of his voice rippled through her and she clung to him desperately. It was growing more and more difficult to deny the passion building between them, and she wasn't entirely sure that denial was what she wanted anymore.

So what *did* she want? Her body answered that question with a will all its own.

A husky growl escaped Drake's lips when she tilted her chin to allow him better access to her neck. One look at the pulse throbbing in the creamy base and he was lost.

His hands encompassed her waist, pulling her hard against his hips, as his tongue tasted the spot that teased him to distraction. The flesh on her throat was cool, kissed by the soft breeze.

Her urgency grew to a demanding ache that could not be denied. Her passion was fueled by the evidence of his desire straining fervently against her. A surge of eagerness tingled in her thighs, seeped up to curl in her quivering stomach.

His fingers slipped down the outside of her thigh, turned inward, and began a much more provocative assault. His calloused palm teased her until a whimper of insistence rushed from her hips. She buried her face in his warm, hard shoulder, insistently straining against his searching caress as her fingers dug into his sinewy flesh. She wasn't sure how much more of this tantalizing torture she could take before surrendering to humiliation by begging openly for release.

Drake never let her reach that point. Sensing her frustration, he slipped one hand beneath her knees, the other beneath her arms, and lifted.

Hope curled into him willingly. Her arms coiled around his shoulders as her tongue darted out to taste the salty expanse of his neck. Every muscle in his body tightened in reaction, and she allowed herself a momentary surge of victory before continuing with the sensuous assault.

Long, sure strides carried them over to the bed—a *real* bed—but instead of placing her atop the downy softness, he paused. Hope raised her head and looked at him through heavy lids. He caught his breath when he saw the dark eyes burning with desire.

"Ah, hell. Why start now?" he murmured huskily. His gaze drifted longingly to the bed before settling on Hope's kiss-swollen lips. He lowered her to the floor.

Suddenly the only thing in the world that mattered was the feel of this man atop her, his muscular body pinning her to the plush carpet.

This time when his hand stroked her thigh, it ascended without stopping. The linen chemise was dragged with it. Hope shivered as the cool air wafted her naked body, but made no protest when the covering was removed and tossed aside.

The sun outside was growing brighter, caressing her flesh as Drake's hungry gaze raked her naked form.

"That's not fair," she said, her voice throaty with desire as her fingers plucked at the buttons on his waistcoat. "You can see me, but I can't see a thing."

His eyes were dark with undeniable passion—and a glint of challenge. "And what, exactly, do you intend to do about it?"

A wicked grin tugged at her lips. "Even up the pot, gunslinger."

He rolled onto his back, allowing her to tug at his clothes. He helped only when necessary, enjoying the feel of her fingers against his flesh much too much to stop her.

As he had done with her chemise, Hope tossed aside each article of clothing she stripped away with a flick of her wrist. When he was naked, she stretched out beside him, pressing her body urgently into his side. Slowly, she let her fingers

295

launch an investigation of their own. A smile of satisfaction spread over her lips when Drake groaned and caught her wrist.

In an instant she was tossed onto her back, her head pillowed by his large palm as his body covered hers fully. The coarse hairs coating his chest tickled her breasts. It was a sensation comparable to none. He pressed against her in suggestive, rhythmic motions, but otherwise refused to relieve her torment.

"Now, Drake," she pleaded when she could bear no more. *"Pleeease!"*

When his knee parted her thighs, she felt a shiver of anticipation course up her spine. Her legs wrapped around his waist, her lips instinctively arching up to meet his powerful entry. He filled her completely, but it wasn't enough. She dug her fingers into his back as she met each wonderful thrust with an urgency that quickly spiraled out of control.

Hope surrendered herself to the wave of sensations crashing over and within her trembling body. At last, she shuddered in blissful fulfillment. Wave after wave of satisfaction rippled through her, prolonged and increased to an almost agonizing pitch with each driving thrust.

His mouth crashed over hers and she clung to his sweat-dampened shoulders. She swallowed his ragged moan as his body tensed and released, tensed and released. Then, when every last ounce of energy had been tapped, he collapsed on top of her.

His lips teased the curl of her ear as she snuggled against him, awash with languid contentment.

"Has anyone ever told you you have beautiful ears?" His warm breath rustled the wisps of hair that caressed her cheek.

Hope giggled, intentionally wiggling beneath him. "Nope. You're the first."

"You keep moving like that and we may never leave this

room," he warned with a throaty growl.

His breath caught as he slipped from her warmth, rolled to the floor on his back, and scooped her pliant body against him. His warm palm covering the hand that splayed his chest. Glancing down, his eyelids thickened when his gaze lit on her lips, still swollen and pink from his kisses. His hand slipped up her arm, over her shoulder. Hope shivered with desire, and a husky groan rumbled in his throat as his fingers buried themselves deep in the silky softness of her hair.

"Why, Ah do declare, Mistah Fraziah," she whispered against his shoulder, "you're insatiable!"

Drake pulled her hard against him, a devilish twinkle lighting his eyes. "The price you pay for keeping me waiting six weeks."

"Ah, well, I don't ever want it said I don't pay what I owe," she replied with mock seriousness. "Eventually."

Her fingers tickled the hair curling over his chest. She found and teased a small, rosy nub to erection. Batting her thick, ebony lashes for effect, she sent him a crookedly suggestive grin. "Besides," she lowered her head and coaxed the tiny nipple with her tongue, "I find I rather like this room. I think I could live here quite happily."

Drake chuckled. "Now who's 'insatiable'?" he mimicked. A shudder ran through him as her hand slipped down the tautness of his stomach. He grabbed her wrist and plopped it back on his chest before he lost all control. "I'm warning you, sunshine, if you keep playing with fire, be prepared to get burned."

A flicker of emotion sparkled in her eyes, but was quickly doused. Drake cursed himself for all kinds of a fool and wished he could bite the thoughtless words back.

Hope stiffened and pulled away. Drake had no alternative but to let her go.

"Hope, I'm sorry, I didn't mean—" He reached for her, but she rolled away too fast.

"It's alright!" Stooping, she withdrew her chemise from the bottom of the wrinkled pile of clothes and slipped it over her head with trembling fingers.

"But —"

"I don't want to talk about it," she replied through gritted teeth. Woodenly, she walked toward the bed and climbed beneath the covers.

She heard Drake's muffled footsteps approach the bed, but she scrunched her eyes closed and refused to open them. The comforter was tightly clutched beneath her chin.

Drake tried everything he could think of to get her to talk. Nothing worked. The only word she would utter was "Leave," and even then, only once.

Eventually, he gave up. Not knowing what else to do, he retrieved his clothes, yanked them on, and left. Hope caught a brief glimpse of the rumpled shirttail hanging to mid-thigh and the polished shoes dangling from his fingers as he gave her a final glance, then closed the door quietly behind him.

She stared at the door for what seemed like hours.

Damn him! she swore. *Damn Drake Frazier for taking something so wonderful and turning it so sour!*

Chapter Eighteen

Drake spent the rest of the night—the early hours of the morning, actually—closeted in the study, pouring over files, reports, accounts, anything he could get his hands on. At seven o'clock, he'd stumbled on the copy of a sealed bid Charles had submitted to buy the lease to City Wharf— Boston's largest and most lucrative block of wharves on the north shore. The wharves would be a definite boost to the floundering business. The problem was, Charles would have a great deal of trouble pulling the venture off without sufficient funds to cover the inevitable expenses. His bankbook was already depleted.

About nine o'clock, less than an hour ago, Drake found an even more incriminating piece of evidence.

The desktop was scattered with discarded files and crumpled papers. Drake ignored the mess as he leaned back in his grandfather's favorite red leather chair. His tired, bloodshot eyes flickered between the two rumpled sheets of paper he held in each hands. The more he looked, the angrier he became.

The Bradfield-Stillwell Home, one declared in bold, black script. Beneath were paragraphs of information regarding a home for wayward boys that handled only the most dire of cases. It was followed by a brief plea for funds to keep it in operation. The other, titled the same and written in the same crisp hand, had two long columns, one, names, the other, figures. The names were easily recognizable. Beecher, Lowell, Webster, Quincy, Frazier — none of Boston's more prominent citizens was omitted. Scribbled beside each name was a dollar amount. The total at the bottom of that column was staggering.

"The fool!" Drake crunched the papers in his fist and slammed them on the desk. The glass mantel clock, ticking rhythmically atop the flat mahogany surface, rattled with the force of the blow. He should have known Charles was capable of using a fictitious charity to draw much needed money. Should have, but didn't. In his wildest dreams, he had never imagined his brother would stoop so low.

He waited for what seemed like hours, until his anger faded to a dull throb, then pushed himself from the chair and moved toward the door with purposeful strides. Once there, he slipped a key from the pocket of his denims and unlocked the door.

It was as he was returning the key to his pocket that his fingers reacted to the silky key ring. Looking down, he saw the lock of chestnut hair he'd stolen from Hope the day of the fight with Larzdon. The dark strands were worked into a fine plait, the reddish highlights glistening like molten copper in the morning sunshine. Absently, he ran his fingers over the braid, his thoughts drifting to the woman upstairs.

Sooner or later he was going to have to do something about Hope Bennett. What, and when, was another question. One that demanded contemplation.

Drake scowled darkly. He'd delayed her leaving by buying her services as his wife. The job was unnecessary. He could just as easily have ruined his brother and sister-in-law without Hope's help. But when it had come time to send her on her way to Virginia, Drake found he couldn't do it. He didn't stop to ask himself why, or question his motives, he'd simply invented a need for a temporary wife. To his surprise, she'd agreed.

At the time, Drake had told himself that his reasons were completely chivalrous, motives his grandfather would have been proud of. Now he wasn't so sure. True, he couldn't bear the thought of Hope making the last leg of the journey alone, but if he was honest with himself, he would also have to admit that his reasons were much more than mere concern. After all, he could easily have put her on the next stage for Virginia the second they'd reached civilization.

But he hadn't. He'd offered her a job and dragged her, not totally unwillingly, back to this godforsaken place.

Why?

The answer hit him like a fist smashing into his gut, and he staggered with the blow. He leaned heavily against the door, his eyes flickering shut as his thoughts were barraged with unbidden memories.

Hope, drunker than a river rat as she collapsed in his arms, awarding Drake his first real look at her enticing curves and innocent profile. Hope, her face draining of color when Oren Larzdon's knife had sliced toward his shoulder. Hope, her hair a tousled mass of chestnut curls upon a bed of sawdust. Hope, her skin moist with the water he'd sponged on her perfect body while she raged with fever. And, at last, Hope, as he had left her, curled and despondent in the large bed that had once belonged to his grandmother.

When did I fall in love with her? he wondered as his fingers crushed the lock of hair in his fist. He remembered her dark eyes flashing with fire that first night in his hotel room. He'd denied the feeling for months, but his love had started then, and had grown over the weeks that followed.

"As always, Frazier, your timing is poor," he mumbled to himself, running the lock of hair against his stubbled cheek. It smelled of dirt and the leather strap that held it tight, but it felt like heaven as it stroked his flesh.

His heart tightened when he realized he couldn't confess

his feelings to Hope and still pretend to be obsessed with Angelique. Once the words were spoken, he'd be lost, and too many years of hard work counted on him being able to convince Angelique he wanted her back. Unfortunately, recognizing his feelings for Hope now would only complicate matters. But it was already too late for that, wasn't it?

There was only one solution.

With a ragged sigh, he shoved the key back in his pocket and stalked to the desk. He snatched up the two bits of crumpled paper as well as the bid, folded them over twice, and stuffed them in his vest pocket. Although he'd planned to prolong Charles's suffering for as long as possible, suddenly that prospect held no appeal. There was no telling how long he could keep Hope waiting before she grew tired of the game and moved on. He couldn't let that happen!

No, his former plan would have to be abruptly revised. He *would* ruin Charles, he'd worked too hard not to, but he'd do it as quickly as he could and take time to savor the victory later. Then, as soon as he was free . . .

He didn't permit himself to complete that thought as he stormed from the room and into the hall. The door was slammed closed behind him and locked. Turning on his heel, he was surprised to find the hall empty.

A scowl furrowed his golden brow. He hadn't expected his brother to give up so easily. Three times Charles had come to the study door, banging and demanding entrance, all the while shouting accusations that Drake had stolen his key. Of course, he was right. Each time he'd shown up, Drake had sent him away. Now, he'd half expected to find his brother camping at the foot of the stairs, pouting the way he had as a child when their grandfather insisted the two boys go out on the *Mary Elizabeth*.

"Damn him!" Drake muttered as he stalked down the hall. He'd see the generous donations returned to their benefactors if it was the last thing he ever did!

Hope eyed Drake cautiously as she slipped a spoonful of oyster stew into her mouth. The oysters were soft and succulent, the potatoes firm, but the spicy concoction might have been made of sand for all she tasted of it.

All day she had been avoiding Drake; an easy task, since he'd been locked in the study all morning and gone most of the afternoon. This, she'd heard from the servants who'd brought her morning and afternoon meals on a tray, as she helped herself to the leather-bound books she found in the library.

On the best of days, Dickens could hold her interest like no other. Today she might as well have been reading a two-bit western. When she thought of it now, Hope couldn't recall if she'd read *A Christmas Carol* or *Oliver Twist*, and she didn't care. Right now about the only thing that interested her was the way Angelique insisted on pressing intimately against Drake's upper arm as he reluctantly recounted some of his tamer adventures in California.

Charles sat at the head of the table glowering. He made no attempt to eat, instead contenting himself on glaring at his brother with an angry, sullen stare as he drank glass after glass of brandy.

And what the hell had gotten into Drake!? All evening he had commented on the wonderful hard rolls, so much like his great-grandmother Bradfield's. Then he'd praised the spices in the stew as exactly the ones his great-grandmother Stillwell would have used. Over and over the two names were bandied about.

Never in all the time she had known Drake had Hope heard these two women mentioned. At first she'd taken his observations as idle chatter used to fill the awkward pauses. Then she'd glanced at Charles. He seemed to pick up on the insinuations — if, indeed, there were any — immediately, and his expression grew more grim with each mention.

"You bluffed?" Angelique gasped with false astonishment.

303

"Why, how clever. I would never have thought to do such a thing."

Drake repressed a surge of disgust and smiled down on her. "Then we should play poker sometime, you and I. It would make an interesting game."

Angelique batted her thick lashes and Hope's grip tightened on the spoon as it clattered to her bowl. "You'd have to teach me, of course." Again, the lashes batted as she smiled coyly. "And, I warn you, it may take a good deal of time. Charles says I am a slow learner, that I have no gift for cards. Isn't that right, dear?"

Charles grunted in reply and looked down at his untouched bowl. His gaze was steamier than the hot stew.

Angelique fixed her attention on Hope. "Do you play?" she asked, then just as quickly answered her own question. "Why, of course you do. I don't know what made me ask. After all, you did live in California, didn't you?"

She stressed the words in such a way that Hope could feel her spine bristle. In spite of herself, she fixed the woman with an innocent glance. "Of course," she said with a wave of her spoon. "It's a state law. Anyone crossing the Nevada border must know how to play a good hand of poker. They won't let you enter California otherwise."

"Isn't that interesting?" Angelique replied, apparently oblivious to the sarcasm of Hope's words. "So tell me," she continued, dismissing Hope as she turned her attention back to Drake, "what else did you do in the West? Surely you did *something* besides playing cards." Her eyes sparkled with a sadistic twinkle that was belatedly concealed. "Did you get into many gunfights? Or fistfights? Did you ever kill a man? Or two? Or three?"

"I was known as a hired gun, for a while," he admitted reluctantly. His gaze locked with Hope's and there was an emotion shimmering in the green depths, unreadable as it was undeniable. "I think we'll skip over that part of my life. It's not a dinner table topic, and I don't want to upset you."

Angelique pouted prettily, but still Drake refused. She gave up quickly, launching into a soliloquy of the people who had attended last night's ball.

Hope recognized none of the names flung so casually about, but inferred, by Angelique's awe-inspired tone, that they belonged to people of prominence. She averted her gaze to the rapidly cooling oyster stew. The silver spoon hesitated beside the bowl. She had suddenly lost her appetite.

"Mutton?" Charles came out of his self-enforced silence to offer Hope the tray piled high with lean meat.

Although her stomach rebelled at the thought, she thanked him and accepted the platter with a wooden smile. Moving the bowl, which was quickly whisked away by a servant, she placed only one succulent slab on her plate. It was one more than she wanted. Passing the tray to Angelique, she resisted the temptation to tip the juicy contents into the other woman's lap.

"Mutton?" she stiffly repeated the offer, holding the heavy platter out until the muscles in her forearm screamed in protest. She had to offer three times before the woman reluctantly acknowledged her, and even then it was with a sigh of impatience.

With a look bordering on disgust, Angelique took the tray. She stabbed several pieces of the aromatic meat for herself, then chose only the most tender slices to ease onto Drake's plate.

He showed no obvious protest at the overly courteous gesture, and the fact that he hadn't galled Hope all the more. Politely, she declined the bowl of mashed sweet potatoes as well as the tender boiled onions. Normally, the small, sweet onions were a favorite she'd longed for in the secluded gold mines of Thirsty Gulch. Today, she had no taste for them.

I have to get out of here! she thought desperately as she watched Angelique rub against Drake for what had to be the fiftieth time this hour. Although she couldn't stand the woman's blatant manipulation, it was Drake's apparent immunity to it that bothered her more.

Hope decided she couldn't sit idly by and watch Angelique use Drake, then cast him aside again — as, she suspected, was the woman's intent. The first time had almost destroyed him. She might not have known him immediately after his affair with Angelique, but she had seen the result of it. She didn't want to see what a second disappointment would do to her proud, arrogant gunslinger.

It will break him, she thought, *and break me right along with him*.

If there was one thing Hope knew she could not stand, it was more heartbreak. Losing her family to the fire had been bad enough. This on top of it would destroy her. Deep down, she suspected the reason why, but she'd be damned if she'd admit it, to herself or anyone else!

With an aggravated sigh, she lifted the bright orange dinner napkin from her lap, folded it, then placed it beside her plate. She stood with such force that only luck kept the delicate chair from crashing to the floor.

"Leaving? So soon?" Angelique purred, a glint of victory glistening in her cat-like eyes as she affixed her arm to Drake's elbow.

"Stay," Charles insisted with a wave of his hand. "If the food isn't to your taste, you can at least join us in an after-dinner brandy."

Hope shuddered. The last time she had tasted liquor she had collapsed, drunk, in Drake Frazier's arms. It had been the biggest mistake of her life.

"No," she said, patiently but firmly. "I'm tired, I have a headache, and I didn't get much sleep last night. I think I'll retire early." It was a lie, but a forgivable one. The last thing she intended to do was "retire," early or otherwise. But there was no good reason *they* had to know that. She stifled a yawn with the back of her hand for effect. "If you'll excuse me . . ."

"Why of course," Angelique purred. She patted Drake's arm and sent him a knowing smile. "She does so need her beauty rest, you know."

Hope thought that if Drake leapt to her defense, she might just stay for that brandy after all. He didn't. Instead he laughed as though the slut had made the most humorous comment he'd ever heard in his life. Hope fumed, caught between anger and betrayal. She hid her churning emotions behind the fists clenched tightly in the pockets of the worn trousers that she refused to trade in for one of Angelique's cast-off dresses. Holding her head high, she swept from the room with as much dignity as the situation — and her ragged attire — would allow. It wasn't until she reached the hall that she felt the sting of tears in her eyes.

She blotted the hated moistness away as she placed her foot on the first carpeted stair. The hand that wrapped suddenly around her arm prevented further progress. Angrily, she spun on her heel, pooling all her hostility into the palm that slapped Drake Frazier's arrogant cheek.

His head snapped back with the blow, but no recrimination glimmered in his eyes. "I guess I deserved that," he said, his hand straying up to the handprint that stood out in scarlet against his sunkissed cheek. "After last night, I wouldn't blame you if you shot me in my sleep." His eyes darkened. "I'm sorry about what I said, Hope. I didn't mean it the way it sounded."

Her lips thinned, her gaze narrowed. "I told you I didn't want to talk about that!" She tried to pull away, but his grip was too tight.

"You'll damn well have to talk about it sometime," he growled, annoyed with her stubbornness. "You can't go around with these feelings bottled up inside you for the rest of your life. One day, you're going to have to let them out. If you don't, they'll destroy you."

"You're a fine one to talk! What about the feelings you've

307

harbored for your brother all these years? Or don't they count?"

He let her arm go, positive she was too angry to flee. Crossing his arms over his chest, he scowled at her angrily. "Oh, they count all right, but the situation is completely different. At least I'm doing something with Charles. And what are you doing, sunshine? You wallow in self-pity over the family you can never have back instead of just dealing with their deaths. You push away anyone who tries to get close. You run in fear every time someone strikes a match without telling you! That's one hell of a way to live, if you ask me."

"No one asked you!"

She spun on her heel, determined to mount the stairs. Again, Drake's hand prevented her. She fixed the strong fingers with a look of utter contempt, which seemed to have no effect on Drake as he abruptly whirled her back around.

"You're getting my advice anyway, like it or not."

She swallowed hard. His face was so close she could see each golden whisker on his sun-kissed jaw. A shiver rippled up her spine as she remembered the scratchy feel of them beneath her palm. She forced the thought away.

"Go ahead," she prompted. "You're so damned fired up to have your say that I don't think anything I could say would stop you. So say it. Get it over with."

"All right," he growled, his grip loosening enough for the circulation to return to her fingers. "I want to know what the hell happened to the spitfire that burst into my hotel room, drunker than a skunk, desperate to find someone — anyone — who would fight in her brother's place. What happened to the girl who was willing to do just about anything to save her precious brother's life? And don't tell me she's standing in front of me now, because I'll be the first one to call you a damn liar."

She flinched when his grip turned hard, his gaze dark and unyielding. "That girl died in Thirsty Gulch, Frazier," she whispered hoarsely. "She found out what it was like to lose everything she ever had and she grew bitter. You'd better get used to me as I am now, because she won't be back."

Drake dropped his hands and stepped away, shaking his head in disgust. "Pity," he said through clenched teeth, "because that's one thing I'll never get used to."

Turning on his heel, he stalked away.

His bootheels clomped over the finely polished floor long after his broad back had disappeared from view. Only when she was sure he was gone did Hope let her shoulders slump in weary defeat. She clutched the mahogany banister, her eyes misting over in tears she refused to shed.

No, she thought. *I won't cry. I won't give the bastard the satisfaction of knowing his words upset me so much.*

She dashed the moistness from her eyes. Again, she realized just how desperately she needed to leave this place. She couldn't tolerate Drake's pursuit of Angelique for another minute, and if forced to endure another confrontation like this one, she would lose what little control she still had.

Hope ran for the front door and threw it wide. Her gait was not unlike a woman running from a collapsing building. She didn't know where she was going as she stepped into the cold, dark night and she didn't care. Anywhere had to be better than here!

Chapter Nineteen

Angelique's black wool coat hung from Hope's shoulders and her head was concealed beneath the generous folds of the hood. She looked about the wharf in confusion. Stretching out before her was a profusion of masts, spars, and crisp white canvas. Merchants hustled in all directions, clogging the wide street — Commercial Street, she thought — which seemed to be a dock in itself.

Salt spray kissed her cheeks and neck, scenting the air with a pungent aroma as it mixed with the tang of citrus, figs, raisins, and the constant odor of fish.

Except for a few odd glances, her presence went unnoticed. And why not? The variety of people milling about this seaswept place were as varied as the people cloistered safely in their grand homes on the hill. Hope would have blended with them even if she'd left the black cloak at home.

No, she quickly corrected herself. Any woman visiting the docks at this hour of the night, decked out in faded trousers and a flannel, was begging for trouble. At least, that's the way the merchants would see it.

Hope sighed in frustration. She'd bolted from the house so quickly that she'd given no thought to what she would do once she reached the waterfront. She was lucky common sense had overrun her when it had. Having reached the stables, panting and breathless, she'd realized that, no matter what her destination, she would need money to get her there. Stealthily, she'd returned to the house, picked the lock on the study door, and, almost childishly quickly, located the drawer containing the safe. The lock there was convinced to open as easily as the one on the door. She had taken only as much money as she thought she would need, appeasing her guilt by telling herself the total was less than what Drake owed her for services rendered, then followed her nose to the docks.

Now she stood stupidly, the salt breeze tossing the cape around her ankles as she wondered what to do next. Her father had purchased the tickets that carried them to the gold mines, so she didn't even know how to go about doing that! And even if she could find someone to sell her a ticket, how would she know which ship to board? The wharves stretched on both sides for what seemed like miles. One ship, though splendid to look at, looked very much like the next, and the next. The names of each, painted beneath the jutting figurehead on the bows, were indecipherable in the pale silver moonlight.

"I won't give up," Hope muttered to herself. In that split second, she felt a surge of self-confidence to rival any she'd felt before the fire in Thirsty Gulch. As quickly as it had come, it was gone. With determined steps, she moved closer to the activity on the docks. She was jostled rudely, and the toe of her boot was trod on twice, but she made it.

"Excuse me," she said to a muscular laborer. The tendons on his bare forearms were rigid as he lowered a heavy crate of lemons onto the planks. He smelled of fish and other things Hope didn't want to know the origin of. The crate dropped to his feet with a loud thud, rattling the shorn timbers beneath her boots. "I—um—I was wondering if you could help me."

"Wi' what?" he demanded briskly. He looked up from his chore, obviously annoyed. He was a dark-haired man with a Scottish brogue, piercing blue eyes, and a crisp, no-

nonsense manner.

"I need to buy passage to Virginia. I was hoping you could help me."

"Ha!" He set his meaty fists on his even meatier hips and glared at her as though she'd just turned into a mermaid. "I load cargo, I unload cargo. I do no' sell tickets."

He turned back to his job, but Hope was nothing if not persistent. Shuffling her feet, she tried again. "I really hate to bother you, but it's important." She rushed to add, "Not that what you're doing isn't, it's just that—"

"Yew are no' gonna leave me alone till I help yew, are yew, lass?" he asked with more insight than Hope would have given him credit for.

She smiled weakly, a gesture that softened the determined timbre of her voice. "No." Taking a deep, steadying breath, she added, "You're the only man around here who looks like he could understand English, let alone speak it. I really wouldn't have bothered you if it weren't important."

"O'Roark!" a voice boomed over the soft sound of slapping waves, emanating from the ship secured at the wharf. "I pay you to work, not talk. Get a move on!"

The one named O'Roark turned toward the ship. Although she could see no one on board who might have uttered the command, O'Roark obviously did. He nodded briskly then turned to Hope.

"We carry cargo, no' people." He nodded to the northern end of the wharf. "Try Lewis Wharf. The wharfinger thar migh' be able tae help yew. Ask fer Davis—and *do no'* tell him who sent yew! It'd cost me me job."

Davis! It wasn't much, but it was a start.

Hope nodded quickly, thanked him profusely, then rushed away. She dodged an occasional groping hand and clumsy passersby. The salt breeze continuously caught at her hood as she rushed down the street. She didn't mind. At least while busy adjusting the coarse material she was spared having to think of what she would say to this "Davis"

312

when she found him.

As it turned out, what she said had little to do with the matter. Davis, a tall, middle-aged, brutish man, refused to listen to a word. He was busy, he said. Too busy to be catering to a flighty young woman looking for a ship. When she'd pressed, he'd briskly informed her that the only ship leaving for Virginia any time that week was leaving Wednesday morning—tomorrow—at dawn, and that the passenger list for it was small and already full. Not even a hammock strung in the crew's quarters remained.

The whole time he had talked, the man's eyes had stayed glued with fascination to the masculine boots peeking out from beneath the cloak's hem. It was almost with relief that Hope parted company with the arrogant man. Almost. She still didn't have a ticket yet.

Deep in thought, she strolled to the dock's edge. She leaned her shoulder against a large, bared tree trunk sticking up from the planks and coiled with rope, and fixed her gaze on the moon as it danced on the rippling surface of the water. The sound of waves crashing and people talking echoed in her ears as she inhaled deeply of the rich salt air. This time when the hood blew back, freeing the cascade of chestnut waves, Hope didn't try to stop it. She was surprised to find that she actually liked the feel of the sea breeze rustling through her hair, grazing her cheeks and making them sting.

"So, you're heading for Virginia?" a worn, cracking voice asked from behind.

Hope gasped and spun around. Barely two feet away stood a woman, her shoulders thick and hunched, her slight form completely enveloped in midnight black. Her lips were so thin it appeared at first glance, that she had none. Her face had more wrinkles than a slept-in cotton shirt. Only her eyes—sharp and clear with the wisdom of age—revealed the feisty spirit locked inside her ancient body.

The woman leaned heavily on her unadorned cane as her

313

shrewd green gaze raked Hope from head to toe. "Heard you talking to Davis," she said, as though the brief explanation meant she hadn't really been eavesdropping. Like her eyes, her voice was crisp and direct. "The ship's all booked."

Hope hesitated. She would have backed up a step, to put some distance between herself and the gray-haired old woman, but the mooring post wouldn't allow retreat. The woman seemed to be waiting expectantly for Hope to say something, but since she wasn't exactly sure what, she said nothing.

"Hmph!" the old woman snorted, her wrinkled nose creasing still more. She waved a crooked hand at Hope, her gaze shimmering with confusion and not a little disappointment. "Bah! Thought I could help you, dearie, but if you can't talk, I'll guess I was wrong."

Help her? What could this crooked old woman do to help her? Hope wasn't sure, but she intended to find out. What the hell, it wasn't as though she had any other options at that point. "Davis did say the ship was booked," she ventured, still leery. "Why? Do you know where I could buy a ticket?"

"Heavens no." The old woman chuckled, a high, cackling sound, and Hope wondered what she'd said that had struck her so funny. "I do know where you'll find an extra bed, though." The watery eyes grew suddenly serious. "If you're interested, that is."

Interested? Right now she was obsessed with the idea of ridding herself of Boston once and for all, losing herself once again in the rolling foothills of Virginia. Only there, at home, could she ever hope to forget her time with Drake Frazier.

On instinct, Hope threw caution to the wind. After all, this was her chance—it might not come around again. "Yes," she said, her voice breathless with excitement, "I'm very interested, Mrs. —"

The woman's eyes twinkled with satisfaction as she leaned

heavily on her cane. "Bentley," she huffed, as though the explanation had been perfected years ago, and was purposely sarcastic. "First name, not last. No Mrs! You can ask me about that later. For now you can call me Bentley."

"Bentley." Hope nodded, testing the name. Unusual though it was, it fit the crooked old woman to a T.

The flesh that should have been lips pursed as she glanced at Hope's feet, and the bare planks. "Got any bags?"

Hope shook her head.

"Didn't think so." One corner of the nonexistent mouth lifted with distaste. "You don't snore, do you? I like company, but I don't like snoring."

"Company?" she gulped. So much for a quiet, secluded cabin to herself! Had she really thought the old woman intended to sell her a ticket? Only now did she realize how foolish that idea had been. "You mean I'd be sharing a cabin with—"

"Me," the old woman huffed. "Of course. Who else would you be sharing it with?"

"I don't know, I hadn't thought about it." Hope paused, a scowl furrowing her brow as she met the watery gaze. "Why are you offering to let me share your cabin?" she asked, suddenly suspicious. Didn't she have every right to be? It wasn't every day that a stranger offered her a favor for no apparent reason. Logic told her that a bit of caution was definitely in order. "I don't mean to sound ungrateful, understand, but your generosity is out of place. Everyone else I talked to looked at me like I had two heads. They weren't willing to help me, so I guess it's only normal that I'm wondering why you are."

"I respect honesty," she said dryly, "in small doses. Do try to keep it to yourself, though, dearie." The spot above her chin cracked into a smile. The expression, not overly sincere, set a whole new variety of wrinkles to crinkle her liver-spotted face. In a way, she reminded Hope of Old Joe. A pang of remorse stabbed at her heart with the unbidden comparison.

"I still want to know why you offered to share your cabin," Hope insisted when the woman again started to hobble away.

She turned back, her cane tapping on the weathered planks. "I already told you," she answered impatiently from over a hunched shoulder, "I like company. I've got a stateroom for two, and now there's only me to sleep in it. You need to get to Virginia, exactly where I'm heading." She scowled, and for a second Hope lost sight of her eyes amidst the wrinkles of sagging flesh. "You ask an awful lot of questions, dearie. Most would just thank me for my generosity and take the bed."

"I am thankful," she was quick to assure her. Now that a bed on the clipper was within grasp, Hope was reluctant to throw the opportunity away. She'd kowtow to the old woman if she had to, if it meant getting home.

It took only three steps to catch up to the slow, stooped form, and as Hope shortened her own strides to accommodate the older woman's hobble, she noticed that the top of the salt-gray head barely reached her shoulder.

The woman named, oddly enough, Bentley, had obviously noticed the difference as well. "Making 'em tall in Virginia nowadays," she quipped, with a devilish smile. She spared Hope only a passing glance as she maneuvered herself around a large crate of spicy smelling tea.

"I'm taller than most."

"And prettier." The observation was said with a frank sort of candor that made it neither compliment nor insult, just a statement of fact. "Could have used you twenty years ago when George put those dern cupboards in the kitchen. Six feet high, they stood—and me only five!" She cackled with the memory. "Never did use the top ones. Couldn't reach 'em!"

"Is George your husband?" Hope asked absently, slipping

a hand beneath the woman's bony arm as she helped her to step over a stray banana peel. A waft of the woman's faded rose scent engulfed her, bringing back bittersweet memories of her childhood and mother.

"One of 'em," she shrugged. She stopped long enough to hold up a hand. Four crooked fingers stood at proud attention from the base of painfully swollen knuckles. "George was the first. George was the best. The rest couldn't compare, although they tried like the dickens. You married, — er — ?"

"Hope."

"You hope what?"

She smiled despite her resolve to be cautious of this stranger. There was something about the crooked old woman that spurred easily compatibility. "Hope," she corrected. "First name, not last. No Mrs.! You can ask me about that whenever you like. But for now you can call me Hope." She smiled devilishly. "And no, to answer your question, I'm not married."

"Oh, Lordy, a woman with a tongue in her head, and who knows how to use it. Heaven help us." She sighed heavily, then ogled the girl head to toe. "Hope, huh?" she said, seeming to weigh the name on her dry tongue before nodding her head in approval. The brittle wisps of hair tumbling from her bun rustled in the salty breeze. "Not married, eh? Pity. Girl your age needs a man."

"I don't," she countered quickly, her voice sounding hollow even to her own ears. Lord, but she was sick of feeling so damn independent. Her lips automatically continued the well-rehearsed phrase. "I don't need anyone."

Again those sharp green eyes raked her, and this time there was a glint of speculation shining in their depths. "Everyone needs someone. It's human nature. No shame in it."

Hope didn't reply as they veered left from the docks, onto a warehouse-flanked side street. Instead, she eyed a group of well-dressed boys gathered around a lamp post. Their youthful laughter sang through the air as they playfully shoved each other around. The moonlight caught on the side of the bottle being passed. Hope tensed, waiting for a confrontation. The boys eyed the two women curiously as they approached, but, thankfully, left them alone.

The old woman seemed not to notice the disturbance, or, if she did notice, chose to ignore it. She hobbled along at the same rate, her gait as precarious as ever.

They walked down one narrow, twisting street after another, always staying close by the waterfront. Bentley glanced up. "Ah, finally," she sighed, pointing a crooked finger at the building to Hope's right. "End of the line, praise the Lord! Got a room here for the night. Where are you sleeping, Hope-who-doesn't-need-anyone?"

Hope's flicker of hesitation made the answer painfully obvious. She rushed to cover the slip. "I — I'm staying with friends in the city," she replied, nervously fixing her gaze on the toe of her boot. She hated lying to a woman who had been nothing but honest and direct — but she also hated the thought of accepting any more of the woman's charity.

"Didn't get to be my age without knowing how to lie and knowing when I'm being lied to," the crackling voice said. The green eyes sparkled shrewdly. "Looks like you need practice there, too. Don't worry, dearie, I'll teach you the ropes." Her crooked fingers gripped the brass doorknob and she looked back at Hope. "Well, come on, then. Wouldn't be able to sleep tonight wondering what happened to you. And I'd probably miss my boat in the morning looking for you, too."

"But I —"

"Bah! Swallow your pride for once, and move that cute little behind. Getting dern brisk out here, and I'm too old to be standing in the cold wind arguing. Keep me out, and it'll be your fault if my rheumatism starts acting up again. Can you live with that on your conscience?"

318

Yes, the woman *did* have a way about her. Reluctantly, Hope followed. She knew better than to protest such a blunt-mannered argument. And, in truth, she was too tired, too drained, to fight. She decided that, just one more time, she would accept Bentley's generosity — and pay her handsomely for it, as well as her passage to Virginia, come morning.

The masts of the clipper ship, *Witch of the Waves,* stood straight and proud against a crystal blue, cloudless sky. Glistening white sails caught the wind, billowing back and forth as though playing with each hearty gust. Her bow was ornamented with the carved figure of a woman in flowing white, the glowing eyes trained seaward. Gracing the stern was a witch floating in a sea shell, at the port, an imp riding a dolphin.

Fanciful figures, Hope thought as she leaned over the rail. The salty wind played with the loose chestnut waves as they floated to her waist in a waterfall of confusion. The black cloak whipped around her ankles.

Her seasickness had passed remarkably fast, considering how ill she'd been on the ill-fated trip to California. Her companion was not so lucky. As she had been for the last six days, Bentley was below decks, curled up on one of the beds in their stateroom. The poor woman suffered from seasickness worse than anyone Hope had ever seen. She lay awake at night, moaning at each groan of the planks, each splash of waves against the hull, as the ship rocked to and fro. More than once Hope had caught her cursing the great-nephew who'd insisted on such discomforts. For an old woman, her curses were imaginative!

Today, however, they had reason to celebrate. This morning Bentley had kept down half a bowl of broth and a sliver of dry bread. Also, the faded-rose color was finally beginning to return to her weathered cheeks.

She sighed, craning her neck and letting the crisp salt spray sting her cheeks. The old woman's bluntness had taken some getting used to, but she had adjusted quickly. In fact, she was finding she actually liked Bentley, sharp tongue and all. Right now, she was waiting patiently for her new friend above deck, ready to make good on her promise of a stroll in the mid-afternoon sunshine — Bentley's reward for finishing her breakfast.

Apparently, the other passengers had the same idea. Hope glanced up at the sound of footsteps and a throaty giggle.

A young couple strolled by, apparently immune to the inquisitive stares their passing elicited. No one talked to the Millers. No one had to. It was obvious from the way they clung to each other, murmured to each other, *looked* at each other, that the two were newly married. And, of course, the time they spent closeted in their stateroom spoke for itself.

She sent the pair a covetous glance as they disappeared through the doorway leading below. Although neither was striking alone, they made a handsome couple. Hope thought that it was the aura of love that seemed to surround them that made the pair so attractive, and so damned enviable.

"Still ogling those two?" Bentley asked as she hobbled over to Hope's side. "Don't see what's so dern interesting about 'em. Seen one young, lovey couple, you seen 'em all."

"I don't know," Hope replied thoughtfully. When the wind blew a thatch of chestnut hair in her eyes, she swiped it back. "It's just — oh, I don't know. I guess I've never seen two people so much in love before. I envy them." She looked at Bentley, confusion mirrored in her eyes. "Is that the kind of love you had with George?"

Bentley's sharp gaze softened as she looked out over the foamy whitecaps. The tumultuous bed of water matched the green eyes to perfection. "Maybe not the same, but dern close to it. But never mind an old lady, what about you?

320

You feel the same way about your man?"

"I never said I had a man," she replied cautiously, her back instinctively stiffening. In the last six days she had shared many secrets with Bentley, but *that* wasn't one of them. This was the third time in two days that the subject had been broached. So far, she had managed to avoid a direct answer. This time, however, she had a feeling Bentley wasn't going to back down.

"Didn't have to tell me. I know love when I see it sparkle in someone's eyes. I know pain when I see it there too. I see both in yours." She squinted at the bright sun, her eyes disappearing behind folds of flesh as she patted Hope's arm. "Might as well tell me about him, dearie. Got four more days on this godforsaken boat. It'd give us something to talk about."

"There's nothing to say," she replied tightly, pulling away from the suddenly insistent touch.

"Bah!" The old woman waved the argument away with a swipe of her crooked hand. "You never want to talk about anything but me. Don't think I've ever known a woman who talked so little! The only information I've gotten from you is what I've forcibly yanked through your teeth. And *don't* say you'd bore me," she snapped, taking the words out of Hope's mouth. "Boring is trying to stay awake at the Ladies' Guild, or," she held up a hand so that a wrinkled thumb and forefinger were only a thread apart, "stitching itty-bitty squares into a wall-sized quilt. *Men* are *never* boring. Besides," the green eyes twinkled with a mischief normally reserved for twelve-year-olds, "I love a love story. Start with his name."

Of course, she couldn't tell Bentley about what had happened between herself and Drake, no matter how badly she needed to talk. So, Hope changed the subject. Or, more correctly, she *tried*. "Speaking of names . . . you never did tell me where you got yours."

"And I'm not going to. Not now. We've got more important things to discuss." The bushy brows rose high in her crinkled forehead. "His name?"

"His name," Hope repeated with a sigh. "Ready for that stroll yet, Bentley?"

"No. I want his name. Unless you forgot it."

"I haven't forgotten," she replied defensively. She caught the slip, but it was too late. The old woman's eyes were shimmering with victory, and it was easy to see Bentley wasn't about to back down until Hope told her the whole sordid story.

Leaning her elbows atop the rail, Hope clasped her hands tightly together, and diverted her attention to the golden rays of sunlight dancing on the glassy surface of the water. *Sun-ripened gold,* she thought. *The exact shade of Drake's hair.*

"Aren't you tired, Bentley?" she said abruptly. "You've been sick, and you really do need your rest."

"Make up your mind, dearie. Do you want to run me ragged strolling the deck or do you want me to sleep? Can't do both at once."

Hope pursed her lips and refused to answer.

Bentley scowled, cleared her throat, tapped her cane, then said, "Aren't you curious to know why I'm going to Virginia? Would have thought you'd ask by now."

"Of course I'm curious."

"Then why didn't you ask?"

A blush kissed Hope's cheeks. The old woman chuckled merrily. She seemed to take great pleasure in shocking people, Hope thought. "I didn't want to be rude."

"Bah! Probably the southerner in you. Don't worry, you'll get over it. You'll learn soon enough that when you get to be my age, you can be as rude as the devil." She smiled sweetly, her wrinkled features lighting up with pleasure. "One of the nice things about being old. There aren't many—nice things, I mean—so I enjoy the ones I've got. So?" she huffed, adjusting her weight on the cane. "You going to ask me or am I going to have to be rude and tell

322

you?"

Hope responded like an obedient child. "All right, Bentley," she said, as she pulled a flickering strand of hair from her eyes. "Why are you going to Virginia?"

"To meet my great-nephew's intended. *Fiancée*," she mocked, the word sounding like a cuss on her tongue. "That's what he calls her, but where I come from, an intended's an intended."

"You're traveling all the way to Virginia to meet one woman? A stranger? It seems like a long way to go to meet someone. Why don't they come to you? After all, you're older and—"

"Feeble," the old woman supplied when Hope hesitated. "Got to learn to be more direct, dearie. If you mean feeble, say feeble. Now, where was I?" She tapped her cane as though to jog her memory and the tip clicked on the polished planks. "Oh, yes. I came from New York, only stopped in Boston—for all of three hours. I was planning to stay there, but my plans changed. It wasn't my idea to traipse to Virginia. Un-uh. But my great-nephew insisted. Said this was the woman of his dreams—don't they all?—and that I *had* to meet her. He also said she wanted nothing to do with him." She leaned toward Hope and whispered slyly, "He thinks I can talk some sense into her. I still haven't figured out why. What can an old lady like me say to change a young girl's mind?"

"I don't know, but your great-nephew sounds very persuasive," Hope muttered.

"Persuasive's his middle name, along with stubborn, arrogant, and dern mule-headed. Never met a young man as headstrong and determined as him."

"But you love him all the same," she teased.

"Course I do. I'm here, aren't I?" She paused, eying Hope appreciatively. "I should introduce you to him sometime. Together, you'd make quite the team. Like me and George. Can't say I'd mind having you in the family, either.

Fresh blood, especially *yours*, would do wonders for Cousin Judd's heart, and it'd give the Ladies' Guild something to talk about for weeks!"

"Please," she replied with forced lightness, "I'm not in the market for a husband. Although I'm sure your great-nephew is very nice, I—" *only want one man,* she finished to herself. A picture of Drake—his hair enticingly rumpled, an endearing, lopsided grin on his lips—flashed through her mind. With a deep breath, she pushed the thought away. The breathtaking image was stubborn, however, and it refused to go quickly.

Hope should have known better. Bentley wasn't fooled for a minute. Again, the cane tip-tapped on the deck. "Back to him again, are we? Didn't think it would take too long. His name wouldn't happen to be Drake, would it?" Hope's cheeks drained of color as she gripped the rail. Bentley just smiled. "Don't look at me like that, dearie, you talk in your sleep. And at the most ungodly hours. I may be old, but I'm certainly not deaf."

"What—um—what else did I say?" *Please, God, let her say "nothing"!*

"About Drake or the fire?"

Hope, in the process of swallowing hard, started to choke. Bentley gave a few clipped shots between her shoulder blades, stopping when Hope started to cough.

"I—*cough*—talked about—*cough, cough*—the fire? Damn! What else—*cough*—did I say?"

"Catch your breath, dearie, you're whiter than those sails up there. My, but they are high. Couldn't get me to climb that skimpy rope if you pointed a cannon at my ankles and swore you'd light it."

Hope caught her breath in record time. "What did I say, Bentley?" she gasped.

"Can't remember it all." She shook her gray head. "I'm old, don't forget. My memory's not what it used to be." She paused thoughtfully and the cane started to tap-tap-tap.

"Let's see. You talked about this Drake, *a lot*. Said he was blond. Said he was tanned. Said things a lady doesn't repeat — though I liked listening to them just fine, even if it was two o'clock in the morning."

"And the fire?" she pressed flatly. "What did I say about the fire?"

"Which one?"

"Oh, God."

The crooked fingers patted Hope's hand, loosening her fingers from their stranglehold on the sea-slickened teak rail. "It's not like you could hide it, Hope. That scar on your back is an open invitation for questions."

Hope leaned weakly against the rail, head down. She'd tried hard to keep her back away from Bentley's prying eyes. Obviously, not hard enough. "Is there anything you don't know about me?"

"Don't think so. Like I said, you talked a lot." She gave Hope's fingers a squeeze, then pulled back. "There's no harm in me knowing," she said in what, for Bentley, was a gentle tone. "The harm's in you keeping all those feelings bottled up inside you. Dern unhealthy, that is, and they won't stay there for long. They'll come out eventually — just when you thought they went away."

"I haven't bottled up anything." Hope wished her voice sounded more confident, less unsure. "I've dealt with the fire, the loss of — do you know about that, too?" Bentley nodded and Hope continued, "The loss of my family, and my scars."

Briefly, she explained about the two fires, her time in the gold mines, losing her family in Thirsty Gulch, her trek across the country, and, finally, about her "job" with Drake Frazier. She left out only the emotions that still rode hard between herself and the gunslinger, as well as the feverish nights they'd shared. She didn't doubt Bentley would piece that part of the puzzle together on her own, however.

"What about this Drake? You say you've dealt with

everything else, but have you dealt with losing him yet?"

Hope's gaze widened. "I didn't talk *that* much!"

"I know, I improvised," Bentley shrugged and she leaned a bony elbow on the rail. "Doesn't take a genius to know either you left him or he left you. Why else would you be on this ship, sleeping in *my* cabin? So who did the leaving?"

"I did. He's—" Hope hesitated. *Oh, what the hell, she knows about everything else.* "Drake's still in love with his former fiancée."

"He told you that?" the fleshless lips sneered. "I'll give him credit for honesty, but not a lick of it for intelligence."

"He didn't have to tell my anything," she sighed. "I have eyes. I could see quite clearly how they looked at each other. I saw the way they touched, the way they smiled. He's still in love with Angelique. Only a blind person couldn't see it. It—it hurt too much to watch them, so finally I left. I know I can forget about him, eventually. Once I'm home again, I'm sure I'll feel differently."

"Poppycock!"

"What?"

"You heard me. Poppycock! I don't believe a word of it." The green eyes narrowed accusingly. "As if the land under foot has a thing to do with the way a body feels! Bah! Things aren't that simple, Hope, though there are lots who wish they were."

"I *will* get over him," she defended tightly. Was she telling Bentley, or herself? Hope didn't want to know. "I just—I need time away, time to put my life into perspective. These last few years have been hard, with one thing happening right after another. I never really had the time to think about any of it." She gave a derisive little chuckle, turning her cheek up to the stinging breeze. "You know, sometimes I think that the only reason I was ever attracted to Drake Frazier in the first place was because he was something I couldn't have. He was a ruthless, arrogant, conceited, good-for-nothing gunslinger, and I was . . . well, let's just say

326

that at the time I was very well aware of the things I could and couldn't do. I guess I just decided to tempt fate."

"And you believe that?"

"Of course I do. It's the truth."

"The truth, as I see it, is that a body can do whatever a body sets its sights to do. You set your sights to run away, and that's exactly what you did. Very brave there, Hope."

"I didn't run away. I'm no coward." The brown eyes sparkled with anger. "I just recognized my weaknesses and I—I conceded to them."

The cane tapped the planks in a rhythm that matched the shaking gray head. As always, the brittle strands that loosened themselves from the bun at her nape whipped in the breeze. "Bah! You ran away, and I think you did it because your young man was trying to get close to you. And you don't want to get close—to him or anybody else." Hope opened her mouth to protest but Bentley cut her short. "Remember that night on the docks? Remember telling me you didn't need anyone? You were quite precise about it."

"Of course I remember, but I *saw* him with Angelique! It wasn't *me* Drake was trying to get closer to, it was—"

"Bah!" The cane lifted, and came down on the deck with a resounding crash. More than one eye drifted toward them curiously. "He saved you from an infection that would have killed you. He dragged you across the country, by his side. He even offered you a phony job to keep you close. Yup, sounds to me like he hates you, all right."

Hope's jaw tightened. "He saved my life because there was nobody else to do the job. He dragged me all the way across the country because he felt bad for me. And he gave me a 'job' to make Angelique jealous." Her balled-up fists were planted on her hips and her eyes sparkled with angry fire. "True love. Ain't it grand?!"

"Lordy, but you don't give your man credit for much! Did it ever occur to you that he didn't tell you the whole story?" she asked, so softly, and so casually, that the question took

Hope aback. "Maybe he had another reason you don't even know about yet. Ever think of that?"

No, Hope thought, *I never have. And I damn well won't waste my time thinking of it that way now!* She'd been over this situation a thousand times in her mind—day and night, backwards and forwards, inside and out—but the ending was always the same: Drake loved Angelique, and, as Charles had so gloatingly put it, there was nothing she could do to stop them.

"You know," the old woman said wistfully, "I miss George more than a tomcat misses his mate. And sometimes I think it wouldn't hurt so bad if I'd never met him. But when I start thinking that way, I start thinking about all the good times, all the chuckles, all the problems. Best years of my life, those were. Wouldn't trade them in for all the tea in Britain."

"That's different. George was your husband. You loved each other." What would it be like to be Drake Frazier's wife? Hope wondered fleetingly. She'd had a taste of it, a small one, and she thought that, if he offered her the kind of love Bentley had shared with George, she would be powerless to refuse it.

"It isn't different," the crackling voice scoffed. "You just see it that way now. Tell me something, dearie. If you could wake up tomorrow, brandspankin' new and an orphan from birth, would you do it? No, don't answer yet, I just want you to think about it. Can't miss a family you never had, can you? Course, you wouldn't have had the pleasure of having known these people, either. No birthday parties, no late night stories, no nothing. Remember, you gotta take the good with the bad," she added, studying Hope carefully. "Well? Would you do it?"

"That's ridiculous," she scoffed. "We're talking about my parents, my brother, my friend. Of course I knew them."

"Humor me," Bentley snapped, the cane beating the deck impatiently. "Pretend you didn't. Would you be so different today? Would you even be *here* today?"

Hope thought for a minute, then turned briskly away. The wind caught her cloak and made it flutter around her ankles. "I don't want to talk about this anymore." In fact, she hadn't wanted to talk about it in the first place.

Bentley caught her arm, reeling her back in. For a feeble old woman, she was strong.

"Well, you're gonna! Seems to me like you've shirked talking long enough. I'll tackle you to the deck and sit on you if I have to, but I want an answer. And while you're at it, think about how your parents would want you to feel."

"What do you mean?" She pulled away from the old woman's biting fingers, but she didn't give in to the temptation to flee.

"Think they'd want their daughter moping around all the time, pining away for 'em? Think they'd be proud of you running away from people for no good reason but that you're scared they'll hurt you? I could be wrong, but most parents I know want better for their kids. I think they'd want you to cut the self-pity and get on with the rest of your life."

"And Drake Frazier is 'the rest of my life'?" she asked skeptically.

"Could be. Way you're going, though, you'll never know."

Hope turned away, raising her cheeks to the tangy salt spray. "I'm scarred," she said suddenly. "You saw my back, you know." She didn't know why she said it, or why she'd said it to this particular person, but the words were off her tongue before she could stop them. Oddly enough, it felt good to voice the thoughts that constantly nagged at her.

"And I have a club foot," the old woman huffed. "So what? I had myself four good husbands, and I'm taking applications for the fifth. Men don't care about those things as much as we women like to think they do—but it does make a convenient excuse to think that way."

Hope shook her head. Her hand strayed inside the parted

329

cloak and she fingered the flannel, thinking of the man who had once worn it next to his flesh. "You don't understand. I couldn't saddle Drake. He's so handsome, so virile, and I'm . . . well, I couldn't even wear a dress that was cut low in back. And the smell of charred wood sends me into a fit of hysteria — although I'm much better with that now." She shook her head and the tangled chestnut mane fluttered at her back. "No, it wouldn't be fair to him. He deserves better."

"Fair?! Bah! You talking fair to him, or fair to you?"

"Both. I'd always feel like he stayed with me out of pity." Her dark eyes misted with unshed tears and she quickly dashed them away. "I hate pity. I've had enough of it to last a lifetime and I don't want anymore. Besides, he doesn't love me, he loves—"

"Her. Right. You go on telling yourself that for as long as you want. Eventually, you're bound to get as sick of hearing it as I am. Either that, or you'll start believing it." Bentley looked around the deck, smiling tightly at the captain as he sauntered past. "I'm tired. I'm going back to the room," she said finally. Patting Hope on the hand, she added, "Think about what I said, dearie. And when you do, remember that the price love asks might may be high, but there's a dern good reason most people are willing to pay it over and over again." Her eyes narrowed and quickly became lost in the folds of her wrinkled skin. "The ones who pay will know what they could've missed."

When Hope didn't reply, Bentley hobbled away. She could hear the clatter of the woman's cane as it click-clicked on the wooden stairs.

Is she right? Hope wondered, shifting her gaze back to the churning ocean. True, she wouldn't feel pain at her family's passing now if she hadn't know them, but just how much would she have missed if that were so? She couldn't imagine a childhood without Luke's gentle grin and boyish escapades. She couldn't imagine a night without her father's bedtime stories. Hell, she couldn't even imagine the state of California without a bulging-eyed Old Joe haunting it.

And what about Drake? Was it possible he had other motives for what he'd done? Motives he hadn't told her about? If nothing else, Bentley was right about one thing; he *had* gone to an extraordinary amount of trouble on her behalf. Once, briefly, he'd even confessed to feelings for her.

But he never said he loved you, she reminded herself.

You never said you loved him, either.

Never had the scar that marred her back obsessed her the way it did now. She thought of Drake's finger — warm and rough — running against the puckered flesh and a shiver of heat curled up on her spine. There had been no repulsion in that touch, only tenderness.

Had she misjudged her gunslinger? Would she ever really know?

"Who the hell do you think you're kidding, Hope Bennett," she muttered to herself, pushing the hair from her brow as she glanced up at the rigging. "It isn't your scars, it's death that frightens you. You're afraid that if you love Drake Frazier he's going to die just like everyone else you ever loved."

There was a crash of waves against the ship's hull. The impact of her words hit her as hard as if she had climbed over the rail and tossed herself into the icy ocean depths. My God, why hadn't she ever realized that before?

Hope pushed away from the rail, deciding to take that stroll after all. A little exercise would do her good. But even wandering the spray-slickened deck and drinking in the crisp salt air couldn't keep her thoughts from straying back to the old woman's words and her own realizations.

Chapter Twenty

The first fingers of dawn were slicing the sky when, six days later, the *Witch of the Waves* slipped into the mouth of the Chesapeake Bay. Slowly, it maneuvered past the bar, drawn like a giant magnet to the strips of water known as Hampton Roads.

Hope watched their progress from the clipper's bow. Her heart soared as she felt the ship rock with the sea's reaction to the bar. She had a hard time containing her excitement. Even knowing that Bentley's stomach was probably heaving with the constant motion of the ship couldn't put a damper on her suddenly high spirits.

Gripping the rail tightly, she took a deep gulp of the crisp salt air, intermingled with the pungent scent of the fish that were being hauled onto the many passing docks. Her eyes glistened as she watched each beloved landmark pass. Fort Monroe on the right, the Castle of the Rip Raps rising up on her left, and the lush, rolling hills edging the place where sky met land.

The docks in Virginia were tame in comparison to the ones she'd left back in Boston. The hustle and bustle was here, but it was on a smaller, more intimate scale. Sweaty merchants hollered across the wharves to each other, exchanging curses as well as jovial conversation. Children milled on the planks, some helping to unload the morning's catch while others darted here and there, perching on crates, or hiding in alleyways before distraught mothers were forced to angrily hunt them down.

It was warmer here, too. The grass was still green, the tips of each stalk browned from the beating sun that had baked it all summer. Even though they were well into the second week of December, no snow threatened in the sky the way it had the day she'd left Boston. That sort of weather wouldn't start for a while here, not until after January. Even then, the fluffy blanket of white rarely covered the ground for more than two or three days before melting away, much to the children's dismay.

The harsh cry of a fish hawk echoing from above caused her heart to quicken with familiarity. She cupped a hand over her eyes and looked up to see the glistening white underbelly of a bird as it swept through the air with ease. The broad brown wings were spread gracefully wide as it circled overhead, searching for its breakfast amongst the rippling waters.

Home! Hope thought with a deep sigh of relief. *I'm finally home!* The only thing that had ever felt this good was . . .

"No!" Her palm slapped the rail in irritation. "I'm not going to think about him now. I have too much to be happy about, and I'll be damned if Drake Frazier is going to ruin this, too!"

"Be tough to ruin things if he isn't here."

Hope whirled around to find Bentley standing barely two feet behind her. She was surprised the clatter of the old woman's cane hadn't given her presence away.

A hand fluttered to Hope's throat. "Bentley! I—I didn't hear you there." Was it her imagination, a trick of the light, or was her friend really smiling so sneakily? Her gaze narrowed. "I thought you'd still be in the stateroom."

"I was. Then I got to thinking." The green eyes twinkled devilishly in the glow of early morning sunshine. She leaned forward, her weight supported on her cane, and confided,

"John, my second, said I always got myself into trouble doing that, but I never listened. Still don't."

"Good for you." Hope grinned. "Men talk up a storm, but they aren't always right. Of course, they'd never admit it to us!"

The gray head nodded, the dry strands flickering in the breeze. Again, the sloppy bun at her nape had more hair out than in. "That's what I was thinking about. Men. One man in particular—your Drake, to be specific."

"He isn't mine, Bentley," she snapped. "And besides, I thought we dropped this subject days ago."

"You dropped it. I don't drop subjects, I just wait until they're ready to be discussed again." Her gaze drifted to the rolling countryside flanking the rails. "This time I don't have time to wait. The ship'll be docking soon, and we'll both be off. Probably never see each other again, although I wouldn't bet on it. Anyway, I wanted to ask you a favor."

"What kind of favor?"

"You never paid me for the room."

Hope scowled in confusion. "You said you didn't want my money."

"Still don't. I want a favor instead." The crooked, wrinkled hands reached out and clasped Hope's. The grip, although not tight, was insistent. "I want you to give your young man a chance. Go back to Boston, Hope. Ask him for the truth."

"Bentley, have you ever seen a fish hawk before? There's one up—"

"Hope?"

She tried to pull away, but Bentley refused to let her go. She relented with a sigh. "Why should I ask him? I already have the truth."

"Until he tells you himself, you can only suspect. You can't really *know*. Now, I don't believe for a minute that your young man would prefer a cunny-hunter like this Angelique over a nice girl like you." The green eyes narrowed shrewdly and the grip tightened. "Deep down, I don't think you do, either."

"I don't know what I believe anymore." Her voice was so soft it might have been made by the salty wind tugging at the sails. "You may be right, but I—I just don't know."

"Did you think about what I said?" Bentley prodded, causing Hope to nod. "And?"

"You're right," she said abruptly, swallowing hard. "After you left that day, I pictured what life would have been like without my family. It wasn't a pleasant thought, but it did make me see that, without them, I wouldn't be me. They taught me so much! I—" Her voice cracked and she looked away. With trembling fingers she wiped away the tears moistening her eyes and told herself she *would not cry*. She waited until her voice was stronger, then continued. "I miss them so much it hurts, especially Luke, but I *am* glad I had them. Even if the time was too short."

"It's always too short, love."

Bentley set the cane aside and spread her gaunt arms wide. Hope almost tumbled into them. Hunching down to accommodate the difference in height, she buried her face in a bony shoulder, scented with faded roses and the tang of salt spray. Hot tears twisted down her cheeks, soaking into the coarse wool of Bentley's cape as she surrendered to her sobs.

"There, there," Bentley soothed as she stroked the long back and arms, "it's all right. Now that you know how you feel, everything will be just fine. I'd stake my life on it."

Hope's voice was muffled against the coarse wool, her breathing ragged. "No . . . it won't. I ruined everything with Drake. He'll never . . . forgive me, or . . . find me. And I don't have . . . enough money to get back."

Bentley chuckled softly, careful not to let Hope see her mirth as she patted the young girl's head. "Don't you worry about that. Your young man sounds smart enough. He won't have a problem finding you." She frowned. "He does

335

know Virginia is your home, doesn't he?"

Hope nodded. Pulling away, she dried her eyes. "But I never told him *where* in Virginia. It's a big state, Bentley. He may never find me."

"So it takes him awhile." She shrugged, brushing a crooked hand over her tear-dampened shoulder. "In the meantime, you saved money sharing my room, so you should have enough saved to get you by until he comes."

"Yes," Hope sniffed. She was starting to slowly feel the tingle of excitement return. Her breath quickened. "Yes, I do. But what if he doesn't come? What if he *can't* find me? Oh God, what am I going to say to him if he *does*?!"

Bentley chuckled as she retrieved her cane from where she'd leaned it against the rail. "Never heard you ask so many questions, dearie, though I have to admit I like it. Nice change." She turned and started hobbling toward the companionway. "Well? don't just stand there, come along. We'll go below and you can help me pack while I answer 'em all — one at a time, if you please."

With a step that was lighter than it had been in months, if still a little cautious, Hope followed.

"Clairmont, you say?" Bentley asked Hope. Her voice quivered with each creak and jostle of the carriage. They'd been riding for what felt like hours, with no stop in sight. She sighed heavily. "Never heard of it, but — bah! why not? Clark, my third, used to say I had a nasty habit of seeing things through to the end. Hate like the dickens to disappoint him now." She reached across the aisle and patted Hope's knee. "I can't stay long, mind you. Got business to attend to. But I'll see you settled first."

Hope fluffed the cloak to conceal her trousers, an item she was beginning to look on as an essential part of her wardrobe. She'd pulled back the curtain at the window and was scanning the fields and houses as they passed.

"Your great-nephew's fiancée," she replied absently. "I didn't forget. Oh, Bentley, look!" she opened the curtain wider and pointed to a towering white mansion, set back from the dirt road and flanked with towering white oaks. "Frank and Hannah Marshall's place. Lord, it hasn't changed a bit! I used to play there when I was eight. Their oldest son, Jimmy, died when I was ten. He was thrown from a horse."

The memory of Tyrone Tubbs shot through her mind. Hope shivered and grew suddenly silent, her cheeks draining of color. *Things change,* she reminded herself as she sagged back against the cushions. And her experience with Tyrone Tubbs had, in some small, indiscernible way, helped to change her.

"Pull the curtain, dearie. You've pointed out every house on that side of the road for the last five miles and, to be blunt, this small town memorabilia is starting to wear thin."

"Sorry." She let the curtain flutter back into place, shrouding the small compartment in shadows, and sent the old woman an apologetic smile. "I'll give my tongue a rest."

Thank you! Bentley mouthed the word no less than twice. If she did it a third time, Hope didn't see her. She'd snuggled back against the cushions and closed her eyes.

She saw Drake, his rugged body wedged in the narrow aisle between her makeshift bed in the rickety old wagon and the potato sack. The lamplight played on his golden head, accentuating the dark circles of exhaustion smudged beneath his sea-green eyes.

Hope squirmed against the seat's plump back. He'd slept on the floor because he was afraid to hurt her. Why hadn't she realized his motive then? Why now, when it was too late?

I thought I'd lost you, sunshine. I don't think I've ever been so scared in my life.

Drake's voice, husky with emotion, echoed in her ears. Her breath caught and she trembled at the feel of his strong arms enfolding her. A bolt of lightning illuminated the deserted way station, and she could see the desperation shimmering in those sea-green eyes.

Why hadn't she seen it then, when it mattered, when it was the only thing she ever really *wanted* to see?!

Hope tossed restlessly against the seat.

Surprised? Didn't you think I'd find you? I'll always find you, sunshine . . . Do you have the strength to stop it, even if you want to? God knows, I don't.

Her heart tightened when she remembered the feel of calloused palms searing her flesh as the cool morning breeze washed over her body. Her lips still tingled with the memory of his kisses, and her blood steamed with awareness when she recalled in vivid detail the heady sensations that Drake Frazier had awakened in her.

The thought of living with only rapturous memories to fill the void Drake had created consumed her with emptiness. She didn't want memories, she wanted the man who had created them. She wanted to go to bed at night enfolded in his warm embrace, and to wake up in the morning clinging to his side. She wanted to bear his children, and to watch them grow.

Oh, God, what's wrong with me? Why can't I think any further than that sun-golden gunslinger?

"I love him!" Her eyelids snapped open with sudden realization. She didn't realize she'd said the words out loud, and with such force, until she saw Bentley's contented smile from the adjacent seat.

"I know that," the old woman scoffed. "I was wondering how long it'd take you to realize it. And he loves you, too. Just wait, you'll see that I'm right."

Hope gripped her fingers tightly in her lap. Her eyes shimmered with confusion, though her voice was steeled with determination. "It doesn't matter whether he does or not. I won't sit around and wait for him to come to his senses. I'm going to visit Lake's Edge and see what I can do about getting it back, then I'm catching the first ship back to Boston. I don't care if I have to steal the money to book passage, I'm going." Her chin rose proudly. "I'll find Drake Frazier and I'll *make* him love me!"

"Shouldn't be too hard," Bentley mumbled with a satisfied nod. She grinned slyly as her crooked fingers reached into the tapestry bag next to her thigh and pulled out a strip of snow-white knitting. She plopped it in her lap, and the ball of yard toppled to the jostling carriage floor. "Nope, not hard at all."

Hope walked alone down the narrow dirt path, her feet guiding her as her mind wandered. The air was heavily scented with the fragrance of wildflowers. Leaves rustled in the ceiling of branches above.

It had been a long time since she'd seen Lake's Edge. Much had changed in the years she'd spent traipsing with her family through the California gold mines. She ducked beneath a low-hanging branch before it could slap her cheek, as she remembered her first sight of her childhood home. She wasn't exactly sure what she'd expected, but it wasn't what she'd found.

The grass had grown in thick over the spot where the house had once stood. She hadn't been prepared for that. She'd wanted a shrine, something—*anything*—to mark the horrendous event that had passed there. There was nothing, only tall, lank weeds and grass. The last time she had seen the spot, the crisp green stalks had been seared charcoal black. Burned timbers had crisscrossed the burnt grass, along with a variety of scattered debris. Now even the bricks were gone—stolen by scavengers.

There was nothing there but open land, nothing to show where the house had once stood. Who had cleared away the rubble was anybody's guess. Hope assumed it had been the new owners.

Her heart tightened. That was something else she hadn't expected: new owners. Her father had never given any indication that the land was going to be sold. He'd always assured her they'd find the money to pay the taxes before that happened.

Unfortunately, things hadn't worked out that way. Her foolish dream that Lake's Edge would always be her home, that no one else would buy the precious land, was shattered the moment she'd stepped from the carriage with Bentley at her side. She'd been wrong, dead wrong. Not only had the land been purchased, the skeletal frame of a new house was in construction on top of the bluff, overlooking the fields already rich with the promise of a tobacco crop, and the glassy surface of the lake.

Hope sighed dejectedly as she rounded a bend in the narrow path that wound up the side of a steep, lush green hill. Although it was out of view, she knew the tiny cemetery would still be waiting at the top. Some things never changed.

Now that the house and lands had been sold, she planned to spend only enough time here to visit the cemetery where her mother rested. Then she would accept Bentley's generous offer to accompany her back to Boston once the old woman's task in Virginia was done. Although she knew Bentley had no real need for a traveling companion, and that her offer was nothing more than charity, Hope was not in a position to refuse. Now that it was out of her power to reclaim Lake's Edge, there was nothing left for her in Clairmont.

She had left Bentley behind with the carriage, explaining her need to visit her mother's grave one last time before leaving Virginia behind. Bentley had not only understood, she had encouraged her.

"Might be the last chance you get," she said, nudging Hope on with a weathered hand between her shoulder blades. "Better take advantage of it while you can. Go on now, and don't waste your time worrying about me. I'll be just fine. Always am."

Hope was now halfway up the hill. Already she could see the tops of the cold, black-veined, marble tombstones. Her breath caught as she forced her feet on. It seemed like years since the last time she had traversed this twisting path, yet, at the same time, it seemed like only yesterday.

Her conflicting emotions grew with each footstep. By the time she had reached the top, her palms were sweaty and her heart was pounding from more than just exertion. She squinted into the bright afternoon sunshine as she lifted the black iron latch. The gate swung open by itself with a mournful creak and Hope stepped inside.

She didn't see him at first. The sun was directly opposite her and blindingly bright. He was between her and the sun, his large body silhouetted and unrecognizable. Except for the sketchy outline of his build, she could make out almost nothing of his features. He was tall, probably standing a head over her, and extremely large-boned. The slump-shouldered stance and curly head reminded her of Luke, and she could feel the sharp sting of tears in her eyes.

Damn! She hadn't cried much in the last three years, yet it seemed like tears flowed down her cheeks at the drop of a hat these days. It was to be expected, she reminded herself—and was quick to discover that, expected or not, she still despised the weakness. Taking a deep breath, she angrily wiped the hated tears away.

The hinges squeaked loudly as she closed the gate, causing the man to turn toward her. Hope ignored him, concentrating instead on putting one foot in front of the other. She'd planned on spending this time alone with her mother, and she couldn't help her stab of disappointment at finding she would be denied even a measure of privacy.

Determined not to let the stranger ruin her plans, she approached her mother's grave, which was set off at the far end of the cemetery. Unfortunately, that was the direction in which the man stood. She could feel his eyes boring into her as she walked, but she pretended not to notice. She feigned acute interest in the other tombstones as she passed, occasionally stopping to read an inscription, all the while hoping he would take her reluctant approach as a hint that she wanted time alone.

When he didn't, she decided that honesty would be her best route. No doubt he was from around here. If so, he could return to the tiny cemetery at another, more convenient time. She had only today. Surely he would understand her request and grant her privacy once she explained how desperate her need was.

But exactly how does one phrase such a rude request? Hope wondered, as she stopped at the foot of Old Man Fisher's grave. What an old tyrant he'd been! Scowling, she knelt beside the overgrown grave and started yanking out thick stalks of the grass that extended halfway up the tombstone. Different tactics on ridding herself of the stranger were considered, then immediately dismissed.

"Hope?"

The voice, so very much like Luke's, caused a ripple of apprehension to course up her spine.

A trick of the breeze, she told herself as she continued to weed the grave. Or was it? She glanced up and noticed that the stranger had neared. She tensed as he took a step closer.

"Hope, is that you?"

The bunch of grass clutched in her fist fell abruptly to the ground. Her cheeks drained to a deathly shade of white and her heart started pounding as she studied the silhouette of the man as he neared.

He was tall, like Luke. And broad, like Luke. His voice was deep and husky, like Luke's. He even had the same mane of curling chestnut hair, like Luke's.

But he can't *be Luke!* she reminded herself harshly. *Luke is dead. You watched the cabin burn to the ground yourself. No one could have survived a fire like that. No one!* And yet a nagging

342

trickle of doubt nipped at the back of her mind. It was countered by breathless, heart-wrenching excitement.

He's dead! she repeated sternly, hands clenched tightly in her lap. *He is dead . . . isn't he?*

The ground trembled as the man cleared the last few steps between them in three long strides. Before Hope knew what he was about, he had swept her up from the ground and into his tight embrace. He whirled her around, the black cape spinning out around her ankles like a pinwheel.

"Luke!" she cried in a voice that shook with the emotions that exploded inside her. The feel of his meaty body pressed against her and wiped away any last doubts she might have had. Tears of joy spilled down her cheeks unchecked, as she hugged him close and let him spin her as if she were no more than a rag doll. She kissed his cheek, his neck, his ear as her breath quivered. "My God, you're alive. *You're alive!*"

His rumbling laugh was her only answer as he set her on her feet in front of him. She tilted her head back to look into those beloved eyes — eyes she'd never thought she'd see again — and smiled through the mist of steadily falling tears. Of their own accord, her hands reached out and cupped his cheeks in her palms, then his stubbled chin, his thick neck. She gloried in the feel of his warm flesh beneath her palm.

"You're alive. *Alive!*" she cried, her voice bubbling with excitement. Over and over she whispered the words, her voice cracking now and again as she kissed his cheek, his ear, his hair. "My God, you're really here!"

He scratched his head in confusion. "So're you. Gee, Hope, you're supposed to be dead."

"Well, I'm not, you big lug. And don't you dare look so disappointed."

He stood there, grinning like a proud schoolboy. And when she threw herself into his arms again, he accepted the added weight as only Luke Bennett could — easily.

After she hugged him tightly for what seemed like hours, she pulled back. Her eyes widened as another thought penetrated her fog of happiness. "And Papa? And Old Joe?" she asked, choking on the words. She was afraid of his answer, but at the same time she found she desperately needed to know.

"Pa's out in the fields," he said, the boyish grin splitting his face wide. His eyes twinkled, as though he could hardly believe his sister was standing here before him. He reached out and clasped her hands in palms that dwarfed hers. "Gosh, Hope, where'd you think he'd be?"

Dead, she thought but didn't say. She couldn't. Right now, death wasn't what she wanted to think about. Besides, no words could get past the thick lump of emotion lodged in her throat.

Alive! Her family was alive!

Relief, joy, disbelief. These were only a few of the tumultuous emotions that sang through her veins as she tightened her grip on Luke's hand and started tugging her reluctant, confused brother toward the wrought iron gate. Like an obedient pup, he followed along. If he had any questions regarding her sudden appearance, he kept them to himself.

The old hinges creaked in protest as she flung the gate wide, then charged down the hill. Her feet floated over the dirt and rocks that crunched beneath her boots, and when a tree branch reached out to slap her full across the face, Hope only laughed. The sweet, fragrant breeze whipped at her hair, and she thought nothing had ever felt quite so wonderful.

"Boy, Hope, I'm sure glad to see you, but can't you slow down a little?" Luke panted, trying his best to keep up with his sister's frantic pace. "Pa ain't — *isn't* going nowhere."

"I don't care," she called gaily over her shoulder. "I have to see him. I can't wait anymore."

His dark head nodded, obviously not pleased, and more than a little confused, but he quickened his pace anyway. Hope had asked him to, and that was good enough reason for Luke. Keeping up with her wasn't easy, but he managed.

"Who's that?" Luke nodded to the glossy black carriage, outlined against the rolling green hills.

If Hope heard, she didn't answer. She, too, had seen Bentley's hunched form standing beside the carriage. But the old woman wasn't alone. She stood conversing with Bart, and their loud voices said they hadn't become fast friends. As though he sensed their approach, Bart's head snapped up and his misty gaze settled on his daughter.

"Hope?" Bart Bennett politely excused himself and stepped away from the crooked old woman when he saw his son and daughter running toward them. Tears shimmered in his eyes as Hope let go of Luke and threw herself into her father's strong embrace. "God forgive me, missy, but I was afraid to believe her." He pulled away, cupping her cheeks in his calloused, trembling palms. The last time she had seen tears glisten in that strong, steel gaze they had been burying her mother. Hope choked back a sob. "It really *is* you, isn't it?" he sighed in wonderment.

"Yes, Papa, it's me," she sobbed, her fingers tightly embedded in his lanky upper arms as his gaze raked her tear-streaked face in disbelief.

"But how—?"

She shook her head. "I don't know and I don't care. All that matters now is that we're together again." Her gaze drifted to Luke, and a beaming Bentley. My God, she could hardly believe it! "All of us. Just like we should be."

Bart smiled, and again enfolded his daughter in his embrace. For the first time since Emma had died, tears flowed freely down his weathered cheeks. But, unlike then, these were tears of joy—complete and utter joy.

Chapter Twenty-one

She'd been here for four hours, but Hope still couldn't get over how little had changed in the brick house Bart Bennett had built for his family after the main house had burned down. Two small bedrooms stood off the main room, one on each side. Neither was used for more than sleeping, since the main room held the kitchen table, cupboards, and fireplace. The floor was plain, its unstained planks unrelieved by so much as a scatter rug.

Although not grand on any scale, this small brick cabin beat the rickety shanties of Thirsty Gulch hands down. It might be the same size as the one they'd shared in the Mother Lode, with an extra sleeping room, but at least she didn't have to worry about a strong wind blowing it down around their heads.

Hope speared another of the "musketballs", as her mother used to call them, with her fork, dipped it in the spicy sauce, then popped it into her mouth. The flaked, salted cod, mixed with mashed potatoes then rolled into tiny balls that were fried to a crisp, golden brown, melted on her tongue.

Luke smiled at her from his place on the opposite bench. She returned the smile, but it thinned when she saw her father staring at her oddly. The time had come. Swallowing hard, she said, with typical Bennett bluntness,

"How'd you manage to escape the fire?" She was careful to keep her voice lowered lest she wake up Bentley, who had foregone supper for a nap on the cot beside the dancing fire.

"Could ask you the same thing, missy," Bart replied poignantly. "Last time I saw you, you were showing your friend Frazier the henhouse. I thought for sure you came back in the house when you saw the flames."

"I didn't see the flames. At least, not right away. By the time I did, it was too late. Drake and I tried to put the fire out, but it spread too fast."

"Hmph!" was all the reply Bart made.

Luke quickly took up where his father left off. "We hid in the root cellar, Hope. Pa said the cabin went up faster'n a matchstick and that we're lucky we made it out at all."

"Hotter'n hell down there," Bart grunted as he pushed his plate away. "Couldn't hardly breath from all the smoke."

Luke nodded in agreement. "Pa made us wait until he was sure the fire was out before he let us go up. That weren't easy, either. The door stuck from all the stuff that fell on top of it. We looked all over for you, Hope, but we couldn't find you."

The root cellar. Of course! She had never thought of that, but it made perfect sense. What better place to hide from a fire of such intensity? A fire there was no apparent way out of. She nodded thoughtfully. "I was gone by then," she said absently, pushing the remaining two musketballs around her plate. "Everything happened so fast — the fire, Tubbs, the gunshot."

Luke's head jerked up. "Gunshot? You got shot?" He scowled, his gaze raking her body in brotherly concern. "You don't look like you got shot."

She smiled patiently. "I healed, you big lug, thanks to Drake Frazier. Say all you want about him, Papa, but he nursed me back to health single-handedly."

"Frazier?" Bart grumbled, raking his fingers through his graying hair. "Should have known he couldn't keep his nose out of things." He glared at his daughter. "Where's this paragon of virtue now? I would have thought he'd follow you like a trained seal."

"I left him in Boston, visiting his brother," she murmured evasively. Suddenly, the food on her plate held great interest, although not a bit of it went into her mouth. What was wrong with her father? Last time she'd seen him, Bart Bennett had thought Drake Frazer was God. Or, at the very least, the next best thing to Him. *So what changed his mind?* she wondered. "You shouldn't be so hard on Drake, Papa. He saved my life."

Bart's gaze hardened. "Drake, is it now? And what happened to 'Frazier,' or 'that no-good gunslinger,' or 'that conniving, low-down rat.' Something changed that I should know about?"

Hope didn't know what to say. Although she dearly wanted to say yes, the truth was, she wasn't entirely sure. She spared herself from answering by changing the subject. "What about Old Joe?" she asked as she reached for a mug of hot, spiced cider. With elbows on the table, she sipped at it, regarding her father from over the chipped rim. "Did he—" she sucked in a ragged breath, "um, make it out of the fire?"

"That old grizzly bear?" Bart chuckled, his eyes sparkling. "It'd take more than a puny old fire to do him in. Stubborn as a mule, and twice as ornery. Got a letter from him last week—Kyle wrote it, 'course—said he was still working the mine and it was paying like a whore with four—" her father flushed and sent her a guilty look. "Sorry, no offense. Anyway, he said it was paying right fine. Better than we'd ever hoped. We should be seeing more of the profits any day now. Joe sends them on when he can. Then I'll see what I can do about hiring on some help and replanting the south field. Do my heart good to see some cotton growing in that dirt again."

Hope frowned. She lowered the mug to the table and for the first time noticed how the last ten months had added a new network of lines to the creases shooting out from her father's eyes. His hair was grayer, too, his skin thicker and weather-darkened. "But if the mine's paying so good, why are you here? After everything we did to get that land, I'd think you would've stayed and worked as much gold out of the claim as you could."

"I did—for a while," Bart shrugged. His long fingers played with the coffee cup in his hands as Bentley's snores punctuated the air. "But things change. I'm not the type of man who likes to wander far from home. You know that, missy. I get damn itchy being away from these hills. So, once we pulled out enough money to pay the taxes, I turned the lead over to Joe. Figured that even if I didn't have enough money to replant, I could pay the taxes. The land would be mine, the way it should be." He scowled. "Only . . ."

"Only what? What happened? Had someone already bought Lake's Edge when you got here?"

Bart shook his head and scratched his stomach. "Noooo, just the opposite. The taxes were paid in full by the time we docked. I had Bat Knowley, he's the county clerk now, check around to see if he could find out who put up the money. I wanted to pay the fellow back. Anyway, Bat came up blank. He tracked the funds to St. Louis, but then the trail went as cold as a rock in winter. I still don't know who did it—or why—but I'm not about to look a gift horse in the mouth, either. I put the money I brought with me to good use. Started building the house and planting crops. That sort of thing."

"I think whoever did it died before he could let anyone know," Luke added his opinion, as he wiped his mouth on his sleeve. "What do you think, Hope?"

"Good question," she replied thoughtfully, studying the

steamy cider as she swirled it in her mug. "That's a lot of money to be pulling out of the bank to help a neighbor or friend. And most people would want credit for their generosity so they could get their money paid back. But if they expected something in return, wouldn't they have asked for it by now?" She sighed, shaking her head in confusion. "I don't know. It doesn't make much sense. I'd be careful if I were you, Papa. This mysterious benefactor of yours could pop up any day to call in his loan."

Bart grinned. "Fine with me. Joe's been sending along our share of the take pretty regular lately. If anyone shows up, I could probably pay him. It'd mean putting off planting for another year, but I could do it."

The cot squeaked as Bentley rubbed her eyes, then pushed her tired old body into a hunched-over sit. "If you ask me, I say keep your money in your pocket until someone asks for it. No sense looking for trouble when there isn't any."

Hope stiffened. As it had all afternoon, tension crackled in the air between Bart and Bentley, as real and as loud as the flames dancing in the hearth.

"Ain't a gentlemanly way to pay back a favor," her father mumbled before taking a sip of his scalding hot coffee. "Not that a woman like yourself would know anything of it, course."

"Bah!" She hobbled over to the bench, her cane patting the floor, and eased herself onto the seat next to Luke. "Know more than you think, old man. I borrowed money in my day, and I lent it. I'm smart enough to know that whoever gave it to you would ask for it back if they wanted it."

She's enjoying this! Hope thought as she watched her father's face flood an angry shade of crimson.

"Oh really?" her father asked with open dislike. His coffee cup slammed loudly on the table. Drops of dark brown liquid sloshed over the side, dotting the dented

350

wood.

Bart launched into a tirade about the benefits of paying a debt, which Bentley wasted no time in staunchly rebutting. The two were deep into their discussion and hardly noticed when Hope rose from the bench and inched toward the door. They barely looked up when the old metal knob creaked beneath her hand.

Stealthily, she slipped into the chilly, starlit night. The Blue Ridge mountains stretched to the west, dark, black mounds jutting the moonswept horizon. To the east, hill and tree dotted the Great Basin as far as the eye could see.

She shivered and hugged her arms close for warmth. Her breath fogged the air with each rhythmic breath.

She considered going back for the black cloak, then dismissed the idea. She had no wish to hear her father and Bentley arguing again. They had bickered back and forth since their first meeting, and their surly banter showed no signs of letting up. If anything, it worsened with each minute one was forced to spend in the other's company.

Oil and vinegar, she thought, as her booted feet crunched over dry leaves and twigs. *Fire and water.* She wandered past a line of white oaks. *Hope and Drake.*

A seagull squawked overhead, its wide wings flapping as her thoughts took an abrupt turn. *Where is Drake now?* she wondered with a distracted sigh. Did he know where she'd gone? Did he care?

Although she would like to believe he did, she had a devil of a time convincing herself. He had, after all, only hired her to do a job, a job she had seen to it herself she was paid for. Now that the job was done, her services were no longer needed, or wanted. He was probably relieved to find she'd left. Why else hadn't he shown up at the docks to keep her from boarding that ship?

Because he doesn't care.

Her breath caught as she remembered his hand caressing the puckered flesh on her back. He had been shocked,

351

but not repulsed. Concerned, but not condescending. Certainly that was not the response of a man who didn't care!

The image of Drake, enfolded in Angelique's embrace, his calloused palm gliding over her smoothly perfect spine, stopped Hope cold. Again, she shivered, although this time the tremor had precious little to do with the brisk night air.

She wasn't foolish enough to delude herself that Angelique would not take full advantage of her absence. No doubt the sly witch would convince Drake quickly of his "wife's" infidelity, deception, lack of feelings — whatever it took to win him back into her bed.

Oh, how she could see that feline smile when Angelique learned she'd left. It was the opportunity the conniving bitch had been waiting for, planning for, *living* for. She wouldn't let it go to waste.

But what would Drake's response be?

It was a question Hope didn't dare contemplate. If she were still in Boston, she would fight Angelique every step of the way. But here, in the hidden valleys of Virginia, there was precious little she could do to stop Drake's seduction.

She walked on, mindless of where she was going. Her feet knew these foothills by heart, she wouldn't get lost.

She thought of her vow to Bentley — her vow to get Drake back. *Could I get him back?* she wondered. *Did I ever have him to begin with? Isn't it a little too late to start fighting for him now?*

"Life won't come to you, little one." Her mother's softly spoken words rang through her mind. How often had Emma Bennett said that? Often enough for the haunting voice to have an immediate response on Hope. "If you want something badly enough, go out there and fight for it like a Bennett. You'll never win a race if racing is the only time you ride. And you'll never ride if you get thrown from the saddle and refuse to get back up."

All her life, she'd taken her mother's wisdom to heart. Back in the saddle she'd always gone, never allowing herself to be defeated — at least, not without a damn good fight.

Is this so different? she asked herself, stopping to lean against the rough bark of an oak.

No, she thought, *it wasn't any different at all.* She'd fallen off the horse that was Drake Frazier, but she'd never gotten back on. She'd hidden behind a cloak of fear, afraid he would hurt her worse than she was already hurt. He couldn't, of course, but she hadn't known that then. She hadn't realized that the prize for fighting Angelique would be the man in all his glory. And the man and his love was what she wanted more than anything in the world.

Fight for it like a Bennett, her mother would advise.

Damn it, but if that wasn't exactly what she intended to do! Hope pushed away from the tree with new resolve. Her strides, as they carried her back to the house, were long and filled with determination.

She hadn't expected ever to see her family again, but she had, proving that miracles *do* happen. Now all she had to do was set about making a lifelong miracle of her own.

A week, she decided firmly. She would spend no more than a week with her family. Then she would return to Boston, with Bentley in tow, and she would fight for Drake Frazier. She'd do whatever it took to make him love her. And if she lost, at least she could console herself with the knowledge that her defeat was not due to lack of effort!

A smile played about her lips as she neared the house, and a plan began to form in her mind. Her steps lightened as her mind whirled to smooth out all the details. The plan was so wonderful in its simplicity, she cursed herself for not having thought of it before.

Everything came around full circle, she thought, and that was exactly where Hope intended to take her relationship with Drake Frazier. Back to the beginning.

It was silly. Preposterous. Perfect! How could he resist? She would simply hand the gunslinger an offer she knew he couldn't refuse. It wasn't as though this was the first time!

"Drake, if you do not stop prowling the deck like some caged animal I'll have you dragged below and tied to the bunk until we reach port. Now, come have a seat, and do try to relax."

Drake ignored his friend as he continued to pace the deck. He sent Elbert Sneyd a heated glance. One look at the small man, leisurely reclined in a lounge chair, basking in the midday sun with a legal journal open on his gaunt lap, made Drake wonder why he had ever chosen this insensitive oaf as a friend. It also made him question his wisdom in having asked the man along, although he knew the logic behind that reasoning well enough. Elbert Sneyd was the only man in Boston Drake trusted, and he trusted Elbert with his life.

Proof.

The single word shot through Drake's mind like a bullet, as he jammed his hands in his pockets and lifted his cheeks to the salty breeze. When he found Hope—and he *would* find her, there was never a doubt—he'd need proof to back up his somewhat wild but truthful explanation. After everything that had passed between them, he couldn't expect her to believe his story simply because he said it was true. If they were ever to have honesty between them, they would have to begin anew. He had to be sure she never doubted him again because, deep in his soul, he knew he'd never give her another reason to.

But first, he had to prove it. Not an easy task.

With a ragged sign, he stopped his relentless pacing to lean against the ship's rail. He read the sky and jagged coastline with an ease born of years at sea. If the storm brewing angrily on the horizon held off, they would reach the Chesapeake by late tomorrow afternoon. Until then, he would wait, worry, and pray he wasn't too late.

God, but he hated to wait!

Spinning on his heel, Drake pushed away from the rail and again began pacing the spray-slickened deck. His agitated strides earned him a grunt of aggravation from his friend. His tight denims, thick chambray shirt, bright red bandanna, and low-riding hat earned him looks of perplexity from the other strolling passengers. The black leather gunbelt strapped to a muscular thigh earned him looks of respect bordering on fear.

He barely glanced up when he heard his name mentioned, with not a little disdain, by an elderly couple strolling by. He was too lost in his thoughts to much care about their shocked reaction, although at another time he would probably have found their suddenly white faces comical.

Tomorrow, he thought. Tomorrow he would see Hope again. His heart sang with the thought and his calloused palms began to sweat. Now that Charles and Angelique had been taken care of, he was finally free to do something about setting his life in order.

Funny, but in his wildest dreams, he would never have imagined that *this* was the way he would go about it. Nor had he ever planned on centering his life, and his future, around a single, stubborn woman.

Things change, Drake thought as his gaze wandered to the horizon. The rain-heavy clouds there reminded him of a pair of stormy, dark brown eyes. Hope's eyes, lids thick with slaked passion. His gut tightened.

Tomorrow seemed like a lifetime away.

Chapter Twenty-two

Hope knelt beside the perfectly groomed grave. Her trembling fingers absently traced her mother's name, and she noticed how weathered the delicate carving had become against the chipped, white marble tombstone.

A light breeze rustled sap-scented air, disturbing the chestnut hair that waved down her back to the cinched waist of her new, mint green dress. She barely noticed. Her thoughts were busy drifting over the time spent lazily in Virginia.

One week had slipped passed, easing its way into two. Her days were spent fishing in the early morning hours with Luke, her afternoons spent cooking meals and keeping house. The early evening hours were reserved for long walks with her father amongst their vast Virginia fields.

It was these times, just before twilight, that Hope cherished the most. Hand in hand she and Bart would stroll, in tune with the sun as it stroked a fiery palette of color over the horizon, the vibrant shadows reflecting on the lush, promising fields that stretched at their feet.

At times, he talked about Emma, her mother, and Hope came slowly to realize how deep her father's feelings ran when it came to the fires that had nearly destroyed their lives. It was a side that Bart Bennett had never before revealed.

He had loved and lost, just as his daughter had. And though both took special care never to mention Drake Frazier's name, both knew they now had a common, if unspoken, bond.

Bentley had left the week before to keep her promise to her great-nephew and talk to his fiancée. "Don't know what good it'll do, but I've gotta try, I suppose," she'd huffed, hoisting her tired body into the carriage with a promise to return for Hope soon. After a callous remark to Bart, she'd left.

Although Hope wished her friend luck and was sorry to see her go, she was glad to feel the tension in the Bennett household ease. Bart returned to his jovial, albeit tight-lipped self, and even their prized cow started giving milk again. Her father swore Old Nellie sensed that the "old prune's finally gone."

Hope sighed. She dropped her hand, pillowing it on top of her lap. The paper tucked snugly in the side pocket crinkled. Her heartbeat quickened and her palms grew moist when she thought of the newly arrived letter.

Her time was up. Bentley had written to tell her that she'd spoken with her great-nephew's fiancée and, amazingly enough, had managed to work things out. Hope couldn't say she was surprised. Bentley did have a way of convincing people of things they might not normally have believed. She could attest to that first hand. What *did* surprise her was that the great-nephew's fiancée would be returning with them to Boston on a ship that was due to leave for the north on Friday. They were waiting for Hope at a hotel in Norfolk.

Friday! So Soon!

Dry leaves crackled in the rhythmic pace of footsteps. Cupping a hand over her eyes to shield out the sun, she turned. A half-smile played on her lips when she saw

357

Luke shuffling his feet as he waited for his sister to notice him.

"Pa said you'd be here," he murmured, dropping himself to the ground by his sister's side. His thick fingers plucked at the fragrant stalks of grass. "He ain't happy you're leaving."

She sighed, raking her fingers through the bristly stalks. "I know. He lectured me for two hours last night, and half an hour this morning. Look, I know you don't understand, no one does, but I have to go. I have to do this or I won't be able to live with myself. The not knowing would kill me."

"It's Frazier again, isn't it?"

She nodded, averting her gaze to the fields stretching lazily beneath the bluff. From this vantage point, she could see the house in mid-construction, the fragile sprouts waving in the fields, and the path leading up the side of the hill. The water of the large lake to her right looked like a sheet of glass as it mirrored flickering rays of sunlight.

"Pa said it weren't none a my business, that I should keep my big mouth shut," he grinned childishly, and Hope's heart swelled as she saw a bit of the Luke he had once been, "but I never did before and I ain't — *I'm not* gonna start now." His dark eyes grew serious as he took her cool hand into his much warmer one. "Do you love him, Hope? Do you *really* love him?"

"More than anything," she whispered hoarsely. She sighed, as though she'd just confessed to committing a hideous crime.

Luke nodded as he released her fingers and clasped his big hands in his lap. "Yeah, I thought so, since Pa won't talk about it. Back in Thirsty, he kept saying the guy was bad news but that we needed him. He said that some

358

morning we'd wake up and Frazier's be gone. I don't know, guess I always thought he was okay. And Old Joe was leery, but I think he liked him. He said Frazier ain't the kind of man Pa says he is, and that life dealt him a dirty hand and that's why he's so hard. Is it? Is that why he acts the way he does, Hope, because he's had it so hard?"

"I wish I knew," she replied with a sarcastic chuckle. "A person only knows as much about Drake Frazier as Drake Frazier wants them to know. He's not open the way you and I are with each other. He keeps things to himself a lot."

"But you spent an awful lot of time alone with him, you should know him pretty good by now."

She shrugged, pushing the hair from her brow. "As good as anyone, but still not good. Not as good as I'd like to, anyway."

"But you still love him?"

"God knows I shouldn't, but yes, I still love him." Luke opened his mouth to ask another, probably more intimate, question. She silenced him by slashing a finger over his lips. "Don't ask me why, Luke, because I can't even explain it to myself. I've tried, but I can't. All I know is that this last month has been sheer hell. I don't think I've ever felt so lost, so empty in my entire life." She smiled at him. "Except for when I thought all of you were dead, of course."

"And Frazier? How does he feel? Does he love you, too?"

"I think the lady should ask me that question herself."

Hope gasped. The grittily familiar voice made her head snap up. The ripped stalks of grass fluttered from her hand, unnoticed, as her gaze shot over her shoulder. Were it not for her brother's look of surprise, she would have passed the vision off as nothing more than a pleasantly haunting mirage.

Drake Frazier had cleared the gate and was closing the distance between them in quick, sure strides that she could feel vibrating through the ground beneath her palm. The tight-fitting denims outlined every sinewy muscle in his firm thighs and hips, and her gaze feasted on the sight. The loosened buttons at his collar displayed a curling vee of enticingly thick hair as it powdered the firm chest below the light blue bandanna. Her hands itched as she remembered the feel of that silky pelt under her fingertips. As always, the cracked leather hat rode low on his brow, and Hope ached to reach out and smooth away the golden strands that were scattered over his forehead.

She was on her feet in an instant, the minty silk billowing around her suddenly weak ankles. Her knees, traitors that they were, were trembling almost as violently as her hands. Her breathing was deep and ragged, her palms moist with nervous perspiration. Her eyes were round, shimmering with disbelief and desire.

Drake stopped, a handsbreadth away, and she could feel the warmth radiating from his body, caressing her flesh as though the impediments of mint green silk and blue cotton no longer existed. His hand reached up to stroke her cheek, but hesitated over the smooth, cool skin. It stayed poised in midair for a split second before dropping back to his hip.

The sea-green gaze, cast in enticing shadows, raked her body, as though trying to commit every delicate curve, every line, to memory.

"Well?" he said finally, his voice husky with pent-up emotion. "Are you going to ask me, sunshine?"

His warm, sweet breath kissed her upturned cheek and her breath lodged in her throat. No matter how hard she tried, words refused to form on her tongue. She stopped trying as her gaze riveted itself to the tiny lines shooting away from those piercing eyes. She thought she had never seen anything quite so wonderful, or so heady!

"Hope, he's talking to you. Hope?" Luke gently nudged his sister's ribs with his elbow, but she didn't seem to notice. He tried again as his gaze flickered between the two. As far as they were concerned, he might not have existed. "She's real glad to see you, Frazier. Ain't that right, Hope? *Hooope?*" He jabbed her again.

Hope managed a fleeting nod, her eyes never leaving Drake. *How long had he been standing at the gate? How much had he heard?* She gulped.

Grudgingly, Drake yanked his gaze from Hope, averting his attention to a beaming Luke. The smile that came to his lips was immediate. "How've you been, Luke?" He reached out with one hand and shook the big man's hand, using the other to clap Luke heartily on the shoulder. Relief mixed with affection sparked in his eyes.

Hope didn't hear her brother's answer over the wild pounding of her heart. The two men seemed to talk for hours, although in reality it was only a few short minutes. Before she knew what he was about, Luke pumped Drake's hand again, welcomed him whole-heartedly to Virginia, gave him a slap on the back that would have landed a lesser man on his knees, then left the tiny cemetery.

Birds chirped high in the rustling branches and the *rat-a-tat* sound of a hammer beating a nailhead echoed up the hill, keeping perfect time with the wild pounding of Hope's heart. Suddenly, she was excruciatingly aware of just how alone her brother's abrupt departure left them. Their solitude was reflected in Drake's darkened glance.

"Come here often?" he asked, nodding to the grave by

361

her feet. His gaze ran over the weathered inscription before returning to Hope. Regret lit his eyes.

"I — yes. Every day if I can." Her voice was weak, but outwardly calm, a stark contrast to the emotions churning within. She buried her hands in the pocket of her skirt and, surrendering to a desperate need for small talk, voiced the first question that sprang to mind. She could have bitten off her tongue! "What are you doing here, gunslinger? You're supposed to be in Boston, ruining your brother and —" *romancing his wife,* she finished silently. Flushing hotly, she looked away.

The memory of her mouth, swollen from his brother's harsh kiss, prompted Drake to reach up and run the tip of this thumb across her full lower lip. A tightening started in his thighs, spread through his loins, and pooled in his gut. "Charles won't be bothering us again," he said. "I saw to that before I left."

She shivered, sucking in a ragged breath. Her senses were beginning to scatter like dry leaves in the wind and her voice weakened until it was no stronger than a whisper. "And Angelique?"

Instinctively, her gaze slipped past his broad shoulder. She half-expected to see the calculating witch awaiting her lover at the wrought iron gate, a feline smile of satisfaction curling her lips. Instead, there was only the towering white oak, and the place where ground met sky before arching back down the hillside.

"She isn't here, sunshine."

"Oh." Whatever else she was about to say was lost as Drake surrendered to undeniable temptation. Gathering her into his arms, he gently lowered his lips to hers.

His mouth was insistent, probing, demanding a response that Hope had no choice but to give. And she responded to their bodies' urgent craving with a willingness that astounded him.

Her hands inched up, encircling his neck, teasing the silky golden curls that tickled her fingertips. With a husky groan, she pulled him closer, willing herself to melt her softness into his firmly worked chest. Insistently, she arched against him. The spicy scent of leather and sweat surrounded her as she opened beneath his searching tongue.

His hands, encircling the indentation of her waist, pulled her closer. Their hips meshed and a stifled moan escaped his suddenly parched throat. He didn't know how much more of this sweet torture he could stand, yet at the same time, he was afraid a more outright advance would scare her away. He satisfied himself with the sensuous thrust and retreat of her velvety tongue, and, holding his desire firmly in check, launched his own hot pursuit of that kind.

His teeth nibbled at her full lower lip, causing a surge of breathless anticipation to tingle up her spine. Her heart sang with desire as she slipped her hands down his upper arms, reveling in the feel of hard muscles bunching beneath her palm. The stubble-coated jaw grazed her cheek as he trailed kisses to the curl of her ear. She tilted her chin up and to the right, basking in the familiar, bristly sensation of his whiskers scraping against her flesh. It was a feeling she had thought she would never experience again.

"Come back to Boston with me, sunshine," he whispered throatily, his breath in her ear.

"You should have waited a few weeks, gunslinger," she sighed through softly parted lips. "That's exactly where I was heading. I—I have another job offer for you."

His tongue lingered over the small shell of her ear tasting, teasing. Slowly, her words sank into his passion-fogged brain. He lifted his head, capturing her gaze. He looked deep into those large, enticing eyes and tried to assess the meaning behind her words. A wave of guilt washed over him. "I should explain about that." He shifted self-consciously. "I guess there are a lot of things I should explain to you."

Hope let him pull back, but refused to let him go. Her dark eyes shimmered with confusion, and her voice cracked. "You can start by telling me what the hell you were doing with Angelique. The way you acted in Boston, I half expected the two of you to kill off Charles, then run off and elope. Instead, you show up here, saying you left her behind! I want to understand, Drake, really I do. You're not making sense! Nothing you've ever done makes any sense to me."

He disengaged her hands from his arms as his gaze scanned their surroundings. A scowl furrowed his golden brow as his work-roughened palm smoothed the hair from her cheek. With a ragged sigh, he entwined his fingers in hers and pulled her toward the gate. "I'll explain—I owe you that much—but not here. I've never been able to talk well in cemeteries."

"Where are we going?" she insisted, panting as she struggled to keep up with his long, determined strides. By the time they cleared the gate, she was out of breath. By the time the reached the bottom of the hill, her lungs felt like they were about to explode. She didn't complain. The feel of his strong fingers wrapped around her hand felt wonderful, more than making up for the minor discomfort.

Drake followed his ears. He dragged Hope through the dense covering of maple and oak, toward the sound of gurgling water. In minutes they broke through the trees and emerged in a lush clearing beside the bank of a river that, further down, washed into the lake stretching lazily beside the house. A waterfall splashed over a jagged cliff of rocks to their right, and rays of sunlight played over the rippled surface of the water that gurgled and twisted away.

How right that he would chose this particular spot, at this particular moment, she thought.

"I haven't been here in years," she sighed in wonder, as she flopped to the ground, panting to catch her breath.

He lowered himself beside her, so near their thighs were touching. The contact, Hope found, was most distracting. She shifted self-consciously, arranging the grass-stained skirt around her legs and ankles. When he made no response, she continued, "I used to come here when I was a girl. Luke didn't know where to find me, and my parents didn't try. It gave me time to be alone. Time to think. I always thought of it as my special place. I'm surprised you were able to find it."

"We can go somewhere else if you'd rather," he offered softly. The gesture was hollow. Drake was reluctant to leave a spot Hope so obviously cherished, thinking the breathtaking scenery might, in some small way, aid his cause. At this point, he'd welcome all the help he could get.

Hope shook her head, her gaze locking with his. She placed a restraining hand on his arm when he started to rise. "No, I want to stay here . . . with you. It feels right." Her thoughts strayed to Angelique and her happiness faded abruptly. He'd left the witch behind, but to what purpose? So he could come here and explain why he preferred his former fiancée over herself? Why bother? Silence would serve the same purpose, and would be much less painful in the end.

Drake watched the emotions flickering openly in the

velvet brown eyes. He knew what she was thinking. His heart tightened in response and his mind raced, searching for the perfect words to ease her worries. He wasn't surprised to find there weren't any. At least, none that came to mind.

"You said you had another job for me," he began, resting his warm hand over her smaller, cooler one. A sly grin pulled at his lips, and at Hope's heart. "Funny, but I came here with one to offer you. I even brought Elbert with me—to legalize it all—but I decided to leave him with your father instead. Now I'm glad I did," his eyes sparkled as his gaze gently caressed her cheek, his palm itching to follow suit. "I like having you all to myself."

"I don't think I want any more of your jobs. You're a hard boss, Drake Frazier, and you don't pay your employees very well." She tried to interject some lightness into her voice, and failed miserably.

"You left before I could pay you. That wasn't my fault, sunshine."

"I *had* to leave." She slipped her hand from his. "You saw to that."

His eyes narrowed. "Did I? Did I really? Are you sure that's why you left? Are you sure you weren't running way from something else? Some*one* else?"

Hope pushed herself to her feet and walked to the riverbank. She focused her attention on the water crashing and foaming beneath the waterfall. "I don't know what you're talking about."

"You were jealous, Hope. Why can't you just admit it?"

"I was not!" she hotly lied. "Why should I care whose skirt you chase? As far as I'm concerned, you could make a fool out of yourself over all the women in Boston if you wanted to," she sniffed in disgust. "I really couldn't care less."

His powerful fingers jerked her around. She came up hard against his chest, and the breath rushed from her lungs in surprise. "Why, you little liar! You care one hell of a lot more than you'd ever admit. Don't you, Hope? *Don't you?*"

"Stop that. You're hurting me," she cried, trying to twist from his grasp. She should have known better.

"I'll do a lot worse than that if you don't start telling me the truth."

"I *am* telling you the truth." She looked up and saw his cheeks darken angrily. "Sort of."

"Sort of?" he demanded harshly.

She wrenched away from him. Chaffing her bruised flesh, she glared into his stormy gaze. "What do you want me to say? That I care? That I hurt? Of course I do. I'm not made of stone."

"I never said you were—"

"How the hell did you think I'd feel when you offered me the *job* of pretending to be your wife? All so that you could romance *her!* Did you think it wouldn't bother me? Did you think I wouldn't care that you preferred Angelique just because she's perfect and I'm . . ." she choked on a sob, "and I'm not? Don't touch me!"

She quickly stepped away when Drake reached out for her. On shaky knees, she retreated to a spot farther down the bank, closer to the cascading waterfall. She didn't look at him. She couldn't. It would kill her to see the pity shimmering in his eyes.

Drake stood, a mixture of confusion and shock rushing through his blood, cementing him to the spot. *Perfect? Is that what she thought? That she wasn't as perfect as Angelique?* His hands clenched and unclenched at his side as he remembered the feel of her puckered scar beneath his palm. Silently, he called himself a blind fool.

When his breathing slowly returned to normal, he approached Hope, stepping in front so he stood between her and the sparkling, clear water. Her shoulders were trembling, though she was doing a valiant job of holding back her tears. He wanted to reach out and touch her, hold her, soothe away her fears, but he didn't know how.

"Go away, gunslinger. Go back to Boston, back to Angelique. I don't need you. I never have." It was the biggest lie she had ever told in her life and it cut her to the quick to be telling it now. But she had no choice. She was foolish to think she could ever win Drake Frazier's love. Fanciful and foolish, she knew that now.

"I'm not going anywhere without you, sunshine." Gently, he reached out and touched her porcelain cheek. Her head snapped up. The moistness glistening in her eyes pulled at his heart and twisted painfully in his gut. "I told you once that, no matter where you went, I'd always find you. And I meant it. You can't run from me, sunshine. You never could. You can't lie to me, either."

Her jaw trembled as she thrust her chin up proudly. Her arms were wrapped tightly, defensively, around her waist. "I'm not lying. I *don't* need you."

"And I still don't believe you. I think you need me. In fact, I think you need me more than you've ever needed anything in your life."

"Why you arrogant, egotistical, no-good—!"

Drake caught her arm before the open palm could slice into his cheek. She cried out with frustration and tried again, but he wouldn't let her go. With a flick of his wrist, he pulled her against him. One hand slipped behind her suddenly rigid back and in slow, languid motions he stroked her spine.

She had no choice but to relax against him. She didn't want to, but she couldn't seem to stop the instinctive

368

reaction any more than she could have stopped the spark of desire his touch was kindling. She lifted her gaze to his, her large eyes sparkling with a confusion of unshed tears.

"Perfection doesn't matter to me, sunshine," he said, his voice a husky whisper. "It never has. Haven't you figured that out yet?" His lips turned up in a slow, knowing smile. "A thousand Angelique Rutlands can't add up to one feisty Hope Bennett."

"But—"

His finger covered her lips, silencing her. "It doesn't matter to me," he repeated, his tone thick with conviction. His hands moved to the front of his shirt and his fingers quickly began to slip free buttons.

Hope's eyes widened. "What are you doing?" she cried, covering her mouth with trembling fingers as more and more sun-kissed flesh was revealed. Her cheeks grew warm and an undeniable quiver of anticipation rippled through her stomach.

"Comparing scars," Drake answered flatly, as he slipped the shirt off his shoulders and tossed it onto a pile of twigs. "See this?" He pointed to a line of about four inches that curved down a firmly tapered bicep. "Hideous, isn't it? And this?" He nodded to a smaller, crescent-shaped one on his taut stomach. "Absolutely disgusting. No woman should be asked to live with such ugliness. Oh, and I almost forgot the best one."

His eyes twinkled as he pried off his boots, then reached for the buckle of his belt. Before Hope could stop him, he had unbuttoned the denims and let them drop to this ankles. He looked like an ancient Greek god as he kicked the pants away and turned his back. He acted like a hunting guide pointing out scenic bits of landscape as he indicated a well-healed hole up and to the left of his tailbone, then three more on the backs of his tantalizingly sinewy legs.

It didn't matter, Hope never saw the scars. She was too busy ogling the superbly developed muscles of his naked hips and thighs.

"This isn't funny," she managed to say once she could breathe again. "I'm warning you, Frazier, if you're trying to embarrass me, it won't work."

"What I'm trying to do is to make you see that the scar on your back bothers *you* a hell of a lot more than it ever bothered me. What *does* bother me is the way you let it drive a wedge between every relationship you have. You can't live in the past forever. Painful things are going to happen. You can't stop them, but you can control the way they affect you." With a ragged sigh, he plucked off his hat, raked his fingers through the windblown golden mane, then settled it back on his head. "Good God, Hope, what do I have to do to make you understand? I love you, no matter how many—"

She gasped. "You what?"

"I said I love you, no matter how many scars you have on your body, or in your mind."

She stared at him long and hard, her gaze searching for the lie, for the pity that she was sure would be closer to his true feelings. Shock surged through her when she couldn't find those emotions in his eyes.

"You love me?" she asked stupidly. It felt like her whole body had started trembling furiously. Her heart soared. *You love me?*

"Yes, I love you. What did you think—that I'd nurse you back to health after you were shot, drag you with me to Boston, then follow you way out here just because I thought you had a cute bottom?"

She wanted to believe him. More than anything else in

370

her life, she wanted to believe him. But she couldn't. Not yet.

Stiffening, her lips formed the question her mind demanded an answer to. "What about Angelique?" she asked flatly. "I thought she was the big love of your life. Don't you think she'll be a little disappointed to find out you don't share her affection?"

"Why the hell should I care what she thinks?" he growled. His angry glare said he was not at all pleased with the course the conversation had taken. "I know what you think, Hope, and you have every right to think it. I realize I haven't done much to convince you there nothing going on between me and Angelique—for my own stupid reasons—but you have to believe me when I say that Angelique Rutland is a sneaking, conniving little witch. I've known that for a long time now, and I can't say I was sorry to see her and Charles go."

"Go?" she echoed stupidly, her curiosity piqued as her heart raced.

"Yes, go. The last I saw of her and Charles, they were on a ship heading for San Francisco, the land of golden opportunity. I made sure my brother won't be able to show his face in Boston again, at least not until he can pay back the debts he so stupidly incurred. Personally, I'd be happy never to set eyes on their miserable faces again."

"Y-you sent her away?" she asked breathlessly. Her heart skipped a beat, then pounded wildly. She was almost afraid to believe her ears.

"Of course I did," he scoffed. Planting balled fists on his hips, he looked at her skeptically. "Did you think I'd want her around so she could come between us again? I'm not that foolish, Hope. I may make a mistake once, but I learn fast enough not to do the same thing twice. Not when I want something as badly as I want you. What are you smiling at, sunshine?"

She couldn't contain her grin. She'd never been so happy in her life. It took all of her self-control not to fling herself headlong into his arms. She bit the impulse back, but it wasn't easy.

Of course, the thought of Charles and Angelique feebly attempting to work a claim didn't help to diminish the smile lacing her full lips. The two would never survive! She could no more imagine Angelique working by her husband's side than she could picture Charles, wearing a pair of baggy denims and a flannel, flinging a pick; or up to his knees in mud as he panned a river, while Angelique whined from the bank about chipping a nail or tearing her skirt.

Hope sucked in a ragged breath when Drake's thumb slipped over her jaw, under her chin. He pulled her laughing gaze back to his. "What are you smiling at, sunshine?" he repeated.

"I was just wondering," she shrugged, an impish twinkle sparkling in her large brown eyes. Her spirit hadn't felt this light in years! "Do you think California will survive after those two are done with it?"

Drake grinned. "Not a chance. The governor will probably be forced to secede the state from the sheer humiliation of having them there."

She giggled, instinctively turning her cheek into his palm. It was roughly calloused, exactly the way she had remembered it in her dreams. "Maybe they'll be lucky and the Indians will revolt again. Or Mexico will—"

Without warning, and before she could finish the thought, Hope found herself scooped into Drake's embrace and being kissed soundly. The hat was knocked from his head, leaving only the sky blue bandanna to cover his nakedness; a nakedness that managed to press and warm every available inch of her front.

"Put me down, you fool!" she cried, swatting his bare shoulders and pushing from his embrace. Try though she might, Hope couldn't stop her hungry gaze from roving up and down his exposed body. She cleared her throat, trying to clear away the breathless passion that clouded her thoughts. "You said you had a job to offer me. What is it? I—I think I might be interested after all."

"Oh really?" he said as his fingers slipped free the buttons lining her back. "And what changed your mind?"

She grinned shyly as she untied his bandanna. She started to look down, then, realizing what was there, decided against it. Reluctantly, she met his gaze. "I—I think I love you, too."

The smile that split his face couldn't have been wider. "I've been waiting a lifetime to hear you say that, sunshine," he groaned as he slipped the minty silk down her arms, then captured her to his chest. His heart drummed rhythmically beneath her palms, his flesh warm and firm against her hand.

"Now, tell me about this job," she insisted, using up the last shred of her self-control. Shifting slightly, she helped him in lifting the white cotton chemise over her head. In less than a minute the cool breeze was caressing her naked flesh. "What does it pay? What are the hours? Is travel included? I'm afraid I don't travel well, although I must say I do a hell of a lot better than Bentley. *Bentley!*" Her eyes widened as she pushed away from him. "Oh, my God, I've got to get to Norfolk and let her know I won't be—what are you laughing at? *Drake?*"

Drake tried to wipe a way his grin with a hand. It wouldn't go. "There's—um—there's something else I guess I should tell you, sunshine. But I don't think you're going to be too happy to hear it."

"I'm listening." Her brown eyes narrowed as she crossed her arms over her chest. Her toe tapped the ground with impatience. "Well? What is it?"

For the first time in his life, Drake Frazier actually looked sheepish. "You don't have to go to Norfolk, Hope. Bentley's already on her way to Boston. She—um—she left last week."

"Last week?!" She shook her head emphatically and the chestnut waves tossed at her waist. "She couldn't have. I just got a letter from her today saying—wait a minute. How did *you* know about Bentley? I only met her three weeks ago. You couldn't possibly have—"

"Yes, I could have. She's—oh boy, this is tougher than I thought it would be—" His cheeks flooded with color and Drake grinned rakishly, hoping to soften the blow. "Bentley Stillwell's my great-aunt, sunshine. Frankly, I'm surprised you didn't see the resemblance. Everybody always comments on how much we look alike."

"Stillwell? Your what?" she asked flatly. She hadn't heard him right. She *couldn't* have heard him right!

"My great-aunt. My grandmother's sister. My mother's aunt. My great-uncle's wife. My—"

"Why you rotten, no-good, son-of-a—!" Hope's jaw tightened as she planted her hands against his chest and pushed for all she was worth.

"Arrrgh!" Drake stumbled backwards and his bare foot caught on a forked tree branch. He tumbled over the bank, landing in the icy river with a splash. He came up wiping the water from his face, gasping for air and shivering. Droplets of water spattered the air like tiny crystals as he shook his head.

He squinted against the sun and looked at Hope on the bank. The arrogant smile was still in place, although the sensuous lips were now etched blue. "Guess this means

374

you don't want to hear about the taxes I paid on your land, huh?" he asked with that endearing, lopsided grin.

"Why, you —!" Hope kicked the ground in frustration, then spotted his nice, dry, clothes. With a sly grin, she scooped them all up and delivered the pile to Drake in the river.

His undershorts were caught by the current and immediately started to float away. Drake swore hotly and dove after them. Her anger quickly thawed and she started to laugh when he stubbed his toe on a buried rock, which caused him to curse even louder — and with such imagination!

"Think this is funny, do you, wench?" he growled, tossing his soaking wet clothes to dry land before wading to the bank. "Well, let's see how *you* like it, shall we?"

Like a panther, he crawled out of the water and stalked threateningly toward her, a menacing grin turning his lips. His wet body glistened magnificently in the flickering sunlight.

Instinctively, Hope backed up a step, then another. Soon she was running. He caught her easily — as if she'd ever harbored a doubt that he wouldn't.

"No, Drake, don't!" she pleaded, pummeling his chest and trying to scoot away.

With one arm under her knees, and the other around her waist, he lifted her high in the air. His cold, water-slick skin pressed against her side, and he laughed when she clung to his neck, trembling.

"No, Drake, don't!" he mimicked, as he reached the bank and tossed her into the twisting river.

The water was ice cold, but Hope wasn't given a chance to notice. In an instant he had joined her, and caught her to him before she could break the surface. They came up kissing, their bodies pressed hungrily together.

Hope splashed a liberal amount of water in his fac. "Be glad your gun's still on the bank, or I'd be sorely tempted to put a bullet through you. How dare you send your aunt after me? Didn't you think I could make it to Virginia on my own?"

"I knew you'd figure out how to catch a ship eventually, but that's not why I sent her." She frowned and Drake smoothed the angry creases from her brow. "I thought you needed to talk to someone about what was bothering you. Since you wouldn't talk to me, I sent Bentley. She has a way about her, in case you hadn't noticed."

"I noticed."

"I figured she'd be able to get you to talk, or she'd kill you trying." He flashed her his most charming grin and pulled her roughly against his body. The current lapped at their naked flesh. "It worked, didn't it? My logic wasn't all wrong."

"Yes," she agreed reluctantly. "It worked. But I still don't like it. Imagine! The woman never even told me who she was, although she did say she was going to meet her great-nephew's fiancée. Constantly, now that I think about it." She smiled weakly as she ran the tip of her finger from his throat to his navel. The cold water, combined with the eternal warmth of his skin, made her tremble. "I should have guessed. There really is a resemblance."

"You're not mad?"

"You bet I'm mad!" She tweaked a chest hair for emphasis. Smiling sweetly, she batted the thick fringe of red-tipped lashes when Drake yelped and grabbed her wrist. "But I'll get over it. Now, tell me what this job is," she insisted as she nuzzled his neck and licked the moistness from his skin. Her hips wiggled against his. "You've

376

you don't want to hear about the taxes I paid on your land, huh?" he asked with that endearing, lopsided grin.

"Why, you—!" Hope kicked the ground in frustration, then spotted his nice, dry, clothes. With a sly grin, she scooped them all up and delivered the pile to Drake in the river.

His undershorts were caught by the current and immediately started to float away. Drake swore hotly and dove after them. Her anger quickly thawed and she started to laugh when he stubbed his toe on a buried rock, which caused him to curse even louder—and with such imagination!

"Think this is funny, do you, wench?" he growled, tossing his soaking wet clothes to dry land before wading to the bank. "Well, let's see how *you* like it, shall we?"

Like a panther, he crawled out of the water and stalked threateningly toward her, a menacing grin turning his lips. His wet body glistened magnificently in the flickering sunlight.

Instinctively, Hope backed up a step, then another. Soon she was running. He caught her easily—as if she'd ever harbored a doubt that he wouldn't.

"No, Drake, don't!" she pleaded, pummeling his chest and trying to scoot away.

With one arm under her knees, and the other around her waist, he lifted her high in the air. His cold, water-slick skin pressed against her side, and he laughed when she clung to his neck, trembling.

"No, Drake, don't!" he mimicked, as he reached the bank and tossed her into the twisting river.

The water was ice cold, but Hope wasn't given a chance to notice. In an instant he had joined her, and caught her to him before she could break the surface. They came up kissing, their bodies pressed hungrily to-got me intrigued."

Drake pulled her away with a husky groan. "I won't be telling you a damn thing if you keep doing that. Tell me about your job offer first. If my memory serves me right, I think I like your deals better—if the first one is anything to go by." His grin would have charmed the skin off a cat, and Hope blushed scarlet at the mention of their first drunken encounter. "The pay-up is fantastic."

"Un-uh, you first. Mine can wait." *For a while,* she thought. When she looked up his expression had grown serious.

"It's a good job, but I want you to think it over before you decide. I—" he hesitated. The words he'd so carefully rehearsed on his way to Virginia seemed to flow away from him with the steadily pulling current. "I want you to be my wife, sunshine." Hope stiffened, and he rushed on. "Let me explain first. This won't be like last time. Last time I would have done damn near anything to keep you near me until I was done with Charles. I was wrong. I should have just told you the truth then, or married you, I'm not sure which. But this time is different. This time the offer is for real." He reached up and stroked the dampness from her trembling jaw with the back of his hand. "I want you to marry me. Say yes, sunshine. Although I wouldn't blame you a bit, I don't think I could stand it if you refused me. I love you, Hope Bennett— more, probably, than I have a right to."

"Oh, Drake." A tear slipped down her cheek, mixing with the drops of water clinging to her skin as she wrapped her arms around his neck. The feel of his hard, wet body pressing against her awoke a burning desire that had been too long denied. "I've never wanted anything else," she sighed against his firm shoulder. "Of course I'll marry you. I'd be proud to be your wife."

377

She hid behind the thick trunk of a maple tree, peeking out at him now and again as he deftly hunted her down. She bit down on her lower lip, trying to contain her laughter.

Drake would find her, of course. She could count on that. He had promised he always would, and with all her heart, Hope believed him.

WATCH FOR THESE REGENCY ROMANCES

BREACH OF HONOR   (0-8217-5111-5, $4.50)
by Phylis Warady

DeLACEY'S ANGEL   (0-8217-4978-1, $3.99)
by Monique Ellis

A DECEPTIVE BEQUEST   (0-8217-5380-0, $4.50)
by Olivia Sumner

A RAKE'S FOLLY   (0-8217-5007-0, $3.99)
by Claudette Williams

AN INDEPENDENT LADY   (0-8217-3347-8, $3.95)
by Lois Stewart

ROMANCE FROM FERN MICHAELS

DEAR EMILY   (0-8217-4952-8, $5.99)

WISH LIST   (0-8217-5228-6, $6.99)

AND IN HARDCOVER:

VEGAS RICH   (1-57566-057-1, $25.00)

ROMANCE FROM JO BEVERLY

DANGEROUS JOY   (0-8217-5129-8, $5.99)

FORBIDDEN   (0-8217-4488-7, $4.99)

THE SHATTERED ROSE   (0-8217-5310-X, $5.99)

TEMPTING FORTUNE   (0-8217-4858-0, $4.99)

Available wherever paperbacks are sold, or order direct from the Publisher. Send cover price plus 50¢ per copy for mailing and handling to Penguin USA, P.O. Box 999, c/o Dept. 17109, Bergenfield, NJ 07621. Residents of New York and Tennessee must include sales tax. DO NOT SEND CASH.

LOOK FOR THESE REGENCY ROMANCES